Reluctant Protector

Elite Protectors, Volume 1

Amara Holt

Published by Amara Holt, 2024.

Copyright © 2024 by Amara Holt

All rights reserved.

No part of this book may be reproduced, distributed, or transmitted in any form or by any means, including photocopying, recording, or other electronic or mechanical methods, without the prior written permission of the author, except in the case of brief quotations in book reviews.

This is a work of fiction. Names, characters, places, and incidents are the product of the author's imagination or are used fictitiously. Any resemblance to actual events, organizations, locales, or persons, living or dead is coincidental and is not intended by the authors.

PROLOGUE

The slow music enveloped my heart. The long dress adorned with shimmering beads weighed down with every new turn I took, while I held the hand of a boy slightly taller than me. A stranger, yes, but he smiled at me as if we had known each other for years.

Magnolia also twirled in her purple, layered dress around the festive hall, decorated exclusively for her prom. My younger sister looked stunning, like a princess with her light hair cascading in waves down her bare back. She was wrapped in her boyfriend's embrace, wearing a passionate smile so contagious that for a moment we forgot about the three men in sunglasses, heavily armed, standing at the edges of the party.

But that didn't matter now. At that moment, all I wanted was to enjoy the company of my sister's charming classmate, who had an unusual depth to him, and the best part... he didn't seem to fear our bodyguards.

"Harry..." he whispered in my ear suddenly, just before spinning me in his arms and pulling me close. "That's my name; I thought you should know since I plan to ask you out after this whole spectacle." He looked over at the party, which was packed with students.

The hall looked like it had come straight out of a Disney movie. Amidst loud conversations and hysterical laughter, several ribbons hung from the ceiling down to the dance floor. A small band played on a brightly lit stage, while in a more isolated area, the teachers watched the students and their guests, likely thanking God once again for surviving another gathering of rowdy youths.

"Harry," I repeated his name with a smile. He gazed at me, his gray eyes sweeping over mine with intensity.

He was so handsome, so charming, and he definitely looked to be my sister's age, meaning Harry was three years younger than me. But who was counting? Certainly not me...

"Where are we going after this?"

"There's a party at Carl's house. A friend from school. Your sister was invited," he whispered in my ear. "Would it be too much to hope you'd come with her?"

"Haven't you been told there are no limits to dreaming?" I smiled, trying to contain my excitement.

Oh, come on! He's 17, but he's definitely a cutie.

"Think you can shake them off over there?" He nodded toward one of our bodyguards, who had practically blended into the decor. The man didn't even budge.

"On a scale from 0 to 100? One percent. That's if a miracle happens." I sighed at the reality, feeling his hand tighten around my waist.

"Relax, we'll figure something out," he said softly. "Our mission tonight is to throw off the MIBs over there. Once they're distracted, I'll finally be able to do what I've wanted since I laid eyes on you."

"And what is that?" My heart raced at the mere expectation, even knowing it was impossible to distract any of those men. I just wanted to imagine that conversation later.

"To kiss you," he whispered right next to my ear. A shiver ran through my body.

A delicious shiver filled with expectation, which, in the next instant, turned into pure panic as a loud sound filled the hall the moment the music stopped.

"Shooter! There's a shooter!" someone screamed. Another loud, sharp sound exploded somewhere in the hall.

Panic erupted. My eyes immediately searched for Magnolia in the crowd. People began to run, trying to escape the hall, and one of them bumped into me, pulling me away from Harry. I looked up and couldn't see him again.

"Stay down!" Arms and hands surrounded me. The bodyguard lowered my head, shielding me with his body.

"Where's Mag?" I tried to rise to look around, but he held me back.

"I'm with Crystal, heading out the side."

"MAGNOLIA! MAGNOLIAAAAAAA..." I began to scream as he refused to let me rise.

"Diamond is right in front of us, focus on staying down, miss," he warned as sounds of breaking things and sharp screams filled the space.

I raised my head just in time to see someone bump into Magnolia in the crowd before the bodyguard once again lowered my face, making me stare at the hem of Magnolia's purple dress dragging just a few meters ahead.

A wave of relief washed over me. Once we got out of there, this nightmare would be over.

I kept moving, barely able to see a step in front of me. Seconds later, we were outside the party hall. The guards started running and urged us to do the same. We were escorted to one of the four identical black cars parked at the entrance. We got into the third one, and it took me longer than it should have to realize what had happened.

"Thank God we're safe." I turned to my sister, who was already seated in the passenger seat. Her hand pressed against her waist, and only then did I see the spreading red stain on the fabric. "Magnolia?" She looked at me, her wide eyes on her delicate, slightly paler face terrified me. "MAGNOLIA! HELP!" I screamed, jumping onto her, who began to thrash and convulse.

"Diamond has been injured, I repeat, Diamond injured!"

"Do something, please! Please, help my sister," I begged as more and more men approached our car. One of them tried to pull me away from Magnolia. "No, I'm staying here." Hardly had I shut my mouth when my sister began to gasp for air, her chest rising and falling as if no air was reaching her lungs. Her lips started turning blue, and that's when the nightmare began.

I had always dreaded nightmares... Being trapped in a place that only caused you pain was terrible, painful, hellish. But there was something far worse than the traps of the mind and dreams... reality.

I watched in disbelief as one of the guards tore Magnolia's dress while she was suffocating.

"She was stabbed, but it's not a fatal wound, so why..." He looked confused at my sister's pale face.

"Help her, do something, for God's sake!" Tears streamed down my face as my body remained motionless, as if I had suddenly lost all my strength. "Help my sister." I sobbed.

I felt useless, my hands tied, watching her suffocate. Her body shook as if she were having a seizure.

"We're going to the hospital. NOW!" one of the guards said into the radio, but before he could finish his sentence, Magnolia suddenly stopped moving.

I closed my eyes, unable to face her. The fear mixed with dread and the pain creeping up my throat froze me.

I didn't want to open my eyes. I didn't want to face the truth.

My worst nightmare had become reality.

CHAPTER ONE

Wolf

3 years later

There was a painful yet pleasurable sensation in solitude. One that I cherished more than anything. This thought invaded my mind as I rolled the phone number the waitress had left on my table between my fingers, alongside the whiskey I downed in one gulp.

I scanned the small crowd crammed into one of the most expensive pubs in downtown Chicago. Young people were enjoying themselves under the incandescent, dazzling lights flashing through the venue's artificial smoke.

I stared at the gray haze and clenched my jaw as once again, the reason I had allowed myself to come to this place gnawed at my mind.

I rarely went out, and when I did, I never chose a place in Chicago, the city where I lived and worked. I always opted for distant towns that allowed me to relax, far away from any possibility of running into someone I knew, but having to face my father the next day was one of the reasons that brought me here. If I didn't distract my mind somehow, I would end up going crazy.

I knew I shouldn't have assaulted my VIP's guest during my last mission, but I hated arrogant people even more than the cowards hiding behind wealth and power.

"Fuck it!" I huffed to myself.

My father would have to understand the situation. He wasn't even my client. The main rule was to keep the VIP intact; no one mentioned anything about his unbearable friends.

I waved my empty glass toward the waitress who had served me minutes before, taking a good look at the woman with plump lips and curly hair framing her face in perfect curls. She approached with a restrained smile and placed a half-full glass on my table.

"If you need anything, anything at all... just call me," she said softly. "Or you can call me." She winked at me and bit her red-tinted lips, aware that I was still holding her phone number between my fingers.

She was attractive, and I could guarantee we both wanted the same thing: a night of sex. But my reality that night was different from the others I had spent in the company of some stranger. I couldn't think of anything but how to escape my father the next day.

"What the hell!" I cursed under my breath, leaning my elbows on the table.

I couldn't control myself at work, and now I was going to hear about it.

I stood up, determined to put an end to this night. I dodged a few people energized by drink, dancing to the music, until I reached the bar and noticed that suddenly, in that hidden corner, the people who had been jumping non-stop were now standing like statues, staring at something amidst the gray smoke reflecting the red light of the bar.

I scanned the area for whatever had captured the attention of all those people to the point they stopped what they were doing, and that's when I saw her. The reason those people felt incapable of looking away, and like them, I found myself trapped by the sight.

A woman was dancing on one of the bar tables. Her shiny black blouse had a deep neckline that stirred my imagination, just like the tattered, tight jeans that hugged her curves. Her perky breasts, outlined by the shimmering fabric, swayed as she spun on her high heels, her long blonde hair cascading over her back and face, her red lips smudged with lipstick, and she smiled in a way that was so... free, that for a brief moment, all I could do was admire her.

Her arms moved with precision around her body, and suddenly she spun on one foot, balancing on her heel with a perfection that caused murmurs of admiration behind me.

The dancer kept her eyes closed as she slid her hands over her chest, neck, and waist. It was an exceptionally exciting and delicious sight. As if she felt the music in her bones. As if they were one.

The woman twirled again on the polished table and then descended in a perfect exit that made me believe she was a professional dancer. I thought I had witnessed the best performance I'd ever seen, but I was mistaken.

She took an unsteady step when the music slowed down and closed her eyes again. She opened her arms and stood there for a few seconds, once more as if the music penetrated her. And for some reason, I couldn't move; I could only watch her. The loose strands caught in her mouth drew my attention to her slightly parted lips, and still with her eyes closed, she moved her arms, and what I saw next was incredible perfection. The girl spun, leaped, and made delicate, sinuous, and very sensual movements.

She radiated such profound energy that it unsettled me. Among the spins, the dancer ended up getting closer to me, and I found myself holding my breath, watching her. Up close, she was even more beautiful. Like a rebellious angel. The high heels didn't hinder her at all, which impressed me. I didn't understand how women managed to walk on those needles all day, let alone dance on one as if they were barefoot.

Suddenly, as if to contradict me, the girl stumbled on something, and her body was hurled in my direction. I instinctively reached out to catch her, and she clung to me like a drunk person would cling to a pole, jamming her hand right in my face.

"Oops, sorry," she whispered, laughing, as another woman appeared right behind her.

"I told you I was going to fall, we better go." The second woman, much shorter than the girl I was holding at that moment, approached with a worried expression.

"Not now..." she replied, lifting her face while still holding onto my arm.

From that distance, I could see every detail of her face. The most fascinating features I had seen in years. Her light eyes looked like two lit lanterns, burning hot. A green so deep it was like jade.

"You..." she whispered, pointing at my face. Her voice slightly slurred by alcohol exuded sensuality.

And I... was paralyzed by the wild and incredibly perfect beauty of that woman. I didn't move until she came to a halt an inch away from me, raised her hand, and looked into my eyes attentively for the first time. I could see when she noticed the difference between them, that which was so characteristic of me that it had become my codename.

Of course, she would notice.

I had never met anyone who pretended not to see. Fuck it, I liked it. I liked being remembered, I liked making an impact. And for some reason, the mysterious girl smiled.

"Your eyes..." She pointed at them. "Either I've had too much to drink... or this one is blue..." She touched my cheek with her finger, holding back a mischievous smile. "And this one is black." She did the same on the other side, and I couldn't help but think that she was the most delightful woman I had ever encountered.

"Almost black," I replied.

"I want to kiss you," she said out of nowhere, wrapping her arms around my neck. The scent of roses and beer soon enveloped me.

"You should take your friend's advice, miss," I said, just a moment before her gaze met mine... bright, lit, enigmatic.

Damn, who was she?

The young woman, who looked like a mirage, smiled, and to my deepest surprise, planted a bold kiss on my mouth.

"Jasmin!" I heard her friend call out as the sweet, deep scent of Jasmin enveloped me. She continued pressing her lips against mine. Her breath, heavy from dancing, brushed against my face, and damn, it felt too good but was wrong at the same time.

"Take it easy, girl." I pushed her away and held her wrists. She mumbled something unintelligible and then laughed. She was way too drunk. "Better get her out of here," I warned her friend.

"I'll do that right now, sorry for this attack." The kiss-happy dancer wrinkled her nose and grumbled as I leaned her once lively body toward her companion. "Jasmin, you shouldn't kiss strangers; I've told you that. Come on, let's get a soda. I'll ask my dad to come pick us up." She supported her friend, who didn't seem satisfied with how the night was ending, and disappeared into the crowd.

I left as quickly as I could. Thoughts of the most unexpected kiss I'd ever received returned to me, and even though it had only been a dry peck, her scent lingered on my skin. Sweet as a flower-filled field.

I paid the bill at the exit and found myself standing in front of the elevator that would take me to the parking lot, taking one last look at the crowd packed in the club, secretly hoping to see her once more. The sly, sensual, intriguing gaze wouldn't leave my mind.

I took longer than I would have liked to admit to pull away from there, but there were few things a man like me should fear. Looks like that woman's—hungry, adventurous, delicious—were at the top of the list.

I stepped into the elevator and went down to the parking lot. I pulled the keys to my bike from my pocket and was mere centimeters from the vehicle when I heard a persistent knock-knock coming from the fire escape. I looked over my shoulder, and like a vision straight from hell to tempt me, there she was.

The girl with jade eyes.

I narrowed my eyes when I noticed her desperate expression as she ran down the fire escape. She glanced in my direction, her delicate face wrinkling in what looked like a plea for help, and just before she could reach the parking lot, a man jumped on her and grabbed her arms.

"I got her!" he shouted, and another man appeared right behind him.

"LET ME GO!" She struggled against the guy's grip, her high heels lifting off the ground as she flailed her legs in the air.

My blood began to boil as anger surged through every cell of my body. I knew I shouldn't get involved in other people's problems, especially with my lack of self-control, but I'd rather die a thousand times than turn my back on a woman in danger.

I ran to her and kicked one of the idiots holding her. The man staggered and instinctively clutched his waist, just like the other bastard trying to restrain her.

So the bastards were armed?

I considered drawing my weapon for a brief second, but I would be putting myself in line for a potential shootout, so there was no choice.

I struck the hand of the man in front of me as soon as he pulled out his gun, so quickly that it took him a moment to register the pain. I spun around and elbowed the second bastard before he could fully draw his weapon. The black object fell to the ground with the impact, and I kicked both guns under one of the parked cars.

The girl escaped and hid behind me. Her hands clutched my jacket tightly.

I clenched my jaw as I imagined what they planned to do with her, and all the thoughts that hit me were horrific, only intensifying the fury I felt in my chest.

They had no idea who they were dealing with.

Now that I was the only one armed, it would be easier to subdue them right there. I reached for my waist, but stopped before drawing my weapon. There were moments when the only thing that contained my fury was the ability to throw some punches. The night for those bastards was over; I would make sure of that. And before calling the police, I'd teach them that you don't lay a hand on a woman who doesn't want to be touched.

One of them, the biggest of the lot, both in height and width, charged at us like a bull. I pushed her aside with one arm to prevent her from getting hurt as I waited for the bastard to get closer.

This was going to be good...

I let him use all his momentum to reach me, dodged his hands, spun at the same moment he did, and landed an elbow to the guy's jaw, who staggered. The second guy threw a punch that grazed my chin. I kicked his leg and landed three consecutive punches. One to the stomach, the second just above, to the plexus, and the third to the face, sending the man to the ground in two seconds.

The big guy wasn't willing to back down and came back with all his strength. We exchanged blows, and finally, I swept his legs out from under him, throwing him to the ground with a thud as his body crashed against the rough floor. I raised my fist, ready to smash that bastard's face in when a third man came sprinting down the stairs.

I jumped up and stood in a second, drew my weapon, and aimed at his head, which he raised his arms instantly.

"MERCY! Let's calm down..." he shouted, staring at the fallen goons on the floor. "What the hell happened here?" The last one was the smallest of the three. Tall and very thin, he also seemed the youngest. It was then that

I noticed they were all dressed similarly. A dark suit and communication devices in their ears.

"And you, motherfucker, are just going to stand there?" I yelled at him, starting to question what these men did for a living.

"Ah!" He looked at his two fallen companions once more. One of them seemed to have passed out, while the biggest one groaned in pain, cursing me. "I'm just chilling here, sir." He shrugged, keeping his hands raised, surrendering.

I kept my aim on his head.

"Who are you guys? Who do you work for? You better speak up now, or say goodbye to your knees." I aimed.

"I love my knees, please don't shoot them," he replied, panicked, his high-pitched voice almost made me laugh.

"The question isn't who we are, you lunatic," the big guy replied, standing up. "Who are *you*, and what were you doing with Ms. Cahill?" *Cahill...* the last name sounded familiar. "We're not the enemy here, can you lower that shit?" he asked, but obviously, I didn't comply.

"We work for her father, idiot!" The man who had been passed out regained his senses and sat up just as the sound of a motorcycle engine I recognized all too well echoed through the area. I froze for a moment. "And shit... now she's stealing a bike, and it's all your fault."

"Damn it!"

I turned in time to see my Spirit GP Sport, a rare and ridiculously expensive model, zooming out of the parking lot like a flash, leaving behind only the blonde hair of that thieving vixen and a wave of unmeasurable fury.

I shoved my hands into my pockets, remembering I had taken the key out at some point, but... where did it go? I looked at the spot where the bike had been parked. The high heels were thrown right there, below space number 14, in the parking spot. That must have been how the bitch found my bike; I had left the parking slip attached to the keychain with the spot number.

Idiot! Idiot! Idiot!

"Shit!" That vixen played me like a fool.

"She stole your bike, huh?" The youngest, the only one who hadn't taken a beating that night, approached me and stood beside me. I was so furious I didn't even respond.

I remembered that woman's hands holding me as if I were her protector. I had thought that once I dealt with these guys, she would be right behind me, scared and anxious, but I was mistaken.

Very, very mistaken, I realized. The feeling of getting punched in the gut hit me.

"We lost Crystal." I heard the big guy say behind me, and I immediately identified them as private security. Only a bodyguard would speak like that about their VIP. It seemed she really was running from someone. From the paid babysitters sent by her father. "Thanks to an idiot, she managed to get access to a bike. We have no idea where she went, surround the area and..."

"The idiot here knows exactly where she is," I replied, huffing indignantly.

I was a naturally skeptical man, rarely trusted anyone, and when I did, I gave no leeway for any type of betrayal. I had dealt with dangerous men of all kinds, and none of them had ever managed to pull one over on me—how had I been robbed by that woman?

"What did you say?" one of them, the second one who faced me, asked, clutching his stomach tightly.

Maybe I would regret not asking first before jumping into a fight with strangers, but that was the only way I knew to solve problems.

Since I was born, the only language I learned was the language of fists. It was the only way I knew how to express myself. A sad path, but one that strengthened me and shaped me into the man I was. But even though I tried to fight that impulse, I had a weakness that destroyed any kind of rationality... women in danger. That drove me insane, blinded me, and always brought me all kinds of trouble, like the one from the night before that I would have to face with my father.

"Do you know where she is?" he asked again when he saw I was silent.

"There's a tracker on my bike, but I'll need a ride," I muttered.

"Oh, you cheeky bastard! After almost getting us killed, you still have the audacity to ask for a ride?"

"He's coming with us," the youngest interrupted the big guy. "We need him; Crystal is priority above all else."

"You're saying that because you weren't the one who got beat by him," the second one said.

I opened my phone while they argued, trying to locate the bike using my GPS.

"If you guys would just think before jumping into fights in parking lots, you'd know who he is." I rolled my eyes at the kid's comment.

"And do you know who I am?"

"Of course I do. Why do you think I kept quiet back there? You're an idol to everyone who wants to be part of Holder Security," he mentioned the name of the company I had known since I was a kid.

"He works there?" The big guy wiped his nose, visibly intrigued.

"He's the Wolf, you idiot. One of the owner's sons at Holder Security. The most sought after for special missions. There's not a bodyguard who joined after him who doesn't want to follow in his footsteps." He took a deep breath and turned to me. His small eyes widening as he smiled. "It's a pleasure to meet you, sir."

"If you want to keep that girl's neck intact, we better hurry. If she crashes my bike..."

"Don't joke! The boss will kill us if she gets so much as a scratch."

"If my bike gets a scratch, I'll kill her myself," I growled. "Let's move."

So many years in the business and no one, absolutely no one, had ever been able to fool me. Until that clear-eyed viper crossed my path. Ah, but by a thousand hells, I was going to teach her not to mess with wolves.

CHAPTER TWO

Jasmin

Holy shit, what bike was that?

The wide, imposing tank made me feel like a tiny ant riding it, the engine roared every time I accelerated. I couldn't even say what all those buttons on the digital panel were for. Even the throttle was different. It was definitely an expensive vehicle, and that man was probably not happy about my brief loan.

He would never understand.

No one understands!

I turned onto one of the main avenues and headed to my destination, accelerating a little more as I entered the North Avenue Beach. The beach that Magnolia loved so much. I blinked several times, the adrenaline flushing out any trace of alcohol still lingering in my blood.

I was so happy that I didn't feel the slightest regret for leaving my friend at the club waiting for her father, who was a strange man that gave me the creeps. I would call Carla later and explain everything; after all, she was the one who helped me sneak away. Escaping from my bodyguards that day had been the hardest mission I had ever faced in my life, but now, with the warm wind and sea breeze brushing against my face under the black helmet that smelled deliciously of musk, I saw that it had all been worth it.

I parked next to a few other bikes and caught the attention of two men who were chatting near one of them.

"Cool bike," said a broad-shouldered redhead with a cheerful grin full of teeth.

I dismounted the bike and took off my helmet. My hair, already a bit stuck from sweat, tangled up, and I had to run my fingers through it to detangle the strands.

"Cool is a cat like this riding a Spirit," his friend added. Unlike the redhead, he didn't smile; he just stared at me with such intensity that I raised my eyebrows.

I glanced at my reflection in the mirror of another bike parked right next to mine. The dark makeup around my eyes had smudged across most of my face, my hair, which I already suspected was messy, looked like a pile of yellow strands, and to make matters worse, my red lipstick had smeared all over my mouth like a circus clown. Oh, and I was barefoot on top of that.

"You need to see an ophthalmologist urgently; your case is serious." I turned to the guy still staring at me and walked away, ignoring what he had whispered in response.

I walked along the shore, watching the coral sand stretch out of sight and meet the vast, dark blue sea under the starry sky that glimmered at the end of autumn. As if a mantle covered the entire horizon, in a canvas that looked like the work of a painter.

I kept walking until my feet touched the cold sand. I felt the grains slip between my toes and closed my eyes, the sensation mingling with the fine breeze that washed over me.

When was the last time I set eyes on a beach?

I couldn't remember.

In fact, I could barely recall when I had the chance to go out alone in life. I think the only time was when I learned to ride, but in the end, I fell, got hurt, and never managed to steal a few moments alone again. The men in black were always there.

But today would be different.

I brought my hand to my mouth, remembering the brief kiss I had given that stranger. That man looked like he stepped out of a movie. His facial features were sharp, the prominent beard around his jaw accentuated his square chin, like a prince. I saw him from afar when I was still dancing with my friend, Carla, at the bar. The dark hair, slightly falling over his forehead, gave him an air of mystery, one that made you lose your soul trying to unravel.

When I saw my bodyguards arriving at the club and tried to escape through the parking lot, I never imagined finding him there with the keys to some vehicle in hand. I thought quickly and snatched the keys, just like I did his bike.

He was going to kill me, oh, definitely... I smiled, remembering the way his eyes had looked into mine. I had never seen anything so different and beautiful. It was like looking directly at a wolf. One of his eyes was a deep, clear, and bright blue, while the other was taken over by an intense dark hue. The combination of those two colors and the lustful look with which he had gazed at me made me wish to be kissed by him at any cost.

I traced my fingers over my lips, clinging to the brief memory that still lingered. A kiss too quick... I closed my eyes, as always, imagining what it would be like to go beyond that point. What would it be like to go beyond a kiss?

I looked up at the sky where countless shining dots bid me goodnight and began to think of her... Magnolia knew what it was like to go beyond a kiss. She had a boyfriend who visited us every now and then, and I didn't even know how she managed to "go further" with the guy since we were always surrounded. But somehow, even though I remained a virgin, she at least managed to steal a few kisses with him. They were completely in love with each other, but after she was gone, I never saw him again. I hoped at least he had visited her at the cemetery more times than I ever could.

"You know if it were up to me, I would visit her every week, right?" I spoke to the nothingness, as I had gotten used to doing in recent years.

Loneliness was one of the worst punishments one could impose on another person, even if it were for love, even if it were for protection. Magnolia and I used to go shopping, to the movies, and to gatherings with friends, always accompanied by our bodyguards. We weren't deprived of going out, but we didn't do it as often as the rest of the world. Unlike that, our days were reduced to studying and dancing. Always together. And I was happy, even deprived of a common life like all the other young girls we knew; we still had a lot of fun together. She was my best friend. My little sister... my sister. But after her death, all that was left for me was loneliness.

My father increased security, and it had been three years since I barely left the house. I spent most of that time drugged up on medications trying to cope with the pain.

Suddenly, breathing became difficult. The pain of longing and memories occasionally stalked me. I tried to push them away; I knew Mag wouldn't want to see me like this, but how could I avoid that endless urge to cry? Today was supposed to be a day of celebration. Of cake, of happy birthdays..., but now, what was left? Many years of life? For whom? For me? No... I didn't want that, thank you.

"If I could, I would trade all the years I have left in this private, lonely life for one more day with you." I stared at the sky, the painful knot in my throat intensifying. "Happy birthday, sister. I will always love you, do you hear me?" I pulled a chocolate from my pocket, the only thing I managed to bring to keep our birthday tradition alive, and looked at the small, round candy in my hand. My eyes misted over. "I promise I'll bring your favorite cake next time." A solitary tear rolled down my face, falling on the helmet I held tightly between my arms. Sadness began to morph again into pure indignation.

He didn't even speak her name. He didn't even remember when her birthday was. I wanted to bring a little cake, even if it was small and just for me; I wanted somehow to show that I still remembered our traditions, like we did every morning on her birthday, celebrating with chocolate cake with chocolate frosting—pure chocolate. But the only way to get to my sister's favorite beach on her birthday was by sneaking out.

"I couldn't even bring the little cake..." I cried, wiping my tears with the back of my hand and feeling like a complete idiot. It had been three years, but for me, it felt like yesterday. I still expected her to come wake me up every morning; I still sat on our porch every Tuesday looking at the stars like we did together; I still missed her so much it felt like I was gasping for air.

The sound of cars braking behind me alerted me to the arrival of my faithful guardians. I wiped my face, donning the armor I had developed over the years, and hid behind a smile. It was time to return to my character.

I turned toward the shore, believing it was my security detail, but the man who appeared in my line of sight was nothing like them. If anger could be seen with the naked eye, I could swear there was a cloud of fury, rage, and aggression coming at me in that moment.

The mysterious man from the club walked across the sand as if fire were spewing from his nostrils. His fists were clenched at his sides, clearly trying to contain the urge to strangle me.

"You!" he growled even before he got closer.

"Good to see you again." I tried to maintain my smile.

He stopped inches away from me and grabbed my arm. I could feel the tremor in his hand, probably controlling his anger little by little.

"That bike is a collector's item, you crazy girl," he cursed under his breath. "How dare you steal it right under my nose? There are only 50 of them in the world; if you caused even a scratch, I swear..."

"You swear you're going to give me another kiss, right? We're not doing anything anyway," I teased, locking eyes with him more deeply, coming to a conclusion: God surely had his favorites.

That man was even more handsome under the cool beach lights, where the dim lighting created a magical and romantic setting. And there was the look I had longed to see again. The irises of different shades blended with the mystery hidden behind the shadow of that gaze and swept over me as if they could see all my secrets. For a moment, I felt exposed, laid bare.

"You're the most beautiful man I've ever seen. What a pity," I said and bit my lips.

"What a pity?" His two-toned eyes scanned my face; his very tense jaw began to relax as his anger yielded to curiosity.

"What a pity that I can't devour you right here on this sand." He coughed and widened his eyes in surprise.

Did he really think he could scare me in any way?

Poor guy, if he only knew what I had faced... that penetrating gaze didn't even tickle me.

"You must be crazy. Hand over the key and the damn helmet," he ordered, furious. I could feel he was on the brink of a breakdown.

"Let's make a deal. I'll return your key, and you give me another kiss," I said playfully, leaning in. "Come on, it wasn't that bad."

"You have no idea who you're playing with, girl."

"I may not know, but I can imagine." I shrugged. "You were alone in that club on a Saturday night. I know at least two women approached you, yet you ignored them. You accepted a kiss from a stranger but pulled away when you noticed I was drunk. And even without knowing me, you got involved in a fight to defend me. I suspect your bike, so expensive and rare, is your only companion in your spare moments. You're a good man; you wouldn't hurt me even if you wanted to, but you're also lonely, and that's why I'm here. To brighten your night." I spread my arms and noticed when he narrowed his eyes at me. I had hit a nerve somehow, and I was glad for the long seasons of *Criminal Minds* I had watched that revealed some aspects of people's traits.

I wasn't Spencer Reid, but I managed when it came to hypotheses.

"You're just a daddy's girl looking for some adventure, aren't you? But let me tell you something..." He leaned forward, getting even closer to me. His breath brushed my face, causing a strange mix of intimacy and anger. "The world doesn't revolve around you, and if you care about your neck, you better hand over that damn key soon."

I tried to ignore the stab of pain I felt in my chest from his angry words and smiled. He had no idea how wrong he was about me, but I wasn't going to explain myself to him. Never!

"How boring, you don't even know how to play." I held up the key in my hand, the same one that held the chocolate I had brought to eat on the beach.

The man lunged for it, and in the blink of an eye, the chocolate fell to the ground, and a strange despair hit my chest.

"NO!" I screamed, and noticed he flinched.

When I saw the chocolate lying in the sand, all dirty, I felt an overwhelming urge to shove a handful of that sand into that idiot's mouth.

"Look what you did! You threw it on the ground, you moron!"

"You're lucky it's not you buried in that sand," he yelled, turning his back to me, broad as it was. I grabbed a handful of sand and threw it at his head.

"Good luck getting that sand out of your hair." I pouted. It was true I really did seem like the spoiled child he had called me, but I usually wasn't like this.

"Ah, you spoiled little brat..."

"I spotted Crystal!" Peter Lyon, nearly 6 feet tall with a crooked pout, advanced through the beach sand communicating with the other security guards, who soon appeared and interposed themselves between me and the unknown man shaking his hair, which had been so clean before.

It was a sin to mess up that impeccable hair, but he deserved it. Who told him to throw my chocolate on the ground? There were things that shouldn't be touched; a woman's chocolate was one of them.

"Miss Cahill, what were you thinking to do something so reckless? You put your life at serious risk today," Lyon reprimanded me as the enigmatic man began to walk off the beach.

"Oh, she threw sand at him," Shaw, my coolest bodyguard, commented with a face contorted in pure horror as he passed by the man. "I'm sorry, sir. She usually doesn't..."

"Keep that delinquent away from me. Next time, I won't be so kind," he growled as a parting shot.

"Delinquent? He called me a delinquent? Well, you..." I made a move to go after him, but Lyon held my arm.

"You stole his bike; you can't blame him. In fact, you should be thankful he's not pressing charges." I huffed in response to Lyon's stern expression, though it soon softened.

Lyon was the strictest of all my bodyguards, but he was also one of the oldest and one of the few who had witnessed everything that happened in our past. He knew exactly why I was there. I looked at his face, red and marked from the scuffle.

"I'm sorry for causing this," I said, staring at my bare feet.

"It's my job to protect you, whether you want it or not, and it was nothing," he said to reassure me. "You don't have to worry."

"Are you okay?" Shaw asked with a slightly affected voice. I looked at the sea, then at the sky, and finally my eyes fell on the chocolate lying in the sand, and for a moment, I felt like it. Abandoned, useless.

In the background, I heard the loud roar of that incredible bike, shaking the air around it, and an overwhelming desire to be on that back seat hit me. I wanted so badly to feel free that I wouldn't mind disappearing with a grumpy stranger like him. If it made me feel alive again, but I knew all too well what my reality was.

"No, I'm not okay, but I will be," was my response before returning to my life as a prisoner.

CHAPTER THREE

Wolf

Bitch, lowlife, deceitful little dog!

I was still furious when I parked my bike in the garage of the building where I lived. A luxurious and exclusive place where I rarely saw any of my neighbors, which suited me just fine.

I took off my helmet and dismounted the bike, observing it for a moment. My chest rose and fell as I tried to control the rage that that... that shameless woman, with her light fingers, had caused me.

There were few untouchable things in the world for me, and my Spirit was definitely one of them. I ran my hand over the wide, black tank, shining like a star in the sky. At the tip of the tank was a small red V mark, representing a brand that was exclusive and one of the most expensive in the world. An acquisition I had fought my ass off to obtain, and that vixen...

I rubbed my eyes and leaned toward the bike. I examined every detail to ensure it hadn't gotten a scratch during that little adventure, and I could only breathe normally when I realized it was still intact.

That said a lot about that woman's riding skills. Not just anyone could handle a machine like this. Even the roaring engine usually scared people away.

"To hell, how did she have the *guts*?" I cursed loudly, completely alone in the parking lot. I still didn't know whether I was more angry, perplexed, or surprised by that crazy woman's audacity to steal from a man like me.

In a way, her bravery fascinated me. The girl had quick thinking, hands as agile as a pickpocket's, and to make matters worse, she was as beautiful as a magazine cover model. And the damn girl surely knew how to use that to her advantage, which irritated me all over again. How could I fall for such an idiotic trick?

I entered the building's lobby, raking my hands through my hair, trying to get the last grains of sand she had thrown at me out.

"Good evening, Mr. Holder," Lucian, the night shift doorman, greeted me, and I noticed the confused look he shot my way when he saw me almost pulling my hair out in anger.

"Good evening," I grumbled reluctantly, continuing my battle against the sand as I waited for the elevator.

I rode up the 16 floors and stepped out of the metal box when the doors opened, entering the hallway of the building that led to the penthouse. A series of lights began to illuminate as I walked over the glossy floor. I stopped in front of the last door in the hallway, dark wood, almost black, just like the entire space behind it.

I lifted the cover of the digital keypad and typed in the door code. The moment I entered my apartment, the anger over my bike's brief theft began to give way to curiosity.

Why the hell was she running from security?

She must be one of the many well-off girls our company took care of every now and then. But those three definitely didn't work for Holder Security. Never in our history had a bodyguard lost their VIP, and in that situation, there were three of them on the girl's tail. THREE! Either they were terrible professionals, or she was a damn good escape artist.

I paused in front of the small bar positioned next to my living room, adorned in shades of black and gray that made the space darker and more inviting. I poured myself a shot of neat whiskey and downed it in one gulp, feeling the strong flavor slide down warm through my throat before refilling the glass. I walked over to the dark gray sofa and sat down, staring at one of the stone walls that adorned the sides of the shelf.

I pressed my lips tightly together, unsure of when I lost control of what happened that night. Was it when I saw her dancing at the bar? Or when that cheeky girl kissed me?

For heaven's sake, that was the worst kiss I'd ever given anyone, so why was I still thinking about it?

The lightness of the touch, the intriguing, enveloping scent. And her eyes... damn, it was the worst memory of that miserable night. Staring at her was like looking directly into a spotlight. The little thief was beautiful, I had to admit, but I was so blinded by rage that I could only grasp that now. When I saw her on that beach, all I wanted was to unleash all the fury I was feeling on her.

For God's sake, I wanted to bury her in that sand! Really.

But when I approached her, she turned to me with a huge smile plastered on her face. A smile that didn't fool me at all. I could still remember as if she were right in front of me. The green spheres, once bright and full of life, looked sad. The makeup, much more smudged than I'd seen at the club, told me she had been crying, and no matter how deeply I hated her, seeing a woman cry didn't sit well with me.

For a moment, I wanted to know what had caused that, but when a grain of sand fell on the carpet of my living room, all doubt vanished and was replaced by the urge to strangle her again.

To hell with why she was crying. I poured another shot of whiskey. She wasn't my problem and needed to remember that the vixen stole my bike. A bunch of tears shouldn't move me, damn it.

But unfortunately, it did...

I leaned back on the sofa, and the problems I would face with my father seemed small compared to everything that had happened that night.

Why were you crying, Jasmin? What happened to you?

I tried to drink a little more, attempting to forget that woman, that scent, that mouth... as much as I tried to erase the flicker of sadness trapped in those beautiful, big eyes. It was no use. Nothing I did would erase the madness the night had turned into. All because of that cheeky little thief.

A SCREECHING SOUND pierced my ears and seemed to stab my brain. I opened my eyes with extreme difficulty. The blackout curtains darkened the whole room, but a small gap allowed a ray of light to enter, hitting my eyes, which irritated me the moment I opened them.

The persistent sound continued ringing, and it took me a minute or two to find my phone, which was lost somewhere in the sofa. Apparently, the successive shots of whiskey had calmed my thoughts, and I ended up passing out right there.

"Ah, damn it!" I squinted my eyes when I found the phone lost in the corner of the couch and saw the name flashing insistently on the screen.

"Dad!"

Hell!

"Hello!" I answered with the best voice I could muster, which still came out sounding like a hoarse duck.

"Did you die or something?" he asked, annoyed. "Do you realize what time it is? Why aren't you at the office?"

"I had a problem last night, Dad. I ended up being late." I tried to explain without going into details. "I'll be there in a few minutes."

"Be quick, Chris. We need to talk about your last mission, and there's no place in this world you can hide," he threatened. "I'm expecting your apologies, and I'll warn you, they better be convincing."

And he hung up... which meant he was pissed at me.

My father rarely lost his temper when it came to his children, and I had immense pride in him. Reid Holder, or R.H., as the employees called him, was always a good man, grounded, and available. He was a born diplomat, always trying to meet the interests of his clients in a professional, efficient, and practical manner. I grew up watching every one of his moves, admiring the man I would come to call my father.

When he started expanding his private security company, no one imagined he would become a powerhouse across the country, with units spread everywhere. Even less did they imagine that Holder Security would rank first in quality in our field and frequently be designated for missions abroad, enabling it to soon become a multinational.

My father worked hard for that company and trained his three children to be the best examples of the place. I understood why he was so upset. Commitment, integrity, impartiality, and discretion had always been the key words that drove Holder Security, and I had broken at least two of them in my last mission, and I needed to face the consequences.

I took a quick shower, put on one of my black suits, and decided to take my bike since I needed to get there as fast as possible. When I got on it, all the thoughts I tried to forget during the night returned with a vengeance. A mix of irritation and concern gnawed at me as I imagined how that clueless girl's night had ended.

Seriously, was I starting to worry about delinquents now? I rolled my eyes and started the bike.

I headed to the central building of the company where my father, my brothers, and I worked.

I was greeted with warm smiles the moment I parked the bike in the lot, as always.

"Good morning, Mr. Holder," the employee in charge of vehicle entry and exit greeted me, and I gave a brief, impatient nod.

My head was pounding. It throbbed incessantly, and I didn't even know what was causing that pain. Was it the whiskey I drank, the anxiety I felt over the conversation I was about to have with my father, or the anger that crept under my skin at the thought of that mysterious girl?

"Mr. Holder!" a brown-haired woman greeted me with a broad smile as she walked past with a handful of papers in her arms. I didn't recognize her. There were so many employees working in that place that even if I wanted to, I wouldn't be able to memorize each face.

I arrived at the turnstile that provided access to the elevators that would take me to the president's office. There was a skinny young guy, broad-shouldered and of average height, responsible for granting entry. We had recently installed a digital recognition sensor, which would help organize who moved through the company and, most importantly, reinforce security. With a badge, anyone could enter; with the new system, it would be harder to fool the security. However, due to a problem, it was necessary to deactivate the software for a few days.

I stopped in front of the turnstile, waiting, as I did every morning since we lost the new program, for someone to open that thing since I didn't use a badge. The young guy raised his small eyes toward me and stared, as if waiting for something. I realized he was one of the many faces I didn't remember seeing around here when he spoke, confirming my suspicion. He must be a new employee.

"Sir, please present your badge so we can allow your entry into the headquarters of..."

"ANTHONY!" The sudden shout startled both me and the rat-faced young man in front of me.

An extremely elegant yet exotic man, dressed in an eggplant suit and matching tie, walked over with a look of disbelief. I knew him well.

"How dare you stop the Wolf?" he cursed as he approached the young man, who stiffened his entire body at that moment. "Mr. Holder, please disregard this young man's lapse of memory." Benjamin, my father's right-hand man at the headquarters, a man of a thousand facets who was always willing to do his best for the Holder family and hated a strand out of place, was almost red with anger. "He started today, and it seems he didn't take a look at the main faces in the place." The young Anthony turned a sickly shade of yellow and leaned on the counter for a moment before opening it.

"Sir, I apologize! I didn't recognize you." He fumbled as he released the turnstile. Benjamin opened his mouth to say something, but I interrupted him.

"Anthony, right?"

"Yes, sir!" he replied, shrinking his shoulders.

"You acted correctly. What you did is part of your job. Identification is mandatory; you don't have to apologize. You're just starting today, and you're probably going to make real mistakes at some point; do your best to avoid them, so you won't have to hear anyone call your attention." How ironic. There I was, about to take the biggest reprimand of my life and advising someone not to mess up. "Take it easy, Benjamin. You've been in the kid's shoes too. And after all, he was just doing his job by stopping anyone without a badge."

"Yes, sir," he replied reluctantly.

"I'll do my best, I promise," Anthony said, looking at me with a different spark in his eyes, rejuvenated. I nodded and walked toward the elevator, not without hearing Benjamin question the young man.

"How many people with eyes that color do you think work here?"

I chuckled and stepped into the elevator with a few other employees from the place, who hurried to greet me.

I ascended to the 14th floor, where the company's presidency was located, and I began to feel suffocated as I approached the presidential office.

I approached the solid wood corner desk where Emma, a woman in her forties with brown hair, almond-shaped eyes, and a very small mouth that sometimes startled me, was looking at me with a smile on her face.

"Good morning, Mr. Holder," she said, opening a wide-toothed smile as she picked up the phone and dialed. "He's here," she informed my father with an upbeat voice. "The president is waiting for the..." Before she could finish her sentence, I was already opening the door.

The sooner the lecture began, the sooner it would end.

I entered my father's office, a spacious and expansive place, just as dark as my home. I immediately looked at the black chair turned away from me, behind a rectangular mahogany desk.

I took a step into the room, filled with the familiar scent of Cohiba Behike, one of my father's favorite cigars, which he regularly received from an old client. An expensive cigar he usually only smoked when he was about to explode at one of us.

I clenched my jaw, preparing for what was to come. I walked between the wide dark gray pillars that contrasted with the navy blue stone floor and matched the bright black walls. The color that represented our organization.

I glanced at the wall to my right, covered in certificates, titles, and awards received in the 25 years since the company was founded, while I patiently waited for my father to turn the chair in my direction.

"Dad?" I called after an endless minute. The cigar smoke rose in waves through the air, like lyrics from a song dancing in the dark room.

He slowly turned the chair, and when he faced me, I noticed he was holding a picture frame in one hand and waving the cigar from side to side with the other. His displeased gaze scanned me from head to toe.

"You've grown up, haven't you?" he commented, placing the family photo on the table, where my two brothers and I held our bodyguard training certificates from the International Security School in Israel, a school considered the best in the world. And my father, who rarely smiled so openly, wore a broad grin alongside us, always in his well-fitted black suit, his graying hair meticulously slicked back. I swallowed hard when he raised his inquisitive eyes, a deep navy blue, like the night sky, in my direction.

My father was a very strong and youthful man. He never remarried after being betrayed by the only woman he ever had interest in. A man detached from love, as many say. But those who truly knew him understood what lay beneath that black suit and his always impeccable military posture.

I had no idea what my fate, or my brothers', would have been if that stubborn, stern man hadn't entered our lives. My old man stood against everything society viewed in kids like us. He saw beyond all the prejudice; Reid saw the pain behind every action we took, and if we had a home and a family, it was thanks to him, who adopted each of us when we had nothing left but air to breathe, and today took us as his own. And if I had one certainty in this life, it was that R.H. was my father.

Reid had plenty of love in that closed heart. If I ever knew that feeling, it was through my father's actions, who took me in when no one else had the courage. Who showed me the difference between controlling anger and being controlled by it. And it was for that reason, for everything we had lived, that my heart felt tight. Disappointing him was worse than losing one of my arms.

"I remember when you used to hide in the rooms of each of the buildings I built just to play pranks on the new employees," he recalled, stroking his jaw. "I wanted to lock you in the house every time that happened." He let out a deep laugh that made me hold my breath. "But I never did that. Not with any of the three of you. The hurricanes I call my children." He lifted his wise eyes, marked by expression lines. "I've accepted and understood a lot, Christopher..." Damn, damn, damn. He called me by my name, no nicknames, no codenames. Things were looking bad for me. "But after everything you've been through, everything you've learned... After becoming one of my best men in Security, the least I expected was commitment."

"Dad, I assure you I had a reason for..."

"To punch a damn SHEIK's guest?" he shouted suddenly, standing up. His muscular body remained upright. "Have you completely lost your mind, boy?"

I clenched my fists tightly, feeling the knuckles tingle. He had no idea what I had witnessed in that place. How could I just stand there and not react?

"Tell me, did you even think about the consequences we would face?"

"I'm sorry, Dad," I said through clenched teeth, "but my only regret is that I only knocked out one of the bastard's teeth."

"You want to die, is that it?" A firm, mocking voice spoke behind me, catching me off guard.

"Damn it, Ghost!" I jumped in place and turned to him, who smiled and shrugged. "How the hell do you do that?" I cursed. "You better stomp your feet when you walk, or I'll punch you for scaring me."

My brother's nickname suited him well, given his ability to move practically unnoticed. When you least expected it, he was there. Like a 6'3" ghost, silent and quick.

"Come on, I was right behind you. You didn't see me because you're too busy facing our dad," he scolded. Despite being the youngest of the three brothers, Ghost was the most sensible and composed. A self-control that sometimes scared me.

"He lives to test my heart. That ungrateful kid," my father said, flopping back down into the chair.

I stared at Ghost, who was watching me with a suspicious look. He pressed his lips together and, unconsciously, touched the scars on the back of his right hand. Some of the many he had on his body. My brother walked over to a glass table next to where my father was sitting, where two bottles of whiskey sat beside some glasses. He grabbed three glasses and opened one of the bottles, pouring the amber liquid into them. Drinking on an empty stomach was a habit for tough days, and by the looks of it, that day was getting worse by the minute.

"Tell me, brother..." He handed one of the glasses to our father and approached me, extending one toward me. "Besides provoking our father and surely having lost your love for life, what led you to do something so stupid?" I downed the whiskey in one go. I needed that stuff to continue the conversation.

"Nothing he says can be tolerated. Wolf exposed the quality of services provided by Security," my father bellowed. "A name I took a long time to build. We are unbeatable. Clients want to hire us, anyone in this field dreams of working with us, and now tell me, how do I explain to these people that one of my sons, one of the most competent professionals in the area, assaulted a VIP guest?"

"Calm down, Dad. There's no condemnation without a trial, is there?" Ghost interjected with his usual calmness. "Come on, Wolf... what happened? And don't bother making up excuses, because I know when you're lying. You don't usually break orders of this magnitude. Something happened."

I pressed my eyes with my fingers, and when I opened them, I stared at my brother's perfectly tailored black suit. He was right.

"Yeah, something happened."

"I knew it!" Ghost smiled, excited, leaning against our father's desk. My father's eyes surveyed my face like an eagle. "Come on, defend yourself." He waved his hands in my direction.

When I received the assignment to protect the Sheik at a party in the VIP's own palace, I knew what I would have to deal with. We always do.

Arrogant, rich, snobby people completely devoid of common sense. Some even get aggressive with the security, after a drink or two they don't want a shadow protecting their damn neck. So far, so normal...

"The event started well," I said. "And as I predicted, many people got drunk during the party, and I had to escort the VIP to his suite." As I recalled what happened, my hand began to tremble, and I started staring at a fixed point on the floor in front of me. "I stayed at that man's door for a good while to ensure no one would enter since the windows were the beta team's responsibility. When the night grew quiet, I began to hear some strange noises."

"Noises?" they asked in unison.

"Yeah." I clenched my jaw. The muffled whimper that terrified me in the nights that followed returned to my mind with full force.

A suppressed cry for help. The suffering in the girl's eyes, the marks on her face. Everything came rushing back as if I could still see her right in front of me.

"Wolf..."

"Damn it!" I shouted when I noticed Ghost standing inches from my face. "Can you stop doing that and just stay still for a moment?"

"I didn't do anything." He widened his brown eyes at me. "I swear! Right, Dad?" He glanced over his shoulder at our father, who was watching me with a deep furrow between his eyebrows. "You were staring into space with a bit of a killer look."

"Tell me, Christopher," my father called suddenly, "what did you hear?"

"A cry for help," I revealed, and I noticed the expression of a mix of curiosity and shock that took over both their faces.

"Help?" Ghost asked.

"Yeah. I followed the sound and found that bastard guest assaulting a woman. The girl looked like she had been pleading for help for a long time. Her face was all marked. She wouldn't stop shaking. When she saw me, she screamed in terror," I revealed, leaning against one of the pillars in the room. "She was a high-class escort, but she wasn't on duty. She was hired to accompany him at the party and leave right afterward, but he took her upstairs and wanted to change the terms of the contract. She refused, and he beat her up. If I hadn't gotten there in time, you know very well how things would have ended, so no, Dad... I couldn't just stand by in front of the shit I saw." I only realized I was shouting when Ghost pressed my shoulder with his firm fingers.

My father raised a hand to his lips, and the silence that followed irritated me. He knew. In fact, both my father and my brothers knew why I would never let that go unpunished, and thanks to the Sheik, our VIP, who understood that the situation could be detrimental to his plans with the investors visiting the next day, I left there with only an assault charge, but the truth was I didn't even know if that bastard would survive the beating I gave him.

Our client didn't tell my father the truth. He said I punched his guest, when in reality I beat the hell out of him, and I'd die before regretting that.

My father tapped the tips of his fingers on the mahogany table.

"I understand why you did it," he said finally. "But you know I can't let you get away with this. Regardless of what you saw, you allowed your aggressive instincts to take over your actions. You knew what the right thing to do was."

"To restrain the man and take him to the authorities. Maybe smash his face against a pillar on the way, but..."

"Zion!" my father yelled Ghost's name, making him jump in place.

"Calm down, Dad. I was just joking." He smiled innocently.

"You need to control your animosity, Christopher." My father ran his hands through his hair and stood up. "And I know just how to do it. I'm taking you off the more intense cases for now."

"What?" I laughed. "You can't do that, Dad. I have three cases locked in. The clients are counting on me and..."

"Ghost will take two, and Snake will take the last one."

"Snake won't accept one of my cases. He barely tolerates the clients I get. You know he works better with a different style of VIP." *The mobsters.*

A bitter taste rose in my throat as I remembered that Snake almost went down a different path from the rest of us, a path I knew too well. The one of hired killers. The damn scum we fight every day.

"He will accept," he assured firmly.

"Dad, I can handle my own cases. I guarantee it was an isolated incident." I tried to gain some confidence.

"It's already decided. I have a specific new case for you, Wolf. And you won't return to missions until you fulfill it." He stepped closer with the cigar in one hand.

"And what case is that?" I grimaced, hating the idea more with each passing second.

"Oh, you're not going to like this at all." Ghost shot me a cynical smile. The bastard was enjoying this.

"Last night, a friend called me to cash in a special favor I owe him from a few years back in Mexico. And given our current situation, I see no way to deny him such a request."

"What is it...?"

"He needs a bodyguard for his daughter," he blurted out, staring at me.

"Are you kidding me?"

"No. You've been assigned to the mission. I need you on this case."

"Do I look like a babysitter? Do I look like a damn babysitter, Dad?" I said, agitated.

I couldn't even entertain the thought of providing security for one of my father's wealthy friends' daughters. Just in the last 24 hours, I had cursed every rich kid who needed our services because of that... light-fingered incident last night.

Damn, this had to be some karma.

"Listen, Wolf, he asked for the best. And you really need to step away from the action for a while."

"Take that as a compliment, dear brother." Ghost smirked. "He asked for the best... and you're the prized sheep." I raised my clenched fist, fighting the urge to punch my brother right there. "Whoa, touchy." He laughed and moved away from me.

"Anything but this. Don't count on me for this shit." My father moved closer and raised his free hand, resting it on my shoulder.

"I understand, son, why you had to do that." He looked into my eyes in that way that made me feel like a kid again, as if I were 13 years old, hiding in a corner of a dark room in the orphanage, with no hope of ever leaving that place. "You know I understand." I took a deep breath; he was right. I knew he understood. "But you are my examples. You are the examples of Holder. I need you to do this so we can erase the previous image. And I promised that idiot I would send my best man."

"There's nothing I can do to get out of this, is there?" He shook his head, denying, and a lazy smile crept up on his lips. "Is this idiot your friend, or do I risk breaking his teeth too?" I reluctantly conceded and followed my father to the table, sitting across from him as Ghost casually sat beside me.

"He's a good man, but you need to be cautious. It will only be 15 days," he warned, and I leaned in, desperate to know what awaited me while simultaneously wanting to get up and flee immediately. "He's the president of a large arms and defense company. He works with big players, provides services for the army and other governmental security agencies in the country. His daughter is his only heir. He's always received threats, but apparently, in 15 days, there will be a merger in the company that has left all the partners anxious. He's worried, especially because the daughter refuses to accept protection. She's unwilling to cooperate."

"What should I expect from her?" I grumbled.

"She's smart. She's already fooled the best men he hired. You need to be on your toes, Wolf. Or she'll give you trouble."

"I highly doubt it."

"Don't doubt it; they say the girl is a real handful."

"Where's the paperwork on this handful?" My brother laughed at the amusing sound of the similar words.

"It's in her father's hands. It's too confidential, and he didn't feel comfortable handing it over to our team. So go immediately to the residence to fetch it, assemble a team if necessary, and start as soon as possible." He clasped his hands and rested them on the table in front of him. "Horrible things have happened to that family, son. Be careful that history doesn't repeat itself and protect the girl."

"You know very well that no mission will fail in my hands. You trained us from a young age. You know my skills." I stood up suddenly. "I've protected all kinds of people and never lost a client. I'm not starting now with some little girl."

"They killed that girl's sister in the same situation she's in today, and I bet the bodyguard back then thought the same thing you do." He caught me off guard, and I swallowed hard at that new information. "It seems that after her sister's death, she gave up on security, and this may seem like a simple case, my son, but it's the hardest one a bodyguard can face. Protecting someone who doesn't want to be protected."

His words hit me hard. I had never lost a life and wouldn't know what to do if I did. I would probably carry that burden for the rest of my existence.

"Consider the job done." I nodded briefly.

"Be careful, son."

"Good luck, Wolf." Ghost waved at me as I was about to leave.

I headed back down to the parking lot and put on my helmet, an odd feeling bothering me. This wasn't just the most pathetic case of my profession; it was an embarrassment to have worked with so many important names and now be reduced, even if temporarily, to a babysitter for a spoiled princess, but even with the anger I felt, knowing her sister had been murdered left me nauseated and ready for anything.

If I believed in a sixth sense, I would say that chill in my stomach as I started my bike was fate warning me that after that day, my life would never be the same, but I didn't believe... and that's how everything changed.

CHAPTER FOUR

Jasmin

The sound of birds singing in a typical hillside euphoria woke me up. I stretched in bed like a lazy cat, wrapping myself in the covers as I recalled last night and my little escape.

I felt happy about the hours of excitement and heart-pounding moments I had experienced. It was as if they had injected a bit of life into my veins. Since I stopped taking the medication a few months ago, I had noticed a significant improvement in my mood and daily energy, which was reflected in the intensity I was feeling.

I got out of bed, still sleepy and a bit afraid of running into my father in the hallways of the house. It had been three days since I last saw him. I only knew he came home very late and left very early due to the changes he was making in the company, and I imagined he wouldn't be pleased after my little escapade last night.

I washed my face in the bathroom attached to my room, still thinking about what I would say to him when the moment came. I went to my closet and rummaged through the mess of clothing piles, aware that I would have to tidy it up myself, since I had asked Ruth, the housekeeper and torturer of souls during her free hours, to keep all hands away from my room. Now the door no longer had a lock. According to Ruth, that was a way to keep me "safe," along with the guarantee that no one would enter without being called.

In recent months, my patience, which was already minimal, had completely vanished. I wanted space and privacy. And since I couldn't have the first option, I would at least resort to the second.

My routine boiled down to getting up, having someone snooping around my room and the amount of my medications while I tried to gulp down some coffee. Studying, studying, and studying every kind of subject related to my father's company and the arms it provided. Walking in the garden, reading a book, having lunch, spending the rest of the afternoon being followed around my own house by bodyguards, and before bed, more medication accompanied by a deep, induced sleep. The next day, the cycle repeated in an endless loop, with minor alterations, like when I needed to go to my father's company. In that case, the whole crew of security would be on my tail, and I usually could barely breathe.

Out of all the times I had to go out with them, I only managed to shake them off twice. One time, thanks to my friend Carla's lack of sense, I was caught trying to hide among the meat pieces in a butcher shop near my father's company. A failed hiding spot that left me smelling like raw meat for quite a while. At least Carla was creative, I couldn't deny.

I sifted through the pile of shoes, which, to no surprise, were also disorganized, and tried to fish out a pair of comfortable low sandals I really liked. Unintentionally, I ended up grabbing one of my pointe shoes. The one I used most during contemporary ballet classes.

For a moment, I stood there, staring at it. It was too worn to keep being used. The stained fabric showed no signs that it had once been pink.

I pursed my lips, gazing at that lonely shoe. I didn't like the pointe shoe for dancing, nor was I a fan of the ballet teacher. I preferred to dance barefoot and feel the roughness of the floor against my feet, or the soft, damp grass, just as I loved to invent free expression choreographies and perform them. Which drove the teacher mad. So, even though I didn't like the shoe, I wore it. Magnolia did too, but every time the teacher left, we would rip off our shoes and dance for hours on end in our home studio.

Dancing...

Last night was the first time I had managed to dance in three years.

I stared at the worn-out shoe, remembering that for a time I had accepted this whole routine. I accepted being dragged from one place to another, having my life decided for me, paving my paths, and once again allowed myself to be locked inside that golden cage known as the "House on the Hill," my father's domain as the emperor of the arms industry. The largest mansion in the area we lived, with a spectacular view of a cliff, where nature painted a living picture.

I had always been in love with that place, but now... I looked over my shoulder at the various bottles of medication on my large ice-colored vanity in my room. Now I would give everything I had to not spend even one more night there. And that's why I was taking the reins of my life. Sooner or later, my father would have to understand that I was no longer his little girl, and that despite fearing the world outside after the cruelty I had witnessed, I still wanted to explore it.

I tied my hair into a high ponytail and checked my appearance in the large mirror hanging in front of the door, with golden edges and slightly taller than me. I looked at the woman in the reflection as if we hadn't seen each other in a long time. Huge dark circles marked my eyes, and my lips, once rosy, were pale, completely colorless. My mood, my energy, everything had been utterly destroyed in recent years; there was very little left of the Jasmin of the past.

I blinked hard and stepped away from the mirror. It wouldn't do any good to linger there, anyway. The more I stared at my reflected image, the less I recognized myself.

"Where have you been hiding, Jasmin?" I whispered, turning my back to the mirror, and a soft knock on the door pulled me from my daydreams. I hastily threw on a T-shirt and the first pair of pants I found. I opened the door and came face to face with a familiar face.

"Miss Cahill, Senator Magowan is waiting for you, and your father is too." Ruth's low and sneaky voice entered the room, and a tightness in my throat forced me to stop breathing.

I glanced at the clock next to my bed, and it was already past 10 AM. My father usually left at 6 AM. Which meant he hadn't gone to work just to talk to me, plus he had brought reinforcements. If Aunt Claire came rushing over from her house across town just to talk to me, things were looking really bad for me.

"I hope you eat something for breakfast when they're done. If you faint from the property, I have full authorization to shove some food down your throat," Ruth added, her kindness akin to a kick.

"If I survive the next few hours, I promise I'll have breakfast. It'll be the meal of rebirth," I joked, trying to mask my panic. Ruth was used to seeing me skip meals, and even with her constant bad mood, she always tried to keep me fed and healthy. It was her way of taking care of me.

Maybe after that morning, she wouldn't have to worry about me anymore, after all, my father was going to kill me, for sure.

"Please ask Aunt Claire to come to my room," I requested.

Ruth nodded her head in acknowledgment and left soon after.

I closed the door and leaned against it. And now, my God?

Sure, last night was exhilarating, but starting the morning off with World War III was not my intention. I thought I would have more time to think about what I would say to my father.

Apparently, my time was up.

Suddenly, the somber yet extremely handsome face of the mysterious man from last night invaded my thoughts. He, just like my father, was most likely also very irritated. I could still feel his fingers gripping my arm with energetic control.

How could someone look even more attractive when angry? I could live a century and never forget those exotic, furious eyes coming toward me.

A light knock on the door announced Aunt Claire's arrival, and it wasn't long before she opened a crack, her platinum hair spilling through.

"Darling? Can I come in?" she called.

"Of course, Aunt. Please come in." I hurried to open the door. Aunt Claire wore an elegant white sheath dress that accentuated her very light hair. Her turquoise blue eyes sparkled in contrast to her bold lipstick. She was exceptionally beautiful.

As soon as she stepped through the door, she placed her bag—also white and looking like it cost the value of a new car—on the bedside table and pulled me into a tight hug.

"What have you done, little Min?" she called me by my childhood nickname, and I buried my face deeper into her neck, seeking the refuge I could only find in her arms, with that citrus scent reminding me of protection. My heart, so desperate, calmed for a moment.

"I just wanted to get out a little, Aunt. I can't stand being trapped in this house anymore." I gestured widely.

She pulled back from the embrace and turned to the pink armchair next to the bed, sitting down and placing her hands on her knees. Instantly, the diamond ring my father gave her sparkled against the light in the room.

Aunt Claire was engaged to my father. They had known each other for many years. From what I was told, Claire, before becoming a senator, was my mother's school friend. They were inseparable. My mother loved her so much that the now-senator became my godmother. That was a gift. After my mother passed away during my sister's birth, things lost their way in that house, but Aunt Claire never abandoned us. On the contrary, she stood by us for years. I didn't remember much of that time because I was too young, but whenever I tried to recall the past, Aunt Claire's smiling face was always there to reassure me. Over time, she and my father became closer. Two years ago, they began a relationship, and I was genuinely happy for them. It felt like my mother had left her here to take care of us.

Claire was also there for us when Magnolia passed away. Even though she had never spent a night in the mansion on the hill, I felt her presence with me all the time. She was my safe harbor, and now I needed her help more than ever to survive my father.

"Mason is furious, dear," she warned, fixing her hair that cascaded just below her shoulder. "We are truly worried about you." She scanned the room until her eyes landed on the bottles of medication scattered on the table. "I heard you stopped taking your meds on your own."

"Oh, Aunt, I looked like a zombie after taking them. They were making me worse," I explained. "Now I'm feeling more energized."

"Energized enough to run away and put your life at risk, huh?" She squinted her eyes and pursed her lips. I took a deep breath, ready for my first scolding of the day. "Dear, you didn't even consult the psychiatrist I recommended before stopping the treatment. You can't just do things like that; it's dangerous. How about going back to your medication? It will ease your father's troubled heart a bit."

I pressed my lips together, aware that she wasn't wrong, but I felt so much better without them; I didn't want to go back to feeling drugged during the day. That was exactly why I decided to stop taking my meds. They were prescribed by Aunt Claire's doctor ever since I started suffering from night terrors after Mag's death. Their main purpose was to knock me out at night and dull the pain I felt during the day. But I didn't want that anymore. Even though the pain was enormous and recurrent, even if a sharp pang threatened to tear me apart with memories, I couldn't stand "not feeling" anymore.

"I'm sorry, Aunt. I don't want to go back on my meds," I affirmed, firmly.

"Oh, kids..." She sighed heavily. "That's why I dyed my hair platinum, to hide the gray hairs you cause me." She smiled. "Still, you're in trouble, young lady."

"At what level, Aunt?"

"What's the limit?" She winked at me and stood up. "I have to get back to work, but I wanted to see with my own eyes that you were okay."

"Thank you." I hugged her again.

"Promise me you won't put yourself in danger again," she asked.

"You know I don't lie to you, right?" I replied sincerely.

"Holy hearts, help me!" She kissed my forehead and paused at the door, about to leave. "Be careful, dear, and come down in a few minutes. I'll, once again, try to calm your father."

I thanked her and threw myself onto the bed, pretending a calm I didn't feel.

I left the room ten minutes later. Last night was more energizing than my last ten years, and if to feel that sense of freedom I had to face my father's wrath, so be it. It was a punishment I was willing to pay. Maybe I just needed to take control of my life to truly start living again.

Our house was divided into two floors by an oval staircase, with two parts that ended in a well-furnished hall full of paintings scattered across the immense entry wall. I began descending it from the right side, the part that was usually more hidden, and before I even reached the bottom of the stairs, I spotted my father standing in the middle of the hall, like a statue.

I slowed my pace, feeling the familiar scary chill in my stomach that always preceded one of our conversations. He was staring out at the mountains through the huge wooden door of the entrance. A cold, gray sun flooded the house, almost touching his feet. When he heard me descending the stairs, he took a deep breath and shoved his hands into the pockets of his navy blue dress pants, matching his suit. His light brown hair was slicked back.

"Good morning, Dad," I tried to fake a smile, but this time I couldn't manage it.

"Good morning, Dad?" he repeated, turning to me. Only then did I realize he wasn't alone.

The head of the security team stood beside him, casting a sideways glance in my direction. Mr. Wood was a strong man, despite being a good ten years older than my father. He had an oval face and a welcoming smile, with a grandfatherly air, which I could only deduce since I never met any of my paternal or maternal grandfathers.

The only thing that bothered me about Wood was that he hid his thousand eyes and 259 hands behind that gentle face, and he usually managed to fool me. It seemed there was no place in this house that Mr. Wood wasn't monitoring in real time.

He was the one who gave me the most trouble among all the security guards. He always caught me before I even reached the front gate.

"Good morning, Miss Cahill," he greeted me politely, despite keeping his body too still, as if he was very tense.

"You have no idea what you did last night, Jasmin?" my father turned to me. He was holding a crumpled newspaper in his hands, and as he approached me, he squeezed the poor thing even tighter between his fingers.

"Dad, I just wanted some air. Can you blame me for that?" I tried to appear calm. "No one got hurt."

"No one got hurt?" he repeated quietly, sneakily, and a sad smile lifted the corners of his lips. "No one got hurt, Wood!" My father smiled in a dark way that sent a chill through my body. He took another step toward me, and in the next moment, all the friendliness in his light eyes vanished completely. "Two of our security guards were injured due to the fight you caused with a stranger. And as if that weren't enough, you had the audacity to steal the man's motorcycle." He threw the newspaper onto the small coffee table in the hall.

"What is this?"

"Look... take a look at the headlines. LOOK!" he shouted furiously when I refused to look at that damned newspaper. "Heiress of the Hill and Cahill multinational is seen drunk, dancing on a table in a nightclub.

Witnesses claim the young woman was in the company of a stranger and left the location on the back of his motorcycle." He let out a sarcastic laugh. "It's hard to understand you, Jasmin. Everything I do is for your safety. Everything I had to deprive you of was thinking about you, and for what? For you to risk yourself in such an immature and reckless way? Do you have any idea how fast the internet is? This news came out on gossip sites minutes after they saw you at that nightclub. Anyone, absolutely anyone could get to you in that place, it only took a quick search and you would be dead."

His voice was as hard as his gaze, and that only ignited a bad feeling I was trying to forget every night. A painful, suffocating feeling that made me want to blame him for everything that happened to us three years ago: pure rage.

"You talk as if you really care about me," I accused suddenly. He looked at me and narrowed his eyes.

"You mean to say I don't care about my only daughter?" he murmured. "That everything I do for you is worth nothing?"

"If you really cared about me, you would know what day it was yesterday." I lifted my chin, as I always did when tears threatened to choke my voice. "If you were worried, you'd know how important it was for me to go to that place. It was the beach she loved most; I needed more than anything to get out of here and..."

"Put your life at risk." My father took a deep breath, as if fighting a long battle and already feeling exhausted. "Do you really think that's what Magnolia would have wanted?"

"She wouldn't want to see me like a caged bird." A tear rolled down my face, uncontrolled. "How could you expect to keep me trapped on her birthday, Dad?" The rare times I had tried to escape always involved Mag's birthday, and he should have known that.

I needed to feel that she was still with me in some way; I needed to show my sister that I would never forget her.

"For you, it might just be another day on your busy calendar, but for me, yesterday was the birthday of the person I miss most in the world."

"I, more than anyone, know what day it was, Jasmin. I was there, over 20 years ago, when she was born. When we lost your mother, and I came home with a child just a few years younger than you, completely alone," he recalled, somber. "I remember that day like no one else. The day I lost and gained in a miserable measure. I was there."

"So where were you yesterday?" My voice came out weak. "I stayed here all day alone, and while I could only think about her, you were only thinking about work. It's always been like this and always will be. So please, don't pretend you care, because we both know what your priority is, Dad."

"You're mistaken." He shook his head back and forth and pressed his eyes with his fingers.

"Look into my eyes, Dad, and tell me that yesterday you weren't organizing your long-dreamed merger? Isn't that why you're so concerned?"

"My concern is for your life, daughter," he said in a burst, his voice loud as it usually was. "You have no idea, Jasmin..." He stepped closer, and when I took a step back, trying to distance myself, my father gently held my arm. "My daughter, none of my friends have heirs who know the company as well as you do without even properly attending it. You've studied for years to take over Hill and Cahill one day, and I live for the moment when we walk out that door to go to work together. And that's why I'm fighting so hard. That's why I'm working every second of the day. The merger will make it easier for you to join the company. That's yours, daughter. All my legacy, all the future of Hill and Cahill, and you can't imagine how many threats I receive every day against your life. Especially since we started creating the J.A.S."

"J.A.S... what a creatively lacking name." I scoffed and crossed my arms. He smiled slightly.

"You always say it's ridiculous, but how could I give it any other name than yours for a creation that is entirely yours?" He touched my other arm with his hand. "How many 23-year-olds do you know who are capable of creating an electromagnetic defense spectrum?"

"Once you understand directed energy and spectrum control purposes, it gets easy," I muttered, pursing my lips.

"It's easy for you, who is an exception, for sure." His voice, filled with a tone of pride, irritated me. It was hard to stay angry at my father when he looked at me with that expression of fascination. "But dangerous people oppose any creation method that complicates the invasion of communication of their targets. And after we launch the J.A.S., things might get a lot worse. I receive countless threats against your life daily. Absurd, senseless, and terrible things that keep me from sleeping without nightmares. All inflamed by the possibility of the merger. I noticed, from the corner of my eye, that Wood, the chief, was getting more tense with every word my father said."

"I can't allow anything to happen to you, Jasmin. You might think otherwise, and I fear that at some point in life, all children think this about their parents, but the truth is that my only concern, the reason I wake up every day with determination, is you, my daughter." I lifted my chin even higher, suppressing the sudden urge to cry. "You, on the other hand, stopped taking your medication, and now... you're sneaking out. Given all the risks you run, I fear that living or dying no longer makes a difference to you."

I wanted to hate him. I wanted to scream that he didn't care at all about me, but the sincerity I saw there disarmed me. My father also had dark circles under his eyes and wore a sad, tired expression. In the end, we were all suffering in some way, but my freedom shouldn't pay for that.

"I stopped taking the medication because I want to start living again. Just like I want to go out again, Dad," I confessed. "After what happened, you increased the security and cut off any outing outside the House on the Hill that wasn't for work. The only time I managed to go to a mall was yesterday. I can't live locked up here forever," I admitted.

"I'm not asking you to stay." He breathed heavily. "Not for much longer." He caressed my shoulders as if I were again his 10-year-old girl asking for ice cream while I was sick. "I know I've been unyielding, even alienated. You and your sister, although always accompanied, went anywhere you wanted. But after losing Mag, even with several bodyguards, fear has settled in my soul, daughter," he revealed, saddened. "Just give me another 15 days, and I promise things will be resolved."

"You've been saying that for many years. Just a few more days, just another month." I looked at my own feet. "I'm tired, Dad."

"I know you're tired, but I won't allow my only daughter to be hurt. We've already lost too much, Jasmin." He took a deep breath, ran his hands through his very neatly styled hair, and turned his back to me. "I hired an extra team to keep an eye on you."

"What?" I must have heard wrong. "Another team, Dad? What is this house turning into, a bodyguard branch?"

"Since you won't listen to me nicely, you'll have to listen to me harshly," he said, just as a thunderous sound reverberated through the mansion, and I could swear I recognized that noise. But what were the chances that...?

"Oh, crap!" I cursed when I saw the wide and imposing motorcycle stop right in front of the house entrance and a large man dismount it.

"Jasmin!" my father reprimanded me. "That's not the education I gave you. You'd better respect him. He is the head of the new team that will work with Wood until the merger and acceptance of the partners is finished. You'd better behave for the next 15 days. You won't have another option under the care of the Wolf."

Wolf?

The man dismounted the motorcycle and removed his helmet. His dark hair was tousled, but his black suit remained impeccably aligned.

Oh my God!

I was dead. Super dead... so dead. He was going to rip my head off as soon as he saw me.

I shrank behind one of the pillars, avoiding his gaze. A strange chill ran down my spine as he entered the house. I could hear his firm footsteps, as if a hundred men were marching to war. I refused to come out of my hiding spot. It might not seem like it, but I really cared about my neck.

"Wolf, right?" my father said. "Welcome, I'm Mason, a great friend of your father."

"I'm only here for that little detail," he said grumpily, earning a laugh from my father, who turned to Chief Wood with excitement.

"They warned me he was a man of few friends. Come, I want you to meet my daughter. This is... Jasmin?" My father wasted no time finding me curled up behind the pillar, fear coursing through my heart.

What would that man do when he saw me?

I could bet that if you looked up "unlucky" in the dictionary, you'd find my name in bold letters as the result. Of all the twists the world could take, this one certainly left me dizzy.

"Jasmin, sweetheart, what are you doing hiding there? Come on!" my father called, and I took a deep breath before I could move. "This is your new bodyguard. Treat him with respect," he emphasized.

I stepped into the man's line of sight, who looked like a bronze statue, standing still, not moving a muscle. His eyes met mine, and I could see surprise giving way to anger, and a glint of wickedness that made me waver. He was going to kill me, I was sure.

"For heaven's sake!" Wolf cursed under his breath, harshly. Those strikingly different eyes scrutinized my face with precision, and I felt as if my entire soul was being laid bare, exposed by the man who exuded danger and aggression. "Of all the people in the world, it had to be you..."

CHAPTER FIVE

Wolf

For all the demons, this had to be a very bad joke, or I had definitely offended some deity in the void. It made no sense. A mix of anger and shock engulfed me as my eyes fell on that...

"You little thief!" I pointed a finger at her, and she bit her lip, running to hide behind her father like the shameless brat she was. The man next to me quickly went on alert.

I narrowed my eyes at her, who was staring at me through the gap between her father's bent arm. I reached into my pocket and got even angrier when I realized I was checking if the key to my motorcycle was still there.

"Do you two know each other?" Mason raised his eyebrows and asked in a concerned tone.

"Maybe I've seen him somewhere," the little brat replied.

"Before or after stealing my motorcycle?"

"Was the motorcycle yours, Jasmin?" Mason shouted, his eyes widening, making her jump in fright. There went her forced calm. The man put both hands on his head and shook his face in disbelief. "I'm going to lose my mind! Yes, I'm already CRAZY."

"How was I supposed to know you'd hire the owner of the bike? Oh, and by the way, it's a fine specimen." She shot me a cheeky smile that sent the very fire of hell down my throat.

"Jasmin!"

"You... you..." I took a step toward that... little thing, exhaling exasperatedly, clenching my jaw even tighter in an attempt to resist the urge to run to her and grab that slender neck with my hands.

For the love of God, what was my sin against the universe?

"Dad, we only have one option now," she said, still using her father as a shield to keep her distance from me, making the man turn in circles in the house. "Get rid of him. As fast as possible." She stared at my clenched fists, her exceptionally green eyes widening a bit more. Green like the little snake she was. "He's going to kill me as soon as he gets the chance. If you love me, get him out of here before he has the opportunity."

"Now you call me sir, huh?" He turned to his daughter.

"No action will be necessary," I growled, trying my best to maintain my composure. "I will withdraw from the mission immediately, since there are conflicts of interest." I pressed my lips together. "I'm leaving this damn place before she can steal anything else of mine." I turned my back and started walking far away from that crazy woman.

"Wolf!" The father of the wild girl ran after me and caught up as I was approaching where I had parked my motorcycle. "Wolf, wait, please."

"I'll send another team. I won't work with your daughter, Mason, not even by decree. But don't worry, there will be a line waiting to work with the Cahill family," I warned, and I saw the man straighten up immediately.

He put his fists on his hips and took a deep breath. I imagined this would be where he started negotiating the mission; after all, Cahill was no ordinary person.

When I heard the surname the night before, I knew I recognized it from somewhere. The Hill and Cahill multinational was known throughout the country. A gigantic conglomerate run by a man who, in society, is an example and a skilled negotiator. It would be natural for him to negotiate, and even more predictable for me to refuse. But contrary to what I expected, Cahill was willing to go further to protect the little rat he called his daughter.

"Please, Wolf, listen to me." He stepped closer, just inches away from me. The very white walls of the house loomed behind him. "Here, in front of you, is not the president of Hill and Cahill. It's a desperate father." He opened a button of his dress shirt. "I know my daughter is difficult to deal with. Impulsive, irresponsible, rebellious..." He took a deep breath and gazed at the distant hills. "But believe me, she's a good girl. Jasmin is all I have, and I don't know what to do to keep her safe. My last resort is the best of the best. It's you, Wolf. That's why I spent my only trump card with Security. Because she is all I have left. Please, don't abandon the mission."

Abandoning a mission...

I ran my hand over my very short beard. I had never abandoned a mission before. No matter how difficult, no matter how impossible it might seem. And now...

I looked behind Cahill and saw a lock of very blonde hair hanging out of the luxurious wooden door at the entrance of the house. The little thief was hiding, watching everything.

"I have a feeling your daughter is much more than just impulsive." He nodded slightly.

"And you might be right," he confirmed. "She is extremely intelligent, creative, and sharp-tongued, which complicates things a lot. Still, I ask you to give us a chance to work with your team." Cahill insisted, and questions began to invade my mind.

I hated when that happened. It was stronger than me. Stronger than refusing a mission was discovering why my work was necessary. And I began to wonder, why the hell was that girl so troublesome? Where did she learn that damn light finger? And worse... Why was her life in danger?

Dangerous questions... that led me to accept the position simply because I wanted to know and, most importantly, not to disappoint my father.

Apparently, two fathers would end the day happy, while I...

"Let's talk. I need to understand the case, and I need you to know that if I accept this mission, I don't want you interfering in my way of working," I yelled. "You know very well the kind of people I'm used to dealing with, but your daughter doesn't. Are you aware that I will do whatever it takes, no matter the cost, to keep that woman's neck in place?"

"Yes, I am," he replied quickly and energetically. "That's all we need, Wolf," he said, visibly relieved. "Follow me to the office. Chief Wood, please," he called to the man who had been waiting patiently for the conclusion of the story near the entrance of the house, "gather the team in the meeting room."

"Yes, sir." He shot me a sideways glance and disappeared shortly after.

"Are you sure I can leave her here?" I pointed at the motorcycle and stared at him. Mason let out a dry laugh and squinted.

"How could she steal your motorcycle?" He opened his eyes, looking older than when I arrived here just minutes before. "How does that girl know how to ride one of those?"

"One of my greatest curiosities."

"Did she cause any damage? I'll pay for any harm that she caused."

"Then you're going to spend a lot on anger management treatment," I revealed. "Come on, we don't have time to waste."

"God help me," he said, turning toward the mansion, which was adorned with beds of yellow, red, and pink flowers, and small shrubs shaped in distinct forms that formed a pathway, like a labyrinth, to the entrance.

I could have sworn I heard a low hiss as I passed through the door again, and I had to restrain myself from turning around and catching that crazy girl hiding back there.

Argh! Never, in all my years of career, had I to complete a mission and protect someone I hated so much.

That... green-eyed little brat, shameless. The worst part was remembering how much I enjoyed watching her dance. As if nothing around me made more sense, as if my eyes existed solely to behold the beauty she was in those high heels, surrounded by a fog of freedom that sparked envy.

"Shit!" I blinked, trying to shake off the memory.

"What did you say?" Cahill asked, already by the entrance to the office.

"Nothing."

"Well, then come in. Make yourself comfortable." He pointed to the dark room. "Do you want a drink?"

"No. I came to get a feel for the environment and to find out if I need to request an extra team. I still haven't received the file folder to study, nor the layout of the house. From the information I received, you were supposed to provide it personally for security reasons."

I entered a room where an entire wall was covered with books, in a wooden library so old that if someone rummaged through it, they might find the entire lineage of Queen Elizabeth, cataloged even before the dinosaurs went extinct. That thing was nearly collapsing.

"Why do you keep this decaying shelf?" Cahill glanced over his shoulder while pouring himself a shot of some violet drink. "It's going to give in."

"This was my late wife's office," he revealed. "It was where she spent most of her time." He took a deep breath and drank the liquid all at once. "My wife was a writer and was almost finished with her first book when she became pregnant for the second time. She loved this shelf. My Sophie loved running her fingers over the spines of the books or organizing them by color, title, or author. She enjoyed it. I believe that of all the places in the house, including the garden and the view from the lookout, this was her favorite." I could hear in his voice a tone I had known while observing others. The sound of love mixed with longing. "She died during the birth of my youngest, and she never finished the book." His eyes drifted for a moment. "Even though my fiancée made some improvement suggestions, I am unable to change it."

"You don't have to take my advice, Cahill, but if you want to maintain security in this house, you'd better do it. Replace the main beams of the shelf and keep the books as they are. I believe your late wife wouldn't want this thing collapsing on the VIP, am I right?"

He thought for a moment and nodded in agreement just as someone knocked on the door and opened it.

Chief Wood walked in, and behind him were three other men who recognized me as soon as they stood before me.

"You!" The burliest of them, sporting a thick mustache and a nice bruise on his eye, pointed at me with a furious expression and suddenly started turning red.

"Oh, you bastard!" Another security guard, the tallest of all, pointed at me and charged toward me.

"Here we go!" I rolled my eyes and squared up, ready for a new fight.

"What the hell are you doing?" Wood cursed, stepping into the fray.

"It was him, chief. He's the one who attacked us yesterday," the mustached one replied. "I'm going to rip that slick hair off you. Come here!" When he lunged forward again, Wood grabbed him by the collar and pulled him back.

"Was he the suspect who cowardly attacked you with a gang?" Cahill asked, and it was my turn to face the liars.

"Uh... that's not exactly how it happened." He lowered his face and smoothed his mustache with his fingers. "Maybe Lyon exaggerated the number of people."

"I was alone."

"He was alone?" Cahill and Wood questioned together, exchanging surprised looks. "Well..." Mason sighed loudly and rubbed his temples with his fingertips. "At least everything I heard about you is true."

"How?" I replied, unsure whether to keep staring down the security guards to prevent any of them from jumping me or to look at Cahill.

"Your name precedes you, Wolf. And if this isn't proof that we're hiring the right person, I don't know what can confirm it." He turned to Wood. "He took out and disarmed three men by himself. Our men." He clenched his jaw.

"But he had his bike stolen by Miss Cahill. Let's not forget that detail," one of them reinforced.

"If only you did your jobs..." I started.

"Enough!" Wood interrupted and turned to me. And that's when I realized...

I was screwed with that ridiculous team as support.

"I will introduce you properly, and be aware that you will work together for Miss Cahill's safety, putting all your personal desires and objectives aside. Understood?"

"Yes, sir!" The chorus of ducks echoed through the room, and I fought the urge to roll my eyes again.

"For those who don't know yet..."

"I know! I know!" I almost hadn't noticed the youngest, and the frailest, of them standing in the corner of the office, bouncing as if his life depended on it.

"Shut up, Shaw!" Wood shouted, losing patience with his daycare. "This is Christopher Holder. More commonly known in our field as Wolf. He will be responsible for Team Alpha from now on."

"Chief, I'm sorry to disagree, but this guy doesn't know Miss Cahill. He doesn't know anything about our routine; how can he take charge of the team?" Lyon, the tallest and also the most irritated, complained.

"An Alpha team must be ready to handle all kinds of situations. You not only lost the Crystal but also got beaten by a single man and put your own lives at risk," Wood cursed, and I watched them shrink with each new angry word that escaped him. "From now on, you will be subject to Wolf's directives. And I think you better come to terms with that, or you'll be dismissed." An unsettling silence followed by a collective "yes, sir" filled the office.

"It's a pleasure to have you with us," Wood said, keeping a serious demeanor. "These are Mark Shaw." He pointed to the scrawny one with very alert eyes, who waved excitedly. "Peter Lyon..." The tallest didn't even look in my direction, and I was thankful for that. "And that's Eric Ray." The mustached one was chewing gum and shot me a dry, sideways smile that looked more like a threat. "We are Team Alpha of Hill and Cahill security. Team Beta is located at the Hill and Cahill conglomerate."

"Team Alpha is now led by a Wolf; isn't that funny?" Shaw laughed loudly.

"I'll rip your tongue out," Lyon murmured to the young one, who shrank back into his suit.

"I usually accompany Mr. Cahill while he's at the company, but when I'm at the mansion, I'm in charge of the surveillance room, or at the exterior point of the house, which I'll show you later, and all actions must be reported to me without exception," Wood explained.

"And what is the threat?" I finally questioned, realizing they referred to the VIP as Crystal. "I want to know every detail. What am I facing, and I also want a layout of the entire house, in addition to the VIP folder."

"Here it is," Cahill interrupted me, sliding a mustard folder filled with papers across his large desk. "I'm the president of a multinational, as you already know." He flopped into the leather chair positioned behind the desk. "Jasmin is my only heir. And when I said she was extremely intelligent, I wasn't exaggerating. My daughter is working on a very important project within the company, something I believe will be successful among government agencies and will upset a lot of people." He clasped both hands on the desk, and his eyes drifted, staring at them. "Jasmin is aware of the danger she faces and used to cooperate for her protection, but a few months ago something seems to have changed her mind. She has lost all sense of danger." He shook his head, as if he couldn't believe what he was saying. "If she only knew the number of threats I receive daily against her life," he confessed.

"Any suspects? Anyone who wants to get rid of the VIP specifically? Who would gain something from that?" I started my routine questions.

"Three years ago, I was already receiving threats like the ones now, but I didn't take them as seriously as I should have, and I allowed my daughters to attend a ball. Something simple and common for young girls their age. I thought they'd be safe, but even surrounded by security, a man managed to attack and kill my youngest," he revealed, lowering his eyes to one of the buttons on his shirt. "He stabbed her." My eyes widened.

"How did he manage to get past the security to stab her?" A gun I would understand; it was hard to find elite shooters in the high rises around any event that the VIP would attend, but a stabbing?

"Someone fired a shot into the air at the party to create confusion," Wood added.

"The killer approached at that moment and did nothing more than bump his body against my daughter," Mason continued. "The knife barely cut the dress. It hardly touched her skin, but in less than five minutes my daughter was dead." He raised his eyes, a deep metallic blue, and I raised my eyebrows instantly.

"If the stabbing wasn't fatal, then how..." I stopped as an idea struck me. But it would be absurd to consider that.

"What I'm about to tell you is confidential. Jasmin has no idea, and I ask that it stays that way. It was very difficult to convince her that the stabbing was fatal. I don't like lying to her, but I didn't want my daughter to live in fear of a mere bump."

"What was the real cause of death?" I was already worried.

"The blade was coated in cyanide," he said. "Magnolia was poisoned." I lost my breath, as if someone had punched me right in the stomach, and I was unable to speak. There was only one hitman who used methods like that. A damned sadistic bastard I knew all too well. "Do you see now?"

Cahill exhaled, exasperated. "Jasmin thinks I'm the monster who hires monsters to keep her from living. What she doesn't know is that there isn't a night I don't have nightmares where she is the next victim of that bastard, and that's how I ended up depriving my daughter of everything." He exhaled. "I need you to keep her away from anyone who could hurt her and, especially, from anyone who might touch her. Keeping distance is essential in this case. Can I count on you, Wolf?"

"I need to speak with you alone, now," I leaned over the desk and requested quietly. This was far from the conversation I had imagined having with Cahill, but with the new information, everything had changed.

He narrowed his confused eyes. I waved my hand toward the other security personnel in the room, and he seemed to understand what I wanted.

"Leave us alone for a moment," he asked, and I heard them grumble something before exiting one by one, leaving us alone.

"Now that you know what happened, are you going to give up on the mission?" Cahill inquired, worried.

"Listen carefully to what I'm going to say. I don't like your daughter. In fact, I hate her with all my strength." He let out an amused laugh. "But know this: from the moment I accept this mission, I will be capable of killing half the world and maybe dying along the way before a single hair on Miss Cahill's head is harmed. So yes, you can count on me," I confirmed. "But you need to understand the scope of your problem. I believe I know who might be behind these attacks."

"For God's sake, man!" he exclaimed loudly, standing up and nearly throwing the chair to the ground. "If you know anything about who might be involved, please, tell me," he begged anxiously. "I've been searching for any clues, any sign of the culprit for three years, and the only thing I find are useless pieces of information." Mason's voice began to tremble. I could see his breathing was getting more agitated, and in light of his desperation, I decided to be as honest as possible.

"There's only one man, if we can even call him that, who is capable of using such devices to kill someone, and I know well the prices he charges. It's extremely high-level work," I revealed, feeling the bitter taste fill my mouth with memories of the past that returned to my mind. Cahill's eyes widened.

"So you know who might have killed my daughter? Tell me who it is, tell me!" he shouted. "I'll put half the world behind that bastard right now."

"He's known as Naish," I revealed.

"Naish?"

"Yes."

"Do you have any more information besides that strange name?" Cahill grabbed a pen and a piece of paper, ready to jot down everything I said.

"I'm afraid to inform you that he has no surname, nor a fixed address. The bastard doesn't even have fingerprints because he removed them many years ago." Cahill opened his mouth, stunned by the new information. I could see the shine of desperation mixed with hope filling his eyes. "He's a psychopath, extremely intelligent and cruel. A serial killer disguised as a hitman." I clenched my jaw, holding back the fury of knowing what that son of a bitch was doing, taking the lives of innocent young people. "If he takes a job, he never abandons it. I recognized the method of murder because he doesn't use guns. He might even be working with some extra team, but his main signature is to finish the job himself, with a knife dipped in cyanide. That's why I have no doubt it's him, and as the crazy bastard he is, he insists on keeping his ritual. If anyone tries to do something against Jasmin, it will be him. And I'll kill him before he even notices my presence."

"How do you know so much about him?" he asked, his eyes distant, as if he were absorbing the information.

Because I almost worked for him once, I wanted to answer.

"Just the nature of the job," I lied. "We'll need more security than I anticipated, but against me, Naish doesn't stand a single chance."

"It reassures me to hear that," he said softly. "I will put all my men on the hunt for that name today and... thank you." He extended his hand toward me, and I stared at it for a moment before accepting it. "It's been a long time since I've searched for a name for the nightmare that surrounds me repeatedly. Now I've found it, and through it, we will find the mastermind behind the crime."

"Don't thank me. Instead, inform me if you obtain any success and don't dare hide anything from me again, Cahill. This is the last time I ask."

"All right," he agreed, anesthetized.

"What happens after these 15 days? If the culprit isn't arrested by then, he will pose a danger to the VIP for as long as he lives, especially if Naish has been paid to deliver her death. He will never stop." A pang hit me in the gut with the hypothesis.

"That's why I'm desperate to get my hands on the culprit soon. I want my daughter to live in peace. And I'm counting on us finding something in that time, but if we're unsuccessful, I will need to reinforce her security, especially to train her in my company until Jasmin is prepared to take it over. That will keep her out of trouble, and I've already asked her father for a fixed team for when that moment comes. I know she needs freedom, and I intend to give it to her, but with security." He paused and suddenly looked at me. "As for this new information about Naish... I'm counting on you to guide my team. They need to be prepared in case this man shows up. Do you think you can create a composite sketch?"

"I've already done it." I turned my back and walked around the office, restless. "But Naish is clever. He's wanted by Interpol in several countries and has never even been captured on camera in his life." I pursed my lips. My racing heart revealed how much considering that Naish might be involved in the death of one of the Hill and Cahill heiresses affected me. "I won't rest until I've used all my resources to find him. I'll show the composite sketch to all your security personnel, but I should warn you it's been almost ten years since I last saw him. Since then, he has become a detestable memory."

"Still, please show it to them." Cahill walked around the desk and stopped right next to me. "After these days, you'll be free from the commitment to us, but until then... I need you to help us with this. I've already lost one daughter, Wolf." He took a deep breath. "I need you to protect Jasmin from that same fate."

"That's my job, Cahill," I affirmed.

I would do anything to protect my VIP clients, even if one of them had stolen from me and was the very embodiment of pure shamelessness. I had one certainty in that moment: even if Jasmin kicked and even hit me along the way, I wouldn't allow anyone to touch the little thief, especially Naish.

"Provide me with all the information you have. Keep me updated on everything, and even if your daughter tries to steal from me again, I'll bring her home tied up and safe."

"I'm counting on you. Chief Wood will explain the entire process and provide any access or information you need," he warned, heading toward the door. "I have a meeting now, but I want my team to get to work on this. Call me if you need anything." I nodded, watching Cahill hurry out the door.

Wood was waiting for me outside, and he didn't waste any time intercepting me as soon as his boss left, nearly tripping over himself. I could see in the man's stern gaze that he wanted to ask what had happened inside, but he held back.

"Follow me. You need to see your new workplace."

I FOLLOWED WOOD THROUGH the mansion, which had a colossal pair of oval stairs right in the middle of the hall, covered in strange and abstract paintings, while he pointed out the main areas of the place, and I didn't catch another glimpse of the VIP.

"On the second floor is the surveillance room; let's go." He led the way and indicated the path.

We climbed the shiny marble stairs and entered a hallway full of doors—and more hideous paintings hanging on the walls, which were a cold, icy tone, almost white. Large crystal chandeliers hung in every corner of the place.

"The bedrooms are to the left," the chief guided me as we stopped in front of the last door in the hallway, next to an impressive and beautiful painting, the only one that depicted in detail the lookout that existed on the property and overlooked a vast forest.

"We found it feasible to keep a support room close to where Miss Cahill spends most of her time, and here we also have the advantage of seeing the entire residence from the highest point," he informed, stepping into the room, where an entire wall was dedicated to various monitors tracking all corners of the house. There were also three black chairs and a bed placed beside a small table with a lamp resting on it.

In some contracts, security personnel needed to spend most of their time at the VIP's house, in long shifts, and in those cases, there were beds in the main surveillance room for them to take turns and rest. In my case, I was hired for 15 uninterrupted days, one of the types of contracts I would only accept out of pure obligation, as was the case. Usually, I only worked on cases that lasted one or two days at most.

"The security staff's lodging is in the house next to the garden. You'll get the key to one of the rooms," he notified. "Would you like some coffee?" He sat down near the only table in the place.

"No, thank you." I watched him pour coffee into a single white cup, and with all the patience in the world, the man turned back to me.

"Cahill has gone to extremes with Jasmin, to the point of hiring extra force to watch over her at such an important time, but to protect her, you need to know a bit about that young lady's personality."

"A very difficult personality, I can assure you," I scoffed, irritated once again by what that woman had put me through.

"Let's say she's... motivated," he recounted. "I've been working with this family for ten years. And even under my command, even with all the effort my team has put into this job, Jasmin managed to escape. We can't let that happen again."

"It won't. We'll keep her safe." I stared at one of the monitors that showed an area near the pool, which looked a lot like an improvised gym, and that's when I saw her. Jasmin was staring into the gym as if some kind of monster was about to come out from inside. "What's she doing?"

"One of the many strange things she's been doing in recent months." He sighed. "That's the dance studio. It's one of the rare spots in the house where there are no cameras inside. She grew up training there with her sister, but since Magnolia's death, Jasmin can't enter. Before, she couldn't even get close to the place; now she does, but she stands at the door as if there were a barrier preventing her from entering."

I looked back at the image. From there, she seemed so small and defenseless.

"She's not alone." He pointed to one of the monitors. "Lyon is standing a few meters behind."

"Big deal. They let her escape once," I grumbled.

"Wolf, Wolf..." he almost hummed. "My men have done everything possible and impossible to stop that girl. Jasmin has the face of an angel, but don't be fooled by her sweet voice. She's crafty when she wants to be and doesn't spare any effort to express her will or impose her opinion on her father. I couldn't expect less from the creator of J.A.S."

"Cahill mentioned the project, but he didn't say what this J.A.S. is about."

"Ask her when you get the chance. You'll enjoy hearing her talk about it. It's one of the few moments we can see the spark that once existed in her eyes."

"I'll pass, I don't want unnecessary conversations with the VIP."

"Crystal," he corrected me, and after a few more technical details about the place, I ended up asking something that was bothering me more with each passing second.

"I'm curious." I sat down in the chair, which felt too small to support my body. "If she knows the life risk she's running, why is she still trying to escape? Does she want to die or something?" The question hung in the air for a moment, as if a ghost hovered over us.

"Listen carefully to what I'm going to tell you." I raised my eyebrows as Wood leaned forward and looked into my eyes. "Three years ago, Jasmin witnessed the murder of her younger sister and only escaped the same fate by sheer luck, perhaps." I suddenly averted my gaze, not wanting to confront the past behind those green eyes or anything that might lessen the anger I felt toward that girl, but apparently, the damn story was just beginning.

"And as you already know, the one responsible for the murder managed to escape," he recounted. "We feared that at any moment he would try to finish what he started with Jasmin, and in light of that danger, Cahill increased security around her even more."

"Has she always lived escorted like this?"

"Yes, she and her sister spent much of their lives behind these walls, at Hill House," he confirmed. "The difference is that now Jasmin no longer has her sister by her side. She's alone and determined to escape and venture out without fear of what might happen to her. I don't know what she intends, but I feel it will repeat."

"Is there any escape route in the mansion?"

"Not that we know of."

"If there is, I will find out." I stood up once again.

"There's another thing I feel obligated to warn you about."

"What is it?"

"She's going to try to get rid of you," he cautioned, his face calm.

"And how would she manage such a feat, if you don't mind me asking?"

"By making your life hell, provoking you in every way. Come on, be creative." He laughed. "She is." He shrugged, seeming to enjoy it. "There's no way to work for so many years alongside someone and be impartial or cold as our job demands. So here, at the request of Cahill himself, we usually interact with her and always try to make her as comfortable as possible. But as I said, she's intelligent. She can discover your weak point with a glance and will likely try to use it against you somehow."

"I don't have any weak points." I rolled my eyes.

"It's good you don't; otherwise, she'll certainly find it. Just wait and see," he warned. "Trying to control her is like trying to fight a lion. You might even try, but there are no guarantees you'll come out alive." I stared at Wood as if he had poured coffee over his own head. That man had to be crazy.

"I'm not an amateur, Wood. I'm a professional and I honor my career," I retorted, sulky.

"You better be prepared, because when she realizes you'll be the next stone in her shoe, you won't have a minute of peace." He sipped his coffee while I still tried to digest that new information.

I wanted to see that little brat try something. I'd lock her in her own room if necessary, but nothing she did would have any effect.

"I'll be back soon." I ignored the subject and turned to leave the room when the chief called me once more.

"Wolf..." I looked at him, already at the door of the communication room. "Have patience with Jasmin. She doesn't handle strangers well and has suffered too much to face severe reprimands."

"I'm used to dealing with all kinds of people, Wood. A spoiled woman like her who doesn't care about her own life is just one of them. We all have a sad story behind who we are; that doesn't give us the right to do as we please," I replied. "I'm not here to coddle her, nor will I be her babysitter. I'll put that girl in her place; just wait and see."

"I deserve this!" He exhaled, exasperated. "Why did they send someone so stubborn?"

I left that house a few minutes later, in possession of the VIP-Crystal-Thief's folder and with my mind racing. I would study the residence that morning to return to the place with the necessary team to carry out the mission, and before anything else, I would use my contacts to see if I could somehow track Naish's whereabouts over the past few months. A strange feeling hit me as I imagined what that bastard would do to her if he got the chance, and I was determined to move heaven and earth to ensure he wouldn't even be able to approach the VIP.

I put on my helmet and was already on the motorcycle when my gaze met hers for a moment. Cornered, she glared at me from beside one of the trees in the garden at the entrance. Her cheeks were red, as if she had been under the sun for hours. She had the audacity to narrow her eyes at me and then turned her back.

Perhaps I would indeed become the intruder she would do anything to expel, which made me feel a mix of pleasure, curiosity, and dread.

I had no idea what the next few days would reveal to me, but I would be lying if I said I wasn't curious to find out.

CHAPTER SIX

Jasmin

I watched, my heart in my throat, as the man who would soon become one of my father's new hires mounted the motorcycle and left without ceremony, but not before shooting me a twisted, threatening glance.

What the hell!

That guy was going to be trouble for sure. I needed to get rid of him if I wanted to guarantee at least a little freedom, and I already had enough reasons for my father to agree to replace him with someone else. Anyone else who didn't have those piercing, deep eyes. I didn't feel comfortable being watched by him, as if suddenly all my fears and anxieties were exposed before a stranger.

What would it be like to live under the same roof as him? In one night, I had shared more with that stranger than I had experienced in my entire life.

Every moment, from the escape to the motorcycle theft, was magnificent and exhilarating, but nothing compared to the brief memory of that quick, firm, unyielding kiss that left me yearning for more. And it was there that I would shudder.

I didn't kiss him because I was altered by alcohol; on the contrary. I kissed him because I felt completely drawn to his rugged, firm, feverish beauty. By those broad shoulders, the beard that framed his square jaw, but most importantly, those eyes. They were like the confluence of two singular rivers, different. A rare, exotic beauty, and my God, impossible not to notice.

I wanted him far away! Yes, far away, and I needed to do something about that situation immediately before he returned and took that spot.

I sat on the garden entrance steps and called my father.

"Jasmin?" He answered on the last ring, worried. I almost never called him.

"Hey, Dad, don't worry, everything's fine," I rushed to calm him down.

I knew what was weighing on his heart, and I understood him, I swear I did. But I couldn't shake the feeling that I was suffocating within those walls. And that lack of air motivated me to want freedom.

I would die in any case if I remained trapped inside. I wanted space; I wanted a bit of the freedom I once experienced. I wanted my life back, even if it meant risking it. I wouldn't wither away there. I couldn't accept it any longer.

"You can't hire that man, Dad," I blurted out when I noticed he was calming down. "You know we won't get along; he hates me, and I admit I gave him reasons for that."

"How did you steal that motorcycle, Jasmin?" He completely ignored what I had said.

"Does that matter when your daughter's life is at stake?" I dramatized, using my best "I'm on the edge" voice. "He's going to want to kill me himself as soon as he gets the chance; don't you understand? I can already feel his hands around my neck. I can barely breathe." My dramatic voice made a dry laugh escape through the phone. "Don't laugh, Dad. I like my neck the way it is. I'd prefer not to be choked, so it's better to let him go."

"I won't do that. You need to accept that he will work with us for a few days." He exhaled forcefully. "We need him, Jasmin. I hope you won't do anything else to disappoint me, daughter. Tomorrow, I need you to come to the office for a new meeting with the scientists from the J.A.S. project, so rest today, calm down, and before you know it, everything will be just as it was before."

I highly doubt it, I thought as I hung up the phone after he said goodbye.

"He's incredible. Maybe he'll recommend one of us to work at Holder Security too. Just imagine?" I heard Shaw's voice and turned around. He was chatting distractedly through the radio communicator. I turned back and pretended not to listen, but I continued eavesdropping shamelessly. Since I couldn't get rid of Wolf, I had to find out everything I could about my new adversary. "Come on, Lyon, you're just upset because Christopher kicked your ass." So his name was Christopher... "No, I'm not getting involved in that mess and risking my pretty little face." I pressed my lips together to keep from laughing. "He's the owner's son at Holder, remember? He can put whoever he wants in there; I hope to show him my work. The amazing Shaw in action. Lyon? Lyon?"

I covered my mouth, stifling the laugh that bubbled up after hearing the amazing Shaw complain about being disconnected from the radio frequency. That guy was a character. I got up and walked past him, and he gave me a silent wave. With his large, almond-shaped eyes and a very white smile, Shaw was the smallest of them all, with skinny arms that disappeared into his always well-fitted suit, but he was charming. He had very straight hair that occasionally fell into his attentive eyes, and he seemed to possess a heart of gold.

I went to my room, ready to study a bit to face my father's company scientists, who, by the way, didn't like me one bit. It was written all over their faces that receiving ideas from a young woman, even if she was the CEO's daughter, didn't please them at all. But who cared what they thought? I certainly didn't.

I threw myself onto the bed with my arms open and fell onto the pile of blankets. My thoughts still stuck on Shaw's brief conversation. So the Wolf guy was the owner's son at Holder Security? My father had been trying to get one of their bodyguards for a long time, but there was a long waiting list for the level of security he desired. Someone who could keep me off the radar. I didn't know what had changed in that equation, but adding and dividing everything, I was in serious trouble.

I SPENT THE REST OF the afternoon with my nose buried in one of my favorite applied physics books, and when I started to see double, I realized it was time to stop. I leaned back in my chair and stretched my arms, yawning. My eyes left the pages of the book. The study desk in my room was positioned next to the window so that I could occasionally admire the living picture formed by the hills outside. It was just what I needed to regain my focus.

The end of the sunset left an orange trail over the treetops that flowed down the very green hill like a river. A sight that looked like it had come straight out of a movie. I was distracted when the sound of gravel being crushed under the wheels of a car caught my attention. I held my breath.

Could it be him?

I jumped up and rushed to the window. A black car with very dark windows stopped next to one of the three cars designated for bodyguards. When the driver's door opened, my heart leaped into my throat and sank into my stomach as I recognized who was stepping out of that damn vehicle.

Wolf slammed the car door and looked around as if searching for someone. He was still wearing the same outfit as before—a perfectly black suit, from the dress shirt to the shoes. Everything was that color, which, to my utter misfortune, made the man even more handsome and accentuated the tone of his skin. Unaware he was being watched, he drew his gun, checked the magazine, aligned the communicator with the radio, and finally, to complete the "MIB Men in Black" look, put on a pair of sunglasses.

Definitely, he had become the most incredible specimen of man I had ever seen. I put my hand to my chest, wanting to throw myself out the window for not having managed to get rid of him, feeling that my upcoming days would be more dangerous than ever.

Wolf exuded danger. Just looking at him sent a mix of sensations crashing over me. Caution, fear, and an insane desire to know what it would be like to kiss him again. Oh heavens, I was lost!

I stepped away from the window and bit my lip. And now?

I AVOIDED POKING MY nose out of the room for as long as I could. I didn't want to run into Wolf in the hallways of the house, much less be watched by him on the cameras. Knowing that man had his eye on me gave me a strange feeling in my chest, so I decided to hide under the shower to see if the water would wash away that fiery, intense gaze that occasionally filled my mind.

I spent a good 40 minutes under scalding water, which only served to make me think more about what I should forget. I stepped out of the bathroom frustrated and put on my kitten outfit, which consisted of a very short top with whiskers and a black short with a pom-pom for a tail. I loved custom clothes, and half my closet was full of them. To complete the look, I put on my headband with cat ears and flopped onto my bed.

My room was one of my favorite places in that immense property. In shades of pink, gold, beige, and a very light gray, my little corner had something special and striking. Several pillows lay on the wide bed, along with some comforters and an old tulle that I didn't even know how it got there but was so warm and cozy that I never allowed anyone to get rid of it.

I glanced at the cluttered little table filled with papers and pens and everything that could fit there, including some scribbles of new ideas I might share with my father in the future, and wrinkled my nose at the books piled right next to them. I needed to tidy up that mess before Ruth completely lost it and stormed into my room. That woman could sniff out a mess, and she would attack my books without mercy if she saw them scattered around.

I got up from the bed, desperate to grab one of the books and maybe spend the night reading one of them. I was just about to pick one up when my phone buzzed with a message. I unlocked the screen and stared at the same words I had seen the night before, a mix of surprise and euphoria washing over me.

Party tonight. You in? I'll cover for you.

I laughed at the end of the message, which was our secret code for "I'll be waiting for you. Figure it out."

My friend Carla was one of the few people I knew who was willing to risk helping me escape from the men in black.

She studied with me, and we were always very close. Carla had been by our side in various situations. In the few moments my sister and I could go out, and in the many times we had to stay home. And even with all the restrictions, she never abandoned us. I knew I could count on her calls, her visits, and especially her help in getting rid of my bodyguards, just like the night before.

I sat back down on the bed, pondering whether to go or not. I never imagined my brief escape would end up in the newspaper.

I twirled the phone in my hand, indecisive, my gaze lost on the scaly rug in the same color as the room, which covered most of the floor.

And now, there was an additional problem I would have to navigate to get out of there: Wolf.

"What the hell!" I buried my face in my hands, weighing my options.

There was one way, just one, that could facilitate an escape if I needed to leave Hill House. It was risky, but I could try.

I tightened my grip on the device between my fingers.

Maybe, if I behaved, no one would even need to know I left. My father would definitely find out, but if we didn't involve the newspapers, he might not lock me away for the rest of my life afterward.

So? 10 PM at the hill?

She sent another message when I took too long to respond. I tried to imagine how irritated Wolf would be if I managed to escape right under his threatening nose, and I smiled at the idea. Pure adrenaline coursed through my veins, and I typed my response without worrying about the consequences.

Count me in. I'll meet you at 10 PM. P.S.: You won't believe who my new bodyguard is. I'll tell you on the way.

Done! It was decided. I was going to face Wolf's fury.

HAIR, CLOTHES, MAKEUP, shoes, escape through the window... drag, drag... I began to visualize my plan and everything I would need to prepare to put it into action. The time was approaching, and I felt so anxious that I had no appetite.

I stopped in front of my messy closet and stuck my hand inside, rummaging through the dresses one by one. I glanced at a white dress and dismissed it right away. I picked up a dark green one and wrinkled my nose, tossing it onto the bed. I did this with about ten more pieces and was just about to throw a fit for not having anything to wear when I found one that I liked buried deep in the closet.

"It's you!" I exclaimed, holding up a black dress covered in shiny sequins, with a bold, expressive neckline.

I glanced over my shoulder at the small graveyard of clothes resting on my bed. I gathered everything in a big hug and shoved it back into the closet. A dry laugh escaped my lips. Poor me when Ruth found that mess.

"She'll stuff me in there with you," I said to the dresses and laughed to myself.

I gathered everything I would need: my dress, high heels, a small purse with the jewelry I would wear, and my makeup. I glanced at the golden clock on my study desk, which read exactly 9 PM. Time to put the plan into action.

I cracked the door open and peered out at the long, empty corridor on the second floor. The only sound ringing in my ears was the rapid beat of my heart. I had wrapped all my belongings in a towel, trying to hide everything as much as possible, but the towel had taken on a strange oval shape, so I tucked it under my arm and tiptoed, wishing to blend in with the paintings I passed along the way.

I walked past one of the mirrors in the corridor and liked the messy blonde hair I saw in the reflection. I tousled my hair even more, pulling out some strands to give the impression of "I plan to stay home" and blah, blah, blah, while also trying to draw attention to the crooked cat ears headband I still wore. Everything was meticulously thought out to divert the guards' eyes from my bulging towel.

I descended the stairs humming and headed toward the kitchen, which, to my relief, was completely empty. I stealthily glanced at one of the cameras watching the kitchen and was sure that if the guards weren't in sight, they were probably gathered, watching me through it at that very moment.

For many years, I had lost hope of eating something without being monitored, so they wouldn't be able to fool me. That was the only escape route from the mansion I had managed to devise after many months studying it. I couldn't afford to make a wrong move; otherwise, it would be my end.

I placed the towel on one of the chairs and, distracted—or rather, pretending to be distracted—opened one of the cabinets and rummaged through it for something I could pretend to eat. It took me a while to find a cookie since Ruth insisted on having everything cooked fresh each day, rarely leaving anything canned around. Even the cookies I ate were baked fresh, but by luck, I found a hidden packet in a corner.

I sat down at the table, opened the life-saving chocolate cookie packet, fished one out with my fingertips, and brought it to my mouth, chewing slowly. Anyone who saw me would never imagine the mini heart attack I was almost having there.

Would that crazy plan actually work?

I had no idea, but if none of the guards had cornered me yet, maybe they didn't really suspect anything.

I finished the cookies, grabbed my towel with the utmost casualness, and headed toward the first-floor bathroom, where my escape route began.

When I entered the bathroom, which was large and spacious, I locked the door and checked the clock. I had exactly 30 minutes to get ready and meet Carla at the agreed-upon spot.

I unraveled the towel and pulled out the dress, slipping the snug piece over my head. To my utter despair, the damn dress got caught on the earring in my second hole, which I never took out, and I found myself spinning in the bathroom, trapped by the dress.

"Shit!" I cursed, already starting to sweat. I shook my body from side to side, but it wasn't working. I huffed, too nervous to think straight.

Nervous? No, indignant!

I paused for a moment, arms stuck overhead, beginning to suffocate, and imagined how much embarrassment I would feel if I had to leave there like this, like a tuna trapped in sequins, and admit that my escape had gone wrong right from the start.

No. No. No!

I couldn't give up. No way.

I wiggled a bit more and, with great effort, managed to free the earring and lower the dress.

I attacked my makeup bag next, focusing on the red lipstick, since I couldn't waste time on the rest of the details, like contouring, eyeshadow, and plenty of glitter.

I combed my hair and a few minutes later checked my appearance in the mirror.

"Wow, you're a ninja of instant makeovers," I said to my reflection, which sparkled along with the dress.

Part one of the plan completed successfully. Or almost! I rubbed my hand over the ear that throbbed from the struggle with the earring...

The next mission was one of the hardest parts. I looked over my shoulder at the long rectangular window in the bathroom. I had never escaped through there before, but that window was one of the rare blind spots in the property, where the cameras couldn't capture movement, and if I played my cards right that night, they would remain clueless about how I managed to slip away. The plan boiled down to jumping out the window, crawling through the property, and reaching the exit without being noticed by them. It wasn't the best plan in the world, but it would do.

I pulled the small cabinet from one corner, stuffed with towels and a bunch of odds and ends. I placed the wooden cabinet under the window and climbed on top of it.

I opened the glass and hung out the window, balancing precariously. I was about to jump when a thought crossed my mind.

If something happens, one of us needs to take care of Dad.

The phrase Magnolia had once told me while we were walking home from school hit me hard. I remember arguing with her all the way home simply because she suggested that one day she might leave me alone. But now, hanging out the window like an inexperienced thief, I started to wonder how much of that request I had heard over the years.

I had fled on Mag's birthday because it was such a special date, and even though I didn't mean to, I ended up not only upsetting my father but also jeopardizing his business by appearing in that damn newspaper. I knew how much he poured his heart into that company, just as I tried to impress those idiotic scientists at every opportunity I had, not to catch the eye of a bunch of arrogant old men, but to make my father proud, to feel part of everything he had built.

It wouldn't be right to run away now, just out of sheer desire to dive into the night with Carla. I had too much to lose. Much more than just my own neck. Magnolia had left Dad in my care, and he, in turn, had entrusted me with a top-secret and very, very expensive project. How could I face him, or even deal with the crowd he called partners if I didn't carry myself like the daughter of a CEO in the arms industry? Like the heiress of that entire legacy?

The night's escape was coming to an end. I needed to be responsible. My last escapade had probably left room for me to be called childish, spoiled, and things like that. I couldn't allow it to happen again, not so soon.

I turned back to the bathroom, carefully spinning in the window. I was holding my heels with one hand and balancing in the window with the other. I tossed one shoe back into the bathroom.

"SHIT!" I yelled as my foot slipped out of the window and I fell backward.

Strong arms caught me before I could land like a potato on the granite floor. I widened my eyes and sucked in air, immediately recognizing the citrusy, delicious scent that flooded my senses. I let out a dissatisfied groan.

"Is this how you usually move from room to room in this house? Through windows?" Wolf held me in his arms, keeping me pressed against his solid chest as if I weighed no more than a dozen eggs.

"What..." I lifted my face, and all the blood in my body rushed to my feet as I looked at him so closely again. I could feel his strong breath brushing my face. "You!" I said weakly in the face of his hard, unyielding expression.

"I can't believe the woman who was capable of stealing my motorcycle thought she could escape by jumping out a window." He chuckled to the side, his expression a mix of provocation and amusement. "I'm perplexed. I thought you were capable of something more elaborate than this." I pressed my lips together and exhaled through my nose.

"Could you put me down?" He scrutinized my face, enigmatic. His bicolored eyes moved up and down, analyzing me so closely that I felt the back of my neck start to heat up. He set me down cautiously, and only then did I feel capable of responding.

My hair had fallen into my face, and part of it was stuck in my lipstick.

"How did you know where to find me?" I spat out a bunch of strands and rubbed my face, trying to maintain some semblance of dignity, the anger simmering in every cell of my body.

"This is the only blind spot on the property."

"Exactly!" I shouted. "How did you see me?"

"The point is blind, I am not." Wolf smiled again and examined my face for a moment. "You're underestimating me, Miss, and you'll regret that." He stepped closer, cornering me against the wall.

His broad body completely surrounded me. I raised my face to meet his gaze and found myself drowning in the depths of his stare.

In the dim light, the blue in his eye became more intense, a deep navy, like a piece of the sky, while the gleam of the brown intensified, giving him a pair of bicolored eyes that seemed to pierce my skin.

"I still haven't heard an appropriate apology," he said softly, too close. The minty gum breath brushed my face, and a sudden urge to kiss him to taste that flavor flooded my senses.

But what the hell!

"And what if I don't apologize? What are you going to do?" I retorted, trembling from head to toe, and he lifted his square chin, marked by a low, stubbly beard that gave him sharply defined contours, and unfortunately, made him look devastatingly handsome.

"Don't mock my abilities, Miss Cahill. I'll be watching your every move inside this house. It's better not to try something like this again." He let his eyes slide down my dress before returning to my face.

"Y-you're going to watch me?"

"Isn't that my job? Keeping an eye on you?" He straightened up, moving his body away from mine. Even so, I could still feel him pressing me against the wall, like an invisible force threatening to take part of my soul. "Looking at your escape plan, I'm starting to believe this will be very easy work," he teased. "If you want to escape, you'll have to come up with something much more creative than this. And even then, I'll be right here, just waiting for you."

"Well then." I tried to regain my villainess posture, which didn't work out very well. "If it's war you want, Wolfie, it's war you'll get!"

I turned my back, about to run back inside, when Wolf grabbed my arm, forcing me to face him closely once again.

"Be careful, Miss Cahill." He opened my hand and placed a round, golden-wrapped package in my palm. Moments later, Wolf turned his back and disappeared into the bushes.

I opened the wrapping, almost tearing the small package in my eagerness to see what was inside. My heart raced to my throat and almost jumped out when my eyes landed on a chocolate truffle covered in sprinkles.

I looked to the spot where I had last seen Wolf, but there wasn't even a shadow of the man.

What was that all about? Did he want to confuse me? Was it some strategy to deceive the enemy?

I climbed the stairs, returning to my room with my head in the clouds. My trembling hands now held the truffle as if it were covered in gold.

I shut the bedroom door, confused. I still felt the firm, hard hands of that unbearable man around me, and all I wanted was to push him out of my mind, but I couldn't.

I walked around the room, clutching the truffle with my thoughts racing.

I still remembered the exact moment he knocked my chocolate into the sand at the beach, but I could never have imagined he would try to make up for what happened.

"What the hell." I took a deep breath and froze when I realized his scent had lingered on me.

And now, my God?

I looked at the chocolate, still in disbelief. I thought he would choke me at the first opportunity he had. Receiving that was by far one of the biggest surprises I had ever experienced in my life.

I took off the dress and jumped onto the bed in just my underwear, burrowing under the covers with the truffle.

"What taste do you have?" I asked the sweet and then bit into it.

I moaned when the flavor of the truffle chocolate enveloped my palate.

Suddenly, I began to wonder what Wolf's lips would taste like. So rough, firm, feverish... For a moment, I wished for more than just a peck on that mountain ogre. And I fell asleep before I could regret that thought.

***

"YOU'RE BEAUTIFUL, YES." Magnolia tossed a small twig at my calf.

"Ouch!" I complained, even though it didn't really hurt.

"You deserved it." My sister laughed. The dark blonde in her long hair shimmered under the weak sunlight. Our garden was our favorite place; the sun caressed our skin with its gentle warmth, and from there, the grass looked much greener, like all the foliage beyond the hill. A magical view.

"I think everyone looks in the mirror one day and thinks they're ugly," I retorted.

"My sister, for you to look in the mirror and think that, you must be having vision problems." She leaned toward me, and when I tried to pull away, Mag grabbed a handful of my hair and gently tugged. "Come here now, let me see if you have a speck in that huge eye."

"Let me go, Mag!" I laughed and kept giggling for what felt like an eternity until suddenly the sun was covered by a dark cloud. "I think it's going to rain." I propped myself up on my elbows. My sister fell silent. "Mag?"

I turned to her and froze at the sight. Magnolia was lying next to me. Her eyes were open and lifeless, staring at me as if pleading for help.

"Mag!" An excruciating pain suffocated me. I brought my hand to my chest, trying to breathe, but I couldn't.

My sister's pale face continued to stare at me, white as marble. The little light that remained vanished. I tried to scream, but I couldn't even move. A shadow emerged from the darkness and came toward me. It was a man.

My God, no. Please! Someone! Someone help me!

I tried to speak, but I couldn't. My whole body was petrified with fear. The man had no face; I could only see his hands and the knife he held in one of them.

"No," I cried. "Please, no." He leaned down beside me, pressed the knife against my side, and that's when my nightmare began.

CHAPTER SEVEN

Wolf

The moment I saw Jasmin walking through the house in a cat costume with that towel under her arm, I knew some scheme was brewing in that mischievous little head of hers.

I was in the surveillance room when she entered the first-floor bathroom, and as usual, I looked for the camera that would show me the outside window. When I realized it was a blind spot, I knew immediately what the little thief's plan was.

I almost didn't let her attempt to escape, just to see how she intended to pull it off, but when I saw her hanging from the window, balancing herself in a tiny dress with her gaze lost on the horizon, I feared she might fall and hurt herself.

I could still feel the scent she left on me, along with a good portion of her makeup glitter. My suit felt like a float in a parade from all the sparkles.

I had to admit that girl stirred a mix of strange feelings within me. Anger, worry, anger again, curiosity... all mingling with the brief memory of the kiss I had given her.

The night we met for the first time, I had accidentally dropped a chocolate that seemed very important to her. I didn't like owing anyone anything, and today, as I was gathering everything to start work at the Cahill mansion, I passed a small shop selling chocolates and couldn't help but remember Jasmin's sad face when she saw it fall.

I knew I shouldn't care. I was fully aware of what she might think about that gesture, but I wasn't known for thinking before I acted, and after seeing the surprised look on the girl's face, I realized it had been worth it.

After that, my Crystal—or rather, the Crystal I was tasked with protecting—went upstairs with the chocolate, staring at it in a strange way that made me doubt whether she would actually eat it, and locked herself away for the rest of the night.

The night came without me seeing her again. Cahill, it seemed, would also be out for the night, probably with his fiancée or caught up in work.

I poured myself a cup of coffee and sat down like a stone soldier in front of the cameras, focused on the only two that gave me access to Jasmin's room. I distracted myself, watching her window from the outside. What was she thinking when she decided to run away? What was wrong with that girl? Did she really not care about her own life anymore?

When it came to Miss Cahill, I had many questions and no answers.

"Wolf, if you want to stretch your legs... we can switch from external to internal." Lyon's head poked through the door opening. He still looked at me with a strange expression, making it clear he didn't like me one bit.

"Sure, I need to take a walk anyway."

I stood up from the chair just as a horrifying scream echoed through the silent house. Part of my soul left my body when I realized that sound was coming from Jasmin's room.

I drew my weapon and ran toward the exit of the room. The screams grew louder and more frantic with each second, but before I could even reach the hallway, Lyon gripped my arm tightly.

"Let me go, damn it. Can't you hear?" Another loud scream rang out. Painful, high-pitched, as if someone were torturing her. I had never heard anything so horrifying in my life.

"Damn it, Wolf, wait!" He kept holding my arm firmly. I jerked away, incredulous that he was actually getting in my way, and immediately a suspicion crossed my mind.

What if Lyon was covering up some attempt on her life?

I drew my weapon and aimed it at his face.

"Are you crazy? We're on the same side."

"I'm not so sure about that." I hurried closer to Jasmin's room while Lyon continued to follow me.

"It's not what you think. You can't go in there. She suffers from night terrors. She stopped taking her medication, and we knew this would come back at any moment."

Night terrors?

I paused for a moment, my hand already on the doorknob.

"We can't interfere." Lyon stared at me as if I were a complete idiot. "It's not up to us, Wolf. Trust me, it will pass."

Another sharp scream echoed through the house, and I couldn't ignore it. Screw what was up to me or not. She was suffering; I couldn't just believe that this would pass.

I burst into the room with a bang, and my eyes widened at what I saw.

Jasmin was thrashing on the bed as if someone were right there on top of her, hurting her somehow. But there was nothing, absolutely nothing. She ground her teeth and squeezed her eyes shut, moaning loudly as if her skin were being torn apart.

"Shut that door, Wolf," Lyon asked at my side.

I was still frozen at the sight of her and the horror manifesting in her screams, which pierced my heart into pieces. It took me a moment to react, but I would never, under any circumstances, abandon her there, alone like that, flailing like a wounded animal.

I entered the room amidst the sharp cries and a compulsive sob that shattered my heart.

"Wolf! What the hell!" Lyon shouted, but I ignored him.

Jasmin kicked off the covers, and in that instant, her round, perky breasts were exposed. She was practically naked, wearing nothing but a very thin black panty.

"Damn it! Don't go in, Lyon," I ordered, wanting to prevent him from seeing her like that. I grabbed the sheet and covered her up. I avoided looking at any exposed part of her body, even though I'd already seen more than enough. "Miss Cahill?"

I knelt on the bed.

"Don't do that, you idiot," Lyon insisted. "Don't wake her up."

"I'm not waking her up, I'm calming her down," I replied, wrapping my arm around Jasmin's waist and pulling the sheet along with me.

Immediately, she turned her flailing arms toward me, as if I had become her greatest enemy. I placed her agitated arms around my neck and pulled her to my chest, trying to control her violent movements. Jasmin's face was drenched in tears, and deep lines marked her forehead from the grimaces she made.

She tried to push me away, her screams becoming higher pitched, and for a moment, I feared I had made the wrong decision. But even if that were the case, I wouldn't regret it. I would never allow her to face that hell alone.

I began to stroke her back and made soft sounds with my mouth. Sounds I had heard often in my youth, after I moved in with my father and woke up nearly every night from horrible nightmares. Sounds I hoped would somehow calm Jasmin's heart.

"Calm down, shh..." I whispered into her damp hair. "You're safe. It's over," I repeated like a mantra.

Jasmin let out a sob and her hands, which had once wanted to push me away, now gripped the fabric of my suit tightly, as if she were channeling all her energy into the fingertips. She gasped, took a deep breath, and buried her face in my chest, falling silent soon after.

I held her for another long minute in complete silence.

I didn't want to have reasons to get close to that little thief. Much less to like her. My intention was to hate her with all my strength until I disappeared from that mansion, but hearing her screams blinded me with despair. I could still feel her pain in my bones, and yes, it would be hypocritical to say I wouldn't wish that on one of my worst enemies, because I truly did; they deserved it, but Jasmin didn't. She wasn't my enemy; she was my charge and was suffering immensely.

Whatever she was dreaming about, it was terrible and painful. I feared just imagining it.

I gently laid her sleeping body back onto the bed. A tired expression settled on her delicate face.

It seemed Jasmin had learned to deal with pain very early on. A point we had in common that didn't make it any easier for me to hate her. I looked over her face again, the anguish forcing me to stare longer than I should have, and I eventually spotted the open chocolate wrapper on the bed.

"So you did eat it," I whispered, shaken by the shock, and I placed the wrapper on her nightstand.

The only thing I could think about was the fear that this episode would repeat itself.

I left the room more confused than when I entered. Lyon was waiting for me, standing in the same spot as before.

"You shouldn't have done that," the man grumbled.

"And what did you want me to do? Leave her in that state?"

"It's what we always do." His answer shocked me.

"She has nightmares like that, and you just let the girl scream and suffer all night?" I questioned, perplexed.

"It's not a recurring factor; it happens now and then and usually doesn't last more than 15 minutes," he tried to explain. "In any case, we can't wake her up."

"BUT YOU CAN CALM HER DOWN, DAMN IT!" I shouted. Shaw was climbing the side stairs and found us arguing at the top.

"That...," Shaw said, breathless, as if he had run there. "Was that one of the nightmares? Has it stopped?"

"At least someone cares," I continued glaring at Lyon, who shot me a venomous look.

"It doesn't do any good for him to stand like a puppy at the door without being able to open it," Lyon accused, and I turned to him, fed up with it.

"I could understand such an attitude coming from a stranger," he narrowed his eyes, "but you, Lyon? How long have you known Miss Cahill? Only Wood has been here for ten years."

"Four years, sir," Shaw replied promptly.

"Shut the hell up," Lyon yelled.

"How can you remain indifferent?" I shook my head, still in disbelief.

"You think I don't suffer with Miss Cahill's pain?" He narrowed his eyes and took two steps toward me. "If that's what you think, you're mistaken, Wolf. Do you have any idea what it's like to hear that and not be able to do anything? This situation is beyond what we can control. She stopped taking her medication; sooner or later this was going to happen again."

"That will change."

"How?" Lyon questioned, and even though his gaze threatened to burn me alive, I could see a glimmer of hope shining in his brown pupils.

"I'll talk to Cahill and request new security here."

"Another one?" Lyon's eyes widened further.

"Not another one. A woman. As soon as my time in this place ends, there will be an opening on the team. I'll ask them to include a woman who can help her when the crises start, since no one here seems to care." Lyon nodded when he realized I was resolute. "They can rest for the rest of the night; I'll remain here, on standby."

Lyon took a deep breath, and I turned my back to him and Shaw, heading back to the surveillance room.

I stared at my trembling hands when I was completely alone.

My God, I couldn't explain the terror that gripped me when I felt the panic and terror that Jasmin was trapped in. Inside her own thoughts.

I grabbed my phone. Something I only did during work in extreme situations, and I dialed the numbers of the only person who might be able to help me. The only one I knew who had suffered from that same affliction.

"I hope you haven't killed anyone, my brother. It's only been two days."

"You're always as optimistic as I am, Ghost." He laughed on the other end.

"Receiving a call from you can't be considered routine, especially at this hour. It's actually concerning, don't you think? What's happened?"

"I need you to tell me everything you know about night terrors."

I grabbed a piece of paper and a pen from the control desk, ready to spend the rest of the night learning everything I could about that crap. There had to be some sort of treatment or something I could do if she had another episode.

I wouldn't rest until I found something to ease my little thief's suffering.

CHAPTER EIGHT

Jasmin

I hadn't even opened my eyes when a pulsating sting bothered me. I rolled over under the warm blankets. My arms and legs felt sore, as if I had been hit by a speeding car. My head threatened to explode in throbbing waves.

I knew that feeling. The one that always attacked me after a night of night terrors. It felt like my mind suddenly drifted into turbulent waters.

I sat up in bed and blinked, trying to fight the urge to hide there for the rest of the day.

I stared at the soft gray blanket, trying to recall something from the night before. I usually didn't remember my dreams. Only a few flashes came to my memory, and I didn't know if that was good or bad. I wanted to at least know what happened in those dreams that left me so physically and emotionally destroyed.

I looked at a fixed point where a beam of light slipped through the curtain and touched the bed. For some reason, I felt that something new had happened during the night. I rifled through my memories for any flash of remembrance. I could remember the fear I felt, yes. Even if I didn't know what it was or what I was afraid of, I felt it deep down. Lurking. I was drowning in that feeling when... *he saved me.*

I sucked in air sharply, suddenly remembering a knight, wearing armor black as night, coming toward me. He was the one who pulled me from wherever I had been. Which was very strange, because I could still feel his arms around me, caressing me as if I were someone very important, and for a moment, I wished I could fall asleep again, just to find him.

Who was that strange yet somehow familiar man?

I got up, using all my willpower, my thoughts still fixed on the mysterious knight. I didn't want to leave the bed, but with the exciting, not to say desperate, meeting waiting for me at Hill and Cahill, I had no other option.

I walked to the mirror and was startled to see the mess my hair was in. My reflection looked a bit faded, colorless, another consequence of a crisis. I usually felt drained when they hit, but at least I would try to look better than I actually felt.

I turned to the bathroom, ready to take a hot shower, but before that, I glanced at the pile of medications on my nightstand and even considered talking to the psychiatrist Aunt Claire had recommended again. According to her, the doctor had taken care of her mental health since she was 20. Still, I couldn't bring myself to like that woman. She analyzed me as if I were a little cockroach she wanted to squash at all costs, and even when I told her I didn't want to take anything that would affect my performance during the day, she insisted on piling me with medications.

I know, I know. Who am I to contradict a trained and specialized doctor? Nobody. But this nobody wants to stay awake and not feel nauseous, which was another horrible side effect those medications caused, in addition to the lack of appetite that made me lose nearly 10 kilos. Maybe, at some point, I should look for another specialist, but right now, even feeling bad about the night terrors, I still preferred to keep my mind intact.

I FINISHED GETTING ready nearly an hour later and stopped in front of the mirror to check my look. I had pulled my hair up into a high ponytail and chosen a fitted white dress with short sleeves and a fabric marked by icy waves that looked like a sequence of codes, with a hem just above the knee. Elegant, yet suitable for the day. I grabbed my white sunglasses and matching jacket, completing the monochromatic look, and put them on. The end of autumn was approaching, and winter was already showing its face with chilly winds. So it was better to be prepared.

I descended the stairs a while later, the persistent clicking of my heels echoing in the air. I stopped when I reached the entrance hall and scanned the place until my eyes landed on the man standing by the door.

Wolf's eyes met mine, and for a moment, I felt trapped there. His impenetrable face looked even more beautiful under that confident seriousness, like someone who could calmly walk through a world on fire. His attention remained fixed on my every movement, making my cheeks heat up. I raised the back of my hand to them as he observed me cautiously.

"Are you ready, miss?" His voice came low, but the rough and firm tone made me hesitate. There was something different about him.

"Y-yes," I stammered, cursing myself internally as he took a step closer, dangerously near.

"Are you sure you feel okay?" he inquired. I blinked, confused, and my eyes widened as I realized that if I had a crisis the night before, Wolf had probably heard everything, and that look, which had once seemed warm and intense, now resembled what I would call... pity?

My face, already warm, ignited. I would admit to any feeling, especially coming from that stranger who managed to provoke every cell in my body, but pity?

"I'm perfectly ready for today," I asserted, lifting my chin.

"Being ready and feeling up to it are two different things." Was he really going to worry about me? Him, my declared enemy? He should save that pity for someone else.

"I enjoy irritating the Hill and Cahill partners; it's one of my favorite activities," I joked, trying not to show how much his witnessing that situation had shaken me. I knew that the crises were more painful for those who heard than for those who actually felt them, and I felt somewhat ashamed for having exposed that vulnerability in front of him. "I can't postpone this commitment, don't you think?" He shook his head side to side, and a side smile, dark and indecent, crossed his face as Wolf adjusted the radio communicator.

"The Crystal is ready. Let's go," he announced into the earpiece and grabbed his sunglasses. Two other cars were parked close to the one I would enter.

"Aren't you going to have breakfast, Miss Cahill?" Ruth intercepted me before I could even move, her shrill voice pulling me from the hypnosis that man had cast on me.

"I'll eat at the office, Ruth, I promise," I informed her, watching her wrinkle her nose.

"As if that packaged food were anywhere near what Judith makes," she grumbled. "You'll get sick and wonder why."

"My dear Ruth, you woke up so sweet today." I smiled at the woman as she turned her back and left.

Wolf opened the car door for me to enter. I walked past him, ignoring the persistent thrum in my chest just from being in the presence of that man.

What was going on now? My heart must have had some problem, it could only be. His presence bothered me. All those taut muscles in that suit, that inquisitive and so different gaze, his rough, low, and threatening voice—everything, absolutely everything bothered me.

I slid into the leather seat of the car.

"Good morning, Miss Cahill!" Shaw said cheerfully, opening the front door of the car.

"I hope it's really good, Shaw," I muttered, taking off my jacket as I noticed the car's interior was warm.

Shaw took the passenger seat while Wolf moved ahead, and after directing the rest of the team, he sat in the front seat.

"Put your seatbelt on, Miss Cahill," he said curtly.

"Oh, come on, it's not that far; it'll crumple my dress," I complained, and the moment Wolf removed his sunglasses and turned to me, I knew I had irritated him.

"Put on the seatbelt, or I'll come over there and tie you up with it," he growled.

I opened my mouth, incredulous, and noticed Shaw flinch slightly in the front seat. No one had ever treated me with such harshness and rudeness.

I took a deep breath and, instead of jumping on him and pulling his hair out, which I felt like doing, I opened a smile, causing a crease to form in the middle of his forehead.

"Oh, but of course. Asking like that, with so much affection." It was good to have received that kickback. That way, I could reconnect with my main target. Irritating him until he gave up that position.

Wolf turned back to the front, and for a brief moment, I gazed out the window beside me. The late autumn sun was weak, yellow, yet there was still a special shine through the hills that pointed to a magical horizon.

The Hill House was such a beautiful place that on some mornings I felt that if there were gardens in the sky, they would look like that.

The first car began to move, and we followed in line, as always. The car I was in was the second of three identical vehicles. Completely black, with dark windows and armored glass. A common technique used by bodyguards to confuse any enemies.

The only difference between those cars and any others Wolf might have worked with was the ability to connect my phone to the sound system without external interference. In other words, even if he wanted to turn it off, he wouldn't be able to.

Maybe that man needed a bit of music to lighten that beautiful face.

I mean, ugly face, horrible.

We were already approaching the main highway when I decided to initiate my plan.

"Are you ready for the party, Shaw?" I questioned the bodyguard, who looked at me with a pale expression and a weak smile, probably fearing that Wolf would explode and throw us down a ravine.

I grabbed my phone and played one of my favorite songs.

"A Thousand Miles," the theme from an old movie that I loved dearly.

"White Chicks."

The music started playing, and being a fan, I began singing along at the top of my lungs.

Making my way downtown
Walking fast
Faces passed
And I'm home bound

"Ta na na na tan taaaaaaannnn." If I'm not going to sing along to the instrumental, I won't sing at all. "Come on, Shaw!"

"Staring blankly ahead. Just making my way... ow!" He stopped when Wolf elbowed him.

"Isn't it enough that this crazy girl is singing like a deranged parrot in this closed car?" he shouted irritably.

"I heard that, you know?!" I complained. "You're so boring." I lifted my nose toward the window, feeling motivated to unleash my inner parrot for the rest of the trip. I sang half my playlist in his head.

When Wolf parked the car in front of the large building where the Hill and Cahill headquarters was located, I could swear smoke was rising from his head, so great was his anger, and he needed all his self-control not to drag me by the feet out of the car.

He opened the door for me to get out. I slid from the seat and exited the car, brushing against his arm on the way out. A little chill ran through my stomach when I felt his subtle touch.

I was still mad at him for mocking me the night before, but I didn't understand how my body and mind could disagree so much. Just brushing against him made me feel all tingly.

Wolf of the inferno!

I looked at the colossal glass building in front of me, transforming the headquarters into a shiny silver skyscraper. Some people were walking around the courtyard in easy conversation, and a few began to notice my presence, which, while rare, was becoming increasingly public. I knew that all my father's employees knew my name, but many had never actually seen me. I guess after making headlines in the newspapers, my face became quite common around here.

I took a deep breath, gathering courage to face whatever came my way, and took an uncertain step toward the building.

"Miss Cahill." I stopped when I heard Wolf call me, and before I could even turn to him, his hands enveloped my shoulders, gently placing my jacket over them. "You forgot this," he warned.

I turned to face him, as close as the night we kissed, and I found myself tracing a path over his rugged mouth, slightly hidden by the well-groomed beard, and up again to the eyes concealed behind his sunglasses.

My chest warmed, and I began to breathe more slowly, as if his mysterious aura left me dizzy. Thank God my glasses camouflaged me;

otherwise, I wouldn't know how to explain the urge to keep staring at him. I felt trapped there, held captive by the delicious image that was Wolf before me.

Oh, God... why did this man have to be so handsome?

"I need you to pay attention to what I'm about to say now. Okay?"

"Y-yes." I was surprised to notice his tone, usually so harsh, carried a strange note of concern.

"I know you weren't happy with what happened last night," he recalled, and I pursed my lips.

"'Not happy' doesn't even come close," I retorted.

"You can hate me as much as you want," he admitted calmly. Shaw was trying not to pay attention to the conversation, while standing behind Wolf. Each of the other security personnel waited in their respective cars. "I'm not looking for your approval; I'm looking for your protection. And for that, I need you to know that from the moment you cross that door, we'll be one."

"One what?" My voice came out hoarse.

"That's exactly what you heard. I will be your shadow. Absolutely no one is allowed to lay a hand on you, do you understand?" he warned seriously, removing his sunglasses. His colorful orbs expanded, like two bright and different stars. He seemed worried. Too worried.

"Is something happening that I don't know about?" I whispered.

Probably, his concern stemmed from what happened to my sister. Magnólia was stabbed by a bastard who got too close. That took my sister's life, and it could surely take mine as well.

"Nothing to worry about." The crease between his thick eyebrows didn't fool me. "Just follow my instructions."

"Do you think someone at my father's company might try something?" I glanced over my shoulder, already paranoid.

"I'm not your bodyguard for nothing, Miss Cahill. Someone can always try something, at any moment." He raised his sunglasses and put them back on. "That's why I'm here. The rules are simple. No one gets closer than half a meter to you. No one will touch you, and you won't be alone for even a moment."

"Even in the bathroom?" I widened my eyes in horror.

"In that case, I'll enter first and assess the location. You enter afterward."

"Oh, my God." Even my bathroom time was now compromised.

"I'll stay with you while the others wait here. Shall we?"

"I guess so." I blinked, confused.

"We're moving," he announced in the communicator, and we began to walk.

This time he was closer, which tangled my thoughts even more.

We entered the headquarters, a very spacious place where every inch of the environment, from decorative paintings to the laminate floor, was tinted in blue, white, and gray. The colors of Hill and Cahill.

"Good morning, Miss Cahill," the receptionist greeted me and allowed entry without even bothering to acknowledge the nearly two-meter shadow behind me. My father probably had already informed her that Wolf would be with me.

"This is where it all happens," I commented over my shoulder as we paused in front of the elevator. "All the projects, from a mobile aviation training simulator to wireless communication systems. Oh, we also have an amazing night vision equipment and ground-space antennas for government sectors. But my favorite is the microwave weapons."

"Microwave weapons? That's new," Wolf said behind me.

"It's a weapon capable of emitting microwaves towards the skin, making the water in our bodies heat to an unbearable temperature," I explained, feeling excitement coursing through my veins. I loved each one of Hill and Cahill's projects. "It's not lethal at all, and can only be provided to the army, but it causes intense pain and the sensation that you're dying. Isn't that exciting?"

"Define exciting, Miss. I wouldn't want to be on the receiving end of that weapon."

"You'd have to be at least 80 meters away, which is its maximum range, not to be hit. Did I mention it's my favorite product?"

"Yes, to the point that I'm quite worried."

The executive elevator arrived, and as soon as we entered the metal box, which thankfully was empty, I was embraced by the usual anxiety of facing 12 scientists who saw me as the spoiled and intrusive daughter of the boss. Indeed, that wasn't the best feeling in the world.

The elevator door was almost closing when someone shoved their hand through the gap, causing it to open again. When I saw who was entering, I had to stifle the urge to roll my eyes.

"Miss Cahill!" Foster, a cheerful and very handsome man, I must admit, greeted me as if we were childhood friends. "Finally, you returned to the company." He stepped closer when the door closed, but Wolf was quicker and placed his hand on the man's chest, pushing him away from me with a fierce look that, for a moment, even made me feel scared.

"Keep your distance," he warned, with a fixed stare at the man.

"You got yourself a guard dog to control your scandalous desires, miss?" he mocked. "Or are you still planning to illustrate the newspapers with your... reduced self-control?"

I widened my eyes when my bodyguard raised his hand, about to grab the idiot by the neck.

"From what I see, Foster..." I touched Wolf's arm, trying to calm him, and saw him clench his fists, glaring at Foster as if he were in a boxing ring. "You still haven't learned to keep your hands to yourself and your tongue in your mouth." I leaned briefly in his direction. "It's better to be careful, or you might end up without one of them," I whispered, and I saw pure hatred flowing through the man's gaze, who smiled as if he hadn't been affected.

Foster was one of my father's partners. He had a small but significant percentage in the company and was one of several partners who opposed the J.A.S. project, mainly because it was being created by me. Men like him were used to giving orders and being obeyed. Since I started the project, both Foster and the others did everything to discourage me, but when they realized I would never give up, all that was left was to accept me down their throats.

He would use all the tricks he had up his sleeve against me, and it was thinking about men like him, and with the intention of protecting my father, that I avoided going out last night.

"It's good to see you," he said, turning to the elevator door, which seemed to be on its way to heaven rather than the 23rd floor.

Wolf remained in the space between me and Foster, and I couldn't help but notice the fury with which he stared at the man. I bit my lip, ignoring the strange flutter in my chest as I saw him protecting me so fiercely.

The elevator door opened, and Foster stepped out without looking back. I pulled Wolf by the edge of his jacket as soon as we set foot outside the elevator.

"Now, the one who needs to listen to me is you," I said softly, already in the long corridor filled with doors that would lead us to one of the laboratories. He raised his eyebrows, waiting for me to speak. "An exorbitant total of two people support my project in this company. My father and my aunt Claire. If you hit anyone here..."

"It'll be for a good reason," he interrupted me. "And I wasn't going to do anything too extreme. Maybe just shake him a little." I struggled to contain my laughter and kept a serious expression.

"Please, Wolf, this is very important." I held his arm and moved closer to him, trying to avoid anyone overhearing our conversation in the corridors of the company. "My father's partners are going to provoke me. It's what they do best, and if you hit any of them, my reputation here will get even worse. So stay out of it."

"And why does your father allow you to be treated this way? You are the heiress of this place; the least those bastards can do is respect you," he said seriously and intensely.

"My father has no idea what happens around here. None of the guards have come into the testing room with me before."

"Why didn't you tell him?" I straightened my posture and turned to the corridor, this time wearing the mask of sarcasm that usually protected my heart.

"I never wanted to be daddy's little girl, Wolf," I replied. "I certainly won't allow a bunch of frustrated, misogynistic men to spread around that I resorted to him because I was too weak. I'll handle this myself and show that bunch of cowards what I'm capable of. Are you coming with me?"

"You're completely insane." He couldn't hold back a smile. "Makes sense. How else would you steal my motorcycle?"

"You will never forget that little mishap?"

"Never!" We walked down the corridor, passing several closed doors marked with golden number plates. We stopped in front of laboratory 6.

"Promise you won't jump on anyone's neck inside this room?" I pointed at the number on the door.

"As long as they don't cross the proximity limit," he said seriously. "Otherwise..."

"Yes, yes, I already know. Blood, bodies... I can imagine." I waved my hands in front of his face. "Can I really count on you?" I questioned, apprehensive.

"You can always count on me, Miss Cahill. I'll do anything to keep you safe," he promised in a low, deep voice that made me hold my breath. "Whatever you face in there, know that you won't be alone."

Oh, damn, don't say that! I wanted to plead.

It became harder each second to ignore the strange pang that his voice caused me, but I forced myself to ignore it. At that moment, I had bigger concerns, and if I messed up in there, I would lose much more than I would like to admit.

"So, let's go." I knocked on the door and waited until it opened, and the games began.

CHAPTER NINE

Wolf

The door opened, and a very short man with long mustaches and a white lab coat that reached his knees greeted us with a smile so weak that for a moment I thought he was suffering from some intestinal ailment.

"Miss Cahill, it's so good to see you," he said, as if it wasn't written in the middle of his wrinkled forehead that he was not the least bit pleased to lay eyes on us.

"It's so nice to see that you missed me." She flashed a mocking smile at the man and lifted her chin, staring him down.

Jasmin calmly removed her sunglasses and opened an even brighter smile when she noticed all the gazes in that room turning toward the door to see her. She looked stunning in that dress; "stunning" wasn't quite right—"radiant" was the more fitting word, and I had to admit I was surprised. Not by her sparkling beauty; far from it.

Jasmin Cahill was breathtaking in any situation, but after the night she had, I expected everything from her, except for her to be able to stand up as if nothing had happened. And after everything I heard her say in the elevator, it was impossible not to be impressed and in awe of her courage, even if I'd rather die than admit it.

Her willpower to face anyone without hiding behind her father's power affected me, and as if she were willing to surprise me even more, Jasmin walked into the room with the relaxed posture of someone among friends, ignoring all the wary glances she received. One by one, the twelve men, who were similarly dressed in white lab coats and casually seated around a long rectangular table made of pure wood, greeted her, and then all those looks fell upon me, standing next to her.

"Miss Cahill, we can't allow strangers into this room. Your project is confidential," one of them said.

"Mr. Jordan, don't you think I would bring someone who would steal my project with me?" The man scrutinized me from head to toe and pressed his lips together.

"I think you're too young to know what's good for you."

"I disagree. I believe you forgot that people like me, heirs of entire conglomerates, need a bodyguard 24/7. He goes where I go. Is there any opposition?" she said calmly, clasping her hands in front of her dress.

I knew that statement was a pure lie. Jasmin would throw me off the rooftop of that building if she had the chance; still, seeing her lie to defend my position at her side brought me a certain pleasure.

"Well then, I think he will be extremely necessary, don't you agree, Jordan?" Another man, the only one who observed Jasmin with a calm expression on his face, nodded toward her, which she reciprocated. Apparently, not everyone inside that room detested her.

"Well, let's get started. We have no time to waste." She walked to the center of the table and grabbed a mustard-colored folder laid out before her, along with a remote control beside it.

I stood a meter away from her, watching her point the remote at the wall. Suddenly, a wide white screen descended, and slides began to be presented with all kinds of numbers that I wouldn't understand in two lifetimes.

Jasmin spent the next hour explaining her project with enviable determination. There, before those men, I barely recognized her. She spoke with absurd authority. She didn't even seem like the same 23-year-old girl who stole my motorcycle and threw sand in my face. No, on the contrary, I'd say that version of Jasmin, lecturing before me, had the soul of a scientist.

She pointed at the screen with enthusiasm, moving more with each second, excited about the conclusion of the presentation that I still hadn't understood. The white dress accentuated the curve of her uplifted breasts, flowing down to her defined waist before flaring at her hips, revealing a round ass that I had to struggle to look away from. That was not the case for those old perverts. Some of them were watching her with visible interest. A sudden urge to gouge out their eyes hit me.

A few minutes later, Jasmin wrapped up her presentation, and Mr. Jordan raised his hand the instant she closed her mouth.

"Tell me, Miss Cahill, do you intend to burn your father's and our money on a project like this just for luxury, or do you genuinely believe that major companies will be interested in buying it?" I clenched my fists when I saw Jasmin grit her jaw, hoping she'd unleash one of the curses she seemed so accustomed to swearing. It would be incredible to see the bastard's face if she told him to fuck off right there.

But, contrary to what I thought she'd do, the only reaction from Jasmin was to smile. Apparently, sarcasm was also a factory setting for the girl.

"Oh, Dr. Jordan, just because you're from Noah's time doesn't mean you can't understand the present." Some of the scientists brought their hands to their mouths, stifling laughter. Jordan's face turned a shade of red, like a ripe tomato. "What I propose is not a simple project. The J.A.S. will be able to expand a spectrum radius with directed energy to identify any threat, internal or external, creating a defense network that will make it impossible for any attacks against systems, radars, and other sensors. If you still remember, there's a significant number of electronic wars our country needs to face. Do you really think no one will be interested in this creation?"

"Irrefutable!" The man who supported her earlier spoke again. "Miss Cahill presents us with facts and tests showing that the probability of the J.A.S. becoming one of our best-selling protection systems is approximately 99%, given our clients' purchasing base," he explained to his colleagues.

"Thank you, Dr. Willian." She turned to him. "Does anyone have anything against the finalization of the project?" Jasmin scanned the faces of the men seated there, and I noticed the restlessness in their concerned expressions, which remained silent, even though they seemed to want to do otherwise. "Perfect. I will send the analyses to the responsible department, and we'll begin production." She took the remote and closed the presentation screen, which slowly rose behind her and disappeared into a panel in the wall. "It's been great being with you, but I'm afraid I need to leave. Have a good afternoon."

"Until next time, Miss Cahill. I look forward to seeing your new projects," Dr. Willian said sincerely. She thanked him and received the not-so-warm farewells from the other members in that room.

We left that place shortly after, and as soon as we stepped into the hallway, I could already feel the atmosphere lightening up.

Jasmin exhaled, exasperated. She looked a thousand times more tired than when she entered that room, and I wished we could get to the car quickly so she could rest.

"Looks like you have more than two supporters for your project," I remarked on the way to the elevator. Jasmin held her sunglasses in her hand and stared at them. The smile from moments ago had completely vanished, and only then did I notice the sad expression that had taken over her delicate face. "What happened? Your presentation was spectacular," I questioned before I could stop myself.

The elevator arrived, and I held the door open, allowing her to enter.

"It's just... too exhausting. They think I don't know they hate me, but I do. And it's really strange to go in there, talk, talk, and talk, only to hear grumbles in response to a project that means everything to me," she revealed, "but it doesn't matter."

"It does matter," I ended up saying, stopping when a man entered the elevator just before the doors closed. I narrowed my eyes and clenched my fists upon noticing it was the same jerk from earlier.

"Working in the elevator now, Foster?" Jasmin didn't waste any time, and I noticed the exact moment she shoved the sad expression off her face.

"Quite the coincidence, isn't it?" The creep smiled and pressed the button for the basement, one floor below the lobby, where we would exit. "I hope your meeting was interesting." The elevator began to descend.

"It was indeed very productive," she said, without looking at him, and I could feel Jasmin nearing her emotional limit.

Since the crisis she had suffered the night before, the provocation from that idiot upon arrival, the intimidation she faced in the room with the scientists—all of it was piling up, and she seemed about to explode. Seeing that only made me want to shove Foster into the elevator ventilation system even more.

"Oh, I'm sure it was. I heard several laughs coming from the scientists' room a few minutes ago; I bet you left a good impression behind. Did you dance on the table? That seems to be one of your standout characteristics."

"You son of a bitch!" I lunged at him, and his eyes widened, but I stopped the moment I felt Jasmin's hand on my arm. He let out a dry laugh.

I could see her face turning shades of red as she tried to control her anger, and I couldn't understand how someone could be as idiotic as that man.

Idiot? No, that was an understatement—he was a total moron. How dare he provoke the future owner of all this? It didn't matter what percentage he had in the company; Jasmin would be the heir to every inch of that place, and for a moment, I wished I could be there when her ownership happened, just to see her toss that idiot into the street.

The elevator doors opened, and I held the door for her to pass.

"I didn't say anything untrue, did I?" he provoked again as she was almost out of the elevator.

Jasmin halted, took a deep breath, and continued walking. The bastard started laughing at her. That was the last straw.

I pressed the button that kept the elevator from moving and stepped back inside.

One of the advantages of having trained in Aikido for over ten years was being a master of short, extremely painful strikes that usually didn't cause a ruckus.

"What the hell..." He stopped talking and gasped for air as I delivered a swift elbow to his stomach, so quickly he didn't even have time to defend himself. I grabbed his shoulders and straightened his body, as if we were old friends while he choked from the pain.

"Breathe, stay calm, and straighten up. That was nothing." I looked him in the eye with a brief smile. "If you provoke her again, I will break every bone in your body, and you'll know what real pain is." His eyes widened, and he braced himself against the elevator's metal railing as I walked out.

Jasmin was waiting for me at the turnstile with a worried look.

"Tell me you didn't do anything."

"I didn't do anything."

"You liar! You hit him, didn't you?" she asked, concerned. "If my dad finds out about this..." Suddenly, her eyes widened as if an idea had infiltrated her mind, and she looked at me with a gaze that seemed to plan world domination, making me shiver. "Did you leave marks?"

"If you're thinking of using this to try to get rid of me, know that I have full autonomy to hit anyone I want to protect you, and I will do so." I connected the radio and switched to channel 3. "I'm with Crystal; we're heading out," I alerted the team.

"I appreciate your interference, but I'm quite capable of solving my problems on my own, and yes, I still want to get rid of you." She glared at me, narrowing her eyes, fierce like a nervous kitten. "You're going to regret accepting this job."

"You seem determined." I stifled a smile.

She wrinkled her nose and walked toward the exit, her high heels echoing a loud thump against the floor.

We walked in silence to the car. I opened the door, and Jasmin entered without ceremony, settling into the leather seat. In the dim light of the sun streaming in that late morning, her eyes sparkled green, making them even brighter. She grabbed the seatbelt and fastened it around her body, and when she noticed me still standing there, staring at her for some unknown reason, Jasmin pouted and raised her nose.

"I'm not going anywhere, Wolf. Look, I already put the seatbelt on."

If she knew the reason I couldn't stop staring at her was far different from any concern for her safety... I would be utterly lost.

"It's Wolf. No diminutives, got it?" I shouted, and she rolled her eyes with a smile. I forced myself to break the connection that kept me tethered to those jade eyes and closed the door.

I brought my hand to my chest as a pang hit me right there, but I had no idea why. Maybe that pain was caused by the tension and worry I felt since Jasmin stepped out of that car earlier. Considering the whole soap opera history that girl had, and the looming risk that Naish was just waiting for the perfect opportunity to strike, I felt a deep concern at the thought of what might happen if she were to run away.

Having the blood of an innocent on my hands was my greatest fear. Now, imagining that blood could belong to Jasmin terrified me.

That was it; that pang was pure worry.

That's what I kept repeating to myself every time I searched for her eyes in the rearview mirror as we made our way back to Hill House.

CHAPTER TEN

Jasmin

The sunlight streamed through the car window, warming my bare legs with a gentle touch. My thoughts wandered as I gazed at the landscape zipping by outside.

Wolf drove in silence, and I could barely bring myself to look in his direction.

Had he really hit Foster because of me?

The thought made my chest burn in an uncomfortable, nagging way. No one had ever defended me against any of the verbal attacks I had suffered in that company. The few people who had witnessed anything never cared, and I had never asked for protection against it; after all, I felt strong enough to fight those idiots with more than just insults, with such amazing projects that not even the most hateful among them could reject. But Wolf made me feel something I had never felt before.

When we were in the room presenting the continuation of the project, every now and then, one of those idiots would throw a new insult disguised as a joke my way. I was used to it and, even in the face of their nonsense, I managed to maintain my composure, always responding with the purest sarcasm imaginable. But Wolf didn't seem satisfied with that way of handling things.

Every time one of the scientists opened his mouth, he would clench his fists until the thick veins stood out on the back of his hand, glaring at them as if he would rip their heads off right there in the meeting. That left me in a mix of worry and surprise.

Wolf's job was to protect me from threats to my life, as well as to irritate me constantly, but he never needed to protect my moral integrity—yet that's exactly what he did.

I still couldn't believe he had actually hit Foster. God, how I wished I could have seen that scene. I smiled at the window, imagining how furious that jerk must have been.

Even if I had asked my bodyguard to keep his hands away from any trouble, I was thrilled to have been defended by him. And that was precisely why I couldn't look him in the eye. A fluttering sensation rose in my chest at the mere thought of standing before those singular, captivating eyes. Wolf was stirring my feelings, and I didn't like it one bit. In fact, I was terrified.

We arrived at Hill House a while later and were greeted by the two security guards responsible for vehicle entry and exit at the location.

One by one, all the guards parked the cars in the strategically reserved space, a point that lay exactly between the house and the main exit. This facilitated an emergency escape if we needed one.

As soon as we stopped, Shaw stepped up, got out of the car, and opened the door for me.

"Have a great day, Miss Cahill," he wished and went to meet Lyon and Ray.

I hurried to get out of sight of the man I intended to avoid, but for some reason, Wolf got out of the vehicle and stood in front of me, blocking my way. All the conflicting feelings I had tried to avoid during the ride surged back with force the moment he removed his sunglasses and calmly examined my face. His expressive eyes sparkled like two lanterns with lights in different shades. Then I had the impression that for a fleeting second, he dropped his gaze to my mouth, but it happened so quickly that I couldn't tell if it was real or just a figment of my imaginative mind.

"You didn't have coffee at the company like you said you would," he reminded me, his strong voice low and deep.

"I—I can't eat when I'm about to enter one of those meetings. I get so anxious I can't even drink water," I stammered.

"Then you should eat something right after leaving there." He tilted his head to the side, and I realized that whenever I was this close to Wolf, I always held my head high, as if looking up at the sky. He was so tall, and from that angle, his mouth looked even more enticing. Suddenly, I couldn't look away from it. "That place sucked half your energy; if you don't eat, you'll end up feeling sick."

"I will eat." Oh, how I wished I could devour him right there. "Damn," I cursed loudly when I realized where my thoughts were leading me, and I saw Wolf raise his eyebrows. "NO, it's not you that's the damn thing."

"I'm glad to hear that." He pressed his lips together as if holding back a smile.

"I must be hungry and confused." I rubbed my face. "Thank you for your help today." His eyes traveled down to mine, plunging me into the hell of following his bicolored irises as they scanned every inch of my face, warming parts of my body that had been quiet until then. "I know I asked you not to interfere, but I was glad you did."

"Miss Cahill..." he interrupted me. "I didn't do anything beyond what is required of me as your bodyguard. Even if you desperately want to get rid of me, it's my job to protect you from everything and everyone, especially from the idiots who can't get physically close but try in the worst way... emotionally," he added, and my heart raced a little more at the seriousness and commitment in his words.

"I still want to get rid of you," I narrowed my eyes and stared at him, "but I won't torment you for the rest of the day. Think of this as a peace offering," I joked.

"You should be careful with your offers, Miss Cahill." He stepped even closer. His enticing scent wrapped around me like a labyrinth, pulling me in deeper. His low voice combined with the dangerous gaze of someone who could conquer a nation in just one afternoon. "I can believe you're starting to like my presence."

"My gratitude doesn't go that far," I scoffed.

He raised a hand toward me. His serious, strong demeanor hypnotized me. I closed my eyes as I imagined Wolf, for whatever reason, touching my face. In fact, I awaited that touch as if my life depended on it, and suddenly, I felt a light flick on my forehead.

"Ouch!" I yelped, opening my mouth in shock.

"Don't put your life at risk again like you did the night before." He pointed a finger at me, like a father reprimanding his rebellious daughter.

"Oh, you..." I couldn't believe I closed my eyes in front of him, waiting for his touch.

How humiliating! Idiot, idiot, idiot.

"Come inside and eat. You're looking a bit green," he teased, flashing me a sidelong grin.

Anger and fury surged up my neck and warmed my face, but I held back the urge to jump Wolf's neck and stomped past him, furious. I bumped my shoulder against him with all the strength I had, but ended up losing my balance on impact against that wall of muscles he called a chest.

"You'd better watch where you're going, Miss Cahill." I grew even more irritated when I felt his hand gently wrap around my waist for support. His rigid arm only withdrew when I regained my balance.

"Maybe it's you who should be careful, Wolf," I whispered, raising my right hand where the key to his car, which had been in his blazer, now dangled between my fingers, right in front of his face.

"What?" He stared at the key, and his expression shifted. First confusion, then surprise, and soon after, his colorful irises turned into a fierce, consuming, fiery gaze, like a raging sea.

He smacked his hand against his clothes, probably checking to see if it really was his key.

"You little troublemaker!" he cursed, shocked, which made me laugh out loud.

"You'd better never show up with your motorcycle around here again, or you know what will happen, Wolf." I tossed the key in his direction, and before he could catch it, I turned my back and started walking as fast as I could toward the house, practically running in those high heels. Wolf's furious voice behind me left me with no other option.

"I'm going to hang you from the chandelier, you..." I didn't hear the end of the sentence, but when I stopped under the crystal chandelier in the entrance hall, I was overwhelmed by a sense that Wolf could really trap me there.

I laughed. If Wolf wanted to provoke me, he'd better be ready because I could very well be a worthy opponent. I just needed to shake off the spell those distinct eyes cast over me.

THERE'S NO BEING IN the world with half the strength of a woman. We are incredibly strong emotionally, and for those who think we aren't physically strong, I'd like to suggest spending just one damn day dealing with cramps. A pain that comes straight from the depths of hell.

That afternoon, my period decided to show up earlier than I expected, and all I could do was suffer.

"I'm going to die, Ruth." I rolled in bed and curled up under the covers. My stomach was swollen, my legs hurt, as did the rest of my body, and I felt so sad it was as if a villain had stolen the world's happiness.

"You survive every month, miss. This one isn't going to kill you." The woman walked around my room patiently, went to the little table where my medications were, and picked up one I hadn't taken yet. "According to the doctor's prescription, if you start taking this birth control today, your period won't last more than two or three days." She grabbed the pack and the glass of water she had brought with her.

"Do you really think that if I take this," I pulled my head out from under the covers, "the next times I menstruate, the symptoms will be milder?"

"Yes, I believe so. My daughter had to take birth control because she suffered a lot from premenstrual symptoms. In your case, they come after she arrives, but I believe the effect will be the same." She tried to reassure me.

I sought a gynecologist a month ago. I could no longer bear all the horrible symptoms I felt during those days. Worst were the mood swings. I went from joy to deep sadness in the blink of an eye, and she assured me that with the right medication, I could get through this period more easily.

"And did your daughter improve?" Ruth rarely talked about her daughter, who, from what I knew, was married and had two daughters.

"She improved a lot. She only stopped taking the medication when she got pregnant, and after the birth of my second granddaughter, the doctor switched the medication to a milder one, since she no longer felt so many symptoms. Maybe you'll feel better after you have a child," she commented, handing me a pill and the pack.

I reluctantly lifted my body. My eyes were already overflowing with tears.

"What if I never find someone who wants to have children with me?" My lips trembled at the thought, and before I realized the countless other methods available for those who want to be single mothers, I was already crying.

Or rather... I was sobbing.

"I'm going to be alone forever. I'm an annoying, irritating woman. I steal things." I sat up in bed with the pill in one hand and the glass Ruth had handed me in the other, throwing my head back, crying as if there were no tomorrow. "I'm going to die a virgin, Ruth! A VIRGIN!" I sobbed at the top of my lungs.

"I'll get you some hot chocolate and a heating pad for your belly. It'll help with the pain, along with the cramps medication I gave you earlier." She tried to sound more gentle, and seeing Ruth, usually a soldier ready for war, trying to be affectionate with me made me cry even harder. "God, I'll be right back."

"O-okay! Come back soon, please." My nasally voice joined my swollen eyes and all the pain I felt.

I felt like a fool, naïve, lonely. I was nothing more than a nerd who would soon need 40 cats to keep me company. I sobbed, cried some more, and then took the medication. I curled back up under the covers. I knew that feeling would soon pass, but I couldn't shake off the sadness and despair that hit me during this time. I pressed the blanket against my face.

All I could do was start thinking about where I could find 40 cats.

LATER, WHEN THE CRAMPS medication started to take effect and I could walk without leaning on the furniture, albeit slowly, I decided to go to the living room to watch a movie.

I descended the stairs slowly and passed by a mirror on the side of the entrance hall. My face was pale, and the high, messy bun I had my hair in didn't help much to disguise it. But at least I felt warm inside the hot pink sweatsuit I was wearing.

I sniffled and dragged myself to the living room, thanking God I didn't run into any of the guards along the way. I would've kicked one of them in the shins if they got too close.

I entered the spacious room, where two gray leather sofas faced a television that took up almost half the wall. I grabbed the remote and flopped down on the couch. Ruth entered the room shortly after, holding a black blanket in her arms.

"I asked Judith to make sweet popcorn," she announced, handing me the blanket, and my eyes welled up.

"Thank you," I said, emotional. I loved sweet popcorn.

I covered my legs with the blanket while Ruth grabbed another remote, the one for the window, and with a click, the automatic blinds began to close. She also turned on only the lights on the TV panel, transforming the space into a cozy little cinema before leaving the room.

I turned on the TV and didn't take long to find the movie I wanted to watch. Twilight... for the hundredth time. Ruth returned a few minutes later with a big bucket of popcorn, filling the air with a delicious sweet scent, and handed it to me along with a cup of soda, which I promptly set on the small table in the center of the room to avoid spilling it on myself.

The movie began, and Edward, as always, made my heart race. I sighed.

Oh, how I wished for a movie romance like that! Where the hero does everything to protect his beloved. He was romantic, gentle, caring, and hot all at once.

I wasn't even halfway through the movie when I decided to grab my phone, sobbing, and call Carla.

"Hey, girlfriend," she answered cheerfully.

"Why do they only exist in movies?" I sobbed.

"What are you talking about, Jasmin?" Her voice sounded worried. "Are you crying? What happened, for heaven's sake?"

"Edward happened!" I cried. "There's no perfect guy like him. In fact, in my life, there isn't even an imperfect guy. There's nobody."

"You're on those days, aren't you?" My friend took a deep breath, and I nodded through some sniffles.

"Girl, you're beautiful, amazing. Plus, you're funny, fun, and loyal. You'll find someone who values every little piece of you," she said kindly.

"I love you, Carlinha." My lips trembled.

"I love you too, my favorite crazy girl," she joked. "Now tell me, what about that guard? The handsome one." After the incident at the window and the candy, I had called Carla to tell her all about the crazy coincidence of running into the guy from the club at my house the next day, on the same motorcycle I had stolen, with a transcendent fury blazing in his bicolored eyes. "What's he up to besides forbidding you to go out with me? He's really cute, girl. Why not distract yourself with him? You're both free anyway. I bet he'll help you forget any *bad*.

"Tch!" I sniffled. "That idiot hates me. I highly doubt he thinks of me in any way other than monitoring my steps."

"What the hell! If he fell for your charm, it would be easier to distract him. I still can't believe he caught you at that window." She sighed, exasperated, recalling the previous night when our plan to sneak out had been thwarted.

What I didn't tell my friend was that I had given up on going out even before being surprised by Wolf.

Carla was an amazing and popular person. With her envy-inducing golden skin, my friend had well-defined Colombian curves, something she inherited from her father, a widower named Matías. Carla, a name similar to her father's, like me, lost her mother at a young age, and that was one of the bonds that united us. Besides being beautiful, she was kind and funny. There was no shortage of invitations for nights out with her, as she was in a constant state of partying. Carla usually went out five out of seven days a week, and partying so often had introduced her to a love for event planning. My friend was studying to become the best in the field, so she would never, ever lack invitations to drag me along.

"You know my birthday is coming up, right?"

"There are still two weeks left, Carla." I widened my eyes, momentarily fearing I had forgotten my only friend's birthday.

"Yes, but my dad wants to travel with me next week, so we're going to celebrate next weekend."

"WHAT?" I shouted. "This weekend?"

"Yes. And you have to come, girl. Even if I have to break in there, grab that Wolf guy, and kidnap you."

"No need to grab him," I grumbled.

"Then you'd better do it." She laughed. "Pick some of that killer lingerie I know you're hiding for the day when 'the special guy' shows up, and strut right in front of him. I doubt this Wolf will stay distant."

"And what if he rejects me? Or better yet, what if he falls for my charm, what do I do?"

"Then just go for it!" Did she really think things were that easy? "Girl, I have to hang up. I'm going out with my dad. I'll call you later, okay? Think about what I said."

I hung up the phone and spun the device between my fingers for a good while, pondering the craziness my friend had suggested.

What if?

No... I shook my head, pushing that thought far away. I must be going crazy to even consider an idea like that, yes. Completely nuts.

"CRAZY, NUTS" I REPEATED the words later, staring at my reflection in the mirror of my room.

Night had already fallen when an idea came to mind.

What if?

That little question inspired me to open my closet and rummage through the space reserved for the lingerie I had set aside. Occasionally, I bought lingerie online, dreaming of the moment when I could be alone with a guy on the night I would lose my virginity, in love with someone who would kiss me until morning... bringing me breakfast in bed and making love until we lost track of time. A beautiful dream that faded as the years passed and nothing changed.

I decided, then, to try one on. Obviously just the top, since I was on my period.

I lifted my gaze to my reflection, observing how the black shorts of the *baby-doll* matched the top, which was also black. However, unlike the shorts, the bra was adorned with ribbons, some crossing over my breasts and descending in ties to my navel, where it would connect to the bottom piece if I were wearing it.

Wolf's gaze crossed my mind.

What would he say if he saw me wearing that lingerie?

"Shameless, brazen" I mimicked his voice in a childish tone to my reflection and laughed.

I turned around, then again, and stopped on the third turn with my nose wrinkled, a bit dissatisfied with my "sexy mosquito" appearance.

"You are sexy!" I tried to inspire myself. "You. Are. Sexy! Ugh, this is never going to work." I looked at my tiny breasts pressed against the elegant bra, grabbed the yellow rabbit robe, and wrapped myself in it. I sat on the bed next, gazing at the twinkling stars through the open window.

I didn't feel sexy; to be more precise, at that moment, I didn't feel beautiful at all either. I took off the lingerie and huddled inside the fluffy robe when I remembered it was Tuesday. My special night with the stars... something that always used to cheer me up.

I closed my eyes, my mood shifting again, making an absurd sense of longing probe my heart.

Sometimes, loneliness made you crave the company of someone you shouldn't. Someone intriguing, unique, and far too dangerous.

In the early hours of that morning, when I was about to begin my ritual of every Tuesday night, all I could think about was the pair of penetrating eyes as unreachable as my freedom.

All I could think about was Wolf.

CHAPTER ELEVEN

Wolf

I tried to rest a bit in the security guard quarters during the afternoon since the night shift would be mine, but the more I tossed and turned on that single bed—so small that my feet hung off the edge—the less I could stop thinking about her.

How could Jasmin manage to slip her hand into my pocket without me even noticing? She seemed like a professional pickpocket, which intrigued me even more.

At what point in her controlled life did that woman learn to steal like that?

The question lingered in my mind all day. I was once again amazed by her precise ability to wrap me around her jade eyes just to invade my pockets.

I stared at the white ceiling until another worry crept in. I raised my wrist and looked at my silver watch. At this hour, I might be able to talk to Snake. So I gave up on sleeping and grabbed my phone, determined to call my older brother and maybe get some relevant information.

I hadn't been able to relax for a second since my first conversation with Cahill. The small possibility that Naish had been hired to end Jasmin's life drove me crazy. I knew that man better than I'd like to admit, and I knew exactly what he was capable of. I wasn't exaggerating when I told Cahill we were dealing with a psychopath.

From the moment I first saw Naish, I knew he was a different kind of man. Something about his perfect smile made me uneasy.

At the time, I was confused, frequently filled with rage, and had once again run away from my adoptive father. I ended up lost. Without a place to sleep, without anything to eat, the only thing I had left was my anger. A feeling my father was struggling to help me control, but I was too stupid and ungrateful back then to realize it. That was when I met Adrian. A guy not much older than me, but unlike me, the Puerto Rican had an enviable sense of humor and joy. He had been living on the streets since childhood and was also the son of addicts, but he found a way not to die out there and offered to teach me how to avoid that too.

He was the one who introduced me to Naish. Adrian worked making small deliveries for the man. Nothing of value, just papers. Even with Naish exuding a dangerous aura, Adrian had the courage to open one of them once, and according to what he told me, he couldn't read a single word. It was either in another language or it was coded. He didn't care, and neither did I. It was a type of easy money with no involvement in drugs, which caught my attention. After seeing what they could do to a human being, I developed a transcendent hatred for them and had no problem doing anything Naish needed that didn't involve them.

I met him once, and the man showed great interest in working with me, especially because of my size. Even as just a teenager back then, I already had well-defined muscles from training with my father and was much larger than my peers who were the same age as me.

I spent a week with Adrian on the streets waiting for orders from Naish to start working, but my father found me first, and I ended up going back home.

A few days later, I returned to the streets to look for Adrian alongside my father. Holder, with his kind heart, was moved by my friend's situation and offered to give him a decent job. I searched the city for him, but I couldn't find him. I only saw Adrian again two years later, at a moment that changed my entire life and turned Naish into my worst enemy.

"Brother..." Snake answered on the third ring, his voice laden with boredom pulling me from my thoughts.

"Are you working?" I asked.

"I think I'm done here." I heard a muffled groan in the background of the call.

"What the hell was that? Is everything okay?"

"Nothing to worry about," he cut me off.

"Don't tell me you're suffocating one of my clients?" I sat up in bed. "In case you've forgotten, we need to keep them alive."

"I wish I could, brother. How do you stand all this monotony? I need something to liven this place up before I die of boredom."

"As long as your fun ends with him alive and intact, I'm fine with it."

"Intact too? Just being alive isn't enough?"

"Snake!" I called his attention. Sometimes I forgot who was older between us. "I'm calling to see if you got my request."

"Yes, brother. I've passed it on to my trusted men, and we've started the search. I also have a contact in Los Angeles who might be useful. He owes me a hand, so he'll cooperate."

"When you say the man owes you a hand, you mean he owes you a favor?" I squinted, confused.

"I mean if it weren't for me, he wouldn't have a hand. Simple as that." His voice was cheerful. "But thanks to my meddling, he only lost a finger. And it wasn't the thumb."

"What the hell, Snake. No!" I shook my head side to side. "I don't want to know what you've been up to."

"Well, you asked."

"Just tell me what you know about Naish. Do you think we'll be able to locate him?"

"Wolf, you know that trying to capture that man is like trying to catch a legend, right?" he said seriously. "He's like a shadow that only exists in people's heads. There's absolutely no one who's seen the man's face and lived to tell the tale, not a loose thread to identify him, besides you, of course." He let out a heavy sigh. "What worries me is if he finds out you're working the same case he is, only on opposite sides, you know what's going to happen."

"He'll become even more interested in killing her soon." I leaned back against the bed and stared at the Cahill mansion through the side window of the room. A suffocating tightness rose in my chest. "That's why I need to find him, brother."

"I sent the sketch to Cahill as you asked," he said, "but I want to make sure you're not going to do anything stupid. Wait for my men's return. You know I have ears under every rock in Chicago, and we'll find a lead."

"I need to find him fast. I can hardly breathe when I'm with my VIP out on the street, away from the mansion's protection." I exhaled noisily. "Just the thought that it only takes a single touch for him to..." I stopped speaking, fearing what I might end up saying.

"I want you to worry about yourself too, Chris," he warned. "You know you've always been a potential target for that psycho. Don't let him get close without backup and put a bullet in that son of a bitch's forehead the moment you have the chance. Don't hesitate."

"When have I even blinked before shooting, brother?"

"I hope nothing has changed. Wipe out that filthy breed." Another scream, now higher-pitched, reverberated through the line. "I need to go." Snake hung up before I had the chance to ask more about that noise.

I tossed the phone onto the bed and continued to survey the very white walls of the mansion. I'd have to prepare for war if I wanted to keep Jasmin, my little light-fingered mouse, safe.

"When did I start worrying so much about you?" I asked myself, my gaze distant.

I was fucked.

AFTER A LONG SHOWER, I was already ready for the night shift, but not before making two important calls. One to Cahill and another to Holder Security.

I left the security guard quarters. The sunset cast a bright orange light over the mansion, enhancing all the greenery surrounding the place. I headed up to the surveillance room, prepared for the night ahead.

"Alpha Team, this is Wolf. I'm taking over in the surveillance room," I alerted on the communication channel.

"Okay, sir," Shaw replied, and shortly after, Lyon and Ray mumbled something in agreement. I quickly switched to Wood's radio channel.

"Wood, this is Wolf. You copy?"

"Yes, Wolf. Any problem?"

"Can you come to the surveillance room? We need to talk."

"Understood."

After what happened last night with Jasmin, I spent the rest of the night talking with Ghost, catching up on everything known about night terrors. There was no one who could help me more than he could; after all, Zion suffered greatly from that same affliction. And although I barely remembered anything about his episodes—my father tried to keep us from hearing anything—I remembered he had struggled a lot with them and might be able to help me.

And I was right. Through Zion, I discovered that night terrors were a very common disorder in children, rarely affecting adults, though it could happen if the person experienced trauma or something similar.

Unlike nightmares, where the person wakes up and usually remembers what they dreamed, in night terrors there's amnesia, along with screaming, aggression, and agitation that can put the life of someone suffering from the disorder at risk.

Jasmin probably had brief flashes of what happened during the night but didn't remember. According to Zion, those who suffer from night terrors cannot be awakened during the episode; otherwise, they'll experience confusion for a few minutes, which would scare them even more. And while it's not considered a fatal disorder, it's extremely necessary for the person to be monitored, as they can end up seriously injuring themselves.

I couldn't understand how that bunch of useless people could leave her alone for so long.

"You arrived early." Wood entered the room with his hand resting on the gun at his waist, walking calmly to the nearest chair. "I heard you had a rough night; you should rest a bit more."

"Did you know she could have fallen out of bed?"

"What?" He furrowed his brows, and several lines appeared on his forehead, as if I had just offended his mother.

"What if there was something sharp nearby, Wood? She could have seriously hurt herself," I scolded, and he looked down at his own feet for a moment.

"You're talking about the episode Miss Cahill had." Suddenly, he lifted his gaze toward me when he understood what I was referring to.

"What else would I be talking about?" I yelled, furious. "Wood, Miss Cahill was thrashing around like I've never seen before, aside from the screams." The man opened and closed his lips twice before finding his voice. "She was at serious risk of injuring herself unconsciously, and no one intended to do anything but leave her to her own despair."

"You're right," he admitted, and it was my turn to widen my eyes in surprise. "Although we've grown closer to her over the years, I've always tried to keep the personal side of the staff separate. Usually, when Miss Cahill had episodes, her father wasn't home. Mr. Cahill has only witnessed two of them, while we..."

"Have heard several," Shaw, who I now noticed was standing in the doorway, completed.

"We need to separate the professional side from the personal, Wood, you're right, but if it involves her safety, it involves us too. She needs our help and professionalism, even when she's unconscious."

"I agree with you," Wood affirmed.

"I contacted Cahill this morning." I gained the attention of both, who were now looking at me with a questioning expression. "I told him about the episode and reinforced everything I said to you." I reported. "I suggested Cahill hire a bodyguard on my recommendation immediately to help during the night shift. That way, she can be responsible for assisting Miss Cahill if the episodes return."

"And what did he say?" Shaw sounded hopeful.

"Victoria Davis."

"What?" Wood asked, confused.

"Victoria Davis, the new hire, starts next week. Until then, if Miss Cahill has another episode, I'll intervene myself."

"Wow," Shaw replied excitedly. "He's amazing, isn't he, boss?" I pursed my lips at the sudden enthusiasm of the guy.

Shaw was energetic; he couldn't stay still for a second, but besides being overly dramatic, he also seemed to have a huge heart.

"I'm glad to hear that," Wood said with a small smile on his expression-lined face. "I hope Miss Cahill finds some peace in this life," he said. "Well, have a good shift. I need to get back to the office. Mr. Cahill needs me."

"Wait," I called as Wood was already at the door, and I approached close enough so Shaw wouldn't hear what I was saying. Although I knew his intentions were good, ever since the night I spoke with Ghost, a worry that felt more like a conspiracy theory had crept into my mind, and I didn't want to spread it around.

"Yes?" Wood looked at me with a worried expression.

"Who medicated Miss Cahill?"

"You want to know which psychiatrist treated her?" I nodded in affirmation.

"I'll get her name for you. I don't remember it right now, but it was a good recommendation from Senator Claire," he said, stuffing his hands into the pockets of his black pants. "The senator has always cared for Jasmin as if she were her own daughter. She's the female figure Miss Cahill looks up to."

"I see." I started snapping my fingers, a habit I had when I was overthinking something. "Please get the doctor's name."

"Are you going to try to convince Miss Cahill to consult with her again? Because that would do the girl a world of good."

"Yes, that's exactly what I'm going to do," I lied.

Wood smiled and left with a pleased expression on his face while all I could think about was the brief conversation I had with my brother.

"What's the treatment for night terrors? How can she escape this suffering, brother?"

"I admit I'm being consumed by pure curiosity about seeing you involved in something so personal with a VIP. You usually keep your distance from us too, brother."

"It's a work matter; it's part of my job," I replied, grumpily.

"Yeah, sure. I understand. And what kind of brother would I be if I didn't help you with your job, right?" He laughed shamelessly.

"Ghost!" I growled.

"Okay, okay," he said, taking a deep breath and stopping his laughter. "The treatment is good old therapy."

"What?"

"That's right, brother. She needs psychological support. Nothing more. She'll be as good as new soon."

"And the medication? Doesn't she need to take anything?"

"In extreme cases, the patient needs to have their sleep induced by medication, usually in the first months of therapy, but they're weak meds, just to help induce a peaceful sleep."

"Did you have to take any of them?"

"Yes," he admitted in a lower tone, "but as I said, they're extremely light, just to induce and not force sleep. Rarely does a doctor use them, especially in her case. From what you said, the episodes are sporadic, right?"

"Yes, the guards said they don't happen often."

"Mine happened every night," I said with regret. "That's why medication was necessary. Her case is different. Find another psychiatrist, and if you want, I can recommend my therapist. She's a specialist, and I doubt your Jasmin will need to take any medication."

My Jasmin?

I cursed a half-dozen times before hanging up that night, but what surprised me was learning about the medication. Something didn't fit into that equation, and if Wood believed I'd influence her to return to that psychiatrist, he was very mistaken. I would do the exact opposite as soon as possible.

"What's the report so far, Shaw?" I asked the young man as soon as I sat down in front of the cameras. "How did Miss Cahill spend her day? Is she okay?"

I wanted to stay updated on every step she took, especially during the moments I needed to be away from her presence.

"Define okay, sir?"

"How?"

"Well... apparently Miss Cahill is in perfect condition, but because of her monthly visitor, she seems about to die from crying."

"Monthly visitor?" I raised my eyebrows, confused, and it took me a few seconds to understand what he was talking about.

"You know. Those days when..."

"Yes, yes. No need to explain." I held back a laugh at the look of worry and despair on Shaw's face.

"Where is she now?"

"Lyon, are you there? Are you seeing Crystal?" Shaw activated the communicator, and I connected my network to the same channel to hear the response.

"Yes, she just entered the room."

"Was she still crying?" I asked, feeling like a fool immediately afterward. What did I care about that girl's tears?

"Yes, sir. It seems endless." He sighed.

"Damn," I cursed, deeply troubled. "Okay. Shaw, head downstairs; I'll take over the surveillance room."

"Yes, sir." He seemed relieved. "If you need anything at all, just let me know." I nodded, and he left the room shortly after.

I settled into the chair in front of the monitors, and it wasn't long before the little thief came out of the room again.

"What the hell?" I stared at the monitor, my eyes wide.

I started laughing to myself as I saw Jasmin in a hot pink outfit that could easily blind someone. She had a very different wardrobe. In the morning, Jasmin looked like a successful businesswoman, living up to the inheritance she would inherit. However, shortly after, she appeared to me in a fluorescent pink set that didn't match that demeanor but gave her a different, lively, cheerful aura, like a little girl.

I kept watching her, but my smile faded the moment she reached the stairs. I switched cameras and zoomed in on the one positioned right next to the stairs. I couldn't see her clearly, but Jasmin had her hair up in a bun that left her face clearly visible. Her cheeks, very red, were from crying for hours on end. A pained expression took over her face as she walked, and a pang hit my chest. I wanted to help her somehow, but that was beyond my reach.

I followed her on the cameras until I saw her enter the room, where Ruth supported her. Jasmin watched a movie, cried, ate popcorn, cried again, leaving me even more anxious, and finally paused the movie to make a call. As usual, she cried again, burying her face in the blanket provided by Ruth.

"You're going to dehydrate, girl." I got up, irritated.

Was all of that due to PMS? Or was there something that had hurt her? Did I say something that upset her?

The thought terrified me.

I had never lived with a woman aside from the horrible experience I had when living with my mother and father, so I had no idea if that was normal.

I was almost about to call one of the agents from Holder Security I usually had more contact with, to try to find out anything, when Jasmin decided to turn off the TV. She was about to go back upstairs when Ruth intercepted her and took her to the kitchen, where the cook served her some soup.

After that, Jasmin, who looked more like a pink teddy bear, practically climbed the stairs and disappeared into her room shortly after.

I found myself anxious, hoping she would feel better soon with the same fervor I hoped Jasmin would at least be able to sleep through the night without any night terror episodes.

I didn't know what was happening to me, but I was more worried about that aspiring Bonnie and Clyde than about myself.

THE EARLY MORNING ARRIVED, and so did the shift change. Ray would take over the surveillance room, but even if I wanted to leave, I couldn't. According to some rumors I'd heard, the man was restless and loved to do the night watch in the courtyard so he could pace back and forth. So, as soon as I saw him come in chewing his usual gum, I had an idea.

"Do you want to do the external rounds and let me stay here in the surveillance room? I can swap with you," I said casually.

He pursed his lips and looked at me suspiciously.

"Are you serious? You really want to swap the outside so you can stay here?" He looked at me as if I were tearing a hundred-dollar bill right in front of his nose.

"Yes, I'm very serious, but if you don't want to..."

"I do, I really do," he said quickly.

"Great. Now, let's get to work." I tilted my head toward the door and watched him almost run out of the surveillance room.

I sat there with my eyes glued to the central screen, where Jasmin's bedroom door was. I was worried and very anxious because I couldn't stop thinking about her, just as I feared that I might have hurt her somehow. The thought that she could be crying over something I said was killing me inside.

I was a difficult person to deal with and often crossed the line. I was aware of that, and that's why I was fearful. What if I was the one to blame?

I remained there for a long time. I pulled out my gun, loaded and unloaded the magazine a good three times, restless, as I usually wasn't. I leaned back in the cushioned chair that grew more uncomfortable with each passing second. Half the time, I tried not to think of her, while the other half, all I could do was think about the damn girl.

I took a deep breath and stared at the monitor, not knowing what to expect for the rest of the night when, to my complete astonishment, the door to Jasmin's room slowly opened. I jumped to my feet and kept watching the screen as if she were about to appear right before me.

I glanced at the clock and realized it was almost one in the morning. Where was she going?

Jasmin wore a bright yellow robe as fluorescent as the sun, and worse, it had a tail and a little hood with long bunny ears attached to it. Only part of the girl's blonde hair escaped over her shoulder, which meant she wasn't trying to go unnoticed by the cameras. At least, that's what I thought. After all, she was wearing a yellow bunny costume. YELLOW!

What kind of bunny was yellow?

I kept watching her. Jasmin descended the stairs, leading me to switch to a second camera and so on until she reached the kitchen.

"What's your position, Ray?" I asked over the radio communicator.

"Standing at the main entrance of the house, Wolf. Shaw will take over the north exit in 30 minutes."

"Great." If she was planning something, Ray would find her before I even announced her whereabouts over the radio.

I remained standing, watching the dazzling bunny rummage through all the cabinets in search of something. Was she hungry?

I was surprised when she found a bag of snacks, those stinky yellow ones that do nothing good for the stomach. I pursed my lips. She'd eaten only soup the entire night, as far as I could tell. That snack could lead to unbearable stomach pain.

"Oh, screw it. That's not my problem." I paced back and forth in the small surveillance room, my eyes glued to Jasmin's steps as she returned to her room with the snacks in tow, her gaze fixed on the ground ahead.

She opened the bedroom door and disappeared inside shortly after. I let out a sigh, exasperated, imagining that from now on, I'd only see her the next day if she managed to sleep.

I sat back down in the chair. A certain calm washed over me, believing that part of the problems had ended. At least we would have a peaceful night.

But who was I kidding?

That was Jasmin Cahill, and apparently, nothing related to her was calm and quiet.

Not even five minutes had passed when I saw Jasmin's bedroom window open on the external camera. I narrowed my eyes, puzzled by the movement, when out of nowhere, the bunny girl climbed up onto the window.

"Holy shit!" For a moment, all the blood in my body seemed to rush to my feet.

What was she doing? If she fell from that height, she might not survive. I froze at the thought.

I jumped up and ran as fast as I could toward her room. All sorts of thoughts raced through my mind. I hadn't even seen her face when she went to the kitchen. What if she were sleepwalking? There was nothing in her file about that, but they had also hidden the fact about her night terrors.

In a second, I was bombarded with horrible thoughts, and one of them genuinely terrified me. What if she wanted to take her own life?

I burst through her door and looked at the window. I held my breath when I didn't see her there anymore, and despair coursed through my veins.

"JASMIN! JASMIN!" I shouted, sticking my head through the window. Fear and pure terror consumed me.

What if she fell?

"If Ruth wakes up to your shouting, we're both dead. Can you stop freaking out, please?" she said quietly and very seriously. Only then did I find the bunny sitting on the roof that divided her room from a secondary one in the opposite direction. "By the look on your face, it seems nobody told you, huh?" She wrinkled her very red nose, as well as her cheeks, probably from crying all day. Her small hands clutched the bag of snacks tightly. "I thought you knew everything."

I bit my lip at her audacity and narrowed my eyes, staring at her. One of her ears was slightly bent, and the hood framing her face gave her such a cute appearance that the anger I had built up began to fade. How the hell was I supposed to argue with someone dressed as a bunny?

"What are you doing up there?" I asked slowly, trying to keep my expression serious. My heart was certainly in great condition; otherwise, by now, I would have been dead from a heart attack on the floor of that woman's room. Jasmin was truly an effective cardiac test.

"It's Tuesday, or it was," she whispered.

"What happens on Tuesdays? Is it climbing day?" She threw her head back and laughed, causing her hood to fall off, revealing her very disheveled blonde hair and a face far more haggard than I could have imagined.

"It's not climbing day." She shook her head as if that idea were the most absurd in the world. "It's star-gazing day," she told me. "Every Tuesday, my sister and I would sit here to watch them, and we always brought some snacks to share. You can guess that Ruth isn't a big fan of them, right?" She waved the blue bag in front of her face. "So we always hid one in the room and ate it here. It's one of the many traditions we had, and I refuse to let it die. Over time, even Ruth gave in, and they now stay stored in the kitchen."

I was thinking of a pile of curses I'd unleash to drag her down from there by force, but... what now? She was repeating a tradition she had with her late sister. I couldn't just pull her down from there. A strange feeling threatened to tear my chest apart at the thought of her being up there alone.

Jasmin was making my mission to hate her increasingly difficult with every passing second.

Damn it, you little thief!

I climbed up to the window, against all my self-preservation instincts, which were warning me to do the exact opposite.

"What are you doing?" she asked in a whisper.

I balanced myself on the roof and sat on the tiles beside her.

"You don't have to stay here with me," she said. "It's fine if you want to leave."

"My job is to protect you," I replied tersely, trying to maintain as much professionalism as possible. "I can't allow you to fall and break your neck." Jasmin let out another laugh and covered her mouth with her hand. I realized I liked that cheerful, lively sound. It was one I rarely heard from her.

"You're actually funny. Where have you been hiding that sense of humor?" She opened the bag of snacks, which immediately released the familiar odor of edible stench.

"I have a reputation to uphold, Miss Cahill. It's hard to build a career as a grumpy bodyguard, so I need to maintain it. It's best not to go around telling others about this."

"I promise to keep it a secret, with one condition."

"And what's that?" I turned to her, attentive and concerned.

"I liked it when you called me by my name. Jasmin! JASMIN!" She reenacted the little freak-out I had when I thought she'd fallen out the window. "Dramatic? Yes, but I liked it so much." She smiled.

"For a moment, I was worried about you. Given your tendency to fall from windows, it's justifiable. Ouch!" I complained when she elbowed my arm, but I felt genuinely happy when Jasmin smiled and I noticed the sad expression I'd seen on her face moments before had completely disappeared.

"Thank you for worrying about me." She reached into the bag of snacks and popped one into her mouth. "And I meant it, I'd like you to call me Jasmin."

"Are you going to keep stealing my keys?"

"Who knows? It's stronger than me." She laughed, and I couldn't help the smile that spread across my face.

"Listen, Wolf..." She took a deep breath and stared at her hands, which I noticed had tightened their grip on the stinky snack bag. "I'm sorry." I raised my eyebrows, confused. "For stealing your motorcycle and wishing you'd suddenly turn into a frog. I'm really sorry, I crossed a line."

"Believe me, part of my job is being hated by clients now and then, but none of them ever wished for me to turn into a frog."

"Has anyone ever stolen something from you?"

"No. That feat is also exclusive to you." I laughed. "What's going on, Miss Cahill?"

"Aren't you going to call me by my name?"

"No." She huffed. "And answer me. Are you thinking about doing something stupid?"

"I'm not thinking about doing anything except stargazing, eating this styrofoam, you want?" I shook my head, denying.

"So what's going on? Did you receive a visit from the Christmas ghosts? I can't believe you're a woman who apologizes easily, especially after telling me to my face that you never would." She smiled with a snack inches from her mouth and bit into it immediately.

"I just don't want to fight with someone who's trying so hard to protect me," she said, as if it made sense.

"You think you're fooling me, Miss? I bet you plan to throw me off this roof the first chance you get." My disbelief was palpable in my voice.

"There he is again! The angry, skeptical Wolf..." She rolled her eyes and somehow managed to look even cuter than before.

What the hell! What was happening to me that I found a snack-devouring bunny cute?

"You must have heard," she said suddenly.

"Heard what?" I was confused for a moment.

"Last night," she recalled. "I know I had an episode. You must have heard it." She curled into her robe. "I'm sorry for what you had to hear. Obviously, I've never heard the sounds I make, but they say it's terrible." She looked at her hands resting on the snack bag, diverting her bright eyes from mine.

"I didn't hear anything," I said when I noticed Jasmin was uncomfortable.

"You might be a good bodyguard, but you're not a good liar," she claimed. "This morning, when I looked at you, I noticed you were staring at me strangely." I swallowed hard. Was it written on my forehead the conflicting feelings I had for that woman? "I understood in that instant."

"What exactly did you understand?" My heart raced, waiting for her answer.

"That not only did you hear everything, but you also felt sorry for me." She pouted, filled her hand with snacks, and shoved them into her mouth. "I don't like people feeling sorry for me."

"If there's one thing I've never felt for you, Miss Cahill, it's pity. Anger, hatred, an overwhelming urge to strangle you... but pity?" She laughed, making me smile along with the delightful sound of her laughter. "Pity, no, never." Jasmin's cheeks flushed even more, and I couldn't stop staring at them. It was the most beautiful thing I'd ever seen.

"Thank you." She ate some more of the snacks, and all I could think about was the moment I hugged her last night.

She had been trembling, terrified, and fear had initially made her want to push me away, but soon after, the arms that pushed me away began pulling me closer, and it was that damn feeling—the feeling of having her in my arms, leaning on me, seeking refuge in my protection—that made me think about her all the time.

I was going to lose my mind at any moment.

"Are you sure you don't want some?" She pointed the almost empty bag in my direction. I shook my head with a smile growing on my lips, and she tucked the now empty bag into the pocket of her robe. "Can I ask you something?"

"If I say no, will it matter?"

"Not at all. I'm going to ask 24/7 until you answer me." She smiled cheekily.

"Then ask, since you're so determined." I narrowed my eyes at the bunny.

"Why did you give me that chocolate?" She caught me off guard, and I was left with no choice but to tell the truth.

"That day at the beach... I ended up dropping your chocolate and noticed you were very upset."

"You really thought so? I believe I'm very transparent with my feelings." She sighed dramatically.

"You threw a handful of sand in my hair." I pointed to my extremely well-groomed brown hair. "It was clear that it was an important chocolate. I don't like owing anything to anyone. That's why I returned it."

"No one should touch a woman's chocolate." She wrinkled her nose.

"What was so important about that chocolate?" It was my turn to question her.

"It was my sister's birthday," she revealed. "We always walked that beach on her birthday. Whenever we could, that is." She twisted her fingers around the tips of her hair and opened a sad smile. "She was addicted to chocolate, and I, the tradition crazy, wanted to bring a piece of cake to eat on the beach in her honor."

"Was that why you ran away that day?" The light from the full moon touched Jasmin's eyes, transforming them into a deep lake of green waves.

"Yes. I really wanted to go there, but since I couldn't sneak out with a piece of cake, I brought the chocolate to eat there." She lowered her eyes to the coral tile.

"And I dropped it on the ground." I cursed myself mentally. A painful knot closed my throat. All she wanted was to eat the treat on her sister's favorite beach. "I'm sorry for my behavior, Miss Cahill."

"Don't apologize; I stole your motorcycle, remember? I deserved it." I was left speechless, staring at her as if I'd never seen that woman before me. An overwhelming need to touch her hand surged within me, but I suppressed it immediately and coughed.

"She's really nice," she suddenly said, leaving me confused again. It was difficult to follow her train of thought, looking at her under the intense moonlight that highlighted every little part of her I wanted to ignore. The heart-shaped mouth was something I would love to trace with my finger.

"What the hell are you talking about?" I blinked, startled to realize what I was thinking.

"About your motorcycle." She laughed.

"Ah... yes. Yes!" I took a deep breath. "It's a collector's bike, as I've mentioned once or twice."

"Ten times, actually," she teased.

"Since we're back to talking about my Spirit... there's something I've been curious about since we first met."

"What is it?"

"How did you learn to ride a bike like that?"

"I had never even touched a motorcycle like yours," she revealed. "I learned to ride on a much smaller one when I was a teenager. A close friend of my dad had a son who studied at a school near mine. We ended up becoming friends, and my dad let me and my sister visit their ranch on weekends. It was one of the few places he allowed us to go without security since his friend already had his own. Things were much more peaceful back then, and that's where I learned," she said excitedly. "You have no idea how many times I fell flat on my face learning to ride. I came home all bruised, but I managed to hide the injuries for a long time. Long enough to improve and stop falling, but one day I got caught red-handed. When my dad found out, he never let us go back there again." She shrugged, pouting slightly. "But it's true what they say. Once you learn to ride a bike, you never forget, and it's the same with motorcycles."

"You adapted your knowledge to ride my bike," I stated, perplexed.

"Yes. I think it all depends on courage. Anyone who rides one type of motorcycle can ride any other, even if they find it difficult at first; it all ends up feeling the same." As soon as Jasmin closed her lips, a silence formed between us, broken by her stomach growling loudly. "Oh my God, that's just what I needed." She covered her eyes with her hands. "Sorry about that, but I think those snacks opened my appetite." She peered at me between her fingers, and I laughed.

"We should go inside. You need to eat something more substantial." I stood up, and Jasmin did the same.

"I think you're right." I extended my hand for her to take.

Her slender fingers touched mine hesitantly, and I noticed they were too cold.

"Hold on to me; I won't let you fall," I warned, and she raised her eyes to mine. Her jade-colored irises regarded me cautiously.

She took an unsteady step, then another, gripping my hand tightly as she walked. I helped her climb through her window, and when I did the same, I found Jasmin sitting on her bed. The memory of seeing her there, thrashing helplessly, struck me.

"There's just one problem," she said quietly, staring at her bare feet.

"What is it?" I moved closer to her, and she lifted her eyes to meet mine.

"I don't know how to cook, and the only ready thing I found in the kitchen was those snacks, so..." She shrugged. "I guess it's better if I go to sleep."

"I can cook something for you." I found myself offering, and my tongue burned as soon as I closed my mouth.

What the hell was I doing?

"You'd do that for me?" A look of surprise crossed her face, and she stared at me with wide eyes.

"Protect your feet with something warm. It's too cold to be walking around barefoot," I grumbled. "I'll meet you downstairs, and you'd better get there before I regret this."

"Thank you, Wolf." She jumped off the bed.

"I'm already regretting it," I said as I left through the door.

It seemed that part of my sanity had stayed on that roof.

CHAPTER TWELVE

Jasmin

I could only believe that Wolf was really going to cook for me when I walked into the kitchen and saw him standing in front of the stove, blazer gone, wearing Judith's apron with a sunflower shining right in the middle.

"What's up?" He turned to me when he caught me trying to stifle a laugh at the sight of him in that. "This?" He pointed at the apron. "It's my work uniform. Please respect it."

"Yes, sir." I couldn't hold back a chuckle and noticed he stretched his lips, as if trying to suppress a smile.

I stepped closer to Wolf and got the impression that the stove shrank in size as he stood in front of it. My bodyguard had apparently already cooked the pasta, which was cooling in a colander, and was now about to finish the sauce.

"Can you make pasta?" I watched him stir a sauce that filled the kitchen with a delicious aroma.

"I can do a lot of things." His broad shoulders, previously protected by the suit jacket, were now more exposed, and I could see the hard bulge of muscle in his arm moving as he stirred the pot.

"I imagine you can." I couldn't help the comment, and he smiled to the side.

Seeing him there, casually wanting to help me, sent my heart racing in a way I desperately wanted to avoid. Still, I was extremely happy for the company Wolf had provided me just minutes earlier. It was the first time I had seen the stars with someone other than my sister.

"I hope you like pasta. I forgot to ask what you eat and ended up choosing my specialty," he said, rummaging through the cabinet until he found a red jar of seasoning.

"Yes, I love it. In fact, there are very few things I won't eat." I drummed my fingers on the island countertop that divided the kitchen in half. "I could probably even eat a rock if I had some water," I joked as Wolf continued his endless search, now sifting through the utensils. "Maybe I can help with something," I offered, restless, as I approached the counter where a lonely egg rested.

"You can grab the..." He barely had a chance to speak before I bumped into the egg, which rolled to the edge of the table right next to the stove. I lunged for it with my hand outstretched, but I couldn't reach it in time. The egg fell to the floor just as I turned and bumped into the salt, trying to catch it, and that's when I smelled something strange burning.

"My hair!" I screamed as I realized a large strand was on fire, and I ended up spilling almost all the salt on my robe.

"Miss Cahill!" Wolf called through clenched teeth, grabbing me by the shoulders. His eyes scanned my hair until they landed on one of the singed ends. Only then did I see the charred tuft of hair. "In less than 30 seconds, you've broken an egg, spilled salt, and burned your own hair. Do us both a favor and sit down."

I shrank back into my bunny robe.

"I'm sorry," I whispered, slapping myself in an attempt to shake the salt off my clothes, "but what was that egg doing there?"

"I put it there when I thought I'd make an omelet, but I changed my mind for something more elaborate that you might like better. Let me help you," he said, grumpily, and turned to grab a cloth. "You should be banned from the kitchen." Wolf started wiping the sides of my robe, brushing off the salt I hadn't even seen. His hand grazed the opening of the robe, and his body pressed even closer to mine.

I raised my eyes to look at him. I could feel his warm breath on my face. His thumb brushed along my neck, and I shivered, letting out a low moan, startled by the chill that struck me.

His attentive gaze caught mine, and he repeated the motion, sliding his thumb along the side of my neck. The sleeves of his shirt were rolled up, showcasing his toned arms covered in dark hair that I suddenly wanted to touch. His heated eyes rested on my lips, wearing an expression of someone fighting against something new, something with a taste of forbidden.

I closed my eyes as another shiver coursed down my spine and parted my lips slightly. Wolf let out a low, deep sound and gripped the back of my neck firmly. I could feel the roughness of his hand against my skin, and all I wished was for it to slide all over my body. The thought made the center of my body pulse with anticipation.

I opened my eyes, brought my hand to his tie, and held it, pulling myself closer to his rigid body.

"Miss Cahill..." He suddenly pulled away, and I sucked in a breath sharply. "I can't. I'm sorry, but I can't do this." His voice was filled with pain.

I struggled to breathe, overwhelmed by a bliss that made my legs tremble, and only then did I realize the camera was right in front of us, recording every second of what we were doing.

Wolf braced his hands on either side of the stove and lowered his head.

"I can't, I shouldn't," he repeated, as if trying to convince himself of that.

"If they weren't watching, would you?" I dared to ask. I really wanted to know if he felt attracted to me the same way I burned just thinking about him.

"What do you think?" he shot back, tearing off the apron.

"I'd say the same, even if we were completely alone," I confessed. Wolf straightened up, and when he turned, he didn't even look like the same man.

Something subtle crackled behind his bright irises, intense and feverish. His clenched fists raised the muscles in his arms, signaling that he was trying to control himself. I could feel the danger with every step he took towards me, and not for a second did I want to pull away.

"There's no one in charge of the surveillance room but me today," he said in a low, husky tone that heated me further. "That's exactly why I'm keeping my distance from you." He tried to step back again, but I grabbed his arm tightly, deciding to voice what had been bothering me the most.

"I can't forget that stupid kiss," I said. My chest rose and fell with my wavering breath. "Even when I hate you, I still remember. And you know what's worse? Being attached to such a simple kiss and still wanting more."

Wolf lunged at me as quickly as the rapid beats of my heart. Suddenly, I felt his arm wrap around my waist in a firm, possessive grip, pulling me close. His eyes dropped to my mouth, the hungry expression intoxicated me, and I could see the exact moment he gave in to the strange, impulsive, delicious attraction that seemed to wrap around us in warm golden threads.

He lowered his head and captured my lips with his in a careful, seductive kiss. His hand cradled my neck, fingers anchoring there, causing a mix of sensations I would never forget. Wolf opened the way into my lips with his tongue, kissing me with an erotic urgency that swept me away.

He tangled his fingers in my hair while holding me in his ardently hard arms, sending a series of shivers through me, leaving me breathless, as his kiss took everything from me.

My sanity, my desire, my soul... everything!

I felt the hard bulge pulsing in my belly and was filled with ecstasy knowing I was affecting him too. He lifted me by the waist and pressed me against the kitchen wall. I wrapped my legs around his waist, overtaken by a desperate, fervent desire. Wolf sucked on my tongue, and my whole body responded to that sensation, cascading over my skin. His calloused fingers grazed my neck and trailed down the valley of my breasts, tracing them over the robe. His hands rose and fell over my silhouette with controlled calm.

I gasped against his mouth, in ecstasy. I had never received a kiss like that in my life, one that heightened my pulse, disoriented my thoughts, and left me at Wolf's mercy, who seemed willing to devour me with his lips.

Having him between my legs, pressing me like that, awakened something primal, obscene, urging me to tangle my fingers in his neatly styled hair and moan when his finger grazed the side of my breast beneath the robe.

But the trembling sound that escaped my lips made Wolf suddenly open his eyes, as if startled, and pull away from my mouth.

"Damn it!" he set me on the floor and cursed softly, bracing his hands on the fridge above my shoulders, surrounding me. The veins in his arms pulsed. "I'm sorry." He pressed his eyes shut with the tips of his fingers. "I promise... I promise it won't happen again." There was so much regret in his voice that I froze. He stepped back without looking into my eyes again.

I watched, disoriented, as Wolf moved to the stove, plated the pasta, and set a full dish right in front of me. The appearance and aroma were wonderful, but suddenly I lost my appetite.

"Eat and rest a bit." The subtle coldness in his voice was back. "I'm going back to work." He turned his back and exited the kitchen quickly.

I let myself fall into a chair and stared at the pasta for a long time, wondering what I could have done to make him act that way, but I couldn't understand. I brought my hand to my swollen lips, marked by him, and closed my eyes.

I could still feel the rough stubble grazing my sensitive skin. His hand sliding over my body, his desire pulsing thick and hard. That had been the most pleasurable sensation I had ever felt.

I sighed, restless with the feeling that no one would ever possess my mouth in such an intense, rough, and extraordinary way.

Of all the men in the world, did it have to be one I could never be with?

I twirled the fork in the pasta and tasted it. I moaned, unable to contain myself, as the flavor spread through my mouth. Not only was he handsome and charming, he cooked divinely well.

Damn!

Wolf

DAMN IT!

I kicked the first chair I found as soon as I stepped into the surveillance room.

"Fuck!" I leaned against the table, staring at the cameras in front of me.

Jasmin stood there, staring at the plate as if it could suddenly come to life before her eyes, and I could only curse myself. I had always looked down on anyone in my line of work who strayed from moral conduct and ended up getting involved with a VIP, and that was why my conscience was killing me in that moment.

But how could I convince my body of that conduct? How could I deny the continuous and desperate attraction that scorched me when I saw her so close?

I still felt the sweet taste of those lips on mine, her timid yet curious tongue exploring my mouth with abandon, the low, breathy moan she made when I pressed my body against hers. Damn it, the rigidity of my member throbbed painfully as the desire to go back there and claim that woman threatened to suffocate me.

I wanted her, hell, I wanted her so badly, but who would I be if I allowed that? What kind of bodyguard would I be if I touched my VIP?

My...

That word had never seemed so distant.

I ran my hands through my hair, aware of the decision I needed to make.

From that day forward, I would keep as far away from the VIP as possible. Even though the attraction I felt for her grew stronger by the second, I would do everything to stay far enough away, no matter how much my body begged otherwise, before it was too late.

Later, with my chest pounding, I watched Jasmin return to her room. She avoided looking at any of the cameras along the way. A knot formed in my throat when she slammed the door to her room.

Maybe she was cursing me at that exact moment. I was.

I threw myself into the chair and buried my face in my hands, hoping she could sleep without suffering any nightmares. I needed a few hours away from those jade eyes to stabilize myself again.

That was my wish that night. For Jasmin to stay far away from my sight. But apparently, some men need to be tested against their weaknesses.

It was past four in the morning when the screams erupted through the house, reverberating against the walls and hitting directly at my heart.

I didn't even think, and before I knew it, I was in her room.

This time, Jasmin was wearing a pink nightgown, which at least didn't leave her naked. She cried more than she screamed and thrashed around with her face contorted, as if she were lost in the middle of hell.

I took a deep breath for a moment. Seeing her like that caused a painful, deep discomfort that I hadn't felt in a long time, not since being adopted. It had been so long since I felt that burning urge to take someone's pain away with my hands.

I took her into my arms and hugged her gently. Her body, heavier than usual, trembled between painful moans. I started reciting the words that had calmed her the previous night. This time, Jasmin didn't push me away. She shivered, cried, and let out low, deep moans, leaving me in agony.

"I'm here," I said into her hair, feeling the sweet scent of wildflowers mark me in an irretrievable way. "Listen to my voice, Jas. You're not alone," I murmured. She wrapped her fingers around the lapel of my coat, buried her face in the curve of my neck, and clung to me, gradually calming down.

I spent a long time there, cradling her body against mine. Jasmin eventually fell asleep again, but I couldn't let go of her. I took a deep breath, savoring more of her scent, storing it in my memory with all my might.

I leaned her body down onto the bed and covered her. Her expression was calm and tired, but she still looked like an angel.

I raised a hand and touched her face, caressing her skin carefully.

I wanted to touch her like I had never wanted before. Until the sun rose, until we forgot who we were to each other, until there was nothing left to stop me from making her mine.

It was an absurd thought that I should immediately dismiss, but the more I forced myself not to think about her, the more I did.

"What do I do now?"

It was already too late.

CHAPTER THIRTEEN

Jasmin

I sat up suddenly, startled, and fell back onto the mattress when I realized I was awake.

"My God!" I propped my body up on my elbows and blinked a few times. My mind was confused and my throat sore, as well as my body.

Once again... I noted.

I gasped and closed my eyes. A sharp urge to cry rose in my chest, but I fought with all my might to hold it back.

I felt so alone in those moments. So lonely that it was suffocating, but a brief, almost surreal memory filled my mind with a glimmer of hope.

The protective arms, the tender, caring touch. My protector, my knight. He saved me again, I was sure. I could still feel his concern on my skin, which started to intrigue me.

How could he seem so real if he was a figment of my imagination? I shook my head back and forth.

My knight must have been an escape created by my mind to free me from those damned nightmares, but I was still grateful to have something to cling to after yet another night terror.

I tossed and turned in bed for a while, lost in my thoughts. I knew I couldn't stay there all day; I needed to study and go over some details of the project. Not to mention the dinner I would have with Dad and Aunt Claire.

I needed to push myself.

Reluctantly, I got up and took a long shower. With every passing second, I tried not to think about what happened the night before, but whenever I got distracted, even for a moment, I was thrown back to the instant when Wolf's tongue invaded my mouth with desire. Just thinking about him made my whole body ignite and a deep sadness filled my chest. It was the strangest mix of sensations I had ever felt.

The only certainty I had was that I couldn't stay holed up in my room all day, so after spending a good amount of time staring at the wooden door, I decided to start my day. If I saw him, I would pretend nothing happened between us, and I imagined he would do the same. So I squared my shoulders and opened the door, ready to face him, or at least I thought so.

A certain disappointment hit me when I went downstairs for breakfast and didn't see him along the way.

I entered the kitchen, which was filled with the delicious smell of freshly brewed coffee.

"It smells great, Judith," I said, noticing Ruth standing next to the cook with her usual business attire, wrinkling her pointed nose in my direction. "Good morning, Ruth."

"Good morning, miss. Did you do any cooking overnight?" I widened my eyes, surprised that she noticed. I had tried to clean everything as best as I could the night before, but it seemed some trace had been left behind.

"Yes, I got hungry in the middle of the night."

"And how did you cook, since you don't know?" Ruth inquired, and I opened my mouth at the woman's not-so-subtle cleverness.

"Well, I made quite a mess." I grabbed a piece of my hair, the one that had singed ends, and showed it to her. "I even burned my hair, but I managed to cook while watching a tutorial online," I lied. "It wasn't that hard," I said casually.

"Poor thing, I'll leave some sandwiches ready in the fridge for when you get hungry," Judith interrupted me, helpful.

"That will be a big help, thank you." I smiled, but I didn't miss Ruth's rolled eyes at me.

I finished my coffee and disappeared from the kitchen as fast as I could. I spent the rest of the morning trying to study, but the words suddenly lost their meaning, just like I apparently had lost my way.

"Damn." I pushed the pile of books off my study table and buried my face in my hands. I felt lost and frustrated. Everything I was was right before me, and not being able to focus on my studies made me feel an absurd weakness.

My eyes fell on a pair of noise-canceling headphones that had been abandoned on the table for a long time. They were tangled, and I couldn't even remember the last time I used them.

I widened my eyes, staring at them, and an idea came to mind.

Ever since I lost my sister, I felt like I lost part of myself. That was the worst feeling anyone could carry, the feeling of being empty, lonely. But the truth was, I had never truly been alone.

I grabbed the headphones and slowly untangled them.

There was something that connected Magnolia and me. Just as there was something that brought me to life, a life I had ignored for three years. My essence, my joy, and also, my sorrow.

The dance.

I grabbed my phone and connected the headphones. I headed down to the garden right after, finding myself alone among the bushes, and put on the first song from one of my favorite playlists. One I hadn't listened to in a long time.

The melody started slow, sentimental, and intensified. I closed my eyes, standing in the middle of the garden, feeling every word enter my cells like a vitamin, strengthening my heart.

I opened my eyes and began to walk, looking at my feet, feeling the music shake my soul, and before I knew it, I was standing in front of the dance studio.

The last time I stepped inside, I was a different person. Hopeful, joyful.

I faced my reflection in one of the large mirrors fixed to the wall and began to wonder what would happen if I entered again. I took a step and then stopped. My heart raced so fast I feared I might have a panic attack at any moment, but the sound in my headphones urged me on, to discover what it felt like to be alive once more.

I wanted so much to feel the music again that just imagining it made my eyes well up with tears I tried to hold back.

I took another step, as if being pulled by the tide into an unknown sea that promised a freedom I hadn't experienced in a long time. Before I knew it, I had one foot inside the dance studio. For the first time in three years. My legs trembled, as did my fingers. The scent of polished wood filled my senses as the mirrors hanging on the sides reflected my very red eyes, a testament to my struggle not to cry.

A mix of pain and longing filled me as I laid my eyes on the speaker in the corner of the room. I walked towards it, half-numb, and noticed a USB drive resting on the table. Before I could second-guess myself, I plugged it into the speaker, took off my headphones, and turned up the volume. I stood in the middle of the room and closed my eyes as the first chord reached me, and an angelic version of *Amazing Grace* filled the entire space.

I opened my arms, feeling the music wash over my body and touch my soul. There was pain, frustration, and nostalgia hidden beneath the surface of my skin, and each of those feelings began to pulse as the music engulfed me.

I lifted my head, the sound wrapped me in a magical cloud where all my anguish and loneliness were exposed. I rose onto my toes and stretched my leg, revealing all my fears.

How I wanted to dance, how I wanted to free my soul from that torment, from all the pain that marked me daily.

It was then that I focused on the lyrics of the song, where a voice, as enchanting as that of a hundred angels, recited calmly and lovingly:

Amazing grace, how sweet the sound
That saved a wretch like me
I once was lost, but now am found
Was blind, but now I see

I sobbed as I felt the moment had come to allow that sound to envelop me. The wetness on my face didn't stop me from rising to my feet, spinning my body slowly as the music washed over me. It cleansed my old, painful wounds.

I jumped over the pain, twirled among nightmares, and allowed myself to express with my body everything I felt in my wounded soul.

Dancing was like flying without wings, and for a long time, I forgot what it felt like to lift my feet off the ground.

The Lord has promised me good
His word secures my hope
He my shield and portion will be

As long as life endures

I sobbed loudly, stopping the moment the music ceased. The silence pulled me out of the magical bubble I had immersed myself in. My entire body trembled from head to toe, but a peace, one I hadn't felt until yesterday, washed over me. It was as if Mag were there, happy for me.

I placed my hand on my chest, fearing that at any moment my heart would stop, and when I finally mustered the courage to open my eyes, I saw Wolf standing in the doorway of the studio, watching me with a furrowed brow and sunglasses in his hand.

My legs turned to jelly, and I lost strength, dropping to my knees on the floor. All the tears I had been holding back for years were released.

Wolf

NO ONE WARNED ME. NO one prepared me for the sight of Jasmin dancing in that place.

I was making my rounds when I heard the music echoing from the dance studio and couldn't believe she might have gone in there. Since I arrived, one of the most talked-about subjects was that. Everyone in that place seemed to be waiting for the moment she would return to dance, and I, the fool that I was, imagined I had already witnessed Jasmin dancing *for real*.

I was mistaken.

I stopped in front of the studio, my eyes glued to the most graceful image in the world. That night at the club didn't compare to what was happening inside that hall.

She had her eyes closed. Her loose blonde hair swayed freely around her face along with the movements she made. Her legs moved from side to side in alternating hops, her arms flowed like ribbons in a vibrant color show, wrapping her body with the melody. Watching her dance was exhilarating and delightful in an almost supernatural way. It was as if Jasmin made it impossible to find beauty in anything else in the universe that wasn't her.

Light, pure, perfect. Yes, Jasmin was truly like an angel.

She jumped high, legs spread wide, and landed on the floor, rolling and getting up with impressive speed, as if she didn't even realize the intense movements she was making. The expression on her face was striking, a mix of pain and relief.

Jasmin was crying. Her trembling lips told me much. She had just overcome one of her greatest traumas. She hadn't stepped foot in there since her sister had passed, and her dance revealed longing, love, loss, and all the feelings I struggled to suffocate in my own life.

I took a while to realize my hand was pressed against my chest, trying to contain the sudden pain that arose there.

She was like music entering my ears, enchanting, addictive, liberating. Jasmin was a splendid dancer, and I felt her dance in the one place she should stay far away from. Inside my chest.

I lifted my hand to my sunglasses and removed them. Unable to look anywhere else. Jasmin made one last spin and stopped the moment the music ended. She opened her eyes, which were now red, along with the tip of her nose, and discovered me there, watching her. I felt when her essence hit me, as if we were connected by a transparent thread through our gaze, a thread that tried to pull me toward her, even though I fought with all my strength. We stared at each other for a long minute, and Jasmin's lips began to tremble. She closed her eyes, lifted her head, and fell to the ground, sobbing.

I don't know what I felt when I saw her drop to her knees. The loud cry hit me. A mix of anger, worry, despair, and agony surrounded me. I didn't think twice. I ran to her, dropping to my knees in front of her. I wrapped her trembling body in my arms. Jasmin buried her face in the curve of my shoulder, as if seeking some form of comfort and protection. Her fingers tangled in my suit, and she cried uncontrollably. A painful scream rose in her throat, making my damn eyes burn.

I could only imagine what it was like for her to step in there again. To dance in a place that had always been meant for two, but now... only one existed.

The pain of loss was something I knew well, just as I knew the wickedness of the world, and I would give anything for her not to have to face all that.

She sobbed, coughed, and choked. And I remained there, kneeling with her in my arms, in the middle of the dance studio, supporting her in every way I could.

"You were brave," I whispered into her hair. "Are you listening, Jas? You were very brave." She nodded, agreeing through her sobs. "It will be alright." I kissed her forehead and widened my eyes in surprise at what I had just done.

I glanced over my shoulder, checking for anyone nearby, and the only two people I found were Ruth and Judith. Both were clinging to each other, watching the scene unfold. Judith was crying, while Ruth did her best to hide the silent tears streaming down her face. They disappeared the moment Jasmin clung to me.

Her hands patted my chest, as if trying to sense whether this was real. I held her hand tightly and she gasped, surprised by something, then hugged me tightly.

"It was you," she said softly, still clinging to my suit jacket.

"What?" I questioned, confused.

"The knight in shining armor." She sobbed. "The one who saves me every night. I'd recognize..." She pulled her face away, looking at me with very red cheeks. "I'd recognize this hug anywhere." I froze in place.

What the hell! She remembered.

"It's you, isn't it? You're the one who hugs me when I have episodes." There was something hidden beneath her tear-filled green irises. Something deep like the waters of a lake.

"I'm sorry, Miss Cahill. I lied," I confessed. "I lied when I said I didn't hear anything. The truth is, I heard everything and couldn't control myself. I'm sorry for invading your privacy, especially after what happened yesterday, but..."

"Thank you." She hugged me tightly, surprising me. "Thank you," she repeated, and cried uncontrollably.

I caressed her back and held her in my chest for long minutes.

"It wasn't your obligation," I said, and she lifted her eyes a while later. "I know nightmares can be more troubling for those who hear them than for those who have them. I'm sorry for what you had to hear." Her congested voice made me smile.

I examined her face, now much redder. Her eyes, even swollen, were beautiful and expressive. I cupped her face in both my hands.

"What part of 'we are one' didn't you understand?" she sighed deeply and managed a weak but genuine smile. I could swear it was the first one she'd given in a long time.

Her eyes locked onto mine, and in that moment, I realized two things: I had an overwhelming desire to taste those lips again. I wanted to devour every inch of that beautifully shaped mouth, wanted to feel her in every corner, and that realization frightened me.

From the moment I accepted the mission, I had one certainty in my heart. I would do anything to protect her, even if I had to kill half the world along the way, and now I was absolutely certain that if I didn't control myself and acted solely as her bodyguard, I would end up with Jasmin in my arms.

I well knew I had already fallen under her spell.

CHAPTER FOURTEEN

Jasmin

I spent the rest of the day in my room. I felt exhausted, both physically and emotionally, and I still couldn't believe everything that had happened.

So it was him...

The knight who saves me every night!

A mix of shame and gratitude filled me. I could still feel his arms around me, protecting me with such tenderness. A tenderness I hadn't expected, especially after the kiss from the day before.

A light knock caught my attention.

"Can I come in?" Ruth asked from the door.

"Yes, of course," I replied, lying on my bed.

Ruth entered right after, bringing lunch for me. The delicious aroma of Judith's cooking filled the room, and my stomach growled loudly.

"Thank you so much, Ruth," I said as she set the lunch down on the table.

"I heard you decided to start dancing again." She cleared her throat, and an intense sparkle filled her dark eyes.

"Yes." I smiled to myself at the memory, which brought an indescribable feeling of freedom. "I think it won't be long before the teacher returns."

"I'm particularly happy to hear that, Miss Cahill." She didn't meet my gaze, but I noticed the low, emotional tone in Ruth's voice, always so tough.

"Thank you, Ruth, for never giving up on me." I sighed.

"Just eat everything, miss, and get well. That's thank you enough." And she left, without looking back at me. I smiled at the covered dish on the table, and for the first time, I felt like I was beginning to see a little light in the darkness that had surrounded me for three years.

I TRIED TO READ A BOOK after finishing lunch, but I couldn't focus. As soon as I started reading, my eyes would wander, and my mind drifted back to the moment I was enveloped in the most comforting embrace in the world. Wolf smelled of danger and tasted like temptation—a combination that left me feeling hot and trembling.

I abandoned the book and closed my eyes, wishing to return to that moment, where his firm hands wrapped around me as if I belonged to him. His low voice whispering in my ear still sent shivers down my spine.

That morning, he hadn't cared about the etiquette he usually upheld; he paid little attention to the rules that kept him away from me. I barely registered when the music stopped. All I could do was collapse to the floor, weak from the surge of emotions coursing through my veins. My mind was confused, dark, my heart ached so much that I wondered if I was having a heart attack. When I thought about having to deal with it all alone again, to my surprise, Wolf stepped into my pain. He touched my wounds with his hands, and even though they still hurt, for the first time, I felt I wasn't entirely alone in that anguish.

I exhaled softly, trying to ignore the strange thudding in my chest—a persistent warmth that left me euphoric.

My phone buzzed, and I received a message. I reached for the device and unlocked the screen. I squinted when I saw it was a message from Aunt Claire.

Don't forget we have dinner tonight, dear. I'm bringing an amazing gift. Your dad asked Ruth to make your favorite apple pie, and mine too :)

I smiled at my phone, imagining my aunt trying to persuade Ruth to make that divine pie.

I couldn't even remember the last time we had all eaten together. What had gotten into them? The dinner was already scheduled, but apple pie and surprise gifts?

I narrowed my eyes, already imagining what might have happened. That blabbermouth Ruth must have told them about the night terrors and my little trip to the dance studio.

Still, I couldn't help the spark of joy that exploded in my chest. Dad would be home tonight, willing to spend time with me. I rolled around in the silk sheets and stopped, staring at the ceiling. Maybe this was the perfect chance to, who knows, get permission to go to Carla's party this weekend. That would be perfect.

I already had the no; now I just needed to seek the yes.

NIGHT FELL, AND A COLD draft swept through the house. I chose a light pink fluffy short dress, warm yet cute. I curled my hair a bit and dared to highlight my eyes with dark shadow. When I finished, I ran to the mirror and liked what I saw.

I would be lying if I said I was getting ready for dinner with my dad and aunt.

In truth, I was thinking about *him*. Even though I knew it was crazy.

A strange feeling unsettled me when I turned toward the door, ready to leave, and I wondered where those butterflies in my stomach were that I always heard about in romance novels. The nervousness I felt, felt more like a stomach ache.

I descended the stairs, glancing around, and I deflated a little when I didn't see Wolf around.

Wasn't it his shift? I bit my lip, realizing that maybe he wouldn't even see me tonight.

I walked into the dining room, where a loud and animated conversation was happening. It seemed they had already arrived.

"Hello, my dear!" Aunt Claire greeted me, her fine face breaking into a huge smile. I entered the room without much expectation and ran to her, throwing my arms around her neck in a tight hug.

"I've missed you, aunt."

"You look lovely, dear," my dad commented, and I turned to him.

"Thanks, Dad. It's good to see you after so long," I teased, sitting beside him. He gave a weak smile and touched his wine glass.

"I've been working more than I should, and I'm sorry for that," he admitted. "I promise things will get back to normal soon."

"That's what I hope. I barely see you, and in a way, we work together," Claire mentioned with a wide, dazzling smile.

My aunt had acquired part of the company shares along with the new partners. Unfortunately, a smaller part, from what I understood, than that jerk Foster owned.

"Aunt Claire, tell me, how are things in the Senate?" I started the conversation.

"Oh, dear, I would bore you with that tedious topic," she joked.

"To me, it's boring," my dad whispered in my direction, earning a playful slap on the arm from Aunt Claire. I laughed, happy to be with family.

"Better than that topic is the gift I have for you." She clapped her hands in front of her face and placed her hand on her lap. Only then did I see a silver box, tied with a small bow of the same color.

"Aunt, you didn't have to." I smiled as I took the box from her hands.

"It's been a while since I've given you a present." She placed her hands, adorned with four rings each, on the table.

I opened the box, filled with anticipation. A pair of earrings sparkled as I lifted the lid. They were two pearls, but unlike the usual white or ice-colored ones, they were a very shiny black.

"They're black pearls," Dad said excitedly.

"Of every hundred pearls produced in nature, only one is black," Aunt Claire added enthusiastically, and only then did I realize the rarity of the earrings I was holding. "They are formed inside the shell by layers of nacre..."

"Nacre, dear," my dad corrected her, giving her hand a gentle pat on the table.

"That's it!" We laughed together. "Nacre."

"These earrings must have cost a fortune, aunt." I opened my mouth, surprised.

"Nothing you don't deserve." I got up and walked around the table, hugging her tightly.

"Thank you so much; I'll wear them wisely."

"They say they attract positivity and energy, so always wear them," she assured.

We spent the rest of the evening engaged in pleasant conversation.

"I bought a ranch in the countryside that you'll love, Jasmin," my aunt mentioned. "One day I'll take you there to see it and, who knows, ride a little."

"I'd love to, aunt," I said, super excited. "I've never ridden a horse in my life. It would be an incredible experience."

"I think the country air will do you a lot of good, dear," Dad added, and I smiled at his calmness. "I heard you're back to dancing," he commented casually, and I nodded. "I'm extremely happy to hear that, daughter." He reached for my hand.

"Me too, dear." Aunt Claire stroked my shoulder.

"It's time to get back to my routine," I commented the moment Judith served the apple pie and I noticed how my dad seemed light.

Maybe my chance was right there, under my nose. It had been a long time since I'd seen my dad in a good mood; I had to seize the opportunity.

"Dad, speaking of routine, remember Carla?" I began, noting that both his attention and my aunt's turned to me.

"Carla?" He squinted.

"My friend," I reminded him. "The one with curly hair and..."

"Who's always involved in your escapades?" He placed his hands on the table.

"Your memory is good." Aunt Claire laughed, and I noticed my dad holding back a smile. That was a good sign. "Her birthday is coming up, and I really want to go."

"What's going on here?" he questioned seriously, leaning over the piece of apple pie served on his plate. "Are you *asking* me to go to a party?" I held my breath for a moment, already anticipating the negative. "Since when do you ask me for anything? Jumping the walls is out of the question? I thought you were going to try to escape." My dad laughed and took his fork, poking the pie.

"The shadows that live behind me don't let me breathe alone." I looked at my aunt, who was watching the conversation with interest, and turned my attention back to my dad, batting my eyelashes. If I couldn't convince him nicely, I'd have to resort to drama. Crying and throwing myself on the floor, maybe? "It's an important party; all my friends will be there, and I miss them so much, Dad," I said sincerely.

"There will be more parties like this after the company merger and the launch of J.A.S., my daughter. It's still too dangerous... um, try the pie, Claire. It's magnificent." He diverted the subject and stuffed another bite in his mouth.

"Dad..." I called and covered his hand on the table with mine, gaining his attention again. "You complain that I don't respect your decisions, but you don't respect mine either."

"Daughter, you know that..."

"I'm 23, Dad. I'm a graduated and very intelligent woman. I know I've made some mistakes in the last few months, and I would be lying if I said I regretted what I did," I burst out. "I'm living a solitary life within these walls. I can't see the few friends I have, I can't study abroad, and I barely have my father's company. So yes, I would run away again if it brought me a bit of joy, even if it put my life at risk. But I'm respecting your concern, and I'm certainly willing to follow the men in black at my heels, but I want to go to this party, Dad; it's important. And if you want me to keep respecting you, I need you to do the same for me."

He looked at me thoughtfully and clenched his fist. He scanned the table and pursed his lips.

"You know why I worry so much, don't you?" he asked. "Every time you walk out that door, I fear you'll never come back, daughter." His voice dropped a tone, and for the first time in years, I saw my dad relinquish the role of tough, unbeatable businessman.

His eyes took on a dark gray hue under the dim light of the room, clearly showing all the insecurity behind each of those words.

"You are my Jasmin. My flower, my jewel." I intertwined my fingers with his, emotional from finding a connection I hadn't felt in a long time. "If I lose you, I lose everything."

"You won't lose me, Dad," I assured. "Weren't you bragging about having a Wolf on your daughter's tail? Maybe it's time to use him," I joked, drawing a smile from my father's lined face.

"She's right, Mason. It's just a party, and she has been deprived for years of going to any event outside these walls. We know Carla, and despite some mischief they've gotten into together, we know she's a good girl. Who hasn't done silly things in their youth?" My aunt came to my aid. "Let her go under the watch of your security."

"Whose side are you on?" My father narrowed his eyes at her, and I smiled, euphoric at the simple possibility of him saying yes.

"Please, Dad!" I whined, as if I were ten years old.

"I don't know. The security team didn't help when..." He stopped speaking, and we all knew what he was referring to: the day Magnólia died. I immediately deflated. My father would never allow me to take that risk. I was almost ready to give up on the idea when he took a deep breath and leaned back in his chair.

"Maybe there's a way it can be safe."

"What does that mean?" The anxiety wouldn't let me stay quiet.

"That if... and only if, Wolf finds the idea I have in mind feasible, you might be able to go to that party. But your treacherous friend will also need to cooperate."

I held back a scream of joy that rose in my throat and nodded repeatedly.

"Are you sure you trust this Wolf? The man seems like trouble; I've said you should be careful with him," Aunt Claire intervened. "I have great recommendations, and we can replace him."

"No," I replied, perhaps too emphatically, and received their gazes on me immediately after. "I mean, he is truly unbearable, but my father took a long time to find someone like him. If Wolf is going to ensure my safety at the party, I can tolerate him for a little while longer."

"Jasmin is right. Wolf can be tough, but he's exactly what my daughter needs, Claire. Ah, Dad... you have no idea how." She needs someone who knows how to face her. I love you, daughter, but you have a difficult temperament, just like your mother."

"And she does, but she's as loving as ever," my aunt added with a maternal smile that filled me with joy.

Now I just had to hope that Wolf would agree to that little adventure. My fate rested in his hands.

Wolf

AFTER THAT TUMULTUOUS morning, I asked Lyon to take my place in the surveillance room and stayed as far away from the house as possible. After the impulse I had when I saw Jasmin crying, I realized I was slowly losing my control and part of my composure as a bodyguard in that place, and that was something I couldn't allow.

Seeing her dance was impactful, exciting, and, damn, it drove me wild, as if she could dance over my reason, with those short jumps and light movements that drove me crazy. I didn't know what those deep green eyes had that kept destabilizing me more and more, but I felt willing to fight against whatever it was, even being unable to get her out of my thoughts. A place that, evidently, she decided to make a home.

At that moment, Jasmin was having dinner with her father and the senator, who for some reason always threw me a threatening look whenever she bumped into me.

I found myself imagining how happy she must be with their presence after days of not seeing them properly, while I stared at a bush.

"Shit!" I cursed when I realized that no matter how much I tried to forget her, all I did was think about her.

"I hope this bush hasn't done anything serious to you." I turned quickly upon hearing Cahill's voice behind me. The man greeted me with a warm smile.

"Good evening, Cahill." I tried to ignore the fact that I was so focused on thinking about his daughter that I barely noticed him approaching. "What are you doing out here?" I glanced at the clear, empty porch behind him.

"I need your opinion," he revealed.

"About?"

I heard Cahill briefly explain Jasmin's plans to go to a friend's party, and I was surprised to see him considering the idea.

"According to her, Carla's house is spacious but has few entrances. Three at most. There's a garden at the entrance and a small underground parking lot." I weighed the possibilities based on the little I knew.

"I need the layout of the place to analyze the danger points. Apparently, it's an easy house to secure," I revealed, resting my hand on the holster.

"I told Jasmin I would allow her to go to the party if you could ensure her safety there. No one can enter carrying anything suspicious. Weapons, sharp objects, nothing. You know what my biggest concern is, but as I've already told you, she doesn't. My daughter doesn't know what the true reason was that took Magnólia's life," Cahill was firm.

"Yes, I remember. And I agree with the fact of sparing her those details. She would only get more nervous with every step she took outside this place. It's better that I have that worry, not her."

"Thank you for your understanding." He smiled briefly and returned to seriousness. "I would like to inform you, in absolute secrecy, that my fiancée, Claire, gave Jasmin a pair of black pearl earrings." I looked at him, trying to understand when that information became relevant. "However, they are not simple earrings." He rushed to say when he saw my confused face. "For a while, I wanted to gift her something that could be tracked, for her own safety, but coming from me, she would soon suspect, so I asked Claire to buy a pair at one of our locations, implant the tracker, and gift it to her. I'll make sure Jasmin wears it at all times, especially at this party." I looked at the man, thoughtful, contemplating the probabilities. "We'll also need to count on the birthday girl's help, but according to my daughter, she will do whatever it takes. Do you think you can ensure her safety given all this?"

So that outing was exclusively depending on my authorization. An intense flame reverberated in my mind, imagining how upset Jasmin would be if I denied her outing. Maybe that was the perfect revenge for us to be even.

Yes, I could simply say no and keep her there, safe and irritated. However, more than furious, she would be very sad, and I didn't want that at all. I would have to analyze our possibilities and if there was any chance of taking her safely, I would do it.

It seemed that over the years, I had become a dull sentimentalist.

"I can guarantee the safety of Miss Cahill; that's a fact, and I would be able to do so even in unknown environments," I assured in a robotic voice. "But I need to consider the aggravating factors we have in this situation." The man straightened his posture in the blink of an eye.

"Yes!"

"First of all, I need Jasmin to tell absolutely no one that she intends to attend this party," I began. "The fewer people who know, the less likely her presence will reach the ears of those we are trying to avoid." Cahill nodded energetically, agreeing. "Next, hire half a dozen more security personnel from Holder Security. Ask for three men and three women. There are no openings, but tell my father it was my direction, and he will get good people," I dictated, running my fingers over my jaw, tracing the stubble and thinking about the details. "Also request all the metal identification materials. All exits will be blocked; we will use only one of the three entrances to the house, where guests will need to enter and exit. We will also thoroughly search each one of them. Miss Cahill will be prohibited from consuming any beverages other than what she brings and that will be served by one of us. I will keep a sniper nearby for safety, and all team members must also be present inside the house, escorting her. I will cover Miss Cahill closely and ensure that no stranger approaches her, especially carrying anything that could harm her. That's all. This way, we can go to the party.

"Holy hell!" Cahill took a deep breath. "All of this..." He smiled, affected and satisfied. "I knew you were efficient. Thank you, I will tell Jasmin she can go to the party and will arrange everything you asked for." He turned to leave.

"If I may ask, Cahill," I interrupted the man, who turned to me smiling. "Why did you decide to authorize something like this? I know I'm capable of protecting her, but with everything happening, what has changed?"

"We are at war, Wolf. Someone is trying to destroy my family. I need Jasmin to fight by my side, and for that, I have to trust her and you." He nodded just before disappearing into the mansion, murmuring something about being excited to tell her the news.

I returned to my post and began plotting some routes and strategies that could be useful in this operation when light footsteps caught my attention almost an hour later. I turned to see who it was and was surprised to find Jasmin's big eyes, green as a precious jewel. They grew larger and even more alive when highlighted by the black makeup she wore.

"Hi." Timidly, she took a step closer to me, then another. As she approached, it became impossible not to admire her.

How could someone look so much like a celestial being?

The thought crossed my mind as soon as I laid eyes on her, dressed in a fluffy pink outfit, like most of the things she wore, and unlike the other times I had encountered her, Jasmin radiated a happiness that struck my chest. Every detail, from her full, perfectly shaped lips creating a graceful arc in the center, to her upturned, rebellious nose... her soft voice like her skin. Everything was perfect.

"Miss Cahill." My eyes traveled down her delicate face to her alluring lips, which made me pulse with desire and curse myself at the same time.

"I just wanted to thank you for what you said to my father." She clasped her hands in front of her body. "If it weren't for you, I wouldn't have his permission to go to Carla's party."

She took another timid step toward me. There were so many unspoken things hanging between our gazes. The sudden kiss in the kitchen, the warm and delicious embrace in the dance academy, the crazy urge I felt to grab her right there, not caring who was watching.

"Don't thank me." I tried to sound as serious as possible. "I'll need your cooperation for everything to go right, and of course, the collaboration of the birthday girl."

"You'll have everything you want." Her eyes rested on my mouth, and she bit her lips subtly, sending a warm, uncomfortable feeling spreading through my body.

Jasmin ran her hands through her very straight hair, and a strand fell onto her face. When I realized, I had already brought my fingers to the soft, very blonde lock. I tucked it gently behind her ear and only then did I see the black pearl earring that Cahill had mentioned.

"It's a beautiful earring. It suits you." My voice came out too low.

"Are you saying I'm beautiful?"

"As if you didn't know."

"At least I've never heard you say it. That's already a win."

"For which battle?" She took another step closer to me. Her hand gently rested on my chest. I lowered my eyes to hers, controlling myself as best as I could to not take her mouth right then, and when Jasmin opened her lips, I felt as if half my world collapsed with her words.

"The one that can make me kiss you again without running away right afterward. I want to be able to feel you, and for some reason, I think you want the same." Her hand rose higher, my heart pounding against my chest. "It's this war I want to win, against what drives you away from me."

I held her wrist cautiously and caressed the inside of her palm with my thumb as our eyes exchanged sparks in an extremely exciting atmosphere.

"It's better to keep your hands light away from me, Crystal," I teased, aware that she didn't like the nickname one bit. "I might consider your idea." She shivered at the comment, and her entire face flushed a delightful shade of red.

"That's exactly what I want," she stammered, confused.

"Are you sure?" I tightened her wrist more, the image of that woman moaning my name until she lost herself filled my mind, and I had to contain the violent urge to pull her to me.

"I am," she whispered, and I released her wrist before I couldn't do it anymore.

"You'd better not play with me, Miss Cahill," I warned. "I'm an impatient man, as you must have noticed." She was staring at me with a strange expression frozen on her face, as if a new toy was right before her eyes, but she didn't quite know how to play with it. "It's better to go inside; they must be waiting for you in there."

"Yes, that's true," she said, turning toward the mansion. "I still hope that one day you'll call me Jasmin." She didn't turn to look at me. "I like how my name sounds in your mouth," she revealed, and a pragmatic energy coursed through me.

She didn't know... not even had any idea that her name echoed in my subconscious every damn second of the day, tied to the overwhelming desire to kiss her all night long, saying that beautiful name at least a million times.

But that reckless desire was far out of my reach, as far as the little angel standing right in front of me.

"Good night, Miss Cahill!"

"Good night, Wolf..." Touché.

Jasmin disappeared into the house right after.

CHAPTER FIFTEEN

Jasmin

The days leading up to the party were the most exciting of my life, but I hadn't seen Wolf, who, from the information I gathered from Shaw, was responsible for the overnight shifts.

He was definitely avoiding me, which left me quite frustrated.

On the other hand, Carla accepted all the numerous rules my father imposed, along with Wolf, for the party, and now I felt restless, aware that my friend had given up the comfort of her own guests so I could be there, which reminded me that this had to be a perfect night.

"You look radiant, Miss Cahill," Judith whispered beside Ruth, as the housekeeper finished curling my hair, which hung down to my waist in a shiny, intense blonde.

The red dress I chose was long but had a deep cut that accentuated my breasts, even though they were small. To top it off, I applied lipstick in the same shade, which made my lips look even fuller.

"The earrings, Miss," Ruth reminded me, and I took the pair of black pearls and put them on.

"If I forget them, my aunt will kill me," I joked, remembering how much Aunt Claire insisted I wear them whenever possible; after all, according to her, anything expensive deserved to be worn as often as possible. A philosophy I had never heard before.

Dad couldn't come home, but for the first time in history, he made a video call just to see me, and although it wasn't ideal, I was happy with it and listened to his advice for the night as well as his compliments.

I went downstairs a while later, balancing on a pair of thin high heels I hadn't worn in a long time. Four cars were parked in front of the mansion entrance, all black and identical. One more than I usually had.

I would probably ride in the third one, where the man who had been haunting my most erotic dreams was standing, showing off his broad back under a completely black suit that fit him perfectly.

"Have fun, Miss." Judith waved goodbye.

"Be careful," Ruth urged, and only then did Wolf notice my presence.

I began descending the entrance steps just as he turned in my direction. His eyes, so different from his own essence, locked onto mine for a long moment before trailing down my dress, lingering on the details. I could see him swallow hard, and I felt dazzled. I hadn't seen him in three days, and that strange flutter in my chest, which felt like longing, intensified as I approached him.

"Good evening," I said to no one specific and glanced at the other bodyguards in the area, feeling Wolf's gaze fixed on my movements.

"Good evening, Miss Cahill. You look stunning!" Shaw said, and I could have sworn I heard a growl from the man beside him.

"What's with that face, Wolf?" I whispered as I got closer to him and surveyed his grumpy expression. "Cheer up, we're going to have fun tonight." I smiled at him, but he maintained his stern demeanor.

"The Miss is going to have fun," he stressed, "and return safely. I will ensure that, now please, get in the car."

I noticed the professional tone he used with me and couldn't contain the slight anguish that washed over me. After the vibe I felt between us last time we met, I could have sworn we were starting to get along, but suddenly he got all serious, strange, and was avoiding me around the house.

I passed him to get into the car while Wolf held the passenger door open, and I was surprised when a whispered voice reached me.

"You look extraordinary, Miss Cahill." My bodyguard quickly averted his gaze, and I widened my eyes, incredulous that he had actually said that.

"Thank you." I slid onto the leather seat of the car, feeling the usual warmth in my chest that I felt every time I was near him.

Wolf got into the car silently, and I settled into the back seat. The anxiety that this day had finally arrived began to overwhelm me, and I twisted my hands together, smoothing the rings on my fingers repeatedly.

"Are you nervous?" Wolf's voice came out soft, concerned.

"I think a little. It's the first party in years that I can attend with my father's permission," I confessed, meeting his gaze through the rearview mirror.

"You're strange." He laughed and put on his sunglasses.

"There's nothing strange about being nervous given my situation," I retorted, and he opened his incredibly white smile even wider. "Why are you laughing?" I leaned closer in the seat to get a better look and give him my best death glare.

"You're brave enough to run away, but you're scared of a party for which you have permission to be at. Are you afraid of being attacked?" He turned to me. His presence filled the car's interior, just like his citrus scent mingled with my sweet one.

"That's just one of my concerns." I exhaled, exasperated. "My dad trusted me for the first time in a long time. I'm afraid that for some reason, I'll disappoint him and end up back in the city's gossip newspapers. Plus, I haven't seen some of the people who will be there in many years. I have no idea how it's going to be, and I don't like that. Oh, and of course, there's the risk of some crazy person trying to kill me."

"As for your friends, I'm sure you'll do well. There's no way it will be different. You manage to hold 12 scientists who don't like you in the palm of your hand. I wonder what you can't do with those idiots." I laughed. "And as for the rest, don't worry. That's why I'll be by your side. I won't allow you to get involved in any scandals, and I can guarantee no one will approach you."

"Thank you." That was all I could say, and the next moment Shaw got into the car and sat beside Wolf in the passenger seat.

"We're leaving," Wolf announced into the communicator, and the first car began to move.

I kept watching Wolf for a moment longer and saw him run his hand over the gun at his waist and disengage the safety that held it in the holster.

"Should I be worried, Wolf?" Shaw asked when he noticed the movement.

"It's nothing," I said, already driving past the mansion's exit. "Whenever I'm with a VIP, I keep the gun unholstered. Car chases are difficult; it makes it much easier to have the weapon free. A second can make a difference."

"Do you really think someone might attack our car?" I leaned my head into the space between the front seats. "Tell me, I want to be prepared. Can't I have one of those?" I pointed to the gun.

"No way!" he exclaimed.

"Are you crazy?" Shaw blurted out immediately. "Sorry, I meant to say no, Miss. You can't have one of those."

I laughed at the guy's panic and rolled my eyes.

"Miss Cahill, could you please fasten your seatbelt?" Wolf asked, and I made a face from the back seat. "I can see you in the rearview mirror if you've forgotten."

"Done, Wolf, are you satisfied?" I pulled the belt and looked in the rearview mirror. Shaw laughed at the nickname. "This thing is going to crumple my dress."

"I don't care about your dress if your safety is guaranteed."

"I should take it off. What do you think? That way it won't get wrinkled," I joked, and I saw Wolf nearly spit out a curse word over the steering wheel.

"Not a good idea, Miss," Shaw groaned. "For our own safety, please stay dressed... or he'll kill us," he whispered the last part through the gap between the seats.

The night was going to be fun.

BEFORE WE EVEN ARRIVED at the event location, we could already hear the loud music coming from there. We turned a corner and came across a gigantic house with tall white pillars at the end of the block, from where some colorful beams of light escaped.

We parked in a space reserved for my security. Wolf got out of the vehicle and opened the door for me. I started to struggle with the dress and heels, trying to get out of the car.

"Come on." He extended his hand toward me, and I looked at him with a suspicious glance. "Let's go, I won't bite."

"Not even if I ask?" I joked and grabbed his hand firmly.

"Control yourself, Miss Cahill." He pressed his lips together in a hidden smile.

I managed to get one leg out of the car, but I tripped while stepping out and was thrown out with the momentum. I ended up hanging onto Wolf with one leg still inside the car and the other outside.

"Miss..." He didn't even have time to finish the sentence.

"My foot!" I shouted, burying my face in his chest for support.

Wolf held me carefully and helped me regain my balance as I straightened up.

"At this rate, I'm starting to think it'll be hard to keep the promise of returning you without a scratch."

"Hell no!" I cursed angrily, glaring at the car as if it were coming to life.

"The vocabulary you adopt when you get nervous is quite interesting." He laughed.

"Don't push it." I straightened up, trying to ignore Wolf's hand on my elbow, ensuring that I was alright and balanced.

I took a deep breath and looked around to check if anyone was watching the scene, and I was glad to see that the entrance to the place was empty, except for the other security personnel.

"Are you ready?" he asked.

"Now that my foot is free..." I confirmed with a nod. "Is my dress wrinkled? Maybe I smudged my makeup, and my hair? Oh my God, I didn't bring a mirror." I turned to the reflection in the car window, running my hand over the dress countless times.

Wolf stepped close behind me, just near enough for only I could hear him.

"Miss Cahill, I don't believe there's a single person as beautiful as you in this place." I turned to him, breathing calmly again.

"Do you really think so, or are you just saying that because you're paid to be by my side?"

"I'm paid to protect you, not to lie," he revealed. The short distance between us allowed me to closely observe the veins running down his thick neck, as well as the arms beneath the perfectly fitted suit. "You are the most beautiful woman I've ever seen. A thief, crazy, and with a dirty mouth? Definitely, but extremely gorgeous." I laughed loudly and opened a smile that seemed to come straight from my heart in a mix of emotion and joy at those unexpected words.

"I already apologized," I whispered, smiling, and Wolf touched my wrist with intensity. The light smile that rested on his lips suddenly vanished.

"Remember the main rules. No one except the birthday girl is allowed to approach you. Half a meter is the limit. I'll be like a shadow at your side, and I'm prepared to drag more than one person out of this party if they disregard the order."

"Yes, I understand. No hugs, no funny business."

"Don't make me rip someone's hand off," he replied through clenched teeth, and a warm flush crept up my neck. "Let's start this madness already." I agreed with a brief nod. "We're moving," he announced into the radio, and all the other security personnel fell into formation.

Lyon and Ray led the way, and Wolf positioned himself immediately behind me, next to Shaw. I lifted my gaze to one corner of the entrance and caught a glimpse of Carla's father with his dark, pragmatic eyes fixed on me. The man looked sharp in a gray suit and waved, lifting the glass he was holding in my direction as soon as he noticed I was watching. I smiled at him, disguising the chill I always felt whenever we met. Matías was tall, with broad, rigid shoulders, and his daughter had inherited several of his strong features, except for the eyes, which were intense and always seemed to be waiting for something.

I blinked, breaking free from his gaze, and found other security personnel at the party entrance, who greeted us with a nod as we passed through the archway, decorated with white balloons, at the house's entrance.

"Jasminnnnnnnnnn!" The shout reverberated over the loud music, and I soon spotted a stunning brunette in the crowd, with tightly curled hair and honey-colored skin that seemed sun-kissed, highlighted in a fitted yellow dress at the bust and loose at the length.

"That's her, right?" I heard Wolf's voice behind me.

"Yes," I whispered back. "Carla!" Before my friend could hug me, Lyon observed her from head to toe, as if she might be hiding a weapon in her cleavage.

The woman shouted and skipped toward me.

"It's so good to see you." I hugged her affectionately. "Happy birthday! Did you receive my gift?"

"Of course, and I'm still fascinated. It's not every day that I get the complete collection of my favorite games." I smiled, happy. Carla had a different hobby, besides the parties she loved to organize. She was a gamer, addicted to rare games, and luckily, I managed to get a few that were missing from her collection.

"I'm so sorry for... you know." I pointed with my nose to Lyon, who had already positioned himself with Ray and Shaw at the designated ends, while Wolf was so close to me that I could even feel his breath.

"Jasmin, my dear, you're the one who's responsible for shaking this place up." Carla looked at Wolf as if he were a piece of steak hanging in the middle of the hall, and that bothered me. I still hadn't confided the conflicting and persistent feelings that man had been causing me, so my friend had no idea he wasn't just the target of my creative torment.

"Hello, Jasmin!" One of Carla's friends, Lia something, I couldn't remember, waved from the other side of the elegantly decorated hall with large crystal chandeliers sparkling with the colorful dots of light that my friend had spread around, not to mention the large area designated for drinks and the buffet, which had bright lights behind each of the arrangements.

I waved at Lia, and in that instant, one of the security personnel from Holder Security approached me.

"Miss Cahill, I'm Morgan, one of your bodyguards for today." The tall woman approached. "Tell me everything you want to drink, and I'll provide it from the drinks we brought." I shrugged, feeling uncomfortable. It wasn't easy to socialize when you couldn't mix your drink with your friends'.

"Fancy people are on another level. If it depends on my dad, we're all going to die poisoned," Carla joked, trying to distract me, and it worked.

A few minutes later, I was feeling a bit dizzy from trying to recognize my classmates' faces in the confusion of colored lights.

Many of my old school friends were there, and even though we hadn't seen each other in a long time, they seemed happy to see me again. I stopped to chat with a few of them during the party, keeping the half-meter distance that each of them kindly insisted on ignoring.

Almost an hour later, I had taken a few shots of rum and was visibly more energized. A Latin song filled the hall as the lights were dimmed slightly.

"I want to dance!" I turned to Wolf, feeling my cheeks slightly warm from the alcohol.

"You can dance alone or with your friend," Wolf said, and I pouted. "I'm sorry, but we're on high alert since the lights dimmed."

I pointed to a spotlight that illuminated the center of the dance floor, making everything more visible.

"Can't you dance with me?" I moved closer to the elegant man beside me. "Please..."

Wolf

THE LADY IN RED BEFORE me was the most delicious and intriguing sight I had ever laid eyes on, and it didn't make it any easier that she wanted to dance with me there. I knew this little one was a natural dancer, and it pained me to have to keep her from that, but her safety came first.

"So with Carla, do you allow that?" she teased and opened a wide smile. Her cheeks were much redder after the drink.

"If your friend wants to, I will allow it, with the condition that she dances close to me."

"Carla!" she suddenly shouted. I thought she was going to object, but instead, she seemed more excited when she saw her friend running toward her. "Dance with me?"

"Only if it's now... Oh, great! Why did I suggest that?"

"Come with us, Wolf." She winked at me and walked hand in hand with Carla into the open space surrounded by the other guards, toward the middle of the dance floor.

I kept half a meter away, ensuring that the show was just for the two of them, and to my surprise, Carla could also dance. Obviously not compared to Jasmin, but together they began to capture the attention of every guest, moving to a light and delightful Latin song.

Jasmin was smiling with her eyes, her lips, her soul. A comforting feeling enveloped me as I saw her there, so free. Once again, I found myself lost in the enchanting movements she made with every inch of her body, twirling angelically and mixing it all with Carla's strong, rhythmic Latin flair. She was a star, shining with her own light, and that brightness began to invade the darkness in which I lived.

A few days were left until my contract with the Cahills ended, and before all I wanted was to refuse that mission, but now I wished for nothing more than for my time beside her not to end.

"Suspected guy in a blue shirt approaching Crystal. Take positions." I received the message on the communicator and immediately reached for my weapon, moving a step closer to Jasmin as the guy entered my line of sight.

I scanned him from head to toe. He was a blonde playboy, of medium height, who entered my list of most hated people the moment Jasmin saw him. She broke away from her friend and opened a charming smile for the stranger. I clenched my fist upon realizing that he posed no danger to her, but I still put my hand on the guy's chest.

"Stay away," I warned, watching him turn a sarcastic smile in my direction.

"We're friends." His gaze shamelessly traveled over Jasmin's body while she said something to Carla.

I felt an immense urge to follow Ghost's advice and smash his face against a pillar in the place, especially when he reached out to her, inviting her to dance.

"Can I?" She turned to me.

"Is he your father?" the bastard asked, and I grabbed him by the shoulders, slamming my hand firmly against the bastard's body while I frisked him.

"Hey, dude, what the hell is this?" I held him by the collar of his blazer and pulled him close, not caring about the attention we were probably drawing.

"I'm not her father; I'm her bodyguard. It's better not to try any funny business. Otherwise, I'll put a bullet in your face." I released him and noticed that now he wore a slightly paler expression than before.

"It's just a dance, Wolf," Jasmin interjected. "I haven't seen him in years." They locked eyes, and the woman smiled at the idiot as if he were missed in her life.

Damn!

"Crystal is safe. He's a friend," I warned on the communicator and spent the next few minutes with my eyes fixed on the two, who were talking quietly in an intimacy that irritated me to the extreme. What were they talking about, anyway? Who was that idiot?

CHAPTER SIXTEEN

Jasmin

Ryan was even more handsome than I remembered, and seeing him there before me brought endless joy to my heart.

"I missed you," I admitted as the music started and he wrapped one arm around my waist, pulling me closer.

I felt the sweet scent of some drink touch my face through the man's breath and remembered that he always liked colorful, flashy drinks. Apparently, nothing had changed. Now and then, I remembered how Ryan and Magnólia seemed made for each other, even though he was a bit older and had very different tastes from hers. My sister's ex-boyfriend was taller, stronger, but the smile and deep eyes were the same.

"I missed you too. You look stunning." He spun me around in his arms. "Very, very stunning." His bright eyes scanned me in a strange way.

"How's life?" I changed the subject, suddenly uncomfortable with something that was probably only in my head.

"I'm working at my dad's company. Construction, remember?"

"Yes, of course. Are you enjoying it?"

"Not at all." He laughed, and I joined in. "I think I want to work in photography."

"That's a creative profession," I concluded, noticing when he pulled his body closer to mine. I glanced over my shoulder just to check Wolf's hawk-like gaze on me. His clenched jaw told me he was also uncomfortable.

"I'm thinking of starting next week. Would you be my model?"

"Me?" My voice came out shrill. "Oh no, Ryan. I appreciate the offer, but I don't handle photos well, not to mention how many times models have to change outfits."

He then opened a strange smile and leaned close to my ear.

"In that case, we can skip any kind of clothing. I can imagine how much more beautiful you would be without that dress." He tightened his grip on my waist, pulling me closer. I was shocked for a moment, my eyes wide, doubting what I had just heard.

"Ryan... what do you mean by that?"

"That time passes and you become more attractive." He squeezed my waist.

"How..." I widened my eyes. "How dare you... how can you say that? You dated my sister! She was in love with you." My body swayed robotically, without me realizing it, and my voice came out in whispers, so shocked was I.

"Magnólia is no longer here, Jasmin." He smiled. "I bet she would love to see us together, even if just for one night. Do you think you can get rid of those bodyguards for a moment?" He pulled me even closer until I could feel his erection against me. "Do you like this?"

"You piece of shit!" I screamed and completely lost my composure.

I pushed him away and clenched my fist. I punched the idiot right in the face, and he instinctively brought his hand to his face. Ignoring the sting in my fingers, I grabbed the idiot's gelled hair and pulled with all my might.

"You bastard!" I spun Ryan around by his hair in the middle of the hall, drawing the attention of the entire party.

"Jasmin!" I felt strong arms wrap around my waist as three other men jumped on Ryan.

"She's crazy!" he shouted, struggling against them. "Out of her mind!"

"I'll kill him! Let me go!" I fought against the arms I knew so well.

"Jasmin!" Wolf spun me around until I was facing him. "Calm down, please, and tell me what happened. Are you hurt? Did he hurt you?"

The steady, firm sound of Wolf's voice brought me back to reality. I looked into his focused face and missed the warmth of his gaze, hidden behind the sunglasses.

"No. He didn't hurt me," I replied, my breathing uneven.

"Let me go!" Ryan shouted, and all the fury I felt returned upon hearing his voice.

"But I'm going to tear this idiot's hair out!" I tried to launch myself toward the fool again, but I stopped upon seeing a flash.

"Calm down, miss." Wolf loosened his tight embrace but kept his hands on my arms.

I scanned the situation. Ten bodyguards surrounded me. The sound of the party had stopped, and all the guests watched the scene with expressions ranging from curiosity to concern. Ryan disappeared into the crowd as soon as he freed himself from Lyon's grip.

Wolf

"WHAT HAPPENED? DID he do anything to you?" I asked, worried, and pressed my hands against Jasmin's shoulders, checking if she was hurt anywhere. She looked into my eyes, her green irises shifting between anger and what I thought was disappointment or sadness.

What the hell had happened?

"Let's go," she said, but before heading toward the exit, she turned to security, Morgan. "Where's the whiskey bottle I saw among our drinks?" The woman looked at me as if she were lost in the middle of a shootout. I nodded, confirming she could bring the bottle, and in less than a minute, she appeared with a full one. "Thanks!" Jasmin took the bottle from Morgan's hand, lifted her chin, and headed toward the entrance of the hall.

Some whispers almost made me turn back and throw some punches, but I was too focused on keeping my hand on Jasmin's back. I could notice her trembling fingers even though she tried to disguise it, and I was worried about what that idiot might have done or said.

"Jasmin, what happened?" Carla intercepted her with wide eyes. "You... punched the..."

"I'm sorry, friend, I guess I'm just not made for socializing." The sorrow in her voice made a hole open in my chest.

"Let's go somewhere else, just you and me," her friend suggested. "I don't care about the guests. I prefer my best friend over any of them."

"Thanks for that, Carla, I love you so much, but I really need to go. I'll explain everything later." She looked at her friend, who seemed to read something on Jasmin's face before nodding and letting her pass.

"I'll wait for a call," Carla shouted from the entrance of the house, and as soon as Jasmin stepped outside, she sprinted in her high heels toward the car, making all of us run after her.

The girl opened the car door and threw herself inside, closing it afterward.

"What was that? Has she gone completely crazy?" Lyon stopped beside me.

"Miss Cahill has a better right hook than you, Lyon," Shaw teased him and received a shove from the man.

"Let me talk to her. That idiot didn't do anything with his hands; I was on top of both of them the whole time."

"He might have said something," Lyon added.

"Something that made her furious. Did you see how she spun him by the hair?" Shaw laughed and mimicked the scene with his hands. "She grabbed him with everything."

"Something happened, and we're not leaving here until I find out what it was."

"Good luck; I don't want my hair pulled." Lyon laughed and walked away.

I opened the passenger door and sat next to Jasmin, who, to my surprise, was tipping the whiskey bottle directly to her lips.

"What's wrong? Never needed a drink in your life, huh?" She wrinkled her nose irritably. "Leave me alone." She took another gulp, and I grabbed the bottle from her hands.

"What happened in there?"

"Nothing," she replied too quickly.

"So you punched a guy and yanked his hair for no reason? I even liked the scene, but there must have been a reason, and we're not leaving until you tell me." That was the last straw that made my little aggressor overflow.

"That idiot, son of a bitch, fucking bastard, spoiled brat, demon spawn was my sister's boyfriend," she shouted inside the car. "She loved that idiot. How could he?" She tried to reach for the bottle in my hands, but I held it tightly.

At that moment, several hypotheses swirled in my mind, and I clenched my fist, feeling the slight calm before the storm take over my body.

"What did he do, Jasmin?" Calling her by name made her look at me.

Her lips trembled, and for God's sake, I didn't care if he just stepped on her foot; I was going to rip that bastard's balls off if she cried.

"First, he came up saying it had been a long time since he saw me." The choked voice made me more irritated with each passing second. "I was so happy to see him, you know? It had been a while since I found anyone who had such an intense connection with my sister. For a moment, I felt so happy that I wanted to hug him. Then in the middle of the dance, he started complimenting me too much, and out of nowhere, he pulled me by the waist until I felt..." She shrugged and stared at her own fingers. "You know... he wanted me to feel that thing that gets excited when a man has his attention on a woman," she said, shyly.

The guy pressed her against an erection? Was that it? Her sister's ex-boyfriend?

"Before that happened, he came with some strange talk, but I thought I might have been mistaken, until he made me an offer."

"What offer?"

"He wanted to take pictures of me... naked. He called me hot, and when I questioned him about Magnólia, he had the gall to say she wasn't here anymore and that she'd be happy to see us together. As if my sister were disposable, as if the love she felt for him had never existed. That filthy bastard didn't care what that meant for me; he just wanted..." She took a deep breath, and I noticed the control she exerted to avoid crying. "He wanted me to get rid of you guys. That's when everything went dark, and I snapped." She pressed her fingers to her eyes and squeezed them shut. "Please, Wolf, take me home."

"Jasmin..." She looked my way, her lost eyes filled with pure disgust and apprehension. "Can you wait for me here for five minutes, my angel?" I asked patiently, my voice as calm as a river on a sunny day that I didn't even realize what I had called her.

"What are you going to do?"

"Nothing for you to worry about. I'll be back in a moment."

"Promise?" She held my hand before I left the car, and I had to take a deep breath to force a brief smile her way.

"Of course, Crystal." Suddenly, looking into those deep, shining eyes, I realized that the nickname suited her as well as that dress.

Jasmin was precious, a rare jewel.

"Shaw, stay with Miss Cahill and make sure she doesn't leave here. I'll be back in a moment." I closed the passenger door.

"This is not good. Not good at all." I heard him grumble, and without thinking twice, I made my way back to the party.

"What do you think you're doing?" Lyon appeared beside me, grumpy as always.

"I'm going to teach that bastard some manners," I yelled, feeling Lyon's hand grip my arm, stopping me from moving. "You better let me go, Lyon; I don't want to hurt you."

"Listen here, you idiot, even though I feel like drowning you in a puddle every time I see you, we're the damn team, so if you're going to play Rambo, at least tell me why," he cursed, releasing me.

"The bastard she punched in there was her sister's boyfriend, and to make things worse, the son of a bitch hit on her," I growled, feeling rage take over every cell in my body, imagining that jerk pressuring Jasmin.

"He hit on…?" It took a moment for Lyon to register, and I saw the instant when his eyes turned darker. "What an idiot!"

"He pressed her against the dress, Lyon, so you better let me go." He seemed to understand what kind of pressure I was referring to.

"I'm right behind you." He nodded, and we both entered the party again.

It didn't take me long to find the bastard, who was in a more isolated corner of the party, laughing loudly with his friends.

"Did you at least touch her?" one of them asked.

"Of course. She jumped when she felt the pressure of my snake." He grabbed himself, showing off to the idiots around.

I clenched my jaw and grabbed him by the neck.

"Sorry to interrupt the fun."

"What the hell! Let go of me!" I shoved him forward, and when he was in front of me, I punched him square in the face, then another, and another. The crack of his nose breaking echoed through my hand.

"Let him go, man!" Someone tried to intervene. I elbowed whoever it was in the face and saw him fall beside me.

I leaned closer to the bastard's bloodied face and tightened my grip on his neck. I punched him in the stomach and watched him lose his breath.

"Want to show your little snake to her again? Want to try, you son of a bitch?" I kicked his legs, and he fell to the ground with a thud, muffled by the loud electronic music.

I pressed my knee into his neck, hidden by the darkness of that reserved space. Anger urged me on, the desire to crush his neck began to consume me.

"S-s-sorry. P-p-please forgive me," he stammered.

That was when I felt Lyon's hand on my shoulder, and his voice seemed to bring me back to reality.

"You've broken him, Wolf. That's enough; let's go." I lifted my knee off the pile of shit and stood up. All his friends, the ones who hadn't taken a beating, were huddled in the dark corner.

"I hope we never cross paths again, you piece of trash." I kicked his leg and heard him groan. "Next time, I'll make sure you never breathe again."

I turned my back, my dirty hands clenched into fists.

"My God, what happened here?" I heard a woman speaking. They probably found the bastard lying on the floor. I didn't turn around; I didn't care. I just wanted to get out of there, just like I wanted that anger to disappear for good.

"I'm not going to say I didn't enjoy what I saw, because I did," Lyon commented as soon as we stepped outside. "That nose is never going to be the same, and it was well-deserved." I was surprised when he pulled a handkerchief from his pocket and handed it to me. "But if you get in the car like that, Miss Cahill is going to freak out."

"Thanks." I gladly accepted the handkerchief and realized that this was the first conversation I had with Lyon without any cursing from either side.

I paused just before getting into the car. Shaw looked anxious.

"What happened? Who hit? Who got hit?"

"No one, you airhead." Lyon covered for me. "How is she?" The man nodded toward the inside of the car.

"Not well. I think she's crying." Both of them pursed their lips, and I realized that, contrary to what I thought when I took that job, none of Jasmin's bodyguards felt indifferent to her suffering.

"I hate when this happens. She's always so cheerful that when she cries, it feels like the world loses a bit of its charm," Lyon commented.

"She was so happy to have a day out, but it ended so quickly," Shaw added, and a crazy idea popped into my mind.

"There's a place..." I said, gaining both of their attention. "It's on the way to the mansion, and I know it very well. It's a private overlook that belongs to Holder. There's a lodge that will be opened soon; it's still inactive but is extremely well monitored, we'll be safe there. What do you think? Shall we take a detour?"

"Are you sure about this, Wolf?" Lyon looked over his shoulder as if to ensure no one was listening to our conversation.

I wanted to take her somewhere different, lively, but Jasmin was in the sights of hired assassins like Naish, and knowing the danger she was in, I had no choice but to take her to the overlook. The only safe place I knew.

"Do you trust me?"

"Of course," Shaw replied.

"Then get in the cars. Let's give her a special night." Lyon smiled without showing his teeth and activated the support point.

"Change of plans," I said the moment Shaw and I were getting into the car.

"Can we go already?" I asked, noticing that Jasmin was looking out the window, clutching the bottle with a desolate look.

That was one of the things that made me angriest at that idiot. He ruined the only chance in a long time that she had to go out and have a little fun, away from that isolated life she lived.

"Please," she whimpered. "My bed is waiting for me." A sorrowful sigh escaped her lips.

"Too bad. You won't see it for now," I said casually, adjusting the route on the shared GPS for the new location we were heading to.

"What?"

"I'm taking you to a special place since the night isn't over yet," I told her, glancing at the rearview mirror just in time to see her mouth form a perfect O. "Unless you'd prefer to go home..."

"NO!" She perked up, the trail of tears and smudged makeup revealing she had been crying. "I'll go anywhere on earth, anywhere at all. I'm in for anything."

"Then let's go!" Shaw chimed in, excited. "To infinity and beyond." Jasmin laughed at the guy's joke, and even I, who minutes earlier was having a blind rage attack, managed to smile at her sudden enthusiasm.

It was then that I realized Jasmin had everything at her feet. Heir to a billion-dollar fortune, probably spoiled since the day she was born, she could buy whatever she wanted. But what she valued most was freedom and the little details that made her an even more beautiful and enchanting person.

"You're different, Crystal. Much different than I thought."

I started the engine, my thoughts focused on the strange, aggressive woman who cursed like a drunk. Sitting in the back seat, now excited like a child about to go to an amusement park, I realized I would do anything to see her smile. Even though that was far from my job as her bodyguard, I wanted to show her what happiness was. And perhaps that was my biggest mistake. But fuck it.

I avoided Jasmin as much as I could, but the truth was if I had to go through hell to free her, I would.

CHAPTER SEVENTEEN

Jasmin

I could hardly believe my eyes. From the high overlook where we were, I could see all of Chicago, lit up like a giant Christmas tree. The countless lights shone brightly, creating a vast sea of pure illumination.

"It's beautiful, isn't it?" Wolf stopped behind me. All the security guards stood a bit farther away, focused on taking in the view from their cars and watching the entrance we had passed through, even though they knew other guards were watching it.

"So beautiful." I smiled, enchanted.

I was extremely grateful when Wolf suggested the detour. I had been sad and downcast about the fiasco that had been the party, but now my mind was focused on capturing every bit of this small freedom.

I tightened my grip on the bottle as a cold breeze swept over me, making the hairs on my arms stand on end.

"Here." Wolf quickly took off his jacket and draped it over my shoulders. "Give me that bottle for a moment and wear it properly. You could catch a cold."

"Thank you," I said, slipping my arms through the sleeves. The scent of the man enveloped my senses and warmed my skin. I turned to face him. His proud gaze was now focused on the city lights, and it took him a moment to realize I was watching him.

"What is it?"

"I'm just... happy," I admitted, taking the bottle from his hands and taking a swig that burned down my throat. "I can hardly believe the unchanging and always reliable Wolf took a detour just to bring me here. It's a really lovely gesture. I almost start to think you like me, even just a little, despite avoiding me at all costs these last few days." I sighed. "I missed you." I didn't know why I said that; perhaps the drink was starting to take hold of my words, and the worst part was that I didn't regret it.

He chuckled softly, shoved his hands into his pockets, and leaned against the hood of the car right behind us. He watched the other guards in an animated conversation across the large courtyard where we were stopped. I followed him and leaned against his side.

"Running away from temptation is much easier than facing it. I'm weak in front of my own desires." He continued to gaze at the horizon, and a surge of euphoria coursed through my neck at the thought that he was also attracted to me. "In the end, maybe I don't hate you that much," he said without looking into my eyes.

"I'm glad to hear that." I smiled, with the bottle's neck held between my lips, and we fell into silence, admiring the view.

I never imagined that words spoken to the wind could move me so deeply.

"I wish we had more time here, but we have ten minutes left, at most."

"Ten minutes with you is all I need." I took another sip and saw the exact moment his eyes searched for mine, a slow smile forming on his lips.

"Do you even listen to what you say?"

"I do. I think you know me well enough to know that I say and do whatever comes to my mind."

"Ah, I know. How else would you have spun a man by the hair in the middle of a party?" Now it was my turn to laugh.

"That idiot!" I cursed. "Oh, Magnolia, my little sister. I hope there's some kind of celestial video editing in heaven that prevents her from seeing the shame he caused." I felt happy for, for the first time, being able to talk about her without that old tightness in my chest that drove me crazy. If she were really watching everything, I bet she'd be laughing right now.

"You could have warned me. In fact, you should have stopped dancing with that jerk immediately and left the rest to me." He turned to me, his irises now a darker shade in the dim light, but I could still feel the intensity radiating from him. "I would have handled it all without putting you at risk. Imagine if he retaliates? If he even brushes a finger against you..." he said seriously, his pupils widening as his rough voice softened. Wolf's eyes roamed down my face, stopping at my mouth. "We'd have a body to bury now."

"I know where we could bury him if the idea is still on the table," I joked, pulling another intense smile from him that swept across his focused face and reached his distinctive eyes.

"Don't give me ideas, Miss Cahill." He shook his head side to side.

"It's hard to talk to you when I'm looking into your eyes," I confessed softly, before taking another sip of the drink that warmed my chest even more. My arm brushed lightly against Wolf's, and a shiver ran up my legs, reaching my core.

"Is it because of the colors? Do they bother you?" The hint of insecurity I detected in his voice broke down any modesty I, still sane and completely in control of my faculties, was capable of maintaining.

I covered his hand with mine on the hood of the car and leaned in his direction. Anticipation surged as Wolf didn't pull away from my touch, and I was well aware that from the angle we were, none of the other guards could see us.

"Do they bother me? Oh, Wolf, you don't know anything." I bit my lips, staring at him. "Your blue irises are vibrant, marked with small darker flecks, like an open sea I would love to explore. I tightened my fingers around his, and I saw him swallow hard. "And the brown hue gives me the feeling of enjoying a sunset at dusk, warm, delicious, enticing." I tilted my head to the side, appreciating the sight of Wolf in front of me, so close, so warm, and as if sensing the exciting energy building between us, he turned our hands until his were surrounding mine. "It's hard to think straight when I'm in front of you like this, because all I want can't be described in words."

"And how can it be described?" The intensity of his voice washed over me, and I realized he was as captivated as I was.

"With gestures I wouldn't have the courage to express before finishing this bottle." I brought my free hand to his firm chest and felt him breathe more intensely.

"I think you've had too much to drink, Miss Cahill." He gave a sidelong smile and tried to reach for the bottle.

"Don't be a buzzkill." I took another sip. "Your eyes are beautiful, that's what I meant to say." I looked away suddenly, feeling my cheeks burn with embarrassment from the compliment.

Even though I had provoked Wolf with spicier comments before, that last one made me uncomfortable because I knew they weren't empty words; they were the absolute truth in my heart.

"Does anyone else in your family have eyes like this?" I tried to change the subject and thrilled when I realized he hadn't let go of my hand.

"No, just me," he began, and I could feel his eyes on me even though I wasn't looking at him. "I have two brothers, but we're completely different from each other. I'm adopted, so... there wouldn't be any physical traits, and I can guarantee that our personalities are quite unique."

"Wow, that's amazing!" I looked at him suddenly. "I've never met anyone who was adopted. Did your brothers handle your arrival well?"

"We're all adopted. We never had issues with it." I widened my eyes, enchanted by a story I barely knew. "I think we need to go." He glanced at his watch.

"Oh no, just a few more minutes. Please tell me about you and your brothers." Excitement washed over me. "I have so many questions."

"I'll only answer one." He pressed his lips together.

"How about we negotiate? I'll share my drink with you, and as a kind thank you, you answer me three questions?"

"That's an unfair deal. I can't drink while working." I moved a little closer to him until our bodies were touching.

"In that case, I'll change the terms." Wolf turned his face, coming within inches of my mouth, and I had to control myself to not leap on him right there. "You answer me four questions..."

"You increased it by one?" He widened his eyes with amusement.

"It's a better offer, after all." I shrugged. "If you answer four questions, I'll stop stealing your keys." He winked for a moment, and his eyes grew wide in a funny way when I held up the car key between my fingers... again.

"You..." He closed his fingers around the keyring. "You really need to stop doing that, light-fingered."

"Here goes the first question." I ignored the accusation in his gaze.

"Just three." I rolled my eyes.

Three was better than nothing, I guess.

"Where did you live before you were adopted?"

"In an orphanage. Next."

"Damn, I should have asked for details," I said regretfully, and he laughed. "Why did you end up in the orphanage? Did your parents pass away?" Wolf's eyes lost focus for a moment, looking at a point behind me, then he stared at the bright horizon in front of us. A strange spark flickered in the bitter smile he opened, and for a moment I regretted the question. "You don't have to answer; I can think of another question and..."

"They were drug addicts," he said, and I held my breath for a moment. "My mother was already using when she got pregnant with me. It was pure luck that I wasn't born with any imperfections. I lived with them until I was nine when my mother passed away and my father abandoned me completely. That's how I ended up in an orphanage." His voice remained steady, but I could swear there was more behind that story he was hiding, and I wasn't sure if I wanted to know whatever it was.

"I'm sorry," I said softly, holding back the knot in my throat as I imagined the childhood Wolf must have faced.

"You have one more question." I just didn't know if I wanted to ask it.

"Um...," I thought of something that wouldn't make me cry with his answer. "Do you and your brothers get along well, even though you're so different?"

"Very well." I felt the intense energy in his response. Maybe he was relieved with the sudden change of subject. "We've had each other's backs since the first time we met. There's nothing I wouldn't do for Ghost or Snake."

"One day you're going to tell me the meaning of those nicknames?"

"You need to earn the right to know." He stood up. "And now that you got your answers, don't you dare touch my keys again." He pointed at my face, and suddenly I wanted to ask a question. Even though I already knew the answer, I felt an absurd need to hear it from him.

"If I may advance a curiosity, what's your real name?"

"Are you sure you don't know the answer?" He narrowed his eyes and cornered me. Damn!

"Maybe I just want to hear it from you," I pleaded, biting my lower lip to gain his attention.

Wolf leaned in my direction. I held my breath when I saw his mouth move closer to mine and closed my eyes in anticipation until I felt his stubble graze my face as he pressed his lips to my ear.

"Christopher," he whispered, and my whole body responded to that rough, penetrating sound. "And now you're in debt to me, Miss Cahill." He pulled away a few inches and slid his thumb along my face, burning the skin where he touched. "We have to go."

"Christopher..." I let out softly, tasting the name on my lips and repeated it in my mind for the entire ride, unconsciously tattooing it in a very risky place. A place that man should keep his distance from.

In my heart.

Wolf

I TRIED TO FORGET THE sound of my name emerging from Jasmin's lips, but I couldn't. The memory of how she whispered each syllable in such a sensual, captivating, and provocative way was leaving me extremely excited. I needed to control myself before we reached our destination, and it was on that goal that I poured all my willpower.

My little thief spent the rest of the ride home sipping from the whiskey bottle, and I kept my eyes on her through the rearview mirror. I noticed she was quite tipsy when we arrived at the Hill House, and the young woman bolted from the car at an impressive speed. She was far too euphoric.

I grabbed her by the shoulders as she was about to rush past me like a jet.

"Come in, take a shower, and rest a bit, Miss Cahill. I'll handle this." I reached for the bottle, trying to take it from her, but the woman hugged it tightly.

"Nooooo, I'm not done yet," she complained. "I want to drink a little more. Maybe dance?"

And she ran off, stumbling toward the dance hall.

"This problem is yours, *Wolfie*..." I heard Lyon tease, causing a wave of laughter among the bodyguards.

"Go fuck yourself, Lyon."

"Good luck, sir." Shaw walked past me. "Magically, I'm off for the rest of the shift."

"And I'm in charge of the surveillance room," Ray added. "So it's all on you, Wolf." I raised my hand, ready to punch Ray, but the bastard quickly joined the other two and disappeared into the dark courtyard, laughing at my face.

"Let it GO! Let it Go!" I heard Jasmin's excited voice singing along the way and arrived just in time to see her sitting on the grass, struggling with her high-heeled sandals. "Can you help me?" She wiggled her feet in my direction, and I had to suppress a smile at the scene.

Her flushed cheeks were highlighted by the dress and red lipstick. I knelt in front of her and held one of her feet in my hands; the contact made the brief smile Jasmin wore turn into an intense, fiery look.

"I don't know how you manage to walk and dance in such thin things." I tried to focus on anything else.

"I should have shoved one of them in that idiot Ryan's face at the party."

"I can't encourage you, Miss, but I would have loved to see that scene." I joked, and she looked at me deeply, her two fireflies shining attentively, fixed on me.

Her hair, slightly tousled around her beautiful face, gave her the appearance of a fleeing nymph.

Holy shit!

Jasmin looked like a doll crafted by an angel's fingers. Delicate, sensual, incredibly attractive.

I slid my hand along the top of her foot and undid the straps of the heel, removing them, but for some reason, I couldn't pull my hand away from her leg and ended up sliding my fingers up her calf. Jasmin almost closed her eyes at the touch, and I needed all my willpower to control my movements on that soft skin.

I withdrew my hand and helped her stand up.

"Shall we dance?" she suddenly asked.

"What?"

"Dance... you know, move to the music." She started swaying her body from side to side. The movements were delicate and precise, even with the alcohol.

"I don't know about you, but I'm not hearing any music." I laughed and shoved my hands in my pockets. "I warned you to stop drinking."

"Tsk!" She rolled her eyes adorably. "The music is everywhere." She closed her eyes for a moment. "Listen... the wind rustling through the trees..."

"I still don't hear anything..."

"Close your eyes," she commanded, bringing her hand to my face, forcing me to shut them.

"Why would I do that?" I huffed between her fingers.

"Please... just close your eyes." Jasmin let go of my face and moved closer to me. She touched my hand with hers, keeping the bottle clutched in her other hand. My jacket covered part of her body, but her breasts, accentuated beneath the red fabric, remained visible, drawing my attention.

There was no way; I had to close my eyes.

"Now listen..." she softly requested. "The wind, the chirping of a cricket somewhere, our own breathing. It's a symphony."

She released my hand a second later and swayed gracefully, spinning around me. I followed her movements, frozen once again in front of that lady in red. She slipped my blazer off her arms and waved it in front of my eyes.

"Dance with me, Wolfie," she asked and ran toward the dance academy, disappearing into the darkness inside.

Go away...

Drag her with you and lock her in the room.

Go away, damn it!

My subconscious tried to warn me, but unlike what I should have done, I started walking toward her as if I were enchanted. A light sound echoed from the dance hall as I stopped at the door; the lights were off, but the moonlight streamed in through the two glass sides. Jasmin was near the speaker, choosing a song, and when she saw I was really there, she smiled widely.

Damn! I had been cursing myself since the day I kissed her in the kitchen. That was inconceivable, but it wouldn't leave my mind to the point where I almost had to relieve myself alone in the nights that followed, simply because every damn time I closed my eyes, my mind flew back to that kiss.

The sweet taste of her lips, the soft and painfully exciting sound she let escape every second, the tentative yet eager touch. Everything... and now I was once again alone with her, knowing there were no cameras inside made everything even more dangerous.

If I stepped into that hall, I was sure I would lose control.

"Aren't you coming, Wolf?" She stopped under the moonlight, and her blonde hair reflected, outlining her angelic face.

Jasmin looked like a magical creature, straight out of a parallel world, and before I realized it, she had entered the dance studio.

She began dancing around me, the long red dress swirling at her feet. Occasionally, her eyes caught mine amid the movements that left me frozen, and the spark of desire I saw there ignited the purest lust within me.

That woman was enchanting me with her movements, free, surrendered, delicious. My member throbbed hard as she bit her full lips and kept her bright eyes on mine, raising her hand to touch my chest, sliding it slowly over me, igniting a flame I couldn't control.

I grabbed her arm, preventing her from pulling away. She stopped eagerly, her uneven breathing excited me, and the barrier I had been maintaining to avoid touching her crumbled completely. I pulled Jasmin into my arms and pressed our lips together eagerly.

I insinuated my tongue between her soft lips, containing the urge to devour her all at once, as I had desired for all those damn days. She emitted a low, wavering sound as I explored the soft depth of her mouth. I caressed her tongue with mine with exaggerated slowness. Her arms wrapped around my neck, pulling me closer. The taste of whiskey filled my palate, infinitely more delicious than I remembered. I sucked and nibbled at her full lips, wrapping one hand around the back of her neck while the other encircled her waist.

The kiss became frantic, desperate, and before I realized it, I walked with her in my arms until we found a wall in the place. I pressed that little nymph's back against it and surrounded her with my body, storing every piece of that moment in my memory. The sounds she made as pleasure grew between us, the scent of jasmine on a sunny spring day that reverberated on her soft skin, the heat of her lips trying to reach mine, everything, absolutely everything.

I slid my hand down the side of her dress, feeling the curves accentuated with my fingertips, as I took everything she was willing to give me in a meeting of tongues, teeth, and sounds muffled by pure desire.

Damn, I was trembling, controlling the urge to take her right there.

I ran my fingers along the smooth fabric of the dress, going over her belly until I reached the base of her hard breasts, and a rough sound rose in my throat at the feeling of her swollen nipples. I closed my hand around one breast. My thumb brushed against the stiff nipple beneath the fabric, and she groaned deeply into my mouth.

"Jasmin, my angel," I whispered, and opened my eyes to see the expression on her face. My member throbbed painfully as I found her half-closed eyes and swollen mouth staring back at me. "You drive me crazy. If I don't stop now..."

"Don't stop," she pleaded in a languid, intoxicated voice. I tried to be rational, but having her there, so surrendered in my arms, swept away any sanity that was left.

Her delicate fingers tangled in my hair at the back of my neck, pulling me in for another kiss. I caressed the tip of her breast, pressing it between my fingers, eager to feel it in my mouth.

"Hummmmm!" she let out, spreading a burning fire throughout my body.

I kissed her fervently and descended my lips along her neck, licking and nibbling at her soft skin along the way. I lingered more at the curve of her neck while pinching the nipple with a bit more pressure, savoring the exciting sounds escaping her lips. I placed my mouth over the tip of her breast and bit it lightly through the thin fabric. Jasmin groaned loudly and tilted her head back.

I took my hand to the strap of her dress and slid it down until her round, rosy breasts were exposed before me. They were medium-sized and perky, not too big, not too small, but perfect for me.

I noticed when she brought her hand to her dress, trying to cover them.

"What do you think you're doing?" I panted into her mouth, holding her wrist and pinning it to the wall.

"They're not..." she gasped, and nearly closed her eyes as I brushed my thumb over her sensitive nipple, now bare for the first time. "So beautiful that I want to display them like this."

I smiled and ran my thumb up to her jawline, tracing the sweet, soft outline with my fingertips.

"You are a set of perfections, my angel," I assured, and descended my lips along her neck, passing over the valley of her breasts until I stopped with my lips right next to one of them. "Delicious." I closed my lips around the tip and sucked it lightly, teasing it between my teeth.

"Damn it!" she groaned loudly and clung to me even more. I sucked at the sides of her breast slowly while torturing the other with my free hand.

"Wolf..." She thrust her hips against my erection. "I'm burning."

"Me too, my Crystal." I wrapped one hand around her round bottom while sucking, biting, and licking her breasts.

Damn, the latent excitement consumed every inch of my body and mind. Jasmin panted and shuddered as the touches became more intense, and I felt I couldn't stop, unless she asked me to. How could I pull away from her now? The insane desire that filled us in that moment was irrational. I wanted to feel her at all costs.

She reached for the opening of my pants, trying to undo them, and I had to gather all my sanity to stop her.

"I can't do this, Jasmin." I kissed the corner of her mouth.

"There's nothing stopping you." She was trembling, hot as hell, and all I could think about was how wet she must be.

"Don't tempt me, girl." As if ready to confront me, she ground her hips against my erection. I took a deep breath, controlling myself to avoid fucking her right there as I wanted.

"That... would happen on the nightclub night if we had some time alone. I knew I wanted you the moment I saw you. I knew it would be you..." she bargained, but something in her statement sounded strange.

"You knew it would be me?"

"The first," she confessed, and it took a second for a hypothesis to race through my mind, freezing me in place.

I pulled away just enough to look into her eyes. Jasmin's face was flushed, her eyes sparkling with excitement.

"How?"

"The first person I would sleep with."

"What?" I exclaimed too loudly, my eyes widening. "You're a virgin, Jasmin?"

Suddenly, the music stopped, and all the lights in the mansion went out, plunging the place into complete darkness. I immediately lifted Jasmin's dress, helping her adjust it as best as I could.

"The lights went out." She looked into the darkness, alarmed.

"Looks like it. Has it happened before?" I asked, bringing my hand to my gun.

"Never."

"Damn!" I held my breath for a moment.

Something was wrong.

CHAPTER EIGHTEEN

Jasmin

A loud, hollow sound sliced through the night. Then another bang, and another.

"They're shooting!" Wolf said, bringing one hand to the communicator while the other shielded me protectively.

My heart leapt into my throat as the noises grew louder.

"Gather the entire team; we need to remove the Crystal. NOW," he shouted, drawing his weapon and turning to me. "They cut the lights; we only have access through the communicators. I've already alerted the team. We're taking you to the safe house. You know the address, right?" He was referring to a safe place where I was supposed to be taken in emergencies.

"Y-yes," I stammered. "My father made me memorize it since only he and I know where it is."

"Good." He placed his hands on my shoulders and looked at me seriously. "Stay behind me until we reach the door. After that, I want you by my side, crouched down. We're heading to the vehicles, understood?"

"Door, crouch, vehicle. Got it," I repeated. He studied me for another second, held my face in his hands, and planted a quick kiss on my forehead.

"I'll get you out of here safely." And the chaos began before I even had time to process everything that was happening between us.

Wolf grabbed his coat and threw it over my shoulders. He pulled out his weapon and started walking toward the door. I followed his lead, and as he surveyed every corner, more and more gunfire echoed from outside the gates.

"Wait," I suddenly said, quickly crouching down and grabbing the whiskey bottle. "Okay, we can go."

"What the hell are you taking that bottle for?" He looked at me wide-eyed as if I had a watermelon hanging from my neck.

"To defend myself, of course. And I plan to finish it if I survive." He growled something and pushed me behind him.

"Beta team, I need cover. We're at the dance academy, over," Wolf said into the communicator, and immediately two red lights appeared on the ground outside the academy. "Let's go." He positioned me by his side, crouched me down, wrapping one arm around my body while holding the weapon with the other.

I clutched the bottle and ran alongside him.

"What are those lights?" I yelled. The gunfire grew louder by the second. "Were they the good guys?"

"They're the snipers. They're part of my Beta team; don't worry about them. Focus on moving as fast as you can."

I kept running. The pebbles underfoot hurt my bare feet. We reached the car, and Shaw was already waiting for us.

"Get in quickly, miss." He opened the door and practically threw me into the car. I had never seen him act so swiftly.

Shaw and Wolf jumped in and locked the doors.

"Buckle up, Miss Cahill," Wolf instructed, and I hurried to put it on. "We have the Crystal. Let's get the hell out of here, NOW!" he shouted into the communicator, and the cars began to move one after the other.

"Beta team, is the road clear?" Wolf continued the conversation, and shortly after, he seemed to switch the communicator, now talking to other security members. "Lyon, do you read? Follow the standard road path; our snipers have secured the way."

"You can relax, Miss Cahill; the cars are bulletproof, as you can imagine," Shaw said, drawing his weapon. "HOLY SHIT!"

"Ahhh!" we screamed together when something hit our car window.

"Accelerate and make space. Come on, come on, come on!" Wolf gripped the wheel tightly. "Get ready, Shaw. I can't see the shooter in the mirrors." Shaw muttered something I couldn't catch and held the gun with both hands. "Now's a good time to give the new address, miss." He turned to me, and after blinking a couple of times, I dictated the address.

I could hardly believe that just minutes before, I had been experiencing one of the most thrilling and surprising moments of my life with the same man who was now driving like a madman, trying to save us from whoever it was.

Damn assassins!

We were speeding down the road so fast I could barely move, but as soon as we reached the main highway, we were enveloped by a suspicious calm.

"Did we shake them off?" Shaw looked back hopefully, and his dark eyes fell on me, frozen in the back seat.

"I highly doubt it," Wolf replied. "We're in three cars; I don't think they've lost sight of us." He activated the communicator once more. "Attention, team, stay alert. We could be ambushed at any moment."

Wolf's phone began to ring, and he tossed it into the back seat without taking his eyes off the road.

"It's your father," he said, and I grabbed the phone with trembling hands.

"Dad!" My voice came out high and shrill.

"Jasmin, are you okay? Did you get hurt? Are you safe yet?" He fired off a million questions, and my heart shattered at the deep desperation in his voice.

"I'll be fine, and I'm not hurt. We're heading to the South House," I referred to the secret location we had been keeping since Magnolia's death. A highly fortified house, resistant to major attacks, with two well-equipped panic rooms. If we could reach it, we wouldn't have to worry for a while.

"Put it on speaker; I need to talk to Wolf."

I did as he asked, and for the next few minutes, my father informed me that Wood was with him in his personal security and that we shouldn't worry about him. He also asked for details that could help identify and apprehend whoever was attacking the Hill House, only ending the call after Wolf assured him twice that he could keep me safe.

"I love you, daughter. We'll be together soon," my father said on speaker just before hanging up.

Wolf

I WAS ABOUT TO TEAR the wheel from my hands. This whole attack felt very suspicious. Why did they let us pass? Why didn't they follow us if the target was with us?

I glanced in the rearview mirror for a moment, and the petrified expression on Jasmin's face made me uneasy and concerned.

All this madness prevented me from processing what had happened between us. I was still digesting the information that Jasmin was a virgin when the gunfire started, and all my thoughts turned into a blur. My only goal was to protect her, and I needed to stay focused on that.

"We're almost there," I warned, recognizing one of the more remote neighborhoods away from the city center, where large mansions were scattered far apart.

We were in three cars. Lyon drove the first, while Shaw and I were in the second, and Ray in the third.

We made the turn and entered a deserted, very dark street. My level of attention doubled.

"Get ready; we're arriving." Hardly had I closed my lips when the loud sound of tires bursting filled the air. The car Lyon was in skidded over a sharp spike hidden in the dark street's protection.

I slammed on the brakes, the tires screeched loudly, and two of them hit the spike, bursting right after.

"Shit! Lyon? LYON?"

"Oh my God! WE'RE GOING TO DIE!" Jasmin screamed from the back seat.

"They'll have to get through me before they reach the lady; don't worry," Shaw responded bravely.

"I'm fine, but the car is done for," Lyon said on the communicator.

"Ray, back up and turn the car around," I ordered the only one of us still with four intact tires. "Get ready for..."

"Wolf! LOBO!" Shaw shouted, pointing to a tree where several men began to emerge, wearing dark clothing, with black masks and caps covering their faces.

One of them was carrying something small and silver in his hands and walked confidently toward our car.

"Can the car withstand any weapon?" Shaw asked, and when I realized what they were carrying, all the blood in my body rushed to my feet.

"The armored windows can withstand bullets of any caliber, but that thing in their hands is a fucking bomb."

For a moment, I imagined I was living some kind of nightmare, and if I didn't think fast, we'd all be dead.

Jasmin

"A BOMB..." I DIDN'T have the strength to speak. The men outside looked like they had stepped out of a horror movie, complete with Freddy Krueger and everything.

"They're getting closer," Shaw said, alert, as one of the men pressed a silver box against the car door.

"Quick, back up." Wolf unbuckled his seatbelt and jumped into the back seat with Shaw. "Buckle up," he warned the other bodyguard and did the same, activating the communicator afterward.

"Ray, Lyon, listen up. When they try to blow the side, the car will hold for a moment; it looks like a low-impact bomb, and then the door is likely to give way. Those bastards will be far enough away not to get hit by the explosion, and we'll use that to our advantage. Lyon, get out of the vehicle and cover us; we'll exit through the left side. We'll need to shoot it out with those bastards to reach Ray's car and get the hell out of here, copy?" he spoke quickly and without pause.

Anxiety suddenly hit me. This was real; we were truly surrounded by a bunch of men who had only one goal: to kill me.

"Jasmin, stay low and do not move away from me under any circumstances. I will get you out of here," Wolf stated with a conviction that almost made me believe him, but the odds didn't seem in our favor. "Hold on. As soon as the bomb explodes, we'll move."

It didn't take long for a loud, excruciating sound to fill my ears, and I found myself screaming as the car was hit by the explosion, lifting the right wheels off the ground before crashing down again with a bang. We went up and down like on a death roller coaster; luckily, the seatbelts held enough.

"Let's go!" Wolf shouted, already opening the door, and as soon as we put our feet outside, they began to shoot.

I held the whiskey bottle tightly in my hand and crouched down as Wolf ordered. I could have panicked at that moment, cried, rolled on the ground, begged for my life, but none of that would help, and I was well aware of it.

I had spent a large part of my life risking being murdered, so this was much more than a battle. It was the war that would be the turning point between living and dying. And I was very inclined to keep breathing.

We needed to confront them to get out of there, so I pushed the fear I felt down under the rug and crouched behind the car's metal.

There was a lot of smoke from the bomb, and I could only see shadows rushing toward us. That's when it happened.

Lyon started shooting and managed to reach our car, joining Wolf, who was aiming, shooting, and hitting with incredible ease despite the obstacles in the way. His aim was surreal in its perfection. He took them down one by one while keeping me so close I could feel the jolt of the gun against his hard body.

"Let's go!" he shouted, and we started running toward Ray's car, which was still locked and intact. The bodyguard then got out of the vehicle and began shooting at everything that moved behind us, just like Wolf, Shaw, and Lyon.

The adrenaline didn't even let me think straight; all I wanted was to get to that car. We were almost there when we were surprised by two men. Wolf shot one of them, causing him to fall to the ground, and did the same with the other, hitting his hand and knocking the crazy man's weapon away, but the second man wasn't willing to give up and jumped on him, engaging in a hand-to-hand struggle that pulled him away from me.

I staggered, trying to hold onto him. A strange sting took over the side of my face, but I didn't even have time to think much about that sharp pain. The bodyguards were focused on shooting at the crowd, which seemed to grow by the second. Bullets ricocheted off the car's metal, and I felt completely lost.

"SHIT!" Wolf roared and managed to punch the man. He grabbed the gun and shot twice at the enemy. I blinked, startled.

My God!

He must have killed about five people there, and I wouldn't be hypocritical enough to say I was upset. I wanted to get out alive, just as much as I wanted my bodyguards to come through unscathed.

"Jasmin!" He wrapped his arms around my waist and pulled me close. "Keep moving. Let's go."

We ran, and in less than a meter, they were surrounding us again, like ants that never stopped appearing. Wolf spun me around in his arms and placed me behind him, but there was nowhere to hide; we were easy targets, camouflaged only by the thick smoke around us.

Wolf focused alongside Shaw and Lyon, even Ray at a distance, trying to take out the new targets before we were hit. I stayed behind the barrier they created, about to run when a voice called my name from right behind me.

"Jasmin Cahill." I turned immediately and saw a figure emerging from the smoke. The man wore a dark hood that obscured his face.

"Who are you?" I shouted over the loud gunfire, looking at his hands, pale as a corpse, and pure fear filled me when I saw the gleaming dagger he held tightly.

"A familiar face. Don't you remember me?" He approached far too quickly, and all I could think was that if I stayed there, he would kill me while my bodyguards tried to eliminate the men shooting at us.

"Fates are meant to be accepted. There's no way to..."

"GET LOST, YOU CRAZY BASTARD!" I threw the whiskey bottle at him with all my strength, satisfied when it hit the middle of his forehead, causing him to stagger and disappear into the smoke for a moment.

Wolf pulled me by the hand, keeping all his attention on the men who continued shooting.

"Let's go!" Lyon shouted, covering our backs.

"They're closing in!" Shaw yelled, and Wolf enveloped me with his arms, hugging me to the side as we started to run toward Ray's car.

We all got into the vehicle. Wolf took the wheel and accelerated hard, screeching the tires as the men began to close in again, and we sped away while being shot at.

The car nearly flew down the highway while I could barely breathe.

"We were ambushed," he concluded, slamming on the gas and checking the rearview mirrors every second. "Who else knew about that house, Jasmin?" At this point, he had given up calling me Miss Cahill.

"Only me, my father, and Aunt Claire, who was the one who recommended the house for us to buy and..." Suddenly, an idea came to mind. "Oh, crap, quick, get rid of the communicators." Shaw and Lyon stared at me with confused expressions. "WHY ARE YOU STARING AT ME? Hurry, they can be traced!" I shouted, frantic.

Quickly, each of them yanked off their work gear and handed it to me, along with Wolf's phone.

"I'm sorry about this." I handed the bundle to Ray. "Throw it out the window."

"Yes, ma'am."

"We need to get rid of this car too. Even though only your father has the access to track it, we have to consider the possibility of an invasion within Hill and Cahill," Wolf added, exasperated as he exhaled.

"What happened back there, Jasmin?" Lyon asked. "I saw you throw that bottle at someone."

"A weird guy tried to approach me, and I threw the bottle at him."

"What weird guy?" Wolf questioned, his eyes briefly scanning me through the rearview mirror.

"The one in the hood with the silver knife in his hands. He came with some weird talk about being a familiar face and that fates are meant to be accepted... oh my God!" I gasped, finally processing what the idiot had said. Putting his words together with the object in his hand, it could only be one person. "It was the man who killed my sister." A strong wave of nausea hit me, and I slumped against the seat.

"Shit, shit, shit!" Wolf punched the steering wheel three times. "I can't believe he was there, and I didn't see him." He punched the wheel again. "I've been hunting that bastard for years."

"At least I managed to hit him with a bottle," I said weakly.

"Whoa!" Shaw turned to me. "You were phenomenal."

Wolf remained silent for the next 15 minutes of the drive. He entered a strange, dark neighborhood and parked the car in a very short alley.

"Get out of the car and stay by the sides of the buildings." We got out silently. Wolf guided us through a dark alley, the buildings in that neighborhood were small, no more than three or four stories high, with red brick walls and some cars parked in garages, just like the deserted streets parallel to the alley we were crossing.

"Jasmin." Wolf turned to me too quickly and held my shoulders.

"What is it?" He studied my face with a worried expression, but soon his attention shifted to my ears.

"Your earrings; there's a tracker in them." My eyes widened, and I froze instantly. "We need to take them off, now." He hurried to unscrew one of the earrings.

"What the hell!" I complained as I took off the earrings. "Who had the brilliant idea to give me such a rare piece of jewelry with a tracker in it?" I could swear Dad convinced Aunt Claire to do that.

I found myself staring at the two black pearls in my palm, a tightness forming in my chest.

"They can find you with that shit." He extended his hand for me to give them to him and threw the earrings across the street. "Now we can go."

We resumed our run, and I didn't even have time to complain about the lost pearls. Wolf kept me pressed against his body and stopped next to a car. He looked around and pulled a key from his pocket.

"What are you doing?" I whispered when I saw him force the car's door handle.

"Stealing this vehicle; any objections?" he said seriously, without looking me in the eye.

"None." I swallowed hard.

We got into the vehicle moments later, and no one commented on the fact that we had gone from victims to thieves in the blink of an eye.

We drove through the night, now free from anything that could track us.

"Shit!" Wolf groaned a while later, bringing his hand to his shoulder.

"Damn it, you're hurt." Lyon, who was in the front seat, noticed what none of us had realized.

There was a tear in Wolf's shirt at shoulder height. My heart raced at once, and I leaned in, sticking my head between the seats.

"You're injured!" My voice came out high-pitched.

"It's nothing; just a scratch." He didn't even look at the wound that was staining his black shirt.

"It could get infected, Wolf, and if you—"

"Miss Cahill, we need to get you out of here. Focus on staying safe," he interrupted me. I could tell he was too nervous, so I held back, even though I wanted to jump over the seats and check if the wound was deep.

We stopped almost an hour later on a highway, where only trucks zipped past us with a loud, swift whistle. Wolf parked near a gas station.

"What are we going to do now?" Lyon asked, and Wolf exhaled forcefully.

"Someone among us is betraying us," he revealed, and a murmur reverberated through the car.

"How can you be sure?" Shaw inquired.

"There's no way anyone from outside knew about the house we were heading to. Think about it." Wolf gripped the steering wheel tightly. "The gunfire at Hill House forced us to leave in a hurry with Miss Cahill, but no one came after us when we fled."

"But they were waiting for us at the new location," Lyon added.

"Exactly. They didn't track us there. They already knew the location."

"They used a bait to draw us out of Hill House," Ray concluded, surprised.

"And we fell for it like idiots." Wolf turned to the back seat. "But now we won't let them manipulate us. Lyon, take the wheel and find Cahill. Tell him I'll take Miss Jasmin to a safe place. Don't reveal our suspicion; just ask him to wait. I'll contact him soon with more information. We need to find out who the bastard who betrayed us is. There are so many suspects that we can't trust anyone outside this vehicle."

"No way!" Lyon interjected. "We're going with you. You can't handle them all alone. What if they corner you? You'll be dead before dawn."

"Lyon is right, sir," Shaw chimed in.

"Either we survive together, or we die together," Ray added, and Shaw groaned, anxious.

"I appreciate the support, but believe me when I say it'll be easier to get her to safety alone, but I need you for the rest of the plan." They exchanged glances, and it was clear they were not satisfied with that. "You need to trust me, and I have no choice but to do the same with you."

"Okay," Lyon huffed. "Count on us, and make sure to come back safe with Miss Cahill." Wolf nodded, his expression softening.

"How will you get her to another place if we keep the car?" Shaw narrowed his eyes at Wolf.

"I have a plan," he said, and a few minutes later, I saw my bodyguards driving away in a small, stolen car while Wolf and I headed toward the gas station.

We went around the back of the place when a light rain began to fall, and I was surprised to see several motorcycles piled up behind the station. There was a man standing under a very old awning, wearing the place's uniform, seemingly keeping watch over both the station and the bikes. Upon seeing us, he gave a short wave to Wolf, who returned it. It seemed they knew each other.

My bodyguard began inspecting each motorcycle for something.

"Do you have a bike here?" I scanned the motorcycles, which looked more like an illegal chop shop.

"I have several bikes at places like this, scattered across the state. I need to be prepared for moments like this." He stopped next to a classic black Harley Davidson, still very imposing.

Two helmets were attached to the side of the bike. He detached one and handed it to me just as the rain started to fall harder.

"I'll take you to a cabin a bit far from here, but it will ensure our safety until I can move you somewhere else tomorrow." He mounted the wide bike, which easily accommodated his body. I put on the helmet but couldn't fasten it. "I'll help you with that." He pulled me close and tied the helmet quickly. He held my hand and supported me as I climbed onto his bike. "Hold on to me like this." He wrapped my arms around his torso. "Don't let go for anything, understand?"

"Don't worry; I won't let go." That was an undeniable truth. I hugged him tighter. I was very scared of what could happen, but when Wolf started the bike and we rode into the cold rain, I knew that even if the world came crashing down around us, he would still keep me safe under his protection.

CHAPTER NINETEEN

Jasmin

We took the road for a long time. The rain intensified, and the drops, aggressive and thick, soaked us from head to toe, but we couldn't stop. My hand, like my entire body, was very cold, but I held firmly around Wolf's waist as he rode as fast as he could, navigating winding curves with skilled control. It felt as if the motorcycle was an extension of his body.

After a while, my chin began to shake uncontrollably, and my body trembled without control. We climbed a steep road where the fog grew denser, and the few lights turned the road into an endless tunnel.

We turned onto a gravel street, hidden among a cluster of trees, and it wasn't long before a small wooden cabin with triangular walls appeared on the cloudy horizon.

Wolf stopped the motorcycle at the cabin's small entrance, which had no more than a window and a door.

"Can you get off?" he asked as he parked.

"I think my legs have frozen." I forced myself to swing my legs over the seat. Wolf extended his hand, gently, keeping the balance of the motorcycle with his own legs as he helped me down.

We rushed into the cabin, and I wasn't surprised to find it was as small inside as it appeared outside. There was no more than a single bed, a back door that I imagined led to the bathroom, and a cabinet next to an old stove, all in the same room.

I immediately took off Wolf's blazer to get rid of the soaked fabric.

There was a strange smell in the air, as if the house had been closed up for a long, long time. I shivered when a cold breeze entered through the door with Wolf. My teeth were chattering.

Wolf approached me and touched my jaw with his fingertips until our eyes met.

"You need to take a hot shower." He observed my face carefully. A shadow crossed his colorful irises and put me on alert.

"What's wrong?" I raised my fingers to my face and felt a sting as soon as I touched the skin below my cheek. "Ow!"

"Don't touch it. You're hurt." The intense look on his face turned serious, with a contained anger that frightened me. "Get in the shower; I keep some spare clothes here, and I'll find something warm for you to wear. It's not ideal, but it will do for now."

"A-and you?" I trembled. "You need to take a shower too and get rid of those wet clothes."

"You go first; I'm fine," he assured, starting to rummage through the only piece of furniture in the place, besides the small cabinet under the stove. "Here." He handed me a towel.

I walked to the bathroom, unsure if my legs would carry me there. No matter how hard I tried, I couldn't stop trembling. The dress felt as if it had become part of my skin, clinging tightly. I entered the bathroom, which was just as small as the rest of the cabin, with a sink, a toilet, and a shower, without a box or any partition.

The window, which was actually a casement, at least gave me some peace of mind. No one could get in through there. I turned on the shower and felt my skin burn from the contact of the water, which, thank God, was indeed hot. Soon the sensation gave way to some relaxation, but I didn't linger. I knew Wolf would only shower when I came out, and he was just as wet, if not more, than I was.

I turned off the shower a few minutes later and stepped out of the bathroom wrapped in the towel Wolf had given me. As soon as I opened the door, I noticed the cabin itself was very cold, and the storm outside wasn't helping at all.

"I set aside some pants, a shirt, and... some underwear if you want to use them." I nearly fell backward when I saw Wolf wrapped in a towel that covered only his waist. "You can probably guess I don't have any panties around here."

Holy muscle definition, he could have my panties anytime he wanted... I thought, but I held back in front of the wave patterns marked on his chest. Wolf was strong, very strong. His fair skin contrasted with the scars scattered across his body, and for a moment, I felt euphoric to have that man there with me, alone.

A fleeting second that went from heaven to hell when I saw the cut on the side of his arm.

"Wolf..." I called, bringing my hand to my mouth. A mix of strange feelings hit me upon seeing him hurt. I wanted to be able to protect him, just as he seemed willing to give his life to keep me safe.

"It's not as bad as it looks; don't worry." He tried to smile when he saw my frightened expression, but I could feel the tension in every word he spoke. Wolf handed me the clothes, and I held them without taking my eyes off the wound. I felt extremely guilty. "I'm going to take a shower. I locked the door; don't you dare come near it. If you hear anything strange, let me know immediately. I won't take long."

I dressed in the clothes, which were indeed warm and completely black, apparently like all of Wolf's looks.

I surveyed the cabin and curled up on the bed for the minutes that passed. The adrenaline was starting to leave my body when Wolf came out of the bathroom already dressed, his damp hair falling on his forehead and wearing an outfit similar to mine, but instead of a shirt, he wore a T-shirt that allowed me to see the wound better.

"I have a first-aid kit here somewhere," he said, without looking me in the eyes, and I waited patiently as he rummaged through the cabinet until he pulled out a small white box with red edges.

I followed him with my eyes as the man, who seemed even bigger in that small room, walked toward me. He sat on the bed, which creaked loudly in discontent.

"Let me see it." He touched my jaw and turned my face toward him. His eyes scanned my skin, inch by inch, pouring all his attention there. I observed his bicolored eyes closely and only then noticed some brown reflections mixing with the blue iris. My heart, which never seemed to stay still, began to race as Wolf's thumb brushed against my sensitive skin. "It's superficial," he said with relief. "I'll clean the wound and put a bandage on it, okay?" I nodded in confirmation.

I spent the next few minutes enjoying his closeness, feeling his wavering breath warm my face more than any blanket could. After he finished cleaning the wound, Wolf carefully applied the bandage and turned to his own arm.

"I'll do this." I touched his hand, stopping him from continuing, and Wolf looked at me warily.

"Do you know how to care for a wound?"

"I can draft a scientific project, and you really think I can't handle a bandage?" I smiled. "Trust me."

I touched his arm gently. The wound was quite red. It looked like it had been grazed by a bullet, and if we went to the hospital, Wolf would definitely get at least one stitch there. The feeling of guilt filled me again.

"I'm so sorry," I said, starting to clean the area.

"It doesn't hurt." He misunderstood.

"I'm apologizing for getting you hurt. I'm so sorry." I exhaled sadly. "If I hadn't insisted on leaving home, maybe none of this would have happened."

"It wasn't your fault, Jas," he said in the same tone he used with me back in the academy, hours earlier. "We weren't ambushed at the party."

"But maybe we would have been. You changed the route at the last minute to take me to the viewpoint. That might be why they didn't manage to ambush us before."

"Ouch!" he complained as I cleaned more deeply.

"Sorry."

"I don't think you're right," he commented finally. "We fell into an ambush the minute we decided to get you out of Hill House. I should have seen that coming."

"If I were you, I'd process who sold you the crystal ball." I finished cleaning and prepared the bandage.

"How?"

"Well, for it to be your fault, you'd need to have predicted that it was just bait to get us out of there. So I imagine you have a crystal ball; otherwise, it seems like no one here is to blame except for those trying to kill me." Wolf smirked slightly, but it didn't last, and suddenly I remembered something that hadn't seemed so important in the chaos but now... "Wolf..."

"Yes?"

"That man, the one I hit with the bottle, could he really be Magnolia's murderer?" He pressed his lips together and looked at me seriously. I had the impression Wolf turned a bit paler at the question.

He breathed loudly and averted his gaze to the mattress. I knew then that something was wrong.

"What is it? Please don't hide anything from me; I need to know." He raised his eyes to mine, and his hand touched mine, as if preparing me for very bad news.

"I know who killed your sister." I held my breath at the honest, direct answer. "And from what you told me, he was indeed the one who was there. That bastard is a hired killer," he revealed slowly. "Your father and I agreed not to tell you anything about it so you could live your life without major worries while we hunted him down."

"So he was there the night of the ball," I said, somewhat lost, recalling the man who accidentally bumped into Magnolia.

"Yes, he was the one who attacked her." All the blood in my body chilled quickly, causing a sudden vertigo. I had to blink hard to absorb that information.

"He stabbed her and intended to kill me the same way." My eyes misted with a mix of hatred, anger, and disbelief. "What kind of sadist does that?"

"There's more to this story that you don't know." He caressed my fingers in circular motions, as if trying to calm me. "Your father decided it was best this way, but now, given everything that's happening, I see no other option but to tell you how your sister died."

I fell silent as Wolf explained things I never thought could escape action and suspense films. A knife soaked in poison? No... that couldn't be real.

"My sister was poisoned? Is that why she died so quickly after the cut?" Wolf confirmed, and I stared at a fixed point on the mattress. "My father had no right to deprive me of information like this." I still felt too numb to scream.

"I'm sorry." His voice reached my subconscious, and I forced myself to look at him. "It's important that you understand the need to keep your distance from that monster. He won't try to shoot you; he'll try to stab you. It's like a fetish, stronger than anything."

"If he had approached me, I would be dead by now." My voice revealed the terror that enveloped me as I absorbed all that news.

"I won't let anything bad happen to you." He held my hands between his. "We'll get him before that."

"How do you know so much about him?" The question caught him off guard, and it took a moment before he began to speak.

"After I was adopted by my father, I spent a good three years adapting, and one day I decided to run away." I nodded, following the story. "I wandered the streets for a while and made a great friend. Adrian worked with small deliveries of strange documents for an even stranger man and ended up introducing me to him."

"It was..."

"Naish!" He clenched his jaw and lowered his eyes to our joined hands. "I even made some deliveries with him. I saw no harm in it; after all, they were just papers. After a while, my father found me, and we went back home. Holder, being the good man he is, wanted to help me find Adrian and give him a decent job, but we searched the whole city without finding him. I thought I'd never see him again, but two years later, I accidentally ran into him. And I was truly happy. I told him about the job opportunity my father could arrange for him, but Adrian said he had gotten a spot on Naish's team and that things would get better. I didn't understand what that meant and left after finding out how to contact him if I needed to."

He barely paused for breath, and with each new word, I felt his breathing get heavier, as if that memory was too painful.

"We kept meeting, and I got even closer to Adrian, considering him a great friend. One day he approached me looking downcast, which struck me as very strange. His high spirits were one of his main traits, no matter what was going on. — He gave a vacant smile. — He said he had gotten the chance to prove he could work for Naish and that he would need someone he could trust by his side. According to him, it was a test, and he needed to pass it to join the team, which paid very well and would turn his life around. I, having already found my own path to freedom, didn't hesitate to offer my help.

"What did you need to do?"

"When I accepted, I thought I just needed to stay by his side," he revealed. "I ended up in the North Zone of the city, in a crumbling abandoned building. Adrian was very nervous. We went up to the fourth floor, where two armed men were waiting for us, but before we reached them, Adrian turned to me and asked me to leave as quickly as possible."

"He took you there just to send you away?"

"Actually, when I questioned him, he admitted that his mission was me."

"You?" My voice came out sharp.

"Yes. Naish was already part of a powerful gang of hitmen, but he still didn't have high resources, and after Adrian discovered who my father was, he mentioned it to the man, who asked for proof that Adrian could indeed work for him. — I stared at him, disbelief flooding through me. — Adrian needed to take me there, where they would kidnap me and demand a good sum from my father."

"What a scummy traitor!" I cursed.

"Adrian was a good person, Jas, but he made bad choices."

"That turned him into a horrible person. You wanted to help the idiot," I continued complaining, "but he preferred to betray you."

"In the end, he didn't succeed." He shrugged.

"What happened next?"

"I freaked out when I saw what he intended to do. Adrian pulled a small gun from his waist and tried to intimidate me into leaving. He apologized, said he regretted bringing me there. He was distraught. And that's when I realized that life had changed him to the point where he lost the ability to see the fine line between being human and becoming a monster." His thumb began to circle within my palm. "For some reason, I couldn't leave him there. I stayed, trying to convince him to come away with me. I told him again that my father would employ him, but the word of an 18-year-old didn't hold much weight, and in a way, he had gone down a path of no return."

Wolf's eyes wandered for a moment.

"In the end, I promised I would get out of there as quickly as possible. Adrian left me on the stairs and went to meet the men. He said he would make up some excuse and would give me cover to escape safely, but I couldn't leave. I saw Adrian start talking to the men and explaining himself. I know I should have been furious with the guy for using me as a bargaining chip, but I couldn't. I was so young at the time, and knowing what Adrian went through on the streets, I felt something for him that bordered on brotherly love," he admitted. "They talked for a brief moment, and only then did Naish emerge from the shadows. He had been hiding, watching everything. He called Adrian until my friend approached the bastard. He said he needed the strongest and that Adrian was nothing more than a useless stone in his shoe." He exhaled. "Then he stabbed him."

"He..."

"Killed him in a matter of minutes."

"My God!" I gasped.

"I was in shock for less than a moment until the rage blinded me. I remember very little after that. I left the stairs and grabbed Adrian's gun. I shot at the two men I saw when I arrived, and Naish used Adrian's body to shield himself from the bullets, but I managed to hit his knee just before two more of his goons arrived. I was shot right here," he placed his hand on the side of his back. I couldn't help but lift the hem of his shirt to see the rounded scar embedded in his fair skin.

"I had to flee to survive, but before I got out of there, I heard that monster scream that I would pay for it. I blinked, feeling a strange burning in my chest with all that story. "I was hospitalized for a long time and almost died. My father pulled every string he had with the police and government agencies, but there was no sign of the man. Only then did we discover that no one had ever seen Naish and survived to tell the tale. He was much more powerful than we imagined, and the end of everyone who worked for him and quits is certain death. But I had seen him and made a composite sketch that, in the end, came to nothing."

"And he's been out there ever since, killing people for money."

"He kills for pleasure, Jas. That's the difference. I believe that today he's so rich that money doesn't make the slightest difference."

"I'm so sorry for your friend."

"You are?"

"No, I lied." I wrinkled my nose. "He almost caused your death; sorry if I'm not inclined to like him."

"Adrian chose his own path, but I can assure you he had a good heart that was deceived." I nodded. "Naish is poisonous, cunning, and knows how to identify an easy prey. And that bastard's time is coming."

"I hope they catch this killer soon. He needs to pay for everything he's done and all the lives he's taken." I sniffled, and only then did I realize that a few tears had rolled down my face, overwhelming my soul with sadness at everything that was happening.

Wolf reached out and caught one of my tears with the tips of his fingers.

"Please don't cry," he pleaded. "It hurts to see you cry. I promise I'll keep you safe."

"I know you will." I tried to sound confident.

"Speaking of which..." He got up from the bed and spread a blanket over me.

"Listen, Jasmin... there are two important things I want to talk to you about, and I need you to pay close attention." He sat down in front of me and looked into my eyes.

There were so many conflicting feelings dancing in his unique irises that I felt momentarily confused.

"From what you told me, the only ones who knew about that house were you, your father, and the senator, right?" I nodded in confirmation. "Do you think that information could have leaked somehow?"

"I wouldn't know how. That house was bought under a ghost name, exclusively to avoid any connection to us." I stared at my hands on the blanket. "But I can't guarantee that. Maybe there's someone infiltrated. Foster, that idiot from the elevator, has access to all the buying and selling plans of the company, as well as the expenses. Maybe he somehow connected the purchase to the company. I don't even know if that makes sense. It's just one of the thousand suspects swirling in my mind." My eyes wandered for a moment, filled with pure indignation when I remembered my precious pair of black pearls. "How could my father put a tracker in my earrings?" I shook my head.

"Your father was just worried about you."

"But he could have at least warned me," I exclaimed.

"Would you have used it if you had known?" He raised an eyebrow and looked at me.

"Maybe not," I said, disheartened by that truth. "I'm tired; I just want this to be over soon."

"Soon, one way or another, we'll know who's behind this."

I opened my lips to express how much I was waiting for that moment, but before I could say anything, my stomach growled, and I nearly burst into flames from embarrassment.

"Yeah... I get hungry when I'm nervous."

"Let's set that aside for now," he said, a smile breaking at the corner of his lips as he stood up. "I'm sorry, but here we only have canned food, at least until tomorrow. I plan to get you out of here to a safer place." He rummaged through the cabinets and returned with two cans of sausages.

"Are they even edible?" I questioned, looking at the reddish, damp cubes inside the can.

"They'll keep you going until tomorrow. I promise I can get something better first thing in the morning." Wolf took his can to the kitchen, where he had placed his weapon, and he looked at it as if it were his worst enemy.

"You look like you're plotting the end of the world." I chewed on one of my sausages, which tasted more like vinegar than anything, but it would suffice. "What are you thinking?" He clenched his fist and exhaled, his expression becoming more serious.

"If Naish saw me at any point, if he knows I'm the one protecting you, he won't stop until he's torn your legs off," he said, and I flinched in fear.

He stabbed my sister and was about to do the same to me. This was terrifying, surreal, and very, very painful.

"I should have shoved that bottle down his throat," I cursed, regretful, staring at the dirt floor and startled when a low laugh echoed through the place.

Wolf came over to me.

"Only you could make me smile in the midst of all this chaos," he commented. "I can't believe you actually hit him on the forehead. Good aim, Miss Cahill."

"It was nothing." I ran a hand through my damp hair. Wolf sat back on the bed in front of me.

"I said I had two important things to tell you..."

"I think I lost count after you told me that whole story." I pressed my lips together. "I thought you had already shared both."

"No, there's still one left."

"What is it?" I startled and straightened my posture.

"Listen... about what happened at the dance academy." My face heated the instant Wolf opened his mouth.

"I thought you'd pretend that never happened."

"I would never do such a thing," he assured, offended. "It was wrong. Very wrong," he repeated, "but it happened, and... it was very good. That's why I ended up losing control." My whole body burned at that brief affirmation. So he liked it? "I shouldn't have let myself get carried away, especially since I was hired to protect you, not to..."

"Take my virginity?" Before I knew it, the words slipped out, and it was Wolf's turn to nearly choke on his own words.

"Uh, well..." He stood up abruptly. "I just want you to know I won't cross that line again." He grabbed an extra blanket from the closet and threw it on the floor, along with an old pillow I had seen lying in a corner. "You take the bed; I'll sleep on the floor."

I thought about screaming that all I wanted was for his hands to glide over my body once more, but I held back. I could spend the night telling Wolf I wanted to feel him more than anything, but I knew it would do no good. That man was quite resolute when he wanted to be.

"That's fine." I was so embarrassed that I curled under the blanket he had given me as soon as I finished the weird sausages.

Wolf turned off the only light in the room, and we were enveloped by darkness. My thoughts began to fly between everything that had happened that day, and I didn't realize I was trembling again until the cold started to bother me severely. I hugged myself tighter in the blanket, but the lack of heating in the cabin didn't help at all. I began to chatter my teeth and even thought I would spend the night awake, freezing, when suddenly I felt another blanket being tossed over me.

I pulled my head out from under the covers just in time to see Wolf standing next to my bed.

"You're going to end up with pneumonia; take this blanket." And he turned his back to me, about to lie back down on the floor, now without a blanket.

I grabbed his wrist before he could move away.

"Lie down here with me," I offered, and he shook his head, declining.

"I'm fine."

"You're not." I pushed the blankets aside. "If you lie down here, we'll both stay warm. Human heat, have you heard of it?" I teased.

"There are certain types of heat that are better avoided," he grumbled.

"Oh, is that so?" He placed his hand on his hip while watching me kick the covers off. "Then we'll freeze together. They'll find our bodies and say we were a passionate couple; we'll go down in history. We'll be more famous than Rose and Jack." A cold breeze touched my skin, and I immediately shrank. "How did she manage to leave the poor guy in the water? Poor thing; did you know they say Jack could have climbed onto the door with Rose and that both would have survived if that had happened? I wonder, maybe if they had taken turns..."

"What the hell are you talking about?"

"About Titanic, of course." My teeth chattered, and Wolf rolled his eyes. "So, what's it going to be?"

I watched the huge man make the bed creak and sink under the weight of his body as he finally joined me. He threw the blankets over us, and it wasn't long before the warmth enveloped us through the fabric.

Wolf kept as far away from me as he could, but the tiny bed didn't help at all. I leaned against the wall and faced him, staring at his silhouette in the darkness.

The day had been too tumultuous. In one single night, I hit my sister's ex, was attacked in my own home, and nearly died at the hands of the same man who took Magnolia's life. Not to mention the details, like fleeing barefoot on a motorcycle in the midst of a storm. Then there was all the uncertainty weighing on me about the next day.

I was freaking out inside, and even though I didn't want to admit it, I felt a lot of fear. I started to warm up under the blankets, but the shivering in my body only intensified as the harsh reality embraced me.

"What's wrong?" Wolf placed his hand on my shoulder. "You're shaking; are you still cold?"

"No, I'm warm."

"Then what is it?" My lips trembled, and I struggled to speak.

"I'm scared," I admitted. "Very scared," I said in a whisper, surprised by Wolf's arms wrapping around me gently, pulling me to his chest. Before I knew it, I was lying on his shoulder, trembling.

"Stay calm, Jas," he whispered into my hair. His arms pressed me against him with a firmness and tenderness that rocked my heart. "We'll get through this; trust me."

He held me until the tremors began to dissipate little by little.

"Ask me one of your questions," he suddenly encouraged, trying to distract me. "I know you have an arsenal of them stored up right here." He tapped the middle of my forehead with his fingertips, and I nestled further into his arms.

"Actually, I do have questions," I admitted.

"What do you want to know?" he said eagerly, impressing me more and more.

"Is this cabin yours or Holder Security's?"

"Mine. I keep it for cases like yours." I don't know why the thought of Wolf bringing another woman to that small, cold cabin infuriated me.

"Have you brought other women here?" I hated the strange, choked sound my voice took on.

"Goodnight, Miss Cahill." He brought his hand to my eyes, closing them. I held his wrist with my hand.

"Christopher..." I whispered his name, and I felt the man stiffen over the bed. "It's a beautiful name. Do you know the meaning?"

"I know my mother probably wasn't thinking of one when she chose it, so I don't dwell on that." He held my hand between his and kept them together, connected.

"My name and my sister's were chosen because they are names of flowers my mother loved. Jasmin means very fragrant flower," I babbled, distracting myself from the fear and the tremors that still lingered.

"You don't have a single strand of hair that resembles your father's. I can only imagine you're like your mother," he said softly, tracing circular motions with his thumb on my wrist.

"I'm a copy of my mother," I confirmed.

"Then she must have been fascinating." I pondered his comment, feeling various pangs in my stomach, and I fell silent for a long time until another question crossed my mind.

"Wolf..."

"Hmm?" he replied without letting go of my hand.

"Do you think the culprit could be someone I trust? Someone I care about a lot?" I didn't know why, but the doubt bothered me. "I wouldn't be surprised if Foster was behind this, trying to kill me to prevent me from taking over the company and throwing him off the third floor the minute after, but I fear it could be someone closer to me than I ever considered."

"Betrayal never comes from an enemy, Jas. It's the people closest to you who are capable of betraying." I shrank back and held his arm close to me.

"I don't want it to be someone with a connection to me." I tried to hold back the sudden tears that burned my eyes.

"I don't want whoever it is to hurt you."

I pulled away from his shoulder and looked him in the dark. I could feel the masculine scent of his body filling my nostrils in a pleasant, warm, penetrating way. I shivered with the proximity and the brief memory of what we had done earlier.

I exhaled through my nose and closed my eyes. Overwhelmed by a crushing sense of desire that confused me, somehow my mouth sought his. I touched his lips with mine gently, and as soon as our skins met, a low growl escaped Wolf's lips, deepening the kiss roughly, voraciously, thirstily, as if he was determined to claim my mouth as his.

His tongue invaded me, taking everything of mine with it. I gasped as one of his hands tangled in my hair at the nape of my neck, while the other wrapped around my waist, pulling me closer against his warm, hard body.

"Jasmin, you're shaken after everything you've been through. We can't..."

"Distract me, please. Feeling you is all I want right now." His breathing became heavier. "We can 'not do this' tomorrow," I bargained.

He let out a muffled laugh in the midst of a kiss and traced a path with small bites along my neck, scratching my skin in a way that drove me mad.

I never imagined a touch like that could trigger so many feelings and reactions all at once throughout my body. My skin tingled, anesthetized by the sudden pleasure that enveloped me.

"You nullify all my reservations with just one word." Wolf brushed his fingers over my belly, slipping under the oversized shirt I wore, and never had a touch felt so good. "This is dangerous," he warned.

I felt the roughness of his hand gliding over my body, and I couldn't help but let out a needy moan into his mouth. His fingers traced a path to my skin, which burned at the slightest touch, reaching my breasts. He pinched my nipple gently, gradually increasing the pressure, making me moan and squirm.

"Wolf!" I arched my body against the fascinating and very warm touch that blended pain and pleasure.

He lifted my sweatshirt until my breasts were exposed to the darkness of the cabin and lowered his lips slowly, firmly gliding over every inch of skin. His thumb grazed my very sensitive nipple, and when his lips approached that spot, I was hit by a surreal expectation. I wanted, with a frightening need, him to suck me there, and from the looks of it, he wanted to as well.

I squirmed, almost begging for the touch.

"Say my name." The command was low, intense, and so deep that it made me hold my breath. He blew softly on my nipple, leaving me in desperation. I gasped and arched my back. "Say. My. Name."

"Christopher!" I couldn't resist, and I swear I even tried.

He closed his lips around the eager nipple, and a jolt of electricity ran through my entire body. I tangled my fingers in his hair, feeling the wet softness of his tongue as he sucked, teased, and tortured. He lightly bit down, a deliciously painful caress. I fumbled in the dark until I found his firm chest beneath the fabric. Everything seemed a bit blurred as my skin burned under Christopher's deep touch.

"This is... Oh..." I didn't suppress another moan, deeper and more intense as he resumed his torture, now cupping my breasts in his hands. My entire body trembled involuntarily.

His hand slid down my skin, and his firm fingers touched the edge of my pants, helping me lower them a bit. I couldn't even think. Christopher's hand descended to my butt. His lips moved up to my mouth, exploring every corner, taking me until I was breathless.

His hands slid between my thighs and gently parted them. I gasped as his fingers moved higher and brushed against my core. He parted his lips calmly, making my legs contract with pleasure.

From what I'd read in one or two romance novels, the first time being touched there was supposed to bring some sort of shame or shyness, but instead, all I felt was an overwhelming desire for him to go even further.

"I want you to touch me." A muffled laugh echoed in my mouth, and for my purest torture, he rubbed his thumb over the pulsing spot that was driving me insane.

"You have no idea how much I want to do this..." Wolf abandoned that sensitive spot and slid his finger to the entrance of my body. "Fuck, you're so hot." His voice, a bit lower than usual, invaded my senses, and I felt compelled to close my eyes, as if opening them would suddenly wake me from this dream. "What do you know about this, my Crystal?" He moved up again, exciting me. I dug my nails into his arm, trembling with the sensation that slowly spread everywhere.

"I know everything there is to know from watching porn," I confessed, breathless. He placed a quick kiss on my lips, followed by a rough laugh.

"That's not what I meant, my little obscene angel." He kissed my mouth and continued to move his fingers in slow, torturous circles. "I wanted to know if you've... touched yourself." The tip of his finger pressed into the center of my pleasure and slid in a little. His finger, now very wet, returned to the spot that seemed capable of making me explode, and he resumed the circular motions that were driving me crazy.

"Hummmmmm!"

"Is that your answer?" He was having fun.

"N-no... I've never touched myself."

"Have you tried?" His voice sounded like a melody in my ears as the incessant rubbing left me numb.

"Y-yes," I stammered. "But I never succeeded." The last word faded from my lips as Christopher increased the intensity of his caresses.

"Let me show you what it feels like." His voice, filled with affection and attention, made me release the breath I was holding in my lungs. His lips brushed against mine, which parted in anticipation. His rough fingers returned to part the lips of my core, and when I thought I might dissolve, weak in his arms, he suddenly slowed his pace. "But first... I want to know something."

"Can't it wait?" He pressed that spot again, making me gasp and cry out in his mouth as he pinched it lightly.

"It has to be now." He tortured as the sensation of intense pleasure began to consume me.

"Anything..." I moaned. "I'll say anything, just don't stop."

"How did you learn to steal things from people's pockets so easily?" I ended up laughing, clutching his shirt as best I could, and earned a light pinch on my nipple when I took too long to respond.

"Do you really want to know that... right now?" I asked, too ecstatic to think straight.

"I've been dying of curiosity ever since I was first a victim of your light fingers." He sank one of his fingers inside me, and a deep moan escaped my mouth at the sensation.

"W-with my sister." I rocked against the steady movement. "Our pastime was... ahhhh." He slid in another finger cautiously, slowly, while still massaging my flesh.

"Was?" I could hear the pleasure in his low, sneaky voice.

"Stealing the bodyguards' keys. We spent the whole day playing tricks on them. E-even... the radios, we were able to take. I perfected the technique over the years, but for the love of God..."

"Yes. Now..." He trailed his lips down my skin until he reached the valley between my breasts, teasing, biting, sucking with fervor.

I lost myself in the sensations, in his firm but gentle touch, in the steady invasion of two fingers moving deliciously back and forth, in the sounds

Christopher unconsciously let escape. His lips came close to my ear, and he started whispering dirty, provocative words that heated me up even more.

One moment, I was lying there on a small bed that creaked with every movement we made, inside a cabin in a completely unknown place, but in the next moment, a feeling of freedom spread through my body in countless points of light. I trembled and arched my back, lifting my hips toward Christopher's hand, which captured my mouth in a deep kiss.

I moaned into his lips and let my body collapse onto the mattress. He withdrew his fingers from inside me and caressed my skin, never pulling his mouth away from mine.

Lost in those intense sensations, I desperately wanted to touch him somehow. I let my hand trail down his chest, resting it on the hard, prominent bulge straining against his pants.

"Oh my..." I parted my lips, imagining he was more than well-endowed, but as soon as I started to move my hand over his erection, his fingers wrapped around mine and pulled me away. "I want to touch you too," I complained.

"I can't allow something I'm not sure I'll be able to control," he warned, his warm, delicious breath brushing my face, flooding my soul.

"I'm not asking you to control yourself. Let's have sex!" It seemed so simple to me. In fact, I was desperate to go further with this man. "I want it, you want it... we're adults. What's stopping us?"

"My angel, I find your practicality incredible." He kissed the tip of my nose. "Even though our involvement is wrong..."

"According to your uptight, moralistic mind." He laughed.

"I can't deny the desire I feel, after all, it's pretty obvious." I tried to touch his erection again, but to no avail. "But you're a virgin, my love. I would never take something so delicate in a cabin in the middle of nowhere. Women don't dream of something like that, I imagine."

"We're not doing anything anyway, I can't imagine anything better than..." He kissed my mouth tenderly, sucking on my lips one by one, nibbling without haste. I sighed, enjoying the tender kiss, aware that this was a battle I had lost, but I still had a war to win. "Alright. For today, you've won." He laughed and pulled me into his arms.

"You need to rest a bit, angel. It's been a tough day, and tomorrow we'll still have a lot to face," he said, playing with his fingers in my hair.

"What if I have an attack during the night?" That fear had been haunting me since we arrived here.

"Don't worry about that. I'll be here to hold you." His comment made my heart race in my chest.

Wolf slowly ran his finger up the side of my face until he touched the bandage.

"Does it hurt?" His low voice hit me, my body still throbbing from the intensity we had shared.

"It just stings a little."

"I'm going to kill him," he said suddenly. "I'm going to wipe that bastard off the face of the earth for hurting you."

"Don't say that." This time, I was the one to touch his face with my hand. His stubble scratched my fingers and caused a delicious sensation. "I know in the world you live in, killing is part of the job, but it's also a path with no return, Christopher. I want that man dead more than anyone, but I don't want to lose you in the process. You're a good man."

"Ah, my Crystal..." He trailed his fingers down my neck. "I want to kill him now more than I did before. I'm not a good man. Don't be fooled."

CHAPTER TWENTY

Wolf

I was already awake when the day broke. The sky was overcast, mirroring the mood of my soul that morning.

Last night, I went from heaven to hell in a matter of minutes.

I traced my fingers down Jasmin's arm and explored her face, now peaceful, recalling the exact moment she had another night terror. The screams were sharper, more painful. Perhaps heightened by everything we went through the day before; I didn't know. But I was fully convinced that my heart felt broken, given the pain that struck it.

Why did someone with so much light have to suffer like that? I couldn't understand.

"It happened again, didn't it?" Jasmin's voice emerged slowly when she caught me watching over her as she slept.

I raised my hand and gently caressed her face; she closed her eyes when she felt my touch, and an absurd need to protect her from her own thoughts consumed me.

I knew that what happened between us was wrong; I knew I shouldn't even be in that bed when she woke up. But how could I resist the absurd urge to witness those jade eyes opening early in the morning? How could I pull my hands away from her?

"I think you were shaken up by what happened yesterday," I softened.

"I'm sorry. It must not have been easy." And it truly wasn't. Watching her suffer, lost in her own subconscious, left me with a terrible sense of helplessness.

"I was worried about you, Jas." I stroked her hand. "There are some types of treatments that might help." I didn't mention that I almost kidnapped my brother to get him to tell me all the possible resources for those suffering from night terrors.

"I don't want to be doped up on medication, Christopher." Hearing my name from her lips sent a strange feeling through my chest. Something good. Too good. "I know you might not understand, but I assure you it's worse to take them."

"There are treatments that don't involve medication. Therapy, for example," I suggested.

"Well, well. A tough bodyguard like you is really suggesting therapy?" She flashed a beautiful smile that wiped the tired expression from her face.

"It's important," I breathed. "You should try it. Consult a doctor of your choice and do the same with the therapist. Don't let anyone choose for you." I tried to keep my mouth shut at all costs.

I needed to keep my suspicions hidden for now, or I would risk revealing the true identity of whoever was behind those attacks.

"I'll consider your advice," she finally said. "Now... can we go eat something? Ow!" I gave a light flick to the tip of her nose.

"We can." She lifted her eyes to mine, lying between my arms so relaxed that it felt completely natural.

I cupped her face in my hands, drawn in by the deep green eyes that sparkled more as the daylight poured into the cabin. Her swollen lips caught my attention, and it was then that I decided to break the promise I had just made.

I took her mouth with mine in a gentle kiss. Jasmin gasped when our tongues met. I wrapped my arms around her waist, pulling her beneath me.

"Chris..." she breathed against my lips as she felt the weight of my body, already rock-hard, on her.

I growled, devouring her mouth. Compressing her body, so small compared to mine, and then I realized that if I stayed there like that, I would lose control, and the moans that escaped that woman every second did nothing to help my decision.

I pulled away from the kiss suddenly and sat up on the bed.

"Yeah, this really needs to stop." I let out a breath.

"I already told you. The solution to our problems is to do... you know." The naughty girl shrugged and bit her lower lip.

"Don't tempt me, Miss Cahill." I laughed and stood up. "We have a busy day ahead." Jasmin rolled her eyes and huffed, dissatisfied.

"Where are we going now?" she asked as she emerged from under the covers.

"To a bar owned by a friend of mine."

"A bar?" Her thin, shocked voice almost made me laugh.

"Yes. I have a safer getaway house than this one to shelter us."

"Does it have heat and food? I could even sleep on the floor with those two things," I said hopefully.

"It has much more than that." I smiled, glancing at my weapon on the small counter at the back of the cabin. "I keep houses like that all over the city for special clients, and I have contacts who keep the keys secure."

"Wasn't it easier to hide the key somewhere near the house?" Jasmin began tying my clothes around her waist to make them a bit smaller on her body, and ended up styling part of the piece, which, by the way, looked very pretty on her.

"It's not just the key this friend keeps," I revealed. "He's also a contact point. Through him, I can reach the only two people I trust blindly."

"Who are they?"

"My brothers."

Jasmin

WE ARRIVED AT THE BAR some time later. The place was in the middle of an empty road. There were no other businesses nearby or any signs of civilization.

My stomach felt like it was touching my back, I was so hungry, but Wolf needed to grab the key before we stopped anywhere to eat.

He parked the loud, oversized motorcycle in a spot right in front of the place, which, by the way, had a very grimy sign, with some burnt-out lights where the words "Walt's Bar" screamed lonely.

Three very rough-looking men were drinking outside and stared at the motorcycle with strange expressions. I shivered when their gaze fell on us, but since Wolf remained calm, I tried to do the same.

"Don't leave my side, got it?" he barked as we passed by the three men.

"Yes, sir! I'll be in your shadow." I linked my arm with his and nearly tripped over the oversized shoes I was wearing. Since I had fled barefoot, I was left with a sneaker we found discarded in the cabin.

"What are you doing?"

"I'm being your shadow," I stated the obvious, and he grumbled, but I was happy he didn't release my arm, a warm flutter rising in my neck.

I didn't know what it was that made my heart race and then slow to almost a stop when Wolf was near me. Maybe it was the memories of what his hands and lips could do, or the infernal heat that pair of distinctive eyes carried with such fury. Whatever it was, it was dragging me into an open and unknown sea, creating a watershed in my subconscious, and with each passing second, one question nagged at me: Should I navigate those waters or not?

We entered the bar, which was partially filled, with half the tables occupied by men as strange and intimidating as the three big guys outside. The stench of rotten eggs wafted through the place, adding to my unease.

"What are all these guys doing in a bar at 10 AM?" I whispered.

"Not everyone works during the day, just like not everyone operates within the law." His cryptic answer made me even more worried.

What kind of bar was this? A den of criminals?

We walked between the tables, gradually drawing the attention of every man in the place. Some had long beards and a host of strange scars on their faces, while others were covered in tattoos, none of them seeming to welcome our presence.

I clung tighter to Wolf's arm.

"Don't be scared," he whispered beside me, his thumb sliding along the back of my hand.

"Easy for you to say when you're not the smallest person here." Wolf flashed a lopsided smile that made his face even sexier, stopping when we reached the bar, where a tall, voluptuous man was shoving some eggs into a jar of dubious yellow liquid.

"I'd like to order a purple drink," Wolf said to the man's back, but whatever that meant made the egg guy stop what he was doing.

He slowly turned around, looking over his shoulder until he found us standing there.

"Coming right up." Without any greetings, he turned and disappeared through a narrow door behind the bar.

"I thought you were friends," I commented, puzzled by the lack of animosity.

"I don't want to kill him, and he doesn't want me dead. So, yes, we're friends." I pursed my lips at that warm assertion.

Soon, the purple drink guy returned with a set of keys, which he handed to Wolf.

"Do you need me to say anything specific?" he asked, rubbing his fingers on the yellowed dishcloth hanging from his shoulder.

"No, just tell him I'm in a hurry." He took the keyring and draped his arm around my shoulders, guiding me away.

We were almost out of the bar when the three rough-looking guys we saw outside came in.

"Is that Harley out there yours?" one of them, the burliest, said as if he hadn't seen Wolf get off it just minutes before.

The other two brutes flanked the big guy, forming a barrier and blocking the exit.

"Get out of the way." Wolf growled. I glanced at his "friend" and noticed the man was patiently washing one of the glasses, oblivious to the chaos unfolding inside.

"That's one hell of a bike... and expensive." One of them approached from the right while the second came from the left. Wolf pushed me behind him with one hand, and I saw him think about reaching for the gun at his waist, but for some reason, he hesitated.

"I want to take it for a ride, Tom." One of the guys, who was quite large, spoke to the bearded man.

"He wants to take it for a ride." The man chewed on a toothpick in his mouth and spat it out.

"I'll take the girl," the one on the right said.

"What kind of hellhole have we ended up in? It's not even lunchtime and already a bunch of drunks are trying to steal your bike and kidnap me. You definitely don't know how to pick a good bar." I took a small step towards the nearby table and rolled my eyes at Wolf, who glared at me furiously, not understanding anything. "Look at them." I pointed with my chin at the bearded man, who stared back at me, seeming to grow a little. "We can't fight all three."

"She's right." The bearded man laughed, his face twisting into a grotesque expression as his eyes roamed my body, as if sizing me up.

"If you fight them, which by the looks of it, haven't bathed in at least a month, you'll end up dying of tetanus."

"What did that bitch say?"

"She called you tetanus, Tom." Their eyes widened, and I had to suppress the urge to laugh. I knew Wolf was armed, and it would only take him drawing his gun for us to get out safely, but for some reason, when the bearded man lunged at him, that's not what he did.

"I'm going to finish that hellspawn!" Tom, the stinky bearded guy, charged at me, but Wolf was faster, landing a punch on the man before he could reach me, and the other two brutes closed in on him.

Wolf grabbed me by the waist and spun me, tossing me into a dark, empty corner of the bar as I watched everything around us transform into a wild west brawl.

Chairs flew, tables flipped, and the floor was soaked with spilled drinks. Some men started fighting among themselves, oblivious to the chaos those three lunatics were causing for Wolf.

I tried to keep up with my bodyguard's movements, but I couldn't. He was too fast and strong. The blows Wolf dealt were precise and impactful. Soon, he took down two of the three idiots. Now only that bastard Tom was left, who had just thrown a chair at Wolf. But it didn't take long before he slammed the man against the wall and started to choke him.

I caught a glimpse of the moment Tom said something to Wolf, which made him pause for a moment. I considered that he might stop the fight then, but I was mistaken. The man lifted his chin, his shoulders adopting a rigid, wild posture, and he began to rain blows on the big guy's face without stopping.

He hit once, twice, three, four times until blood began to pour uncontrollably. I covered my mouth. He was going to end up killing that idiot.

"Wolf, stop!" I rushed to him and tried to grab one of his hands. He pushed me away and continued to punch the man, causing more blood to splatter everywhere. My eyes welled up at the violent, uncontrollable scene.

Had he already knocked him out? Was he really going to take his life?

"Wolf, STOP, for God's sake, you'll kill him!" I shouted, hanging onto his arm. He pushed me again, and that's when I panicked. Without thinking twice, I shoved him, placing myself in front of the bastard, who now had a beard full of blood.

Wolf was blind with rage, his disturbed expression terrified me. He raised his hand to throw another punch but stopped midway when he finally recognized me.

Only then did he blink a few times and stare at his bloody hand, then lift his eyes to mine, looking very confused and shaken.

"I'm sorry, I... lost control," he said quietly, looking at his own hands.

"We need to get out of here, Wolf." He straightened up, resuming the posture from minutes ago, escorting me through the shattered glass and didn't look at me again until we reached the motorcycle.

His hands, very red, made my stomach churn.

I climbed onto his bike again, feeling like I had witnessed a dark side of Wolf that he seemed to struggle hard to hide.

CHAPTER TWENTY-ONE

Jasmin

We stopped at the first store we found after that chaos. We got off the bike, and I intercepted Wolf as soon as he started to walk.

"You're not thinking of going in there looking like that, are you?" I pointed at Wolf's hands, which, despite being wiped on his black hoodie, were still visibly dirty.

"I won't leave you alone," he stated categorically.

"Then let me pick the items while you keep your hands in your pockets. I don't want to end up in a police station right now. Though with a man your size, hands in pockets, and that look like you're about to kill someone, it's also going to raise a lot of suspicion." I watched him raise his eyebrows at my comment. "How about a smile? No?" He growled and positioned himself behind me.

"Let's go."

"God help us." We passed through the parking lot.

Just before we reached the entrance of the store, I spotted an elderly man in tattered clothes with a shopping cart full of junk, parked at the end of the lot. I couldn't even remember the last time I had encountered a homeless person like him. I patted my pockets, unconsciously looking for some money to give the man in an attempt to help him somehow, but it quickly hit me that I didn't have a dime to spare, not even for myself.

"Good morning!" he said as we passed by. Wolf grumbled a low response, while I tried to flash my best smile at the old man, whose face was heavily wrinkled but held a genuine, albeit flawed, smile.

I was still thinking about the old man when we started shopping. I didn't know how much money Wolf had, but maybe he could give something to the old man outside.

We began our shopping in the clothing section, where both Wolf and I picked out some pieces for the day.

"Which color do you prefer, Wolfie, pink or red?" I held up two pairs of panties between my fingers and turned them toward him, watching him turn a bit red while muttering a curse in response.

"Don't make me tie you to a display, Miss Cahill, and hurry up with that."

"Red then..." I laughed at his serious, irritated face.

We reached the checkout almost half an hour later with so many items that I feared we wouldn't be able to carry them on that bike. Was my bodyguard planning to spend the whole winter with me in hiding?

"Put those purchases in two separate bags," he requested from the cashier, pulling his hands out of his pockets to pay.

"Ma'am, your hair is fantastic. What color do you use?" I pointed to the cashier's bright burgundy hair. I wanted to distract her from Wolf's dirty hands, and I was being sincere.

"Oh, thank you," she said with a smile, and spent the next few minutes focused on explaining more about the dye.

I thanked her, satisfied that I had diverted her attention. Wolf grabbed the four bags, and we walked outside.

"Are you sure we need all this?" I barely closed my mouth when the old man we had seen earlier entered my line of sight. "Listen, Wolf..." I was about to ask the man walking briskly beside me for some money to give to the old man when Wolf abruptly stopped and handed two bags full of food to him.

"Oh!" the old man exclaimed in surprise, peering into the bag with curiosity. "God bless you, God bless you very much," he said happily, and a tightness gripped my chest as I saw him rejoice so much for receiving food from a stranger.

Wolf gave a nod and handed the man some bills.

"Is there a shelter nearby that you know? On Ashley Lane," Wolf asked.

"I know it, sir. I sleep there sometimes."

"Do you like it there? Do people treat you well?" He continued with the questioning, and I found it strange.

"I'm always welcome there. I also go to the Van Buren shelter, a great place."

"That's good. Sleep somewhere warm; the night will be cold," he said, and the knot in my throat that I was trying to hold back became even more painful.

I walked toward the bike with my thoughts swirling from the old man to Wolf's attitude. He hid a heart different from anything I had imagined. My father, even with the money he had, never stopped to help someone on the street, nor did he allow me to do so, but Christopher was different, and his uniqueness made my heart race.

"Can we go?" he asked after we settled on the bike.

"Yes," I said from inside my helmet, and he revved the bike with a loud, lethargic roar.

After a long time balancing on the back with a few bags and a roaring hunger, we arrived in a very green neighborhood, with wide, empty streets, too peaceful. There was absolutely no one on the streets, which were lined with colossal houses. We stopped in front of one of those houses, almost at the end of the street.

"Are you sure we're in the right place?" I questioned, incredulous, as I saw him insert the key into a large steel gate.

"Were you expecting another cabin?" He tried to smile, but all he managed was to show his perfect, shiny teeth.

"This time I was ready for a cave. With food, anywhere would do. Wow..." I gasped as he opened the gate to reveal a small mansion behind it.

I stepped into the spacious yet unkempt courtyard, as if no one had set foot there in a long time, while Wolf parked the bike and locked the gate. The place was enormous. It had several windows, most of which were barred. I could have sworn we'd find some kind of panic room there.

"Let's go. You need to eat." I followed closely behind him through the place. We entered through a door that led to the living room. All the furniture was covered in sheets, easily transforming its interior into a haunted house.

Wolf searched every room to ensure we were truly alone and locked most of them, finally stopping in the kitchen.

I helped him remove the sheets covering the stove and refrigerator, and we spread all the bags on the large island that divided the space. I noticed that Christopher was so distracted, mechanically pulling products from the bag while staring into nothing.

His hands were still dirty. I looked around and found a somewhat grimy cloth, but it would have to do. I washed it in the faucet, filled a bowl with water, and added a bit of old soap I found around. I brought everything to the counter and pulled out one of the tall chairs.

"Let me help you with this." I suddenly took his hand, and Christopher looked at me confused, as if remembering at that moment that he needed to wash them.

"I can do it." He tried to pull his hands away, but I insisted.

"Sit down and don't resist." I pointed to another counter and almost laughed at the strange expression that took over his face. "You know I'm persistent."

"You can be sure I know that."

I dipped the cloth in the bowl of water when he sat down and started scrubbing his hand gently. The more I dipped the cloth into the bowl, the redder the water became.

"Why didn't you draw your gun when they came at you? You could have ended that mess in the blink of an eye."

"It's prohibited to carry any kind of weapon inside that bar. An old rule that no one, from either side of the law, dares to break," he explained. "You must have noticed it's not an ordinary place."

"Yeah," I agreed. "It's full of crazies."

"I think you're right." I continued scrubbing, and after a moment of silence, I decided to speak again. Something was wrong with this story, and I needed to find out what it was.

"What did he say?" I asked, rubbing the cloth on his skin again.

"What?"

"The smelly bearded guy..." I reminded him, lifting my eyes to meet his. "I know he said something that angered you to the point of almost killing him. Come on, tell me, what was it?"

"That idiot..." He clenched his fist tightly, and I could feel the anger filling his pupils, making them even larger.

"Calm down, it's over." I caressed his hands with mine. Wolf exhaled, exasperated, and stared at the floor beside me.

"It had to do with eating you," he confessed suddenly. "Only with some rather... provocative words."

"Provocative?"

"Yeah. I was tempted to kill him."

"That man was a scumbag... argh!" I shook my head, a shiver running through me. "You should have hit him with a bottle too." Wolf smiled slowly, but soon his face returned to seriousness.

"I'm sorry you had to witness that. I don't usually lose control easily, but just imagining what that pig intended to do with you... I got blinded," he confessed, looking at his fingers, now almost clean.

"Has it happened before? Not being able to stop?"

"To be honest, I only took your case because I lost control on a mission I accepted." He shifted his body impatiently. "I'm not proud of any of this, but it's stronger than me. When I see a woman in danger, everything changes. My vision turns red, and I just can't stop, and that feeling becomes even more uncontrollable when it's you." He squinted his eyes and kept them closed for a moment. I studied his face cautiously. There was more beneath that story, I was sure, but still, my chest burned with the sudden revelation. "Are you afraid of me?" His eyes met mine carefully.

"No... it's not that."

"If you are, I'll understand."

"I'm not afraid, Christopher." He swallowed hard, his Adam's apple rising and falling at the mention of his name. Since last night, I had noticed that Wolf reacted differently when I called him that, and it pleased me greatly. "I can see the remorse you feel for going too far; it's clear to me."

"You're mistaken, Jas..." And there it was, my weakness. That low, rough tone, whispering my name in a devoted, warm way. There lay my downfall. "I feel remorse for having let you see something like that, but after what that bastard said, nothing in the world, except for you, could stop me. He wanted to rape you. All I could think about was killing him, and..." Wolf's hands started to tremble; his fists clenched told me he was beginning to lose control again, and without thinking, I stood up and wrapped Christopher in a tight hug.

At first, he kept his hands stiffly away from me, but as I didn't give up, his arms gave in, and he enveloped my body in his, burying his face in the curve of my neck.

"I wasn't like this," he said into my hair, and I let him speak without interrupting. "Not before going to the orphanage."

"What happened to change that?"

"Remember I told you my parents were addicts?"

"Yes."

"When I lived with them, I witnessed three things every day." He exhaled through his mouth. "The hunger we suffered, the filth we lived in, and the countless times my father beat my mother." My eyes welled up, imagining a helpless little boy going through that. "He hit her constantly, and I could do nothing but cry and take hits myself. Until one day, he started beating her, and I, scared, hid and watched. That bastard beat her until she passed out. Then he grabbed some of his things and left. I believed for a whole day that my mother just fainted, and I stayed by her side until a neighbor came to our house and found her body."

"He... killed her? Your father killed your mother?" My voice came out broken and loud. I pulled away from him, desperate to find his gaze.

"Yes, and he ran away immediately. He probably died of an overdose shortly after." He breathed heavily. "I ended up in the orphanage, but I was far from the ideal kid for adoption. Aggressiveness began to take shape through the fights I picked with everyone there. Then I ran away and lived on the streets for a while until I went back to the orphanage with the same reputation as a mafia boss, which didn't stop the bigger kids from trying to strip that reputation from me at all costs." He attempted to make a joke.

"Earlier, at the store, when you took food to that old man..."

"I know what it's like to be hungry, Jas." He tapped my hand on the counter. "I help whenever I see someone in those conditions."

"Have you ever been to that shelter you mentioned?"

"I own it."

"What?" I coughed and stared at him. "You own the shelter?"

"Yes, there are four, for now. Each of my brothers has one. My father opened the first after adopting us, and we followed his example. It's something very important for us, to help homeless people." He pursed his lips and looked down at the floor. "We all went through similar situations, and there's nothing worse than feeling cold and hungry."

"Does your father... Mr. Holder, know everything about your past?" I tried to disguise my choked voice and the mix of emotion and pride I felt for Wolf at that moment.

"Yes. My father is my best friend. That man fought hard for me when I was just a troublemaker. If I were in his shoes, I would have returned me at the first opportunity." He shrank back a little more. "I wasn't grateful to him for many years. But I managed to regain my sense of gratitude in time to make him proud, although I still relapse now and then."

I opened and closed my mouth countless times. I didn't know what to say.

"I'm impressed..."

"You wanted to know my story, Crystal..." He called me by my nickname, and warmth flooded my legs. Was that idiot really going to make me like that word? "I didn't want to sour your day by recounting the sordid details of everything I've faced so far, but I feel obligated to explain what you saw today. It's stronger than I can bear, more than I can contain with my own strength." He looked down at the counter. "I'm sorry this story isn't a fairy tale."

"Fairy tales weren't made for people like us," I added, recalling my own horror story. "At least that makes us stronger than we can imagine, and if today you have issues with anger, it's because you became a survivor and have scars that need to be treated, just like I do with my night terrors." I touched his hand with mine. "I think I'll need to look for a psychologist who can deal with us. You need therapy too." I patted his shoulder.

"I think you might be right." My stomach growled, and I couldn't hold back a laugh. He did that all the time.

"We just need to eat first."

"I'll prepare something right now. It's already past lunchtime, so let's skip breakfast, okay?" He stood up.

"I can help with something," I offered eagerly.

"Thanks, but we don't want you to set the house on fire."

I stared at him, hiding behind a smile all the surprise I felt getting to know a little more about that man full of mysteries and a past as painful as mine, if not more. Full of marks, scars, and pains I could hardly imagine. Behind my colorful-eyed Wolf, there was a wounded man who also needed help to face his demons but who, above all, wanted to protect me.

My eyes traced down his broad back as he started preparing our lunch, and a painful pang hit my chest as I realized that with his harsh words, rough demeanor, and piercing gaze, he was winning a piece of my heart with every second we spent together.

Ah, Christopher Holder... how do I not fall in love with you?

WE FINISHED LUNCH, and Wolf busied himself locking up the place and activating the security system.

"It should take a day for my contacts to get back to me." I didn't understand anything he said. I was too distracted by my new discovery.

"Did you know there's a bathtub in this house? With steaming hot water." I clapped my hands. "I think I even found some old bath salts in the cabinet."

"Go take a bath and rest a bit. It's been a hectic day, and we don't know what awaits us. It's best to be prepared."

"You should be the next one to take a good bath. I was serious about that guy being a walking tetanus." He laughed, and I hopped up to take the longest bath I've had in years.

I stayed immersed in the warm, delightful water for almost an hour. I tried to relax, but even if my body could, I was sure my mind never would.

How could I be at ease knowing someone was trying to kill me? And worse, knowing that person could be someone from my father's company or even someone close to me. That's the only way they could find the exact location of this house.

I exhaled and bit my lower lip, considering all the possibilities. Would Wolf be able to find any information? I hoped so. He was my best chance of unraveling this mystery and getting out alive.

I finished my bath and only realized my new clothes were downstairs when I wrapped myself in a towel and didn't see them around.

What the hell...

I left the bathroom to look for them and immediately felt that Wolf had turned on the heater enough to walk around without freezing. I was about to head down the stairs to the first floor, determined to find my clothes, when an ajar door at the end of the hallway caught my attention. I walked over, step by step. Wolf had locked the doors to all the rooms except the bathrooms and the one we would share at night, which was already giving me the creeps just thinking about it. So why was that door open?

I got close and looked through the crack. I was surprised to see Wolf shirtless, with his back to me. His slightly damp hair told me he had just come out of the shower, and for a moment, I was mesmerized by the sight of his well-defined torso, with a few small scars on his fair skin and a shape that took my breath away, just imagining being wrapped in that embrace.

I opened the door wider. He jumped at the noise and turned with a gun in hand, aiming it right at my head.

"It's me!" I shouted, raising my hands. The towel I was awkwardly holding fell to my feet, and I found myself completely exposed in front of him.

"Damn it, Jasmin!" he yelled and quickly turned his back to me.

"What the hell!" I cursed, pulling the towel back up to its place. My whole body felt like it was on fire, overwhelmed by pure embarrassment. "This is your fault!" I pointed at his back. "Who aims a gun at someone's head?"

"You came up behind me without making a sound. What did you expect?" He braced his hands on a table that I had just now noticed was filled with small weapons and even one very large one, alongside some ammunition. Wolf shook his head back and forth.

"I'm sorry, I didn't mean to scare you." I moved closer to him, surveying the space that was nothing like a regular room. There were no windows, and the entrance resembled a safe door.

"You should really feel sorry." He went back to handling the weapons.

"Is this the panic room?" I stopped beside him.

"Yes. There are canned goods, water, a first aid kit, and even radios for communication with the outside, in case the place loses signal." He didn't look back at me, keeping his attention on the armament in front of him.

"That's cool. And these weapons?"

"I left them here in case I needed them. They could be of great help." He picked up a black gun and checked the magazine.

"Can you teach me how to use one of them?"

"Are you going crazy?" His eyes searched mine, and I shivered at what I saw there: tension, doubt, anger... but what caught my attention the most was the heat radiating from his irises toward me.

"I've never been more serious in my life." My voice came out low as I started tightening the towel around my body, as if that would keep me sane in the face of Wolf's penetrating gaze. The small movement didn't escape his attention, and he glanced down at my fingers. "Given everything that's happening, don't you think it would be useful for me to know how to defend myself?" I reached for one of the guns, but Wolf grabbed my wrist midway and loomed over me.

Up close, his bare chest was even more muscular than I imagined.

"You could end up getting hurt, Crystal." His firm voice intoxicated me.

"I can learn to take care of myself, Wolf..."

"I hate when you call me that." He stepped closer to me.

"And I... hate feeling this overwhelming urge to kiss you." Where did that come from? I had no idea, but the muffled sound that escaped from the lips of the man in front of me pleased me greatly.

Christopher moved toward me with determination, as if breaking through an invisible barrier. His hand enveloped my neck, pulling me close until our tongues met in a hurried, desperate, urgent kiss. All the hot spots of my body began to throb. He wrapped his arm around my waist and lifted me onto the table. I felt his firm, slightly rough fingers glide up the side of my leg as he surrendered me to him in a deep kiss.

"You have no idea how many promises you make me break," he declared, burying his lips in my neck, nibbling at my skin until a low sound escaped my lips, which he soon reclaimed. I could feel his hard, throbbing erection through the light pants he was wearing, and all I wanted was to drop the towel and give myself to him completely.

I let go of the fabric, which slid down to my waist, leaving my breasts exposed. A certain shame washed over me, but the latent desire to have him touching me there chased away any hesitation.

"Some promises are meant to be broken," I gasped when his fingers reached my sensitive nipples. He leaned me back and licked my neck down to my aching breast. "I want you, Wolf. I want you so much," I moaned loudly as he bit the nipple of my breast, a mix of pain and pleasure sweeping through my body.

"You don't know what you're asking for, little one." He pulled me to the edge and settled between my legs until his sex pressed against mine. "It's already hard to keep control without seeing you like this." His eyes traveled down my bare chest, and when I lifted my hand to cover myself, he held it. "You're too beautiful," he breathed against my mouth.

"We don't know what might happen tomorrow," I bargained. "We only have today, Christopher. Make me live something I'll never forget."

"Damn!" he cursed and pressed his forehead against mine. I could feel his hesitation and the doubts swirling in his mind. "You know we can't, Jas," he said without pulling away. "I can't kiss you anymore and keep control. This has to be the last time."

"How many last times do we need to have for our first time to actually happen?" His colorful eyes searched mine with a depth I hadn't seen before. I knew at that moment he had made a decision.

I wrapped my legs around his waist as his mouth claimed mine, eager and desperate. He lifted my body with him and supported me with his hands on my backside, carrying me until we reached the bedroom.

"Are you sure?" He tried to persuade me before we entered the room.

"I've wanted this moment since the instant I saw you at that club. I want to be yours, Christopher."

Lust and desire filled his gaze, and he closed the door behind him with a new promise dancing between our lips.

CHAPTER TWENTY-TWO

Jasmin

Christopher captured my lips with his and carried me into the room in his arms, kissing me in a different, intense way, as if he were taking part of my soul with his tongue.

He held the damp towel still trapped between us, and soon the fabric was thrown to the floor. His gaze probed mine with devotion, and a violent desire consumed me as he laid me on the bed and positioned himself over me. My skin burned as I felt him pressing me against the mattress. His bare chest now touched my breasts. Skin on skin in a delicious mix of wavering breaths and heated looks.

I felt his fingers glide along the side of my face, and I closed my eyes, savoring him. Christopher moved back just enough to gaze at my naked body. I felt my cheeks flush as his eyes settled on my intimacy, but I didn't pull away, and a wicked smile curved his lips.

"So perfect..." he whispered against my mouth, already swollen from his delicious, firm kiss.

I gasped as his stubble brushed against my skin.

"I need to control myself; otherwise, I'll devour you all at once," he growled against my mouth, and without realizing it, I raised my hips towards him, seeking any contact I could.

"I don't want your control. I want you to devour me, and soon." I grabbed the back of his neck and dug my nails in, grinding against him shamelessly.

I didn't know what was happening to me. The urgency that had overtaken me was surreal. I needed him to touch me soon, or I would explode.

"Ah, my little naughty one..." He descended upon my mouth and sucked my tongue in a delicious rhythm, then ran his fingers along my neck and continued downward until his hand closed around one of my breasts, which begged for attention.

His fingers squeezed and circled my nipples. I squirmed in his strong arms, completely lost in the little shocks that touch radiated throughout my body.

Wolf left my mouth and began kissing my jawline; I could feel him hard, pulsing against my belly. He went down a little further, leaving hickeys, bites, and caresses across my skin, which by then was already on fire.

"Christopher..." I gasped and moaned softly as he clamped his teeth around one of my nipples. The anticipation left me breathless. He kept his teeth there, torturing me, holding the sensitive bud between them and began licking it without letting go.

My God, what was that sensation?

I moaned, frantic. The pain mixed with the wet, delicious touch left me dizzy.

"There's no sound more delightful than your voice calling my name." He trailed his lips down below my breast. "I want to hear you all night long." He kissed my belly and licked my skin slowly, inch by inch.

With one hand, he opened my legs, and for a moment, I tried to close them.

"What are you doing?" My voice came out weak.

He searched my face, and the shadow of a wicked smile crossed his lips as he went down further and further.

"I want to savor you, my angel." His firm palm stayed on my thigh, and slowly he slid a finger all the way through my intimacy, making me writhe on the mattress.

"Ahhhhh, Christopher!" I arched my back as he buried his face between my legs and blew on my center. His tongue glided over the pulsing spot that was about to drive me insane.

I trembled with the wet yet incredibly warm touch; the sense of shame faded, and I began to move my hips as he bit, sucked, and devoured all of me. His stubble scratched my skin, creating a deep and intense sensation.

He penetrated me with one finger, and all the control I tried to maintain until then went out the window.

"Delicious!" he yelled against my skin, pushing in another finger and returning to suck that little button with firmness and possession. He knew exactly what he was doing.

"Chris!" I whined, and he continued with more strength, more desire, more pressure until my whole body exploded into hundreds of stars.

I was overcome by a delicious tremor that, instead of calming the fire I felt, only intensified it.

The purest desire took hold of me. Wolf trailed a path of little kisses back to my mouth. His tongue invaded me, making me taste myself on his lips.

I reached for his pants, and he helped me take them off. As soon as I saw him for the first time, I had to suck in air at the sight of his large, thick erection, veins pulsing. I bit my lips, imagining him inside me, but I wasn't even sure he would fit.

"We can still stop if you want." He touched my face.

"Now I want more than ever," I confessed.

"It might be difficult, little one, and even a bit painful." He held the back of my neck and placed a warm kiss on my lips. I wrapped my hand around his member, and the sound that vibrated on Wolf's lips excited me even more.

I moved my hand slowly up, and I saw him blink slowly. Christopher leaned down to retrieve his pants and pulled out a wallet from one of his pockets, from which he fished out a small pack of condoms.

A prepared man, I thought, trying to avoid imagining why he was carrying a trio of condoms in his wallet.

"Let's take it slow, okay? We can stop at any moment." He laid down on me, strong, masculine, and opened my legs, fitting himself between them. "Tell me," I felt the tip of his pure member, skin against skin, rise and fall at my entrance—"everything you're feeling," he whispered against my lips and pressed the broad head against my clitoris, rubbing in a slow rhythm that drove me insane.

Quickly, my intimacy began to spasm, craving him deeply. I wrapped my legs around his waist and lifted my hips, the slow movements igniting every inch of my skin.

His lips took mine, and I lost myself in his warm, voracious kiss as he tore open the condom and put it on.

Something told me that all his movements were restrained; I could see the veins shining on his arm from the effort he was making to control himself. I had the impression that Wolf was an aggressive, strong, intense lover, but he was holding back so he wouldn't hurt me.

"Chris..." I felt the tip of his member touch my entrance, and a mix of fear and pleasure washed over me.

"Relax, my angel." He caught one of my nipples with his lips and sucked. One of his hands slid down my butt, opening me a bit more. His colorful eyes locked onto mine. "Damn!" he growled as he began to enter me, filling me up.

"Ahhhhhhh!" I opened my legs wider as he pressed on my clitoris, torturing it in circular motions, thrusting a little more, and then more, until a sharp sting hit me. "Ouch!" I held my breath, and he stopped moving.

"Are you okay?" He placed a kiss in the corner of my mouth.

"Yes, yes." I blinked slowly while Wolf played with my body, using his fingertips, tongue, and voice in gentle caresses at the nape of my ear.

He pushed in a bit more; I could feel the extent of his thick member opening me, stretching me. He thrust deeper, and the pain became intense for a brief moment, right when he took my virginity.

A tear rolled down my face, and Christopher kissed it tenderly. I lost myself in his unique eyes as he pulled out only to enter again, slowly.

"Did it all fit? Really?" The doubt made him smile.

"No, my angel." He kissed me, pushing in a little more and growled in my mouth in a delicious and exciting way. "We won't go all the way today; it's already delightful," he said.

"We can try other ways and..." I closed my eyes as his lips returned to kiss my breasts gently.

"It's what your body can handle; it's perfect for me." He whispered the words against my skin.

His hands became more eager, hungry, delicious. Fingers, lips, teeth... Wolf marked me with every thrust, opening me a bit more. Loud growls escaped his lips and mingled with mine. His hand wrapped around my neck, and I realized it was trembling. He tried to maintain control while penetrating me so as not to hurt me, and that excited me even more.

I kissed his mouth as the peak of pleasure swept over me once again, compressing his member deeply within me.

"Damn, that's delicious!" he roared in my ear, panting. I closed my eyes, overwhelmed by something new, sensational.

I felt light, happy.

Christopher carefully pulled out of me, removed the condom, and pulled me into his arms. I rested my head in the curve of his neck, enjoying the scent of fresh soap on his skin.

"I might have hurt you, little one." There was pain in his voice. "There's a bit of blood. Are you feeling okay?"

"I stopped listening to the rest when he said the word 'little.' I like it..."

"You've always been my little one."

"Always?" I propped myself up on one elbow and narrowed my eyes at him.

"Yes. My little thief." I laughed and let myself fall back into his arms.

"It was really nice," I whispered, my eyes growing heavy, and I allowed myself to close them for a moment. The exhaustion from the last day hit me all at once.

"Too much..." He stroked my back with his fingertips. His ragged breathing caused his chest to rise and fall in a soothing rhythm. I was going to sleep in his arms. "I avoided this moment as long as I could, and now that I've tasted you, I don't know how to stop. You stole much more than my keys, Miss Cahill, and I didn't even realize it..."

I felt a kiss on my temple, but I no longer knew if I was dreaming.

WHENEVER I SUFFERED from nightmares, my body would wake up sore the next day, and aside from those terror-filled nights, I usually woke up electric, anxious, or even lethargic. But when I opened my eyes, all I could feel was a lightness that made me sigh.

I stretched under the covers, not even remembering putting them over myself. I opened my eyes and was startled to notice the room was slightly dark, with just a small crack at the window.

It was still daytime, I thought, staring at the cloudy weather outside. I looked at the bed with white sheets and noticed one side was rumpled. The memories of what happened before I completely blacked out came rushing back, and I couldn't help the smile that formed on my lips.

It had happened.

It had really happened!

I bit my lips and burrowed under the covers only to discover I was still completely naked.

"Oh my!" I covered my mouth with my hand. The sound of the door opening made me peek over the covers.

Christopher entered the room wearing only pants, the same ones from the night before. His athletic chest muscles stood out, and his tousled hair gave him a beautiful, messy look. He was carrying a small tray.

"Good morning, Miss Cahill," he joked with my name and gave me a smile as warm as hell.

"Good morning?" I sat up abruptly. My hair was all over the place.

"You slept after..." My face flushed, and I covered my eyes with my hands. "What's wrong? There's nothing to be embarrassed about." I knew well that it was something natural when we felt attracted to someone, but recalling the sounds I made while in that man's arms made me blush.

He placed the tray on a small table beside us carefully and sat on the bed in front of me. His hands held mine, forcing me to meet his gaze.

"It was incredible." He placed a kiss on each of my hands. "You seemed tired, so I let you sleep. How are you feeling?" He touched my face with the back of his hand, and his eyes settled on mine, filled with care and concern.

"Couldn't be better. I'm ready for another round." I bit my lip eagerly when I realized what I had said impulsively, and I noticed Wolf's eyes fixated on the movement.

"You need to rest, my troublemaker."

"I've rested enough; more than that, only when I die."

"Don't say such things." His hand reached my neck, and the familiar warmth that hit me every time he touched me warmed my heart. A very dangerous place, by the way. "Are you sore?"

I thought about lying for a moment, knowing that if I told the truth, he might not touch me again, but when I faced his bright, intriguing eyes, I knew he would draw out any truth from me.

"Just a little," I confessed.

"I brought something that might help." He leaned over the breakfast table and took out a small bowl with some ice cubes.

I opened my eyes wider, watching curiously as Christopher held one of the cubes in his hands. His attention fell on me, and I stayed still as I watched him climb onto the bed and sit, leaning back against the headboard beside me.

"Come here, my angel." He opened his legs and touched my waist, encouraging me.

I crawled across the bed, unsure of what he was thinking. His arm wrapped around my waist and lifted me until I was between his legs. I closed my eyes, enjoying the sensation of his muscular curves pressed against my back.

"Maybe this can help." He raised the ice cube in front of my face and placed a kiss on my neck that sent little pulsating points across my skin.

"What do you plan to do with that?" I gasped as I felt his fingers, wet with the cold water, touch the sides of my legs and open them slightly, leaving me exposed.

"Shh, trust me. This will help relieve it." With great care, he touched my sex lips with the cold finger, making me nearly jump onto his lap from the cold contact. "I'm going to press an ice cube right here to ease the discomfort."

As soon as the ice touched my already wet flesh, I couldn't hold back the strange sound, almost like a mewl, that rose from my throat, and I writhed, throwing my head back, resting it on Chris's shoulder.

"This feels so good." He moved the ice up and down, and new sensations began to tingle in my belly.

I moaned deeply as he brought the ice down to my entrance and pushed a piece of the cube inside my intimacy.

"Christopher," I called, impulsively.

"The intention is to relieve you," he growled in my ear, spreading a burning flame through my body, "but if you keep calling me like that"—he brushed his thumb over my clitoris, playing with it—"it's hard to keep my concentration."

"This is different." I gasped and felt the ice water melting in the heat of my wet flesh. Christopher's prominent erection pulsed steadily at the base of my back.

"Is it good?" he asked, uncertain. "If you want, I can stop, and..."

"No!" I protested immediately. "Please, don't stop."

He laughed in my neck and left a bite there, making me shiver.

His fingers played with me until the entire ice cube melted away. I opened my legs wider when one of Christopher's hands reached for my breast, sliding his fingers along the sides until he reached the nipple that begged for his touch. I dug my nails into his thigh, over the fabric of his pants, and leaned back when he penetrated me with one finger. His thumb remained rubbing against my clitoris, which was very soaked from the ice water, mixing with my own lubrication.

Holy God, what was that? The sensation was even stronger than what I experienced the day before, as if my whole body was about to spontaneously combust. Wolf's seductive voice whispered in my ear while his hands continued to caress me. Just as I was about to reach orgasm, he grabbed a new ice cube from the metal bowl. It was still considerably large but starting to melt.

"Come for me, my angel. Let me hear you moaning my name." He slid the stone into my core, moving in a delirious back-and-forth rhythm. His fingers stimulating me drove me wild.

I was overwhelmed by a visceral impulse. I needed to be filled by him. I wanted to feel him entering me, claiming me as his own. I reached for the waistband of his pants, struggling to pull them down. Christopher caught my fingers, trying to restrain me, but I persisted nonetheless.

"Are you sure?" I realized he was just as enraptured as I was.

"More than anything."

I felt the hardness of his member pressing against the base of my back, and a new wave of desire consumed me.

"Jas, my little one... lie down here," he whispered against my neck, pulling my body with his to the bed. He guided me to lie on my side, keeping my back to him.

His firm hand wrapped around my leg and lifted it, and his fingers quickly resumed their caress, tracing a constant path of pleasure.

I heard the sound of him reaching for something, and the tearing of a wrapper sent a rush of euphoria through my chest. The tip of his member touched my entrance, and instinctively, I arched my back to meet him. He growled something unintelligible as he slid inch by inch inside me. The thick head slowly stretched me, molding to my body little by little, and unlike the night before, all I felt was the most intense pleasure.

Christopher caressed me, bit my skin, and drove me wild. I writhed, seeking more, yearning to feel him completely inside me, while he played with my sex. I twisted as pleasure consumed me, taking in the full length of his erection inside me for the first time. The sensation was indescribable. It was as if his entire being had become part of me, filling me as if we were one.

"Fuck!" he roared, thrusting deeply, holding me by the waist while his hands continued to caress sensitive spots along the way. Just when I thought I had reached the most intense climax of my life, I was overtaken by a powerful, overwhelming sensation that surged through my legs, belly, and chest, overtaking my senses and igniting me.

"Oh, Christopher," I screamed his name, assaulted by an immense wave of pleasure. He thrust with even more force, revealing the intensity he felt, and bit my neck with a rough, trembling groan.

We stayed there for a long time, unmoving. Chris's uneven breath brushed against my neck, just as irregular as my own. He wrapped his arms around me, holding me from behind without pulling out.

"Little Wolf..."

"What is it?" He planted a tender kiss on my shoulder.

"Do I scare you when... I make those sounds?" I asked hesitantly, closing my eyes, savoring the feeling of his thick member pulsing inside me. "It's just that it becomes more uncontrollable than I can handle."

"No, my angel." He stroked my arm, his fingers gliding slowly across my skin. "It's by far the most delicious sound I've ever heard. One of the countless charming details I've only found in you. You make me afraid, that's the truth."

"Afraid of what?" He fell silent for a moment, and then his lips captured the sensitive lobe of my ear, making me close my eyes.

"It's just a thought, nothing serious." He slid his hand up to capture one of my breasts.

Every thought faded away right there, under Christopher's fingertips.

HOURS HAD PASSED, BUT I could still feel him in every part of my body, as if he had tattooed my skin with his.

I left Christopher at the entrance of the house, excitedly looking at something on the motorcycle, and went to the kitchen to get a glass of water. I had spent the entire morning in that man's arms and still couldn't believe it was real.

I filled the glass with water and drank it all at once, placing it on the counter afterward. I noticed a forgotten frying pan on the stove. A smile crept onto my lips. He was going through all that trouble just to satisfy me and, of course, to keep the house safe from any explosions, I should add.

I turned to go find him at the entrance of the house when I came face to face with a strange man standing right in the middle of the kitchen.

"SHIT!" I grabbed the frying pan without thinking. How had that man appeared right behind me without making a sound?

"Miss Cahill, I presume." I ignored the charming, bright smile he gave me and charged at him.

I attacked the intruder with the frying pan and started hitting him non-stop. If they wanted to kill me, they were going to have to fight.

"Ouch! Miss, for the love of the gods, stop!" The intruder tried to trick me, but I didn't stop hitting.

When I turned, about to flee the kitchen, I found another stranger blocking the door. This one, unlike the first, was as big as a bear, his wide arms barely fitting in the doorway, and he had tattoos up to the base of his neck. A mobster, for sure!

A sudden fear made me hold my breath. I screamed and hurled the frying pan at him.

"Damn! What a crazy woman!" he cursed as the frying pan hit his head.

I grabbed another pot I found in front of me and aimed it at the tattooed giant and the elegant, light-footed assassin.

"CHRISTOPHER!" they yelled, and it took no time for my bodyguard to appear in the kitchen with wide eyes as I wielded a pot like a sword.

I blinked in confusion, watching Wolf's expression shift from concern to amusement in an instant.

"I warned you it was better to knock first." Christopher looked at the first man, who had nearly given me a heart attack, and laughed loudly while the strangers stared at me with clear curiosity and concern. "Jasmin, these are my brothers. Ghost and Snake. Please lower the pot. We don't want anyone getting hurt."

CHAPTER TWENTY-THREE

Wolf

Never in my life did I need to hold back laughter as much as when Jasmin found Ghost and Snake in the kitchen. My brothers had been there for less than five minutes, and I had left them alone for even less time than that. That was all it took for them to wander into the kitchen.

I arrived just as she was attacking them with a frying pan, and now my little warrior, brave wallet-batter, was pointing another pot at the two men, who stared at her with horrified expressions.

"Looks like you're quite well-prepared for any invasion," Ghost tried to straighten his suit again and brought a hand to his jaw, where she had hit him squarely with the frying pan.

"You didn't tell us you were dealing with a wild one," Snake retorted, irritated.

"Wild? Oh, you tattooed idiot... I'll shove this pot down your throat." I reached out and wrapped my arms around my mini warrior while Ghost laughed at the whole scene.

"You surprised her, Snake; you can't expect a different reaction, especially after everything she's been through."

"You're lucky to still have both your eyes," she huffed in my arms, and I couldn't help but smile at her defiant little nose and her cheeks flushed with anger.

When I looked at my brothers, I noticed they were watching me with suspicious looks, and I quickly returned to my normal state, closing my expression.

"They came to help," I informed, and I saw Jasmin's green, attentive gaze scan each of their faces before she set the pot down on the counter.

"I must admit, out of all the tricks they've tried to use to kill me, I've never been attacked with a frying pan." Ghost laughed at the situation. "I admire your courage and creativity." He made a brief bow toward Jasmin, who raised her eyebrows and only then seemed to notice the scars running up Ghost's neck.

"If you're not planning to kill me..."

"You were the one planning such a thing. A death by frying pan, no less. How audacious." Snake exhaled, exasperated, but soon a mocking smile appeared at the corner of his mouth, seemingly disarming my little one a bit.

My...

The word made me pulse. I felt possessive since I took Jasmin on for her protection, something I had assimilated was due to the job and all the risks she might face, but now, after everything we'd experienced, that feeling—of possession mixed with desire and the need to keep her safe—embraced me fully.

"In my defense... I'm a bit worried. Someone wants to kill me."

"A plausible justification, for sure," Ghost supported her. "I'm glad to know that you would defend yourself so well." She smiled.

"Do you really think so?" Jasmin bit her lips, excited. "I've always liked throwing things. Oh, I hit a whiskey bottle in the face of the man who tried to stab me." In an instant, both Ghost and Snake turned their eyes to me.

"That's exactly what you're thinking. She hit Naish with a bottle."

"Fuck!" Snake looked at her again. "The girl has guts." I could see admiration growing in his gaze.

If I was unsociable, my older brother was infinitely worse. He had no friends and rarely opened up to us. He was a brave, aggressive man, but unlike me, not impulsive at all. One of the things Snake hated most was cowardice and betrayal. Similar to mafia principles, I must emphasize. My brother had traits that sometimes worried us, but he knew how to recognize and value courage when he saw it, and that was exactly what I saw in his gaze as he stared at Jasmin.

"He deserved it," she shrugged.

"Brother, I'm curious..." Ghost stepped forward. "What was Naish's fate after that splendid bottle hit?"

"Did you kill him?" Snake stepped forward, very interested.

"No." I pursed my lips.

"Did you seriously injure him?" Ghost's hopeful tone almost made me emit a grunt of dissatisfaction.

Jasmin kept her eyes on both of them, jumping from one to the other like in a game of ping pong.

"We need to talk," I warned and made a brief gesture toward her. "Can you give us a few minutes?" I asked Jasmin, who looked at me with a furrow of concern.

"Sure. I'll be in the living room if you need me."

"I'll find you soon." I touched her hand from behind the counter so my brothers wouldn't see. As if what we had to face wasn't enough, I didn't want to hear any lectures for now. Though I knew that at some point I wouldn't be able to escape it. "Try not to throw anything at anyone until then." I smiled at her, and she left the kitchen shortly after.

I turned to my brothers. They were both watching me with their arms crossed. Ghost had a serious, irritated expression.

"What's up?"

"Brother..." My youngest pulled a hundred-dollar bill from his very black and neatly tailored suit pocket and handed it to Snake. "You just cost me a hundred bucks."

"Don't blame yourself, Ghost. Wolf is as clear as day to me." Snake smiled to the side and tucked the money into his pocket.

"What the hell are you talking about?"

"We bet some cash that you were involved with the VIP."

"As mature men we are..." Ghost rolled his eyes. "I was coerced by him," he nodded toward Snake, "but I believed you would keep your word in front of a VIP, brother. I'm disappointed."

"You deduced all that just by looking at me? You guys are crazy?"

"Besides the interrogation you did to Ghost about the girl's nightmares and your absurd need to turn the world upside down looking for Naish, it's hard to ignore the weird looks exchanged between you two." Snake pursed his lips. "It's obvious, and you'd better prepare to deal with the consequences because they are coming."

He was right. I knew that the moments I was living with Jasmin would soon stop being a dream and turn into reality. And I feared that, in that reality, there would be no way for a relationship between a VIP and her bodyguard to work out.

Just the thought of my contract ending and not being able to lay my eyes on her again drove me crazy.

"No matter what the consequences are, you know what I think about these rules," Ghost stepped forward and spoke quietly, ensuring Jasmin wouldn't hear him. "I've never seen you with that look, brother. You seem happy, something you rarely allow yourself. So you have my blessing."

"Don't say foolish things, brother. Blessing for what?"

"To face our father." He shook his head as if the answer was obvious. "I enjoy the expressions you make when he's about to choke you, but this time I'll stand by your side. Accept my help; you're going to need it." And he truly would.

"You disgust me," Snake growled.

"Don't be cynical, brother. Just because you don't believe in love doesn't mean it doesn't exist."

"Who mentioned love?" I whispered, startled by the word. "Are you crazy, Zion? I've never felt that for any woman. I can guarantee it's not the case here."

"You may have never loved someone as if your life depended on her air to breathe, but I have, in case you've forgotten," he confessed beside me, his serious expression hitting me hard. "Your stance doesn't fool me, brother. Miss Cahill has bothered you ever since she stole your precious bike. No one usually confronts you, but she did. I think she caught your attention there, and the way you look at her—as if you're about to encase her in a golden dome—leaves no doubt. Not to mention she broke one of your most untouchable rules."

I remained silent for a long time, analyzing what Ghost said, and quickly changed the subject when I confronted the truth in each of his words.

"Don't talk nonsense, brother. Save your creativity for figuring out who's behind all this." I deflected the subject.

"If that's how you prefer it..." Ghost pressed his fingertips together, and Snake rolled his eyes. "Well, putting aside all the moral rules broken under this roof..." Ghost leaned against the counter and then stepped away, eyeing it with a funny expression. "Is it safe for me to lean here?" I knew what he was thinking and had to stifle a laugh.

"Start talking already; we don't have much time."

"So be it." Ghost took a deep breath and handed me a small box containing two disposable phones. "Call our father; he's worried. And keep the second phone to contact us."

"Why didn't you kill Naish when you had the chance?" Snake approached. My brother was a bit taller than me, with a serious demeanor and so many tattoos it would be impossible to count them. Even though he wore a very black suit, the designs on his hands were still visible, as well as those climbing his neck and behind his ear.

"I simply didn't see him. It was Jasmin who found him and hit him with a bottle before he had the chance to get close to her."

"Fuck, are you serious?"

I confirmed with a disheartened nod.

"We were ambushed while relocating the VIP to a secondary safe house. Naish had planned everything. They slashed the tires and forced the VIP out of the armored car using a low-impact bomb. I haven't encountered such an organized gang in years. It wasn't amateur work; those men are professionals."

"So he saw you," Ghost inquired.

"Probably yes, but I don't think he knows I'm aware of his presence. He was wearing a hood covering his face."

"That's good. At least it's an advantage. But now we need to kill him regardless; otherwise..."

"He will chase you for the rest of your life, brother. It's the least we can expect from a psychopath like him." Ghost brought a hand to his jaw. "What do we know about this ambush?"

I began recounting every second of our day, obviously hiding the details of the heated exchanges we had in the dance room. Wolf and Snake listened intently.

"The only people who knew about that house were Jasmin, Cahill, and the man's fiancée, Senator Claire."

"Do you think the senator might be involved?" Snake raised the question.

"I don't know. There are too many suspects, and her father's company deals with tracking and locating items, which doesn't help at all. We have no idea how much access a stranger might have within the company, and we need to investigate without them noticing."

"Wolf..." Snake approached with that tone of voice that preceded one of his bizarre, convoluted plans, which usually put our lives at risk. "You know Naish. He's been working under the radar for years. He has no fingerprints and always changes his face through illegal surgical procedures, according to my sources. And now, brother... he saw you. He knows full well that the last time you met wasn't forgotten. He's coming for both of you; you need to get ahead of this. We need to separate him from that team. Alone, he's too weak."

"I know you want revenge for your friend's death, but you need to think coolly when facing him, brother, otherwise... he will get what he wants."

Thinking coolly... I could still feel the urge to kill that bastard in my bones.

"What you have goes far beyond what we can handle in normal cases. There's a personal bond, and that bastard won't stop." Snake slammed the table, serious. "And there's only one way to capture him."

"Come on, brother, don't leave us curious. Tell us your idea." Ghost leaned against the counter, and I feared whatever Snake was thinking.

"Naish isn't the type of man who easily falls into an ambush. But he's extremely meticulous. He doesn't take a step that could harm him and only risks himself if it's to hit the target."

"What do you mean by that?" My voice came out low, cautious.

"You need to give him what he wants. Otherwise, you'll never be able to find him." My entire body stiffened when Snake suggested that. "You know I'm right."

"Are you telling me to use her as bait?" I shouted too loudly. "You must be completely insane. I'm never going to put her at risk like that; we're talking about Naish, for fuck's sake." The thought of having Jasmin near that man drove me to desperation. "I'm not considering that shit, Snake."

"I'm in!" The dim-witted voice came from behind me, and I turned to her, suppressing the sudden urge to strangle her.

"Were you eavesdropping, Miss Cahill?" I narrowed my eyes, a certain fear creeping in as I wondered how much she might have heard.

"Did you really think I would just sit here like a faded statue waiting for you to finish the meeting that was probably deciding my life? I tried, I swear, but when I heard the voices getting heated, I couldn't hold back." She glared at me defiantly, and apparently, she had only heard the conversation from the fight we started having, which gave me some relief. "I don't know what the plan is, but if you guarantee I'll come out of this alive, I'm in."

"Give this woman a frying pan, and she'll be able to rule the world," Ghost pointed at her, thrilled.

"Even you, Ghost? The most rational of us all? Do you really think she should put herself in danger?" Confusion overwhelmed me. Those two must be completely out of their minds. "Not over my dead body."

"Brother, you're the one who needs to be rational. The idea is that none of the inhabitants of this kitchen should become a corpse."

"No, Ghost. Jasmin is not going to submit to that."

"It's not you who gets to decide which battles I will fight." She clenched her jaw. "That bastard killed my sister. He took something from me that I will never be able to get over, and now he's trying to kill me. I will respond in kind, Wolf, whether you like it or not."

"She's actually quite interesting," Snake whispered to Ghost.

"I can still hear you," I growled.

"Relax, brother." He walked over to me and placed his tattooed hand on my shoulder. "We're strong apart, but together we're unbeatable."

"And I have a plan," Ghost concluded.

"I'm in for anything," the little one reminded.

"Then you better sit down, because this story is going to be long."

MY BROTHERS DECIDED it was time to leave almost in the late afternoon. Jasmin was excited about their visit and I could even guarantee that among them, Ghost was her favorite. Especially when he revealed his interest in literature and even romances. Jasmin got into a long, animated conversation with my youngest brother, which made me contemplate the idea of throwing him out the window with all that charm he exuded so naturally.

"Keep the phone on. We'll find Cahill and..."

"Don't forget to talk to him alone," I interrupted Snake. "We can't risk absolutely anyone finding out about this meeting," I warned.

"No one will know anything," Ghost confirmed.

"Thank you both for everything you're doing to help me." Jasmin passed by me and hugged each of my brothers. "Once again, I'm so sorry for..." She raised her hand, mimicking a frying pan.

"The more improbable the bonds, the stronger they become. No one has ever attacked me with a pan; I believe we'll be good friends." Ghost extended his hand toward her. "By the way, my name is Zion. And this grumpy guy beside me is Cedric."

"I didn't mean to mention that," Snake muttered through clenched teeth. Jasmin laughed and waved as they left us alone.

I looked at her, so smiling and hopeful, that a pain probed my chest. I feared that none of this would work and that Jasmin would end up getting hurt, or worse.

The thought terrified me.

I grabbed her wrist and pulled her into my arms, pressing her body against mine.

"I'll protect you, my little one. Nothing bad is going to happen to you." I kissed the top of her head and pulled back to gaze into her bright jade eyes. "Do you trust me?"

"With my life." She smiled at the pun, and I couldn't resist. I touched my lips to hers and kissed her passionately, hoping that, for just a moment, I could stop feeling that sensation of losing something bit by bit.

As if each of Jasmin's breaths became more precious as time passed.

The reality was that Ghost was right. I had been involved with that little light-fingered dancer since the first day I laid eyes on her. I wouldn't know what to do if I lost her.

CHAPTER TWENTY-FOUR

Jasmin

"They're really nice, even though I'm not so sure about Snake being a bodyguard or a wanted man," I said, wrapped in his arms, with a burning desire not to leave that spot. Wolf laughed, the deep sound echoing in my ears.

"Those two and my father are all I have." His heavy voice fell on me, just like the lingering kiss he placed on my forehead. "It's easy to like them once you get used to Snake's restless and sarcastic humor and Ghost's sudden appearances." Christopher ran his fingers down my arms and held my hand, guiding me back into the house.

"I'm shocked by how easily that man moves without being heard. Has he always been like that?"

"Ghost had a very sad past, where he learned that to survive, he couldn't be noticed." He walked to the sofa and sat down, pulling me beside him. I tucked my feet up onto the soft furniture and curled into his embrace with a naturalness that startled me. "You have no idea what it was like to live in the same house as him. Every day brought a different scare. No nickname ever suited someone so well."

"Yours suits you, too. When did you start being called Wolf?"

"The heterochromia earned me that nickname as soon as I entered the orphanage for the first time, but that wasn't the only reason." "I not only had different colored eyes, like some wolves, but I was also aggressive and untamed. I lived in the dark corners of the place, and when the older boys came to tease me, I always retaliated, even if I got beaten up; I never accepted a provocation in silence. Gradually, I became known in that place."

He placed a tender kiss on my shoulder, and I nestled even deeper into his arms.

"How did your father choose you? Can you tell me? Only if it doesn't bother you..."

"Of course. It's actually a funny story."

"Did he find you setting the place on fire? I can just imagine you upside down, hanging from a chandelier, while your little gang terrorized the place." I laughed softly, picturing a mini version of Wolf that must have been adorable.

"Your imagination is quite fertile." It was Wolf's turn to laugh. "Actually, when my father arrived at the orphanage, I had just gotten into a fight with another boy, much bigger than me, over the apples served in the cafeteria. Every now and then, someone would steal my food to provoke me. I was one of the youngest residents there since I had run away from the first orphanage they sent me to, so all the veterans thought they had the right to chase me. At first, I got beaten up a lot, and often spent the whole day hungry because of it, but as time went on, I began to fight back more fiercely and became even more aggressive than I already was."

"That doesn't sound like a funny story to me." I propped myself up on one elbow. My heart raced, and a knot formed in my throat as I imagined him small and alone after witnessing his mother's death, starving in a place that was supposed to shelter him from the world.

"Don't be sad, my angel; the funny part comes now, I promise." He ran his finger down my back and stopped at the base of my spine, almost touching my butt. "That day, I reacted, releasing all the anger inside me; I broke the boy's nose, but ended up with a beautiful black eye and a punishment. I went to my room hungry while the other boys played."

"I still don't see the humor." Damn, now my eyes were tearing up. I curled up against his chest so he wouldn't see.

"Holder arrived at the orphanage that very afternoon. He sought out the administration, which started showing him the best options in the place. I was far from being introduced to him, of course. I was considered uncontrollable, aggressive, and erratic from the moment I set foot in that place." He laughed bitterly. "Holder evaluated all the boys in the orphanage; some were playing near my dorm, and the same boy from the apple incident decided to gather his crew and seek revenge on me for the cafeteria chaos. When he arrived with his friends at my room, I was already waiting for him with a broken broomstick I managed to steal and hide under my mattress. I couldn't do much with that, but at least I could defend myself. There were five boys, if I remember correctly."

"Cowards!" I cursed. "Tell me you gave them a Jackie Chan-style beating. Please!"

"I really wish I could say it was an insane martial arts fight, but the truth is that I snapped and don't remember much of what happened. I seriously injured one of them, and the others got scared and ran to tell the caretaker, who happened to be right next to Holder. The woman even tried to dismiss my father, but he followed her as she went to my dorm to see what had happened to the other boy," he continued, his eyes lost in a fixed point as if he were reliving the scene in his head. "The woman went immediately to help the boy I had hurt, while I stayed huddled in a corner of the room. I knew that from then on, things would get even more dangerous for me in that place, and I hadn't even noticed the man standing in the middle of the room until he knelt in front of me. He said something and extended his hand toward me."

"And what did you do?" I stared at him expectantly.

"I bit his hand." Wolf burst out laughing, and I opened my mouth, too surprised.

"You... bit his hand?"

"Yes. I was too scared. Holder got up, and I thought I would never see him again after that, but the man refused to leave without taking me with him. I remember the phrase he said when he informed the woman that he had found the young boy he wanted to adopt. Upon learning that I was the chosen one, she started questioning him about his certainty regarding that decision. She pointed out all my flaws and made it clear that she wouldn't accept returns. Holder turned to her calmly and said: he will never step foot in a place like this again. Now the boy will be my son; let me handle any problems he may have."

"He's such a g-great man." I sobbed, unable to control the urge to cry. "You suffered so much." I sniffled and buried my face in his chest.

"My angel, I didn't tell you this to make you cry." Christopher sat up and enveloped me in a tight hug. "This is the truth behind my story. My father chose the worst boy from three different orphanages; Snake was the first, I was the second, and Ghost, our youngest, was the last. Each of us with our scars, with our dark pasts. With problems that a normal family would hardly accept, and it took years for him to break through the barrier I put up to try to protect myself. My father never gave up on me or my brothers. Any one of us three would die without a second thought to protect him. Reid Holder is all we've ever had. Our family isn't conventional, but it's stronger and more united than anything that exists in this world. That's the truth. Even though each of us carries our mark, just like me, still struggling to control my anger, we are happy in our own way."

"That's the most beautiful story I've ever heard." I wiped my eyes with the sleeves of my shirt. "Was it your father who taught you to fight and shoot like that? You're so quick that it's hard to keep up with your movements." He laughed and showed a certain pride in his colorful, bright eyes.

"Yes. I trained in Aikido for many years. A martial art focused on short, efficient strikes. In addition to the exhaustive target shooting training," he shared. "When I began to focus my anger on the aim of the gun, everything changed. That's when I found the perfect balance."

"Are you sure you can't teach me anything about guns?"

"Given your fervent skill in the kitchen, I can't imagine how that could be of great help. It would only end up putting your life at risk, and I can't allow that." He traced a finger along my face. "Perhaps, when all this is over, you could take some shooting lessons in a safe place."

"Do you really think so?" The expectation excited me.

"With good supervision, I believe you'd become a great shooter." He brushed his nose against my neck and placed a chaste kiss on my nape, causing me to shiver. "You have all the qualities of one."

"What qualities would those be?" I whispered, caught up in the small, brief kisses he was placing on my skin, around the base of my neck.

"You're persistent enough not to give up on your first attempts..." He kissed my earlobe. "Stubborn enough to try to improve as you start learning more, without wavering or staying stagnant at just one level, like most people who practice target shooting out of pure curiosity and stop trying to perfect their technique as soon as they hit the target just once. And above all—" he kissed my cheek, causing a delightful pop—"you're a confident woman." His deep eyes landed on my mouth. "I doubt anyone in their right mind would face you with a gun in hand, even if you didn't know how to shoot, just because of the stance you maintain. That makes a big difference."

"You're back to using formal titles for me?" The slight heat rising in my body from Wolf's touch expanded as he leaned in closer, his warm breath brushing against my face.

"And when was it that, since the moment we first saw each other, you stopped being my *miss*?" I shuddered and closed my eyes as Wolf's mouth brushed against mine slowly, causing an avalanche of sensations across my skin. "I can't kiss you." He suddenly pulled away.

"Why not?" I questioned, frustrated.

"There's not a kiss from you that doesn't make me want to take you to bed, Miss Cahill." His eyes overflowed with the purest desire, reflecting what I felt in my soul.

"Do you really need to hold back when we don't even know if we'll be alive tomorrow?" He cupped my face with both hands, staring at me with a desire that threatened to suffocate me.

"I already told you I won't allow you to suffer even a scratch." I could feel the difference in his tone, which had become determined and fierce.

I climbed onto his lap and wrapped my legs around his body, fitting him there. His member pulsed beneath me.

"So there's no reason for us to worry." I wrapped my arms around his neck, leaning against him. His attentive eyes stayed locked on mine. "Can't you feel it? This heat, this... urgency?" Wolf let out a low, husky sound.

"I feel that every time I think of you. I'm starting to get worried." His hand gripped my neck, and without realizing it, I began to grind against his member, rubbing my intimacy against him with an overwhelming need. "How can I stay sane near you, my angel?" With his free hand, Wolf touched the edge of the waistband of my pants and began to lower them. I lifted my body to help him and settled onto his lap in just my panties.

I gasped in anticipation when he dug his fingers into the flesh of my butt and guided my movements over his firm, thick erection, highlighted beneath the thin fabric of his pants. His lips claimed mine with fervor in a clash of teeth, tongues, and pure lust. Every point in my body started to pulse. His fingers slid up my waist and touched my blouse. Christopher undid the fabric slowly, leaving me exposed on his lap, wearing only my panties. His eyes rested on my breasts with devotion, the incandescent glow in his irises made me shudder. He cupped them in his hands, enveloping my entire breast slowly, then leaned over and blew on one of my nipples.

"Christopher..." I whispered his name as a hot tremor surged through my body. I squeezed my thighs and began rubbing myself against his member again, desperate for more.

"I love it when you say my name." He flicked his tongue over the tip of my nipple and trapped it between his teeth, alternating the affection that drove me insane. "Do you like this?"

"Y-you know I do." I leaned in closer and tangled my fingers in the soft hair at the nape of his neck, mussing it up.

"I love it when you talk..." He sucked on my nipple eagerly and slid his hand down my skin until he found my intimacy. His finger slipped inside my panties.

" *Chris!* " I couldn't hold back a loud moan when I felt the rough skin touch the pulsating point that was driving me to the brink of madness.

"Ah, my delight." He increased the caresses on that oh-so-sensitive spot. Rubbing it with a firm, steady rhythm, slow and delicious, his mouth traveled over my breasts, alternating kisses, bites, and sucking. His stubble scratched my skin, adding to the already intense sensation.

I needed him inside me urgently. I opened his pants and fumbled, trying to pull them down a little. Christopher came to my aid, lowering them just enough for his thick erection, veined and pulsing, to be exposed.

I was trembling, crazy with desire.

"Calm down, my angel, I need to get the condom from my wallet..."

"Fuck me now. I'm going to explode, Christopher." I panted his name and saw his expression change from excited to something more dangerous, uncontrollable, and extremely appetizing.

He didn't hesitate. His hand pushed my panties aside, and he aligned his member at my entrance. The skin-on-skin contact, pure and raw, made me stifle a scream between my teeth.

"Fuck!" he growled, pushing a little further. The thick head entered, plunging me into an atmosphere of extreme heat. Wolf invaded my mouth with his tongue, while his thumb continued to caress the spot that gave me the most pleasure. I opened my legs to take him in completely. With his other hand, he gripped my butt tightly, pulling me toward his desire. "Damn, what a delight," he growled into my mouth.

My body moved back and forth, sliding over his thick member with every thrust. The most delicious sensation I'd ever experienced, for sure. Or at least that's what I thought.

Christopher picked up the pace, I could feel he was beginning to let go with me, revealing a primal, animalistic desire that consumed and excited me in equal measure. His hand slid over my butt, spreading it open.

I threw my head back when his finger found the most improbable part of my body, a place I hadn't imagined could bring so much pleasure. He caressed the center, spreading my butt open wider and I couldn't take it.

The orgasm came fast, extreme, devastating. I screamed, grinding down on his member, feeling it throb inside me. Christopher suddenly lifted me for a moment and pulled out of me, his hard member falling against my stomach, and his teeth sank into my neck with such intensity that it caused a delicious mix of pain and pleasure. I gasped when I felt the liquid of his pleasure drip onto my belly.

"Damn..." he panted into my hair, pulling me into his arms. Neither of us cared about the mess between us, and it felt so intimate that a sharp pang arose in my chest. I nestled my head on his shoulder, feeling his breath rise and fall in a pleasant rhythm. "That was incredible... and shit, dangerous," he said, and I was sure he was talking about the condom.

"Sorry about that. I was feeling something kind of uncontrollable." My face burned with shame, and Christopher flashed a dazzling smile.

"Don't apologize, my angel. It's my fault. I should have stopped it, but I couldn't either. Just imagining feeling you without any barrier drove me crazy. But even though I'm a man who takes care of himself and there's no risk to you, it can be dangerous." He caressed my mouth with a brief kiss.

"Why does it have to feel so good to feel you like that?" I pouted, and I saw his gaze turn lustful again. The rigidity of his member hadn't even diminished, on the contrary, Wolf seemed ready for the next round, and that enticed me.

"It feels amazing," he admitted. "You can see I couldn't hide my desire to stay inside you even if I wanted to," he referred to his erection, making me laugh. "But from now on, we're using a condom, okay?"

"Fine by me, as long as it happens again..." I leaned in and kissed his mouth, sucking on his tongue just like he had done to me the night before, and things started to heat up again, but we were interrupted by the phone that Wolf's brothers had left with him, now playing a loud, constant, and annoying song.

"I think my brothers found your father." He spun me around on his lap, pulled up his pants, and reached for the device.

Less than a minute later and a few words like yes, no, and okay, Wolf hung up.

"We need to get ready. The cavalry will be here in a few minutes."

"Cavalry?" He smiled and reached for a handkerchief from one of the thousand pockets in his pants, wiping my belly with a casualness and tenderness that made me sigh.

He looked up at me, but before saying anything about that information, he inspected my neck and slowly widened his clear and distinctive eyes.

"Shit!"

"What is it?" He ran his finger along the base of my neck.

"I think I went too far. There's a huge mark right here, fuck!" Christopher ran his hands through his hair, and I had to hide the pleasure that surged through me upon hearing that.

"Don't worry, I can hide anything with makeup."

"Are you sure? I don't want to cause any trouble for you, but damn it," he cursed again. "I've been trying so hard not to leave marks on you, but I guess I overdid it without realizing."

"I hope I get to meet this other side of you soon, the one that promises to leave me all marked," I teased and bit my lips.

"You like it, don't you? You little tease." He laughed and kissed my forehead.

We got dressed as quickly as we could, and before we left, Wolf stopped in front of me and cupped my face with both hands.

"Things are going to get tough from here on out, but don't worry. You'll never be alone." I tilted my head toward his touch and smiled.

"As long as you're by my side, I know I have nothing to worry about."

WOLF WASN'T EXAGGERATING when he said the cavalry was on the way. Less than an hour after the call, which made it clear that Ghost and Snake had managed to contact both my father and their own, an exorbitant number of armored cars surrounded the house we were in.

"Mr. Holder, is everything alright?" A man, dressed in a pumpkin-colored suit, got out of one of the cars in a panic and ran toward us.

"Miss Cahill, this man about to have a heart attack is our manager, Benjamin." Wolf introduced him with a light smile on his face.

"It's a pleasure, miss." He made a quick bow. "You weren't hurt, right? I brought the entire available team. Each of the cars is armored and has two heavily armed bodyguards." I glanced over the dark-tinted cars, barely able to see any of their faces. "We'll take you to safety."

"Excellent work, Benjamin." The man seemed energized by the compliment.

"They are waiting for you at the Hill House," he informed. "You'll travel in car number 6." He pointed to the long line of black cars.

"Have them retrieve a motorcycle I left here and prepare the place for a new season," he said, and I wondered if by "new season" he meant that the place would soon serve as a hideout for another VIP, but I chose to ask what seemed more important.

"And your brothers?" I whispered.

"They're taking care of another matter, but we should see them again soon," he replied attentively. "Shall we go? You must be missing those incompetent people you call security," he joked.

"I bet you are too." I didn't know how Wolf would act around other people; I imagined he would firmly ignore me, but I was surprised when I felt his fingers seek out mine, and he gently entwined our hands.

"I have no one to curse at without Lyon around."

"And no one to flatter you without Shaw on your tail." I smiled, a smile that seemed to emerge from the depths of my heart, as we walked together to the car designated for us, engaged in a conversation that felt exclusively ours. Too intimate to be true.

I sat beside Wolf in the back seat while he greeted the two security guards in the front and exchanged brief words. I caught myself admiring him for a moment. In contrast to everything I had seen of him so far—always elegant, with perfectly styled hair and a sharply pressed suit—now my Wolf was without his jacket, his disheveled hair falling flat over his forehead in well-cut layers, the sleeves of his shirt rolled up to his elbows revealing the thick hair on his forearms, and even his beard showed signs of very dark, thick stubble.

I could only wonder how he managed to look even more handsome and virile.

Oh heavens...

I brought my hand to my chest as a wave of heat washed over me while I watched him. I could feel the irregular beating of my heart racing through all my senses. I feared I was falling in love with the enigmatic man beside me, but now a new fear overwhelmed me with the prospect of feeling something much stronger, more intense, and real. A feeling I still didn't know how to handle.

WE ARRIVED AT THE MANSION a long time later. Wolf didn't let go of my hand throughout the journey, which left me a bit dizzy and confused. He opened the door for me to get out when Holder's security parked in front of the mansion.

"Thank you," I said just in time to see Shaw running toward me as if his life depended on it.

"Miss! MISS!" he shouted, quickening his pace. I smiled when the young man gave me a quick hug and then looked me over from head to toe. "Are you okay? Didn't get hurt? My God, thank goodness you're back." From Shaw's words, it was clear he was a religious man. Every time he got startled, he would exclaim a resounding "mercy," which made me laugh.

"I'm fine, Shaw. Thank you for your concern." Wolf stared at the young man as if he were an ant he intended to crush.

"Mr. Wolf, thank you for keeping her safe," Shaw expressed, and before my bodyguard could respond, a commotion surrounded us. All the staff came out of the house, including Ruth and Judith, bombarding us with a barrage of questions.

"Jasmin!" The crowd around us fell silent as my father appeared at the entrance of the house. He looked very worn out, dressed in wrinkled and disheveled clothes, which made me catch my breath. Dad must have been through hell since the attack on the mansion, all because he was worried about me.

"Dad!" My eyes burned, and I ran to him, throwing myself into his arms.

"Oh, my daughter, I was terrified. I feared for your life. Thank you, my God, for bringing her back." Suddenly, my father pulled away from the hug and looked at someone behind me. "Thank you, Wolf, for protecting her as best as you could. I can never express how grateful I am to you for what you did for my family."

"I said I would do anything to keep her safe." Wolf's eyes fell on me, affectionate, revealing the secret that lay between us.

"I need to speak with both of you, now," my father requested. "Let's go to the office."

"Looks like you really do keep your word," Lyon teased Wolf as he passed by him, in a cheerful voice.

"I still haven't fulfilled my promise to break one of your teeth."

"When did you make that promise?"

"At this very minute..." Wolf laughed, and Lyon joined in.

We entered my father's office, always very dark, and sat in the chairs in front of his mahogany desk.

We spent the next few minutes explaining everything that had happened to my father, who, despite having heard the same information from Christopher's brothers, still wanted to hear it from us.

"Did Ghost tell you the details of the plan?" Wolf inquired when he finished explaining everything, or almost everything.

"Yes, and I'm very worried."

"You know I would never put your daughter's life at risk, especially knowing who we're up against. You can believe me when I say we found no other solution but this." He leaned forward, getting closer to the table. "If we don't capture Naish, Jasmin will never be able to live in peace. That bastard won't stop until he gets what he wants."

A pang of distress hit my chest as I saw my father's expression grow even paler.

"It's not fair." My lips trembled, and before Wolf even realized we were in front of my father, he entwined my fingers with his. Thick tears streamed down my face. "Our family has never harmed anyone," I sobbed. "Why are they pursuing us? Why did they take away all our peace?"

"Human beings are evil by nature, my daughter," Dad said with a tender sorrow. "Money, status, envy... there are so many reasons that we can't even measure. And I agree with you, Wolf." He turned to the man who had slowly released my hand. "This has to end. My daughter and I need to live again."

"So trust the plan and leave the rest to us." Wolf tapped a finger on the table. "We will catch him and find out which of our suspects is the culprit."

"Do you think you can extract that information?"

"I won't be the one interrogating him. That man is a psychopath; the techniques I've used before, which I'm not proud of, would be useless. This is a job for my brother."

"Ghost?" I turned to him with a knot in my stomach, wondering what "techniques" Wolf usually used to extract the truth.

"Not Ghost. Snake." He flashed a sideways smile that sent a chill of bad omen down my spine. "Trust me; if he knows any relevant information, we'll find out."

"I will meet with the press later today and announce that Magnolia's murderer tried to attack Jasmin and was arrested. One of my contacts in the FBI will issue a press release."

"How many bodies did they find at the ambush site?" Wolf cast his eyes down at me with an implicit apology for the question, and I nodded; we needed to know all the details.

"Four dead," my father replied.

"Great." Wolf crossed his arms. "Naish definitely didn't come back to check if any of them were actually alive. The man doesn't care about anyone, especially not those who become a burden in his way." His eyes wandered for a moment before he looked at my father again. "Let's make him believe that one of them survived and that we think he's the murderer. Just that information circulating through the major news sites will leave Naish furious. He values his dirty work above all else. He'll hate to think that someone is taking credit for something he did."

"Don't forget about the party, Dad. It's the most important part," I reminded him. "Announce the event for this weekend, as a celebration for the arrest. He'll be even angrier. Let him think we don't even suspect anyone else is behind all this. We'll need a fast and flawless organizing team." A bright idea flashed in my mind as I remembered that I knew someone who could organize an event of that magnitude in a timely manner, provided she had the right team. "Maybe I already know who can help us," I thought of Carla.

"Does it really have to be a masquerade ball?"

"It's essential that it is," Wolf replied. "We'll expose Jasmin's disguise in the newspapers so that he can locate her in the crowd." A cold sensation filled my chest. The truth was, even though it seemed foolproof, I feared that plan wouldn't work.

"So..." Dad sighed deeply, "let it be. I'll do it right now." He stood up and turned to Wolf. "She is my most precious treasure, Wolf. I'm trusting my daughter's life to the entire Holder family."

"There's no better family to trust." That was my bodyguard's assured response.

I CALLED CARLA AS SOON as I finished the meeting with my father and noticed that I had about 20 missed calls from my friend.

"For the love of my strong-hearted saint, where have you been, Jasmin?" she yelled on the phone at the second ring. "I found out what happened through the newspapers. How could you not call me?"

"Friend, I'm sorry for the delay; I just got a secure phone now." I began to tell Carla about the ambush we suffered and summarized the story without going into detail about the plan we were devising.

"My God, this sounds like a movie," she whispered on the line. "Where did you hide during this time?"

"I don't know where that cabin is, but..."

"How do you not know? You must have seen some sign or something familiar. Friend, I want to know where this place is in case you disappear again. I need to know where you'll be; I didn't sleep a wink, you know? As soon as they announced that you had been attacked, I panicked." Her voice cracked, and my heart ached for not being able to tell her the whole truth.

"I'm so sorry for worrying you, and if I knew the address, I'd tell you right now, but it was raining too hard. I focused on not falling off the bike."

"At least you got to hold on to the handsome guy?" she sniffled.

"Carla!" My face flushed as I recalled everything Wolf and I had done.

"Don't even try; I know there's something going on."

"I'll tell you the details later, but first I want to know if you have room in your schedule to organize a masquerade ball for the weekend."

"The weekend... THE WEEKEND?" she shouted when she realized the short deadline we had.

"If anyone can do it, it's you, and the good news is that we have no budget limits."

"Well, no limits is another story." We laughed together, and I started telling my friend what the party would be like.

Carla believed it was a celebration event, and I felt bad lying to her, but I preferred to keep the truth hidden for a little while rather than put my friend's life and the safety of the plan at risk.

I hung up a while later with a single certainty. The week would be very busy.

Wolf spent the following days away from the mansion, fine-tuning all the details of the plan, which ended up distancing him from me and causing a painful, ongoing longing. The weekend approached, and I hadn't heard from him again, which began to worry me.

The party would take place on Saturday, the next day, and when night fell, I received a worried visit from Aunt Claire, who hadn't been able to visit me earlier due to her intense work schedule. As soon as she saw me, she spent hours lecturing me about all the dangers I faced and accusing the security team for everything that happened.

"Aunt, if it weren't for them, I'd be dead by now."

"Don't say that." She hugged me tightly. "Don't you understand? We couldn't bear it if anything happened to you, my dear."

I spent the rest of the night calming my aunt down and was happy to feel so loved and important. She left a while later, and my thoughts returned to the man who seemed to be tattooed in my mind.

I missed my Wolf. He was probably very busy having meetings with the Holder security team, who seemed to have moved in en masse to the mansion. I had never seen the place so full of them. Shaw took advantage of the bustle and spent much of the week extracting as much information as possible from the guards, hoping to one day secure a position in the company, which made me laugh from time to time, but I still felt weak remembering everything I experienced in that house with Wolf, and not seeing him there bothered me to no end.

It was past eleven at night when a restlessness hit me, and I began to wander around the room with a blanket thrown over my shoulders. I felt a strange emptiness in the absence of that man, a discomfort that felt like it was stealing my breath away.

The next day would be very important, and I might not see him until then. But what about after? If they captured Naish, the risks around us would decrease. Wolf, in any case, had a time limit as my bodyguard, but would he disappear from my life after everything?

The thought cast a deep sadness over me. What if I never saw him again?

I felt like a silly, lovestruck teenager, with the only difference being that I had never fallen in love before, until I met him. I bit my lips and went to the window. Several guards wandered below like little tin soldiers. I climbed onto the window and crawled onto the roof, wrapping myself in the blanket even more. I looked up at the moon and realized that even its glow reminded me of him. The stars sparkled in bright dots across the sky, and my thoughts flew back to the night he climbed that same roof with me.

I was so distracted that I didn't notice I was being watched.

"Don't you ever get tired of scaring me?" A deep voice came from my window, almost making me jump.

It was him! In his usual perfectly fitted black suit, just like his hair. Back to the routine.

My little Wolf...

I jumped up and ran to him, unable to control the longing I felt. I threw myself into his open arms with fervor. Christopher held me briefly, given that the window was still between us.

"I missed you," I admitted quietly.

"I missed you too, my little troublemaker." He helped me climb through the window, and soon his lips took mine with desperate urgency.

"I thought I wouldn't see you until tomorrow."

"You won't get rid of me that easily, I thought I made that clear after your countless attempts to make me give up this job," he joked, sliding his finger across my lips and capturing them again with his. His warm tongue invaded my mouth and set the center of my body on fire.

"I don't want that anymore. No way." I surrendered, completely. "I was afraid that after everything, we wouldn't have time for... us." I gasped softly when he pulled me against his body, pressing me against the erection prominent between his legs.

"Do you have any idea that I spent every second of this damned week thinking about you?" He lowered his lips to the sensitive skin on my shoulder and slid one of his hands down my waist, pulling me even closer to his body, which seemed to burn, just like mine.

Pure desire.

"It would be an understatement if I said I did the same." He brushed the back of his hand over my nipples, protected only by the thin fabric of the nightgown. "Christopher..." I softly panted.

"Ah, my angel, you have no idea how much I want to take you right here. To feel your skin and kiss you until I lose myself in you." He breathed heavily, touching me with his fingers. "But we need to be careful. The house is full of security, and your father will probably sleep here tonight."

"I don't care what they might imagine. I don't care about anything, I just want you." He slid both hands down my butt, pushed up the nightgown, until his cold fingers touched my core, making me moan deeply.

"Fuck!" he growled with his mouth pressed to mine. "So wet like this, it's even harder to say no."

"I know how to solve your problem. Just say yes."

"You little tease!"

"I am, for sure... now come here." I pulled him by the tie, which made him look even sexier, like a government spy.

Wolf hoisted me up by the waist and carried me in his arms to my study desk, knocking all the books off it in one go, and placed me sitting there, fitting himself between my legs. We didn't have time, and we both knew it—at any moment, he could be called on the radio, and we'd have to stop, which just the thought of made me anxious.

I spread my legs wider and let Christopher explore every inch with his mouth, teeth, and tongue. I couldn't describe the pulsing, agonizing, delicious, and deep sensations he caused me. I tried to stifle a moan when Christopher penetrated me with his fingers, licking and biting my exposed breasts. I grabbed his waist and opened his pants. I felt hot, burning, more than ready to take him fully inside me.

Christopher took the last condom from his wallet and put it on, his eyes filled with lust as they lingered on the mark he'd left on my neck, slightly visible, before locking onto mine.

"Make me yours," I begged. He kissed me and thrust deep, all at once, making me scream into his mouth with sudden and intense pleasure.

"You already are mine, angel."

CHAPTER TWENTY-FIVE

Jasmin

The big day finally arrived, and as we expected, the announcement my father made during the week reverberated throughout Chicago. Not a single newspaper was circulating without the news that the murderer of Magnolia Cahill, one of the heirs of the famous Hill and Cahill, had finally been captured and now posed no danger to the family, which would host a masquerade ball in celebration for a large number of guests.

Carla kept me updated on what was happening with the event management team and organized every inch of that place down to the smallest details. So far, everything was going as planned, and Ruth had just left the dress I would wear that night on my bed, along with the mask and hairpiece that had been chosen with great care.

If all went well, we would know that night who was betraying us and have the chance to capture a globally wanted serial killer.

I was getting ready for the shower that would follow the event when there was a knock at my door.

"Yes?"

"It's me." The familiar voice made me smile.

"Come in, Wolf." The tall man stepped through the door with that sideways grin, but I noticed the worry on his face. His eyes darted away from mine to scan the very extravagant dress carefully laid out on the bed. He took a deep breath.

"It's going to be hard to see you in that dress without being able to touch you." I rushed to him, who didn't hesitate to welcome me with open arms and plant a tender, quick kiss on my lips.

"It will be for a short time," I assured him. "The party will end soon."

"That's what I hope," he said, holding my hand. "I want to talk to you when all of this is over," he warned, making me hold my breath.

"Something serious?"

"Yes, but nothing to worry about right now." He tried to reassure me, which only made me more anxious. "There are other matters that deserve your attention more urgently." He held my hand and guided me to one of the chairs at my study desk. "Please sit."

"Good news never starts with 'please sit,'" I observed, suspicious, and saw Wolf leaning his body on the desk beside me without letting go of my hand.

"My angel," he cautiously brushed his thumb across my face, "if I asked you to list all the suspects you have in mind right now, even if the chance is slim, what names would you say?"

"I would start with Foster... that one doesn't fool me." I brought my fingers to my mouth, thinking of the next names, and mentioned 11 of the 12 scientists from Hill and Cahill, along with some random names that came to mind. "Oh, and there's also the project analysis head. He hates me deeply."

"Right. Sixteen names." I nodded in confirmation. "All these people become, from this moment on, suspects."

"Yes, extremely suspicious."

"Now I want you to listen to me and pay close attention to what I'm about to say." He took on a lower, careful tone. "Every person on your list has an obvious motive to harm you, so it's easy to suspect them, but I want you to broaden your scope and start thinking about other people. Those for whom you would put yourself in danger to protect. Those you love."

"I don't think anyone close to me would be capable of betraying me like that, Chris." I froze inside at the thought.

He entwined my hand once more. The gentle, cautious touch helped my racing heart return to normal.

"That's what you think, sweetheart." He kissed the top of my head. "But we all have our share of darkness. Some more than others." I shivered. He caressed my back and sat beside me, enveloping me in his embrace. I took a deep breath, feeling his scent fill my lungs and tried to focus on that smell, seeking to calm myself. "Be suspicious of those you love, not just those who hate you."

"That's very difficult."

"I know you can do it." He touched my chin and lifted my face until our eyes met under the dim light of the room. "I need your best sarcastic version today. Can you pretend everything is fine?"

"I've spent a long time doing that. I won't have any trouble." But the sudden sadness and fear I felt in my chest that this crazy story could become true was about to suffocate me. I trusted very few people, couldn't believe that one of them was betraying me, but I felt Wolf's concern was not in vain. Something was happening. "Still, I'll hope that by the end of the day you're wrong."

"Me too, sweetheart. I hope you won't get hurt when all of this is over."

Wolf

"DID I REALLY NEED TO choose such a sweet-smelling perfume?" I complained beside Shaw.

"It's a special night; I wanted it to be memorable, sir, but I had an accident with the perfume bottle and it spilled on my suit." The scent of almonds could be smelled from miles away. "I'm so sorry."

Cahill, standing next to me in a very luxurious suit, laughed, though he seemed tense about the plans for the night. Wood was in charge of organizing security at the party, but Ray and Lyon were by our side, all five of us standing like statues in front of the stairs, waiting for Jasmin to descend.

"So we're going to use these instead of masks, right?" Lyon asked, lifting the night vision goggles I had handed to each of them.

We only entrusted the real plan to the three bodyguards who were there. I would count on them to keep Jasmin protected at all costs while everything unfolded.

"Yes," I replied. "You already know our priority, so don't deviate from the mission under any circumstances." They nodded, and only then did I turn to Cahill, who was holding his navy blue mask, matching his suit. "Where's the senator? I thought she would arrive with you at the event."

"Claire will have to come straight from work; we'll meet her there."

"I understand." I pursed my lips and straightened my posture. "Did you keep her out of the plans as we agreed?"

"Yes. Even though it bothers me, I need to prioritize Jasmin's safety. If Claire has trusted any information to someone else, it could unintentionally hinder us."

Or intentionally, I thought.

Senator Claire didn't sit well with me. Although she was a very sweet, caring, and kind woman with Jasmin, who seemed to love her as if they shared the same blood, she left me confused with some strange behaviors and was the only one, besides Cahill, to be involved.

Maybe I was overreacting. My sense of trust never worked completely. I always found it easier to suspect someone than to do the opposite. And yes, the senator could be manipulated, or she might not have anything to do with the attacks, but she, like Judith, Ruth, or even Carla, Jasmin's friend, were, unfortunately, suspicious.

"She's ready," Judith shouted from the top of the stairs, and we all turned to look.

Jasmin appeared beside Ruth, who didn't even try to hide the smile on her face.

"My goodness," Shaw said, and I tried to find words to describe what I was seeing, but not even in two lifetimes could I manage.

Jasmin descended the stairs, step by step, with grace. As if she danced on each one. With every step she took, my heart beat harder and faster.

The dress, very white, had an elegant bodice with a deep neckline, and its skirt cascaded in robust waves to her feet, resembling the contours of a princess dress. The white lace mask was adorned with white pearls, just like the lavish headpiece full of white feathers in her hair, which flowed in lush blonde cascades down to her waist. She resembled a queen, majestic, breathtaking.

I lost my words, desperate to touch her. I brought my hand to my chest with the pain that stirred there as my heart raced harder and faster. I felt like I had lost my way in life as she approached. Her striking eyes beneath the mask watched me cautiously.

"You look incredible, my daughter." Cahill offered her an arm. "A work of art, isn't it?" The man turned to me, and for a moment, I forgot how to speak. The words simply vanished from my mind.

"Yes." I coughed, trying to regain my composure. "You look splendid, Miss Cahill."

A chorus behind me echoed in agreement, but the only thing I could focus on was the sweet, delicate, and insecure smile she gave me.

"Have a great party, Miss," Judith shouted from the entrance, and I opened the door for Cahill and Jasmin to get into the car. The man entered first, and I brushed my thumb lightly over her wrist as she passed by me. I needed to touch her somehow or I would end up dying.

She smiled at her father, but she knew very well what I meant with that touch.

My sweet Jasmin… my princess.

WE ARRIVED AT THE EVENT, which, as I imagined, was packed with photographers. We created the perfect scenario for Naish. In that bastard's mind, he would kill Jasmin that night, and her death would make headlines. His name would be branded the main murderer, and he would disappear soon after. That's what I envisioned.

What he didn't count on was me using his main trait against him: his egocentrism.

We escorted Jasmin and Cahill, who was now wearing his party mask, through the small crowd gathered in front of the venue, stopping only when we reached the safety of the ballroom, which spanned two floors and was extremely well decorated with bright garlands interspersed with crystal chandeliers.

Soon, a woman in a stunning red gown with a matching diamond-studded mask approached us.

"Claire, dear." I noticed the apprehensive tone in Cahill's voice.

"Is everything okay?" She scrutinized the man's face, suspicious.

Damn it, he couldn't hide it. The man was terrified at the thought of Jasmin being in the same environment as Magnolia's killer, and I imagined how hard that must be for him, but for that torment to come to an end, he needed to cooperate.

"Aunt Claire, you look beautiful!" Jasmin exaggeratedly complimented, bringing her hands to her mouth. "Dad, you better open your eyes. Aunt Claire is more stunning than anyone at this party." She scanned the guests scattered around the room with her eyes.

"Oh, darling, I doubt that. Just look at you." The woman turned to her with open arms. "You're radiant." Jasmin beamed at her aunt, drawing her attention away from Cahill's anxious face. I pursed my lips, trying to contain my smile at the woman's cleverness. "I hope you enjoy the party after the fiasco of the last one."

"I will, aunt. For sure."

"Shall we get a drink?" Claire turned to Mason, who glanced at his daughter one last time before following the woman away.

"You did great, my angel. I couldn't keep my composure like that." From my peripheral vision, I saw Ray, Lyon, and Shaw find Wood in a corner and position themselves. "You look truly calm."

"Should I say that I'm proud of how fake I can be? Because I am, very much so." She tried to joke, but I could feel the tension in her voice. "I'm terrified."

"It will be fine; don't get nervous." I positioned myself close to her. She smoothed her dress a few times, and when her eyes rose to meet mine again, I found myself frozen, trapped in her deep green irises. "You are the most beautiful creature I have ever laid eyes on. Perfection in its purest form." She broke into a wide smile.

"You make me pulse in strange places when you say things like that, my Wolf." She gazed at my mouth and bit her perfectly shaped pink lips. "Especially here." She placed her hand on her heart, and a strange sensation punched my chest. One that urged me to send all those people around us to hell and take her right there in my arms, not caring about anything else, because I knew my heart was crying out for her, begging for Jasmin every second of the day. "I'm sorry, I shouldn't have said that."

Only then did I realize I was staring at her as if she were doing pirouettes around the room. Damn it, she completely misunderstood.

"Jas..."

"It's fine, this is just one of my flaws, Christopher. I talk too much when I should stay quiet."

"No, sweetheart, I didn't..." I was interrupted by loud music that signaled the start of the masquerade ball, and I knew our plan began there.

Some lights dimmed, leaving only the dance floor lit. I held Jasmin's arm and looked her in the eyes.

"I was flustered for a moment, but I can assure you that what I said was nothing short of perfect," I told her, and she continued to gaze at me with an unsure look. "My angel, I..."

"Jasmin!" An agitated voice called her, and I couldn't finish what I wanted to say. I quickly spotted Carla, wearing a long black dress and holding a clipboard, walking briskly toward us. "I'm glad you made it." She hugged her friend tightly. "Everything is going as we organized, and if we don't have any unforeseen issues, this will be my first flawless official event."

"And have you organized any event that wasn't flawless?" Jasmin asked with a smile.

"At my last event, a girl spun one of my guests by the hair. So..." Both women laughed and stopped when Lyon approached us with a very serious expression.

"Wolf, it's time. Everything is ready," Lyon said.

"Time for what?" Carla asked, confused.

"Friend, I need you to come with me." It was obvious that Jasmin wouldn't leave her friend in a risky place like that, and I had expected this when I learned she would be at the event.

"But... the team needs me." Carla's eyes widened. "Where are you going?"

"Trust me. You'll be safe." She pulled her friend, who began walking beside Lyon, suspicious. I took the opportunity to touch Jasmin's fingers and catch her attention.

"We'll continue our conversation later, okay?" She nodded in agreement. "Let's go to the bathroom. Our night has begun."

TWENTY MINUTES LATER, I took my position alone in the corner of the ballroom. The woman in white dress and blonde hair moved with a certain grace across the floor. I kept my eyes on every step she took.

A few minutes later, she danced with Cahill but didn't approach anyone else, just as we had agreed. The dim lighting helped mask the details and made it easier for more people to enter the dance floor.

Thirty minutes passed with slow dances and, now and then, faster ones. Some women chatted loudly beside me, but my eyes and senses were glued to the woman in white, giving it her all on the dance floor, even though that wasn't her strong suit.

"Are you keeping an eye on the Crystal?" I activated the communicator.

"Yes, sir. The whole team has their eyes on her," Shaw replied, and I felt more relieved.

"Watch those eyes, kid," I teased, and Shaw laughed.

I looked around and noticed the crowd in the venue starting to grow significantly.

"Wood, keep Cahill in the back of the ballroom and be discreet. Take more guards with you," I instructed, when a small commotion began at the entrance of the event, and suddenly a single shot echoed through the room. "Damn!"

My blood boiled as I realized that bastard was here.

He used the same method when he killed Magnolia, as I learned. A single shot to panic the crowd and create chaos, making it easier for him to find his target, but what he didn't know was that the type of crowd inside that party wasn't afraid of the sound of a gunshot.

"Turn off the lights," I requested over the communicator, and a moment later, they went dark, leaving only the red emergency lights on, which caused some muffled screams, just as we had planned. "Stay alert; he's here."

"We've got the shooter, sir. His accomplice was armed at the fire exit. We're checking if there's anyone else," a voice from one of Holder's bodyguards echoed through the communicator.

"Take him to the van," I ordered.

It wasn't Naish who fired the shot, as I had imagined. A psychopath so adept at a precise routine like his rarely changed his *modus operandi*. He intended to assassinate her with a single stab laced with cyanide.

Bastard from hell.

"The show has begun," Ray said over the communicator.

"Don't take your damn eyes off her, understood?" One by one, they agreed, and I put on the night vision goggles that gave me an advantage in the darkness.

The woman in the white dress stood in the center of the dance floor, shifting as if she were lost and didn't know what to do. Some people around her ran from side to side, creating the confusion we meticulously programmed, until a medium-height man stood out, walking with calculated calm toward the center of the floor, unaware that as he walked, people were parting to let him through.

It was him. Damn, it was really him.

I drew my weapon and started walking toward him. My fingers tightened around the grip, and it took immense control to stay calm and not shoot him in the head right then.

"Turn towards the back exit and go there. He will follow you," I whispered through the communicator, guiding the woman via the earpiece I had placed on her. With the few lights in the place, it would be hard for him to see that she wasn't being closely followed by the bodyguards, as usual. I could bet that the man believed he could stab her just like he did Magnolia. Right in front of the bodyguards. He had no fear at all, but that didn't matter. His end that night would be the same. Prison.

She began to walk at once, and Naish quickened his pace, staying close to her, unaware that I was right behind him. I noticed he was limping on one leg, probably the one I had shot in our last encounter. I remembered Adrian and the end he met, and for a moment I feared something could go wrong. I aimed for his head as assurance that no one would leave that place injured, except for Naish. If he put that woman in danger, I wouldn't have much choice but to kill him; after all, it would only take a scratch from that blade to ensure death.

She passed through the door that led to an empty room where the back exit was. He approached the woman and drew the knife to strike her, but Petrova was faster, and before he could even understand what was happening, she hit him in one swift move. He stumbled to the side, and the knife flew from his hand to the ground.

"Don't move, Naish. Or I'll kill you." I subdued him. "Turn on the lights. I want to see the face of this bastard," I ordered, and the lights were restored immediately. I kept my gun trained on Naish's head and kicked the knife toward Petrova.

"You!" The man glared at me. His pale face seemed frozen, expressionless from all the surgeries he must have had over the years. His once-pointed nose appeared to have lost some cartilage and looked horrible. I could hardly believe we had managed to do this, especially without any deaths.

"Good job, Agent Petrova," I congratulated, stunned.

"Your brother will pay dearly for putting me in this dress, Mr. Holder," she shot back, her thick Russian accent rolling the r's.

Winnie Petrova was a CIA agent, specializing in disguises. She was one of the most random contacts Snake kept on his priority list. I had no idea what kind of relationship existed between the two, but it didn't seem good. Like enemies with a peace treaty sealed on trust, something that threatened to rupture at any moment. And it couldn't be any different, since Miss Petrova belonged to the law, and Snake protected the big names in Chicago's underworld. They lived on opposite sides.

"How dare you get in my way again?" he questioned angrily, drawing another knife and throwing it at me without any fear that I might shoot him.

"Damn!" I dodged the knife and noticed he was pulling out two more. I aimed for his knee and shot. The man howled loudly and leaned against the wall.

"I'll make you regret this until the last day of your miserable life," he threatened through his groans.

"I have a debt with you, Naish. And I intend to pay it." I landed a blunt strike to the bastard's face, trembling so much that I had to lean against the wall as soon as he passed out.

The party we orchestrated was completely fake. All the guests were bodyguards from Holder Security, there solely to create an impact. We asked Miss Petrova to disguise herself as Jasmin to lure Naish while the real Cahill heir waited in safety, surrounded by our trusted guards.

A crazy plan, but damn it, it worked.

"Let's get him out of here before he wakes up and puts on a show," Petrova requested, going to the door for help.

Two other agents from Holder, disguised as guests, helped us carry Naish's unconscious body out through the back of the ballroom, where Snake and his men were waiting in a black van.

I noticed a slight change in my brother's usually distant demeanor when Miss Petrova approached. Something flickered in his light eyes, but I couldn't begin to imagine what it was. I hoped he wouldn't jump her throat before they could extract anything from that idiot.

The shooter lay unconscious at the back of the spacious vehicle.

"I thought he managed to hit you," Snake commented when Petrova's green eyes fell on him. She ripped off the blonde wig, revealing her intense red hair.

"I didn't come here to make you any happier, Snake. Hide that smile; I don't intend to die today," she retorted, making him laugh. One point for the redhead.

"It really is a lovely dress to waste on you dying in it. At least change before," he teased, helping the other men toss Naish's body into the van with unsettling ease.

"You won't find it funny when I shove it down your throat," she shot back. Point for her. But what the hell was happening here?

I diverted my attention from those two when I noticed the tip of a paper emerging from Naish's pocket and pulled it out to see what it was. My world shook as I realized it was a photo of Jasmin, pierced by several small, round marks, as if it had been burned with a lit cigarette. Her smiling face was circled by a red line, like a target, and all the fury I had been trying to control up to that moment slipped through my fingers.

"Looks like our guest is waking up," Petrova said, and everything around me lost focus as Naish's treacherous eyes opened. I walked toward the van, holding the photo between my fingers, and stepped inside.

His eyes had a lifeless gray tone, devoid of emotion. This only fueled my anger toward that demon. Imagining that he intended to do to Jasmin what he did to Adrian and Magnolia left me breathless. Rage clouded my vision, and all I could feel was a homicidal frenzy.

He tried to speak when he saw me, but I silenced him with a punch to the mouth.

"It's over, you pig." I unleashed a flurry of blows. "You'll never touch her, you piece of shit!"

I felt the flesh give way with each punch I threw, spraying droplets everywhere until I broke the bone of his jaw with a dry crack. I could only think of the people he had hurt and the endless trail of pain he had left in his wake.

I kept hitting, blind and frantic, until I felt hands and arms pulling me back.

"Brother, leave some for us." Snake jumped into the van alongside Petrova and two other men, while the driver started the vehicle. The Holder security eased the pressure on my arms when they noticed I was beginning to calm down.

"I just wanted him to know..." I gasped. My hands were covered in blood, and when I looked at him, I barely recognized the face now supporting my gaze through an incredibly swollen visage—"...that I was the one who sentenced him to the worst of all punishments. I sentenced him to defeat."

"He'll have plenty of time to remember that where he's going." Petrova tapped the man's leg, who tried to curse and spat blood, passing out shortly after. "We need to go." She reached for a laptop that had been left on the counter and started searching Naish. "We have some accounts supposedly belonging to this man. If I can confirm this information, we'll have the name of who hired him in a few minutes. So expect a call soon."

"I'll take care of him in 30 minutes if she can't," Snake surveyed the man, grinning. "Woman killer, right? This will be fun."

"*Sadist*," Petrova sang, teasing my brother before shutting the van door.

"All good, Mr. Holder." One of my father's security guards patted my shoulder. For a moment, I thought I was dreaming.

"We got him. Attention, we got him," I alerted the internal team over the communicator and stumbled to the wall. I leaned against it, disbelieving. He had actually been captured. I looked up at the sky, an immense relief filling my chest.

"Congratulations, sir. That was a perfect performance. No one was hurt, except the murderer himself, right?" The guard laughed.

"I need to get back to the ballroom." I tried to straighten up.

"Why don't we stop by the bathroom first?" Another guard suggested, and I looked at my hands, stained bright red with blood.

"I think that's a good idea. Let's go."

I ran to the bathroom and washed my hands hurriedly. I was eager to share the news with Jasmin. We finally caught the killer of her sister. She and Cahill could have peace as soon as we knew the contractor's name. Now it was just a matter of time.

I returned to the ballroom, where the lights had been turned back on, and the music resumed. We had agreed to maintain the facade, should everything go as planned, especially to avoid causing unnecessary commotion among the crowd of photographers outside.

Jasmin, the real and only one, stood in the middle of the dance floor. Smiling at her friend as if sharing a secret, probably recounting the plan behind the entire party. Cahill approached his daughter and wrapped her in a tight embrace, one I knew signified victory. They spoke briefly, and soon he stepped back with renewed energy and distracted himself with Wood in the opposite corner. Lyon, Ray, and Shaw stayed close to Jasmin, but it was evident the smile the three tried to hide was one of success.

Jasmin spotted me in the crowd as I navigated through the people to reach her. The corners of her lips lifted, but her attention was diverted when someone called her name. The senator stopped beside her and pulled her into an embrace with a smile.

My world stopped the moment I saw the glint of a knife pass from the senator's hands to Carla's.

"No! Jasmin!" I shouted in panic.

I was too far away to protect her.

CHAPTER TWENTY-SIX

Jasmin

It had been many years since such great joy had filled me. He had been captured. My God, Magnolia's killer would now rot behind bars, and even though we hadn't discovered who was behind it all, that was already a huge reason to celebrate.

"I can't believe this!" Carla looked frozen when I finished telling her about the plan we had orchestrated for the party. As soon as we arrived, I took my friend with me to the security room where my bodyguards would keep me until everything was over, and it was very difficult to keep her still there with me. My friend was extremely professional and tried to leave the security room at all costs to guide the event staff, but the guards wouldn't allow it, which left her quite irritated.

"Can you forgive me for lying?" I smiled, unable to hide the joy I felt. "The good news is that we caught my sister's killer, and soon we'll know who's behind all of this." She blinked, confused, probably processing the information.

"Jasmin!" My father approached and enveloped me in a warm hug. He looked more charming than ever with that mask covering half his face. "We did it, daughter," he celebrated.

"Yes, Dad. I can't even express how radiant I am with happiness."

"I told you Wolf was a good hire." He smiled, and I felt my face heat up.

I had been thinking about what my father would think of my involvement with Wolf, fearing that he might disapprove, which would be a problem. I wasn't willing to let anyone, not even my father, come between us.

"Dad, when we get home, there's something I want to tell you. It's about Wolf and..."

"My daughter," he smiled gently, "you have all the characteristics of your mother, and the strongest of them is how clearly I can read your feelings. You can try to deceive others with your somewhat... acidic and sarcastic demeanor, but all it takes is a single glance at you for me to know how you're feeling. And I do know."

"Know what?" He patted my hand.

"What you feel for Wolf." My eyes widened. "We'll talk at home, but I hope it's mutual; otherwise, I'll be forced to use one of my microwave gun prototypes on him," he mentioned one of my favorite weapons produced by our company.

I hugged him, emotional, needing all my strength not to cry and smudge all that makeup.

"You're old enough to decide what you want from your love life, daughter, and I won't dictate the rules of your heart. I've interfered enough by keeping you sheltered all your life, and I'm ecstatic to know that even so, you consider my opinion." He kissed my cheek. "I love you more than anything, Jasmin."

"I love you too, Dad, and I know you meant well. You just wanted to protect me." I hugged him tighter, and when I pulled away, I needed to ask.

"Dad, is this written across my forehead?" I asked, fearful.

"To me, yes." That was his reply before he joined Wood on the other side of the ballroom.

I looked at the crowd that was starting to return to normal with a slow, casual dance on the floor, until my eyes landed on the tall man, broad-shouldered, with the posture of a warrior marching to war. Wolf pressed his lips together, and a wicked smile spread across his face, sending shivers through my body, but above all, I noticed he was trying to hurry to get to me.

Was he also eager to see me as much as I was for his touch?

"Jasmin, darling!" A melodious voice broke my eye contact with Wolf.

"Aunt Claire." I broke into a wide smile upon seeing her. I was dying to tell her all about the adventure we had secretly lived that night.

My godmother pulled me into a hug, and I didn't hesitate to throw myself into her arms with all the affection I had for her.

"Aunt, I have so much to tell..."

"Jasmin—" Carla called me, and I turned to her abruptly. I sucked in a sharp breath as a piercing pain shot through my body. My eyes widened, and I froze in panic.

"I'm so sorry, friend." Carla yanked the knife out with a strong pull and tried to stab me again. I raised my hand to stop her, but she ended up hitting my leg.

I toppled and fell to the ground amidst the sound of gunfire. My vision blurred rapidly.

No.

It couldn't be, my God.

"Be suspicious of those you love, not just of those who hate you."

Wolf's words infiltrated my mind like a note tucked in a planner meant to remind me of what should never be forgotten.

But I had forgotten.

Wolf

BEFORE I COULD EVEN blink, Carla plunged the knife into Jasmin's abdomen, and the air stopped entering my lungs.

"Lyon, shoot the senator. NOW!" I shouted when I saw that Carla was out of Lyon's line of sight, and I tried to reason through the distance between us. I began pushing through the crowd, which parted as they sensed something was wrong. My whole body felt paralyzed, but my aim remained intact. I raised my weapon, aimed at the bastard Jasmin called a friend, and fired twice.

"Damn," Lyon cursed when he saw what was happening and didn't hesitate. He shot at the senator, who fell to the ground.

Jasmin fell backward, and I rushed weakly toward her. Her white dress started to stain a dark red that dragged me into the depths of despair.

God, please! I pleaded, as if the world had suddenly entered a slow, torturous atmosphere. I found myself dropping to my knees beside her, her very pale lips and closed eyes telling no lies.

I could hear my own screams somewhere distant in my mind as I pulled her limp body into my arms.

"Jasmin." I hugged her, trembling uncontrollably, and struggled to keep my focus.

"Wolf... it's so cold." Her voice dragged out without her eyes opening.

"Don't talk, my love, save your strength." Jasmin fainted in my arms, and purest terror enveloped me. I jumped up, holding her, lost and delirious. Cahill was roaring behind me like a wild animal, frantic.

"My God, my God!" Shaw was running his hands through his hair in panic.

We had left an ambulance on standby in case something went wrong at the back exit, but I needed to remain calm to reach it and have a slim chance of saving Jasmin. In the face of Cahill's desperate struggles against several guards trying to restrain him, I had to find the coldness within my chest. Jasmin's life depended on me.

"Shaw, take care of Cahill. Calm him down and get him to the hospital. Jay, apply pressure to her abdominal wound, and Ray, to the one on her leg." I could see the thick trail of blood running down Jasmin's pale skin.

I checked her pulse, and the only certainty I had was that the knife wasn't laced with cyanide; otherwise, she would already be dead.

We ran to the exit, escorted by other Holder security. Jasmin's skin grew colder and paler, and I realized that even though they were applying pressure, the amount of blood she was losing was too high, and with every passing second, the purest fear seeped into my mind. We needed to reach the ambulance and rush to the hospital, or she wouldn't survive.

"There, sir, the paramedics," Ray indicated with a nod.

We ran over and were soon surrounded by multiple hands. The doctors lifted Jasmin from my arms and placed her on the stretcher in the ambulance.

"She was stabbed twice. Once in the abdomen and once in the leg; she's lost a lot of blood." I tried to speak without trembling.

"We're going to the hospital," the doctor said, and I stepped into the ambulance, unable to think of anything else.

As they started the engine, I saw Cahill rush into the car with Shaw. They sped after us.

"What's your relation to her?"

I'm the bodyguard, I thought of responding, only then realizing she meant much more to me than perhaps I meant to her.

Jasmin was the reason I woke up every day excited, eager to put my eyes on her and see what challenge her creative mind would force me to face. Her beautiful, curious smile haunted my thoughts from the moment I opened my eyes until I closed them again to sleep. She showed me a strength I had never seen in anyone else, and I felt that everything between us was too fast, intense, abundant, as if I were destined to find her. As if Jasmin belonged to me from another life. She was the missing piece of my puzzle, and without her, I would be incomplete.

"She's all I have," I replied, sincerely, and held Jasmin's very pale hand. A burning knot formed in my throat. "I wish I could trade places with you, sweetheart." My voice broke. "Forgive me for not being there, forgive me, forgive me." I rested my forehead against her hand.

Anger, fear, sadness, hatred, resentment... everything mixed together, and I went mad. My heart beat hard against my chest, and I feared it would stop at any moment.

We arrived at the hospital, and I didn't leave the stretcher for a moment, running alongside the paramedics.

"It's going to be okay, my love. It's going to be okay." I held her hand and repeated those words as if by saying them enough times, they would actually become reality.

"Sir, you need to wait here; we're taking her to surgery," the doctor blocked my way, placing her hands on my chest.

"I need to stay with her," I pleaded, weakly.

"I'm sorry; it's the rules," she said apologetically and disappeared down the corridor leading to the surgical room, just as the hospital door swung wide open.

I staggered to a wall as Cahill rushed into the hospital, shouting questions with Wood and the other guards trailing behind him. I could barely breathe.

Almost an hour later, a doctor came to us and asked to speak with the family. Cahill, like me, couldn't even move, and the doctor had to start telling us what was happening right there.

I heard distantly as the woman informed us that Jasmin's condition was very serious.

"The knife pierced her abdomen and caused a laceration to the liver, which has already been corrected; fortunately, it didn't hit any other organs. However, it did hit an important vein, which caused severe internal bleeding. The doctors are still working to fix the injury. Adding to this, with the blow she received to her leg, your daughter has lost a lot of blood and suffered a cardiac arrest early in the surgery." I lowered my head and buried my face in my hands. My chest felt torn apart, hurting so deeply it became impossible to breathe. I felt a hand rest on my shoulder and had to cling to the touch to focus on what the doctor was still saying. "We managed to reverse her condition by a hair's breadth, but the surgery is still risky."

No one said anything, and I forced myself to lift my head. I found Cahill in a catatonic state of deep sorrow. Lyon kept his hand firmly on my shoulder, and I wished I had the strength to thank him for that.

"Doctor, she will survive, right? Jasmin is strong." I was startled by the tremor in my voice. "She'll be okay, right?"

"That's why I'm here, sir. I need you to understand the gravity of the situation. We're working with the best medical team in Chicago, and we will do everything we can to save her, but I can't make any guarantees."

From that point on, I experienced hell like never before.

THE SURGERY WAS TAKING too long, and the early morning arrived without any news. Cahill huddled in a corner of the hospital, staying there for hours on end. The man looked much older now, as if each minute had taken a year off his life.

Shaw prayed nonstop with his face buried in his hands, while Wood, Lyon, and Ray tried to maintain their composure, but their red eyes and trembling hands left no doubt. We were in a state of panic.

I felt restless, unmoored. All I could think about was the moment she placed her hand on her heart and confessed her feelings just before the party began. It was so natural, so sensitive. That gesture made me happier than I had ever been. But why didn't I reciprocate? Why didn't I send all those people around us to hell and tell her how I felt?

When we were in Jasmin's room, I told her that when it was all over, we would have a serious conversation, and my intention was to reveal everything I felt—the nervous, euphoric sensation that washed over me when I saw her, how I longed for a moment to touch her, and the desperation I felt when her lips met mine, as if they fit perfectly. Something I never imagined I would find in life.

I would tell her that I loved her traditions and wanted to share each one with her. Watching the stars every Tuesday with that stinky snack, going to eat chocolate cake at the beach once a year, dancing without any music playing, and holding her in my arms, inhaling that clean scent of roses that thrilled me and made my heart race. Remembering her smile was almost painful, and I didn't even know where.

God, I loved her.

I loved everything she was and everything she wanted not to be. Her qualities, her flaws, the way she would hit people with a frying pan, or how quickly she stole my keys.

My eyes burned with despair.

Why didn't I confess my feelings?

"Why?" I whispered, a sharp pain closing my throat, shaking my head back and forth in disbelief.

"It's not your fault." Cahill's voice reached my ears, but I lacked the strength to look at him. "It was mine." He gasped, and suddenly the man broke into compulsive sobs. "It's all my fault, I let that woman get close; I allowed her to come near my daughters. I lost Magnolia and I'm about to lose Jasmin, my God." He sobbed. "How could they do this?"

In that moment, Mason Cahill was not the CEO of one of the largest companies in the country. He wasn't a powerful man, let alone a dangerous one. There he was, a desperate father.

I looked at the man who pulled at his hair and rocked his body back and forth incessantly. Only then did I realize there were about ten security guards in the corridor besides us, and there were probably twice as many outside containing the reporters.

I forced myself to stand and sat next to Mason. I touched his shoulder for some reason and thought of a million things I could say, but I couldn't utter a single word. I couldn't console him at that moment when all I wanted was to wake up from this nightmare.

"I noticed how my Jasmin looked at you," he suddenly said, catching me off guard, but I didn't pull my hand from his shoulder. He needed it, and I think I did too. "Every time I saw her, she always mentioned something about you. At first, she kept asking me to fire you." He laughed bitterly. "But later, everything she said had a joyful tone. A sound I feared I would never hear again after Magnolia's death." He took a deep breath. "My daughter is very transparent to me. The way she radiated when your presence was mentioned made many things clear. I think she ended up nurturing other feelings for you."

I swallowed hard and stared at the granite floor.

"Was it mutual?" he asked, and my whole body stiffened at the question. "I need to know if she at least fell for someone who felt the same way about her. That she at least experienced love before..." He broke down.

"She's not going to die, Mason," I assured him with shaken conviction. "And I would give everything I have to trade places with her right now. Everything." The man searched my face. "Even if you come to dislike it, or fire me as soon as we walk out that door, you need to know that there's nothing more reciprocal than the feelings I have for your daughter, Cahill."

"What do you think she would do to me if I fired you?" His voice sounded soft, curious, and his eyes lost focus on a point ahead.

"She would definitely blow up one of your labs." He smiled.

"Or set fire to my favorite Porsche."

"I can picture her doing that," I whispered. "Do you believe she attacked my brothers with a frying pan?"

"That tattooed one?"

"Both of them."

"That's so like her. My brave girl." He began to laugh in a frantic way that quickly turned into desperate sobbing.

"I'm sorry I can't say anything that comforts you," I said without removing my hand from his shoulder. "I don't know how to put into words everything I'm feeling right now. It's as if I'm about to die."

"That's already enough," he whispered.

We sat in silence for a long time, waiting for any news. Mason's blood pressure rose, and he started feeling faint, but he refused treatment.

"You need to be well to receive her, Mason," I advised.

"Take the medication, sir," Wood insisted.

"Are you going to stay here, Wolf?" he asked anxiously.

"I won't budge from here." He nodded in confirmation, then followed Wood to the elective care room and was soon medicated, but didn't want to stay there and returned to the spot beside me.

I leaned my head against the wall. Lyon and Ray sat across from me, their expressions as lost as mine, when a murmur began among the various security personnel waiting in the hallway.

I turned to see what was happening, and all the stupor I had been in gave way to a sharp, urgent pain spreading through my chest when I laid eyes on the man in the black suit with gray hair, standing rigid next to Ghost at the end of the corridor.

"Mason, I'll be back in a minute or two," he agreed as I stood up.

I passed through the other guards, and a few of them offered me a low, nearly inaudible greeting.

My father and Ghost took a path that led to the stairs, and I followed them. We entered a dark, stuffy place. The door creaked behind us, and when my father turned to me with a worried expression and placed his hand on my shoulder, I became that scared boy again, getting beaten and feeling hungry every day. Once more, like when he adopted me, I had no expectation of a future. I was clinging to a faith I had never had, aimless, lost.

He hugged me, and I felt somewhat dizzy.

"I'm so sorry, son." A strange tremor overcame my body; my eyes burned uncontrollably, and I found myself fighting against the overwhelming urge to cry.

"We're with you, brother." Zion rested his hand on my shoulder, and I had to blink incessantly to chase away those damn tears.

I leaned against the wall in the stairwell; my father was on my right, and Zion on my left.

"From what I learned coming here, the senator was hit by two of the three shots fired at her, most of them in the legs, and she's going straight to jail as soon as she leaves the hospital. Everything was recorded, and we have enough evidence. The young woman who stabbed Miss Cahill died at the scene," my brother informed me, and once again I felt like a fool, an idiot. I had always suspected everyone around me, especially when I was with a VIP, and Carla was undoubtedly one of the possibilities. But she became such a remote suspect that I ended up losing sight of the details and let her get too close. Now Jasmin was fighting for her life because of those two traitors.

"I thought the senator was dead too. I should have checked to make sure." I was overwhelmed by pure resentment and a sudden desire to kill that woman at any cost. She had never fooled me, but Carla? I still felt nauseated thinking that the bastard managed to slip under my radar like that.

"Let fate take care of that, son. She will pay for what she did, but I'd like to understand what led the senator and that girl to attack your VIP in front of so many witnesses," my father wanted to know. "They identified themselves as murderers and still took the risk of dying."

"There's only one feeling capable of making a person give up everything they have and act impulsively like that." Ghost clenched his fist, lost in thought.

"Fear," I completed, and he nodded. "There must have been some connection between the two that we still don't know about."

"The senator must have found herself in a bind. Perhaps she thought the outcome of attacking Miss Cahill in that place, in front of Holder's entire security team and even the young woman's father, would be better than what she would face if she left there alive."

"That could be."

"Leave that to Snake. He'll uncover the motivations behind this whole story," my father concluded. "Ghost told me about the fondness you have for that young woman." I pursed my lips, unsure of what my father would think about that.

I had avoided meeting with my father during the week I spent organizing the security details for that party precisely because I knew what he would end up questioning, and I wasn't sure I was ready to have that discussion with him, but there, in light of everything that happened, all I wanted was to tell the truth.

"It's more than fondness, Dad," I admitted. "I know what you think about it, and I also know that maintaining a professional relationship with the VIP was one of my most absolute rules, but I broke it and ended up getting involved with Jasmin," I revealed in one breath. "And I don't regret it. I'm sorry."

"There's nothing to be sorry about, son." He touched my shoulder. "I would condemn anyone of you who had a frivolous relationship with a VIP, it's true, but what I see here is not something fleeting. You seem to genuinely care for the girl, and who am I to deprive you of one of life's most exquisite feelings?" I raised my eyes to my father, who had loved one woman in his entire life. A woman who betrayed him, and now he didn't believe in love as much, but apparently, that didn't stop him from rooting for me. "All I want is for you and your brothers to be happy, but don't use this as an example, understood, Zion? If you get into trouble with a VIP, you'll have to deal with me."

"Don't worry, Dad. I'll never do something like that. Let Wolf be the prized sheep once again." Zion tried to lighten the mood, but a second later, the painful knot was back, suffocating me.

"Have faith, Christopher," my father said.

"I don't know what I'll do if she doesn't survive. Just imagining it is... too suffocating to bear." I brought my hand to my chest, the pain penetrating every inch of my skin.

"She'll be fine, son. Keep your hopes up."

"I thought you'd fight a bit more about my involvement with a VIP." I looked at him, eyebrows raised.

"I promise to rip off one of your ears only when she's recovering in her room, but until then, we're here to support you." I hugged him tightly, leaning on the only place I had ever felt safe in life. Next to my father. "You're a good boy, son, you've been through a lot in life. I'm not the one to decide who can or can't mess with your heart. But however it is, I can see in your anguished gaze how important that young woman is to you."

"Lean on us, brother. Everything will be alright, and soon Miss Cahill will be around wielding her frying pans." A shadow of a smile crept onto my lips, and I felt grateful to have that family by my side, so different from the conventional one, yet perfect in its own way.

"Thank you." I tried to keep my posture. "I need to go back in case there's any news."

"Yes, of course. I also need to have a word with my friend in there." He referred to Cahill, and we returned to the waiting room.

My father sat next to Mason, and they spent a long time there talking while Shaw stared at my father and Ghost as if witnessing something supernatural. I could almost laugh at the fascinated expression on the young man's face if it weren't for the constant worry that made me hold my breath from minute to minute.

"Mr. Cahill?" a doctor called from the entrance of the surgical center, and everyone, including the four security guards of Jasmin, rushed to her. "We just finished the surgery. Now we're counting on the..." Before she could finish speaking, a high-pitched sound reverberated through the corridor, and the doctor turned, alarmed, toward the incessant beeping. Nurses and other doctors began to run toward a specific room, and for a moment, I felt as if my heart might stop.

I couldn't explain how, but somehow I knew it was her. The doctor seemed disoriented and asked us to step aside. The lights inside continued to flash, indicating something I didn't want to accept, and before I could regain control, I ran down the surgical corridor, ignoring the prohibitive warnings, and heard more footsteps behind me.

The luxury hospital housed several operating rooms, all with transparent glass walls, and it didn't take long for me to find her. My eyes began to burn the moment I saw her. Jasmin looked smaller lying on that stretcher, her eyes closed, and several wires connected to her sent me into a panic. The frantic beeping warned that something was wrong.

"Jasmin," I whispered weakly as they brought in the defibrillator. Another cardiac arrest. My girl was fighting for her life, and I felt useless, unable to help her. "Jasmin, respond!" I pleaded, pressing against the glass as I watched her chest rise and fall with the force of the machine. Several doctors surrounded her, injecting medications, trying every possible way to save her. "Please, my love, respond!" I shouted, begging her to wake up, for that damned constant sound to return to pulsate with her heart.

I could hear the men around me crying, trying to control themselves while supporting Cahill in some way, as my father and brother stood firmly by my side. But nothing and no one could tear away the despair tattooed on my skin as I saw she wasn't coming back.

The pain in my chest began to spread through every cell.

"Please come back. Come back to me," I cried, trying to deny what was right before my eyes.

CHAPTER TWENTY-SEVEN

Jasmin

I continued climbing the verdant hill, feeling the gentle wind play with my hair. The sun touched my arms, and a sense of lightness hung in the air, except for the endless kilometers I kept ascending, without stopping.

"They should have installed an escalator here." I heard a laugh and turned my face in search of the sound. There was no one.

I kept climbing until I finally reached the top, where a lush forest spread across the horizon, with a large waterfall in the background.

"How beautiful," I whispered to the wind. An indescribable peace filled my heart.

"It's beautiful, but it's not your place, Jasmin." I jumped in place when Magnolia's voice hit me like lightning.

I found my sister holding our mother's hand across a great chasm between two hills. My eyes welled with tears, and I began to cry.

"Mom, Magnolia." I moved toward the chasm. All I wanted was to hug them.

"No!" Mom shouted, stretching out her hand. "You can't fall into the chasm, my daughter. Go back the way you came; this is not your place yet."

My eyes were locked on hers. Both shimmered in the sunlight, like two angels watching over the earth. Magnolia looked stunning, with a beautiful smile gracing her delicate face, and my mother... my God, she really looked like me.

"I want so much to be with you, Mom." I turned to my sister, who watched me with a gentle smile. "I've missed you so much, Mag. So much..." I sobbed. "I think I climbed the wrong hill; I'll go down and climb the other one. I want to be with you."

"Jasmin," Magnolia called, "we've never stopped being with you, but your story is different. You need to change that world a little."

"It's time to be free, daughter." Mom raised her delicate hand toward me, and Magnolia did the same. "Go back and be happy. We will wait for you."

"But don't rush," my sister added, and I placed my hand on my chest, struck by the sudden pain that hit me there.

I screamed and fell to my knees with the burning sensation that felt like it was consuming every inch of my body, and a moment later, everything transformed into a calm, painless darkness. I was embraced by a deep silence.

2 days later...

I opened my eyes and gasped for air. The bright lights threatened to blind me.

"She's awake again," a female voice said.

My head was spinning, and my whole body felt like it had gone through a grinder. My mind wandered through fragments of memory, as if I had woken up in the same place a few times before actually realizing I was there.

"Hey, welcome back, warrior," another, even happier voice completed. "Now she's conscious." A man moved a bright light close to my eyes. "Miss Cahill underwent emergency surgery two days ago and is now recovering in the ICU. Stay calm; the worst is over."

"Can you tell me your name?" the woman asked as she approached me. "I think she's going to go back to sleep, just like the other two times she woke up," she whispered to the man, as if I couldn't hear her.

"Jasmin... my name." I tried to swallow, but the simple movement caused me pain and extreme fatigue.

I blinked and turned my face. Before I could understand what was happening, my wandering eyes landed on a large glass window on the side of the room, where several people were leaning. Many of them were crying, and it took me a while to recognize my father among them. There was also a tall, robust man. He was crying profusely, leaning against the glass. His red eyes still highlighted the two points of light of different colors, and he was saying strange things I couldn't understand, but for some reason, they made me smile.

My Wolf...

I closed my eyes, too tired to keep them open.

I WOKE UP IN A SPACIOUS, well-ventilated hospital room, adorned with flower arrangements and even a stuffed bear at one end. My father was sitting beside the bed, his eyes pressed by his fingers preventing him from seeing that I was watching him. I blinked a few times and began to notice him. He looked thinner, infinitely more worn, and memories of what had happened at that party returned to my mind.

"I warned you it was better to change the routine at work. Look at you, a wreck." My voice emerged low and very hoarse. He opened his eyes in a sudden burst and widened them comically.

"Jasmin! My God, you're awake." He stood up and wrapped his arms around my shoulders. "My little girl." The choked voice moved me. "I'm so sorry for everything that happened. Forgive me, please, forgive me."

"None of this was your fault, Dad," I spoke slowly. I still hadn't fully regained my composure, and the constant pain in my chest was crushing me. "Those vipers had been infiltrated among us for years. Even the security wouldn't have suspected them. When they were hired, they were already part of our lives; don't punish them, please."

"I wouldn't do that for anything." He kissed my hand.

"I don't understand, Dad... what was the motivation? Why did they do that?" My eyes overflowed with tears as I realized that my aunt, whom I loved like a mother, and my best friend, whom I considered a second sister, had betrayed me in such a filthy way. The pain was devastating. Physically and emotionally, I couldn't comprehend how those two could have crossed paths in some parallel universe. I had never noticed any closeness during the rare times Claire had seen Carla at the mansion.

"Let's not talk about that now, okay? I promise to tell you everything when you're a bit stronger."

"No, Dad," I insisted, blinking repeatedly in an attempt to clear my tears. "I need to know. Anything will do; I need... she was my friend, Dad. Since we were in school, and my aunt... my God, it doesn't make sense. I need a glimmer of hope, even if it's brief; please tell me anything that makes sense." He scrutinized my face cautiously. Some lines formed between his thick eyebrows, and for a moment, his eyes wandered. He knew me well enough to understand that I wouldn't give up on discovering the truth.

"We know very little so far," he revealed. "It seems Claire had a lover." He smiled bitterly. "Carla's father, a man named Matías."

"What?" I breathed weakly. The man with the darkest eyes I had ever seen was her lover?

"Snake managed to access several messages and transactions involving the two. It appears they've been together for many years. They might have even known each other before Claire came into our family. Everything we've uncovered so far is that the man worked for one of the most dangerous cartels operating in Chicago." He patted my hand, trying to comfort me in some way.

"So Carla was also part of all this." It wasn't a question.

"I'm so sorry, dear. We believe from the investigation line that Carla was deliberately inserted into your life. As a backup option in case everything they tried went wrong."

"For so many years? How could she pretend for all that time, Dad? How..." I began to breathe heavily. A sharp pain settled in my throat. "She cried with me, she... was always by my side during the hardest times. Are you sure it was her, Dad?" He hugged me, and I released the painful tears I had been holding back. Everything felt so surreal.

"I'm so sorry you were deceived this way, my daughter."

"And—where is she? I need to hear from her, Dad. I need that fake to look me in the face and tell me why, after so many years of friendship, she decided to stab me at the damn party I entrusted her with," I exclaimed, taking a moment to realize the curse I had just uttered. "Sorry about that, but I still want to see her."

"My daughter," he sighed heavily, "Carla didn't survive. And I would be a hypocrite if I said I wished it were different because I didn't. She tried to take what I hold most precious, and I couldn't allow that." He looked at a fixed point on the floor. "I believe Claire orchestrated everything. After all, if Carla killed you and died shortly afterward, she would never be accused of anything. Her misfortune was that there were night cameras installed in the place in case Naish tried to escape. They recorded everything. Claire was also shot, but survived and was sent to a place from which I hope she never leaves."

My lips trembled, and my father leaned in again, enveloping me in his protective embrace until I calmed down.

"Promise me you'll keep me updated on any progress they make in the investigation? I want to understand every detail and how they were able to camouflage themselves in our lives."

"I promise, but until you're recovered, we won't talk about it again, alright? Look at how much you're shaking, daughter." He cradled my face in his hands. "We have too many reasons to celebrate; don't let them steal the happiness we worked so hard to achieve. I know you feel destroyed by the betrayal from both of them, and I understand you; Claire was my fiancée. I was going to marry her, but luckily we discovered the rotten apples before bringing them into our fridge."

"What kind of saying is that?" I narrowed my eyes, and he laughed.

"What I meant is that we were fortunate enough to uncover who they really were, even after all these years. All the weeds have been pulled, daughter. From now on, we can live in peace." He stepped back and squeezed my hand. "Everyone's anxious to see you soon." I sniffled, composing myself as best I could, which didn't mean much.

"And the..." I tried to sit up, but the simple movement made me groan.

"Stay still, okay?" My father tried to adjust the pillows around me, looking anxious. "I think you wanted to ask about Wolf." My heart, which felt a bit weaker than normal, thudded painfully.

"Did he come to see me?" The foolish hope that arose in my voice irritated me.

"Did he come to see you?" My father laughed. "You spent two days in the ICU and a day in this room, and at no point did he leave your side. He stood in front of the glass of the ICU room until he came to your room and left this bed for only a few minutes. Christopher spent all that time here with you, my daughter. And I tried to convince him to at least go rest a little."

"Are you calling him by name?"

"We've gotten pretty close these last few days." My father smiled, and the door behind him opened.

"Mason, Wood asked me to check..." He stopped walking and fell silent the moment he laid eyes on me.

"I'll see what Wood wants and ask a doctor to come check on you. I'll be back soon, my daughter." Dad kissed my hand and gave a quick nod to the man who was staring at me, petrified, near the door.

The emotion that tore through my chest upon seeing him made my eyes well up. Brief flashes of Christopher crying through that glass returned to my mind. He also looked worn, with deep dark circles under his eyes; a thicker beard descended ruggedly along his jaw.

"Christopher," I called his name, and he came to me almost running.

"My love." He inhaled sharply, his arms starting to tremble. "My God, thank you!" He wrapped his arms around my neck and kissed my forehead, frantic. "Thank you," he whispered against my skin, and tears began to stream down my face uncontrollably. My own heart seemed to cry in a mix of relief and despair. "You have no idea how afraid I was of losing you." He shivered, and his mouth sought mine in a chaste, restrained kiss. He touched me as if I might crumble before his eyes. "Forgive me, Jas, for leaving you alone. I never should have done that, I... my God." I held his hand between mine and tried to smile.

"What's going on in the world that everyone is asking me for forgiveness?" I joked, but I noticed his eyes turning very red, as if he were exerting himself not to cry, and I swallowed hard, too emotional. "You did your best. It wasn't your fault. Don't apologize, Wolf." I cried even more when I saw his tear-filled eyes scanning my face with such care and protection.

"Don't cry, my heart." He embraced me. Wolf smelled like home, love, happiness, and I clung to him for long minutes, both seeking comfort in each other's arms. "I was so afraid you wouldn't wake up again." He leaned in and planted another kiss on my lips.

His eyes dropped to the bandages on my abdomen and leg.

"How are you feeling?"

"It hurts everywhere, even when I breathe, but I'll be okay."

"I'll make sure you are." Christopher held my hand, and I noticed he was still trembling. He realized I had noticed and his expression turned serious and intense. "I thought I had already lived through a good amount of bad things in life and that nothing would ever shake me again, but I realized I was wrong." His intense eyes continued to probe mine. "When you have no hope, anything that happens in your life is acceptable, but when you gain something good and precious, your life changes completely. And I gained you, heart, and now it's easier to wish for death than to imagine losing you. You are the light in my darkness, and I've discovered that without you, I feel lost and disoriented."

"It's not good to make a freshly operated person cry." Tear trails descended my face, and he touched each one with his fingertips.

"I love you, my angel. I didn't know how to put the feelings I had for you into words until I found them, and I feared more than anything that I wouldn't have time to tell you." He kissed my forehead for a long time, while my heart remained strong, beating rapidly with each new word he spoke. "I love you, my troublemaker. Please, never scare me like that again in life."

I smiled and wrapped my arms around his shoulders. The love I felt for that man pulsed strongly in my chest, and I couldn't contain the sensation of having found a piece of heaven to call my own.

Wolf

I SPENT THE NEXT HOUR in the room with Jasmin while the doctors evaluated her, along with Cahill, who looked visibly more relaxed, just like I was.

Jasmin gave me quite a scare. I had never felt so terrified at the thought of losing her, and now, just being away from that girl for even five minutes made me anxious and desperate, but she was well cared for, and I had something very important to do.

I hurried down the hospital corridor and stopped when I found Jasmin's four bodyguards having coffee in the hospital's reserved area while watching a basketball game on the TV set up for visitors.

"Mr. Holder!" Shaw jumped up as soon as he saw me.

"Jasmin is awake," I revealed with joy, and soon a cheer erupted in the room.

"Shh, do you want us to get kicked out?" Wood scolded the three of them, and I had to suppress a smile.

"Let's go visit her!" Ray jumped to his feet and was almost passing by me when I grabbed him by the shoulders.

"Before you go see her, I need you to answer one thing."

"Yes, sir." One by one, they replied, and Wood took a sip of his coffee before stepping closer to me.

"What question?" the man asked.

"Is your passport up to date?" They exchanged glances, confused.

"I don't have a passport, sir," Shaw replied.

"Then I think you'd better get one. Wasn't it you who kept saying how much you wanted to go to Israel?"

"What do you mean by that, sir?" Shaw asked, leaning forward with an amused frown.

"Well, during my time working with you, I've found unique qualities that make you excellent bodyguards, even if a bit... clumsy." Wood coughed, and Shaw laughed. "But the truth is that your unity and commitment are exceptional." They looked at me with a mix of confusion and surprise. "Yesterday, I had a conversation with my father when he came to the hospital to see how Jasmin was doing, and I want to know if you would like to work for Holder Security. If you accept, you will all receive training courses for bodyguards at the International Security School in Israel, with all expenses paid, of course."

"HOLY SHIT!" Shaw shouted, ecstatic, causing all of us to burst into laughter.

CHAPTER TWENTY-EIGHT

Wolf

45 days later...

My feet tapped against the floor in a constant, repetitive rhythm. Lyon and Ray covered the entrance to the main hallway of the clinic we were in while I waited for Jasmin to finish her first official therapy session since the incident.

My little one had received initial treatment while in the hospital and was referred to therapy as soon as she recovered from the attempt on her life. This would be of great help, as the days following her discharge were extremely painful for Jasmin. She was still coming to terms with the betrayal from those she loved so dearly, and watching her try to climb the wall of pain that had afflicted her since the attack left me anxious, worried, and deeply unsettled.

I also didn't like to think about that cursed day. The mere recollection filled me with pure panic. Almost losing Jasmin opened my eyes to something I had always known but often ignored: life is but a breath. Sometimes we lose people who take away a great part of our heart, and I knew well that if she had died that night, I would never be the same again. I was left with nothing but gratitude that she had survived.

I felt as if I was reborn that day, and after we left the hospital, I returned to the Cahill mansion and ended up taking a leave from Holder Security—something I had never done before—to be by her side during her recovery. And now I was a bit anxious knowing my days with Jasmin were coming to an end.

The truth was, I was becoming more and more attached to her, and I was already devising a thousand plans to see her after I started working with other VIPs. I would have to come up with an excuse to show up at the Cahill mansion every night, or I would go crazy being away from her, who, by the way, had put up quite a fight during her recovery.

Jasmin didn't understand that resting meant no sex, and I used all my self-control and persistence to not cross that line, even though I was dying to inside.

All I wanted, with all my heart, was for her to recover quickly. I knew well that even with the passing years, Jasmin would never forget what happened. The loss of her sister and the betrayal from her aunt and friend would always linger in her mind, but I hoped that over time, those memories would stop hurting, and I was willing to do absolutely anything to help her in that process.

"Thank you, Dr. Tucker." She came out of the therapist's office with a broad smile on her face.

The pink floral dress was complemented by the cascade of her strikingly blonde hair, which fell in waves over her bare back. She widened her smile the moment she saw me, and the doctor, a petite blonde woman, also narrowed her gray eyes in my direction and opened a jovial smile. She must have been in her 40s, but I had the impression that her mind held at least a millennium of knowledge.

"Dr. Tucker," I greeted her.

"Hello, Mr. Holder. It's good to see you again," she returned the greeting.

The woman, recommended by Ghost, had advised me to seek another therapist last week, a trusted friend who specialized in cases like mine. And though I was confused by some of the things she said, I felt like a point of light had been found in the darkness of my mind, and I just needed to follow it to discover the right path.

I hoped my Jasmin would find it too.

"Wolf." She came up to me and stood on her tiptoes to kiss me.

"Hello, my Crystal." I kissed her lips tenderly, enjoying the scent of floral essence on her skin. "How was your first time?"

"I feel like you're present in all my firsts." Her face flushed at the comment, making me smile as I traced her delicate cheekbones with my thumb.

"I always want to be your first if that's what you desire," I whispered.

"More than anything." She hugged me, and we left for the car.

This time, we were in two vehicles. Ray and Lyon in the front car, and Jasmin and I in the back. Shaw wasn't with us because he had to resolve some pending matters with Wood to issue the necessary documents for the trip they would make soon. Everything was happening so fast, but I really liked that acceleration.

Jasmin waited until we got into the vehicle to start speaking.

"Christopher, I need you to take me somewhere before we go home."

"Where do you want to go, miss? Just say the word, and I'll take you." I smiled, looking at her through the rearview mirror.

"To the penitentiary."

"What?" I turned to her with wide eyes. "Are you crazy, Jasmin?"

"I was talking to the therapist and ended up making two decisions." A certain fear filled me. "The first is that I need to know why Claire did that. Especially if she knew she would be caught. I'll never get an answer from Carla, but at least Claire can tell me something significant."

"What's that going to help now? It doesn't change the fact that she tried to kill you and you just recovered, sweetheart. I don't want you to expose yourself to that kind of stress." She slid across the seat with that little face that made my chest tighten and touched the tip of my nose with her finger.

"You have no idea what happens inside here when you call me that." She brought her hand to her heart and smiled. "I know you want to protect me, and I feel like the luckiest woman in the world for it, but I need closure for my story. An ending, or I'll spend the rest of my life wondering why they did this to me, you know?"

Shit, and the worst part was that I understood. Even though I wanted to tie her down with the seatbelt and take her back to the mansion, I knew I shouldn't interfere. It was a matter she truly needed to resolve, but not alone.

"Okay, we'll go to the penitentiary, but with one condition."

"What is it?"

"I'll stay by your side the whole time, and I won't accept any obj..."

"I agree," she interrupted me.

"Seriously? That quickly?"

"How could I bear to face her without my safe harbor by my side?" All the fear that had arisen in my heart at the last moment melted away, and I leaned in to kiss her between the seats. I savored her soft lips with affection and all the devotion of my heart.

A LOT HAD HAPPENED while Jasmin was recovering. I told Cahill the whole truth about the discrimination Jasmin faced from some men at the company, and he began to get rid of them one by one. He quickly and efficiently renewed the team, calling in long-forgotten favors, just as he had done with my father. I don't need to say that my little troublemaker wanted to be there when those idiots were fired, but she was too fragile for that.

Snake was keeping us updated on the discoveries made by Agent Petrova, our contact in the CIA, after Naish's arrest, who, by the way, would never be seen again now that he was in the agency's custody. According to my brother, he would never be able to hurt anyone again, which brought me profound relief.

Aside from that, Agent Petrova decoded and analyzed all the accounts linked to the senator and discovered two new overseas accounts that had mysteriously been cleaned out. She also managed to trace each of the transactions the woman made, connecting everything to Carla's father, who was one of the arms of a famous Colombian mafia operating in Chicago, and was arrested a day after we captured Naish, trying to flee the country. Apparently, whatever bond existed between Claire and Matías was severed the moment she was arrested.

I didn't know if Agent Petrova had the legal backing to do that kind of thing, but a CIA agent wasn't exactly a stickler for the rules, was she?

And I didn't care what she did, only the results she would achieve. With all that research, Petrova managed to list at least 20 important names linked to the senator, and with proof of their crimes in hand, she ended up arresting 17 of them.

Senator Claire was the mastermind behind everything, negotiating with Colombian cartel owners operating statewide, and selling weapons, both physically and virtually, that could only be supplied to the government for use by the army and armed forces, with Matías's boss being her biggest and most dangerous client. Apparently, the woman pocketed a sum greater than eight digits, but at that point, all her accounts must have been frozen, and I believed she was going to face a long time in prison once all of that was exposed—if she survived behind bars, which I truly hoped she wouldn't.

I never said I was a good man.

"Are you sure you want to do this?" I stared at the walls of the place, high and surrounded by barbed wire.

"Yes, I need to look that snake in the eye at least once." I touched her hand with mine.

"I'll be right behind you."

Jasmin

THE VISITATION ROOM was strange and suffocating, even though it was spacious. Two chairs were placed in front of a large wall that was half glass and half concrete. We sat there side by side. There were a few holes in the glass for communication between visitors and inmates.

I started fidgeting with my hands, not knowing what I was doing there. The days had flown by, but the truth was I had thought about Claire every single one of them. There were so many questions I wanted to ask her. So many whys. But at the same time, I didn't know how I would feel seeing her. Anxiety, fear, and apprehension surrounded me, and I only realized I was holding my breath when Christopher placed his hand on my shoulder.

"You can do it, heart." I exhaled, a little unsure.

The door opened, and she stepped through the threshold, guided by a guard. The woman hadn't left her senate position, but she would be tried like any ordinary citizen, as the rules of our country dictated, and knowing she was behind bars gave me some satisfaction, which didn't negate the frustrating feelings I had toward her.

Claire looked infinitely paler in those khaki pants and white shirt. Her light eyes met mine, and a shadow of a smile crossed her face.

"I'm not accepting this visit." She turned to the police officer and was about to leave through the door when I stood up from my chair.

"You were never a coward, Claire." She paused at my comment. I knew I had hit her. "Or has prison changed you?"

She approached, walking elegantly, her posture straight and impeccable, like a model strutting down the runway, if it weren't for the slight hops she made with her right leg, the one Lyon shot twice.

She sat down in front of us, a mild smile on her face, with her hands cuffed on the table.

I held my breath when I found myself staring into her eyes. I couldn't explain the pain that surged in my chest and paralyzed me for a moment.

I had never been a woman who shrank away from any revelation or danger. The will to survive always propelled me to react. I wore armor that helped me pretend to be normal in a room full of extremely intelligent men who only intended to belittle every word I said. And it was that thick shell that forced me to be brave enough to throw a bottle at a killer to defend myself and even use radical means, like a frying pan, to attack anyone who wanted to hurt me. But there, in front of the woman I had such affection, love, and care for, I felt lost.

A flood of emotions suffocated me. I hated Senator Claire with all my might. She not only killed my sister but also tried to murder me, yet the painful tug I felt in my chest was for looking at a face I had never seen as a murderer. She was my godmother, my Aunt Claire.

I truly loved her, just as I loved Carla. What proved that those women had deceived me perfectly.

"You're quite hard to kill." She smiled at her own atrocity, and I felt Wolf tense up beside me. I placed my hand on his thigh, trying to calm him.

"I don't like people dictating what happens with my life. Especially when they want to decide whether I should live or not. You know how it is; I've always been an incorrigible rebel, Aunt Claire," I called her, and a look of disgust crossed her face.

"Don't waste your breath calling me that; I've had to endure it for many years. Spare us the time and just tell me why you're here." She rolled her eyes, and I tried to contain all the surprise that surrounded me upon seeing this side of her that I never suspected existed.

"I came because I was curious," I admitted. "What drove a woman like you, a senator with a glorious career ahead, to commit a foolish act like ordering Carla to stab me in front of all my bodyguards and my father? It was obvious you'd get caught, maybe even killed, which ended up being Carla's fate. As much as I try to understand her, I don't think your intelligence would allow you to do something so... stupid," I praised, intending to stroke her ego and keep her engaged in the conversation.

Claire started laughing, and I narrowed my eyes, confused.

"You don't know anything, Jasmin. I'm a player. Every one of my moves was carefully planned, and having to kill you in front of whoever was definitely one of my options. In a game of chess, there are moves where the queen must sacrifice herself to protect the king. And that's what I did." She leaned back in the chair, relaxed. "You all were so ridiculously childish. How could you create a fake party to capture that idiot Naish?"

"I can guarantee our plan was a complete success; otherwise, you wouldn't be here."

"You're right," she agreed, keeping a smile that started to irritate me. "But did you really think you could fool me with that poorly made copy of you? I knew it was an imposter as soon as she started dancing. You and your sister always danced in a unique way."

"How dare you speak of her, you..." I stood up and slammed my palm against the glass separating us. Claire jerked back in shock, and Christopher quickly grabbed my wrist.

"Calm down, Jas," he whispered. "You won't get anywhere like this." He, more than anyone, knew that anger only harmed us.

"You two are the most improbable thing I've ever seen." Claire rolled her eyes, and I made a motion to stand again, but Wolf's firm hand kept holding mine.

"It was never a coincidence, was it?" I cut in, and she looked confused for a moment. A painful ache throbbed in my chest. "You insisted that I go to Carla's party and even helped convince my father. You gifted me a pair of earrings with trackers, and shortly after that, we fell into an ambush in a place only I, my father, and you knew. Not to mention that psychiatrist.

I pulled her history, and after the police started the investigation, we discovered she wasn't even a doctor. You had been poisoning me all that time."

"You're really very naive." Claire stood up.

And that's how I felt. A sentimental fool. I was so shaken by encountering her that I lost myself in my own questions.

"I won't waste my time with you." She was about to leave, and a piercing desperation shook me.

"Wait, I still have questions."

"I don't want to answer them, just as you can't force me." I opened my mouth to try to convince her, but Wolf was quicker.

"How about a trade?" The woman's eyes fixed on him.

"You have nothing that interests me," she scoffed, but I could see the curiosity in her wicked eyes.

"Answer all the questions she wants."

"And? What do I gain in return?"

"A piece of information," he bargained, and she laughed loudly.

"There's nothing I want to know, especially from you." She turned to leave.

"Maybe you want to know something about Juan Esteban." She stopped walking, and when she turned to us, a pair of wide eyes stood out on her face.

"Who is that?" I whispered.

"The king of her game." He looked at me patiently. "Matías's boss and probably her best client."

"What do you want to know, Jasmin, dear?" She adopted the persona she used to deceive me for so many years, and I felt nauseous, but I didn't hesitate to fire the questions that had tormented me for days on end.

"What would you gain from my death? And since when did you plan to kill my sister and me? Had you wanted that since you met my mother?" I paused to breathe and kept my eyes on her, though the pain of looking at her threatened to suffocate me. "When did Carla enter your plans?"

"Those are a lot of questions. I hope the reward is equally proportional." She looked at Christopher.

"You can be sure it will be. Now, answer."

"Don't take it personally, Jasmin. It was just business." She sighed, as if tired of it all. "Your mother and I were friends in college, and I met your father a month before she laid eyes on him. I thought about marrying Mason as soon as I learned he owned Hill and Cahill. I already knew Matías back then and had some important contacts in the field he worked in. I knew I needed the Colombians' support to reach the government and expand my business. It would be much easier to access all the material that company produces exclusively for the army if I were his wife." Then she was stealing samples of weapons intended for military organizations right under our noses? "But when your father laid eyes on Sophie for the first time, I knew things wouldn't go as I wished. Mason fell in love with your mother, my then best friend..." She curled her lips. "I thought I might need to get rid of her to get where I wanted, but I hit the jackpot when that bitch died some time later, yet in return, she left her two little brats for me to care for." Claire rolled her eyes. "Carla was a huge stroke of luck. The girl's mother was involved in trafficking and ended up dead. Matías, being a good negotiator and investor, bet on the daughter to get close to you. She spent her life being prepared to be our plan B, even if there were risks. And don't be mistaken, for the sum she received for the help she gave her father, Carla was more than willing to put an end to her own life," she said calmly. "And I saw her as an escape valve. If those damn cameras hadn't been working, as I had imagined, she would take the fall for everything alone, and as you know, the dead don't tell stories." She opened a cheerful smile that made me shudder. "But the idiot was unable to kill you."

"You're a monster," I said, feeling dazed. The pain began to spread through my chest as I faced the woman I loved and admired my whole life, now awakening pure hatred within me.

"That's not who I am. I waited until your father proposed to me, long after your mother's death, to finally rid myself of you all."

"How could you?" I spat the words. "How could you betray us like this? Magnolia loved you like a mother, and so did I," I said with disdain.

There was no sadness over the betrayal. No disappointment. I could only think of how much my mother trusted her, how much my sister loved her, and my heart was filled with the deepest rage.

"Jasmin, only the strongest survive in the world we live in," she warned. "I work for people infinitely more dangerous than I am, Matías and that idiot Naish combined. People who need access to your father's company's projects at all costs; otherwise, my head will be served on a platter in so many different ways that a quick death from a bullet by one of your bodyguards or some years in prison were the least of my problems that night." She shrugged, with the logic of someone closing a deal.

I had to take a deep breath to keep from starting to pound the glass between us.

"As soon as I saw Wolf drag Naish out of that place, I knew he would turn me in at the first opportunity to make a deal," she continued calmly. "But the death of the Cahill heiress would trigger a drop in your father's company stock, and he would be forced to sell part of it, which would be bought by the right people."

"Not to mention the large portion that was already in the hands of your partners, right, Senator?" The woman's face turned pale at Wolf's question.

"How do you know that?" she inquired.

"A little bird told me there were some infiltrators within the company. It seems you intended to use them to keep supplying army weapons to your contacts without being discovered, and in exchange, they would not only make you a billionaire but would keep your neck safe, wherever you went, even in prison," he continued, fixing his gaze on her. "Do you have any more questions?" Wolf asked me.

"No." I stood up. "I just hope she pays for everything she's done."

"Oh, she will. No doubt about it." Wolf shot a sarcastic smile at the woman, who lost a bit more color as she saw us get up.

"Wait, what information do you have about Esteban?" Wolf smiled and intertwined his fingers with my trembling hand.

"The same little bird that told me about your infiltrators also managed to decode all your accounts."

"Impossible." She stood up.

"Not for a CIA agent with no moral concerns when it comes to criminals." Claire's eyes widened as she understood where this was heading. "We found your bank accounts and all the links tied to them. Hill and Cahill spent the last few days under audit and managed to discover every weapon you smuggled. But do you know what impressed me the most about all this?" She remained frozen, and I, who didn't know that information, because since I left the hospital I had been placed in a golden dome, followed every word attentively. "Each of those weapons had a tracking chip, and it was natural for you to remove those chips as soon as you sold them, but that's not what you did. Instead, you changed the frequency with the help of one of the scientists and created a unique sequence that only you could track. I believe you used that information to your advantage; after all, that's the only way you could keep all the cartels in your hands. If they made a slip, you could track each of the weapons you sold." He smiled widely. "But your mistake was creating a single code." He shrugged. "Once we discovered which weapons were missing and located the infiltrated scientist, it was easy, with a little help from Naish, to find a single example of the stolen weapons, and through it, we managed to locate all the others."

"You're bluffing," she whispered, her mouth losing more color with each passing moment.

"If that's what you want to believe..." He shrugged. "The information I have about Juan Esteban is that he was arrested in possession of several illegal weapons, in addition to being apprehended with an entire shipment of drugs. I think it was a ship with seven containers, if I'm not mistaken." She slumped back in her chair, and Wolf continued. "Matías cleaned out some of his accounts abroad and tried to flee the country. It seems he was going to abandon you to your fate with your old boss but was arrested before he could escape." She was paralyzed, staring at him. "Because of you, three of the main names in the Colombian mafia operating in the country earned a one-way trip to prison, with enough evidence to keep them there for the rest of their lives." He hugged me.

"You know something, Claire..." I spat her name with scorn. "The path you chose is cowardly. There's no honor in it, only sadness and pain. Two things I only learned because you introduced me to them." I breathed, trying to calm myself. "But that's our big difference. I only walk the path of truth and have learned through pain to be brave. That's why you are there, and I am here."

"If you want advice, you'd better not close your eyes tonight. And not in any of the others either. You know how Juan is temperamental and vengeful."

"Bastard! You filthy bastards." She lost her composure, and we left there under her shrill screams.

"Do you know this Juan guy?" I asked when we returned to the car.

"No."

"And how do you know he's temperamental and vengeful?"

"What mafia member isn't?" He brushed his thumb across my chin. "Are you okay after all that?"

"Before coming here, I only had a blurred image of what it was like to have my friend stabbing me." I pursed my lips. "That didn't make sense. I needed to hear that truth from her, and now, no matter how confused I am, I feel better. Thank you for staying by my side."

"I'll always be here, heart. You're my most precious crystal." He leaned in, kissing me fervently.

CHAPTER TWENTY-NINE

Wolf

We hit the road in the late afternoon, and I knew the day hadn't been easy for Jasmin. Hearing all those words from someone she loved so much must have hurt like hell, and her lost gaze through the car window confirmed my suspicions.

"Let's take a small detour," I said when an idea popped into my mind.

"Where are we going?"

"To a place you know, which is quite safe, by the way." I entered the highway that would take us to the overlook of the future Holder Security unit and asked Lyon and Ray to wait with the second car at the entrance. I wanted to have a moment alone with Jasmin, without any interruptions.

I drove into the large yard and parked close to the overlook, which revealed a stunning sunset on the colorful horizon.

"Oh my God, the sunset from here is so beautiful." Jasmin smiled, and I noticed that in this part of the new unit, there wasn't a single guard. Everyone was focused at the entrance, just like Lyon and Ray.

I got out of the car and opened the back door, sitting next to her. I wrapped her in my arms, enjoying her delicious scent of freshly picked flowers. She lifted her eyes to my face, her pupils dilating as she watched me cautiously, then closed them when I brushed my mouth against hers slowly.

I slid my tongue along her lips, moistening them, then took them in a deep kiss.

"You are the bravest woman I've ever met." I nibbled her chin and went back to her lips. The slightest touch from Jasmin left me hard, making it even harder to maintain a rational conversation.

"I think I only look brave. I was trembling from head to toe." I caressed her skin with my fingertips, descending slowly from her neck, down her arm, until I grazed the side of her breast beneath the fabric. Damn, how I missed touching her.

"That's fear, sweetheart, and we all feel it." She let out a low moan as I brushed her hardened nipple under the thin dress fabric. "There are two types of people: the cowards who choose the easiest and often the wrong path to escape, and the brave who face anything, even trembling with fear." I kissed her ardently and deeply, tasting her mouth.

"Sorry, but I haven't understood a word you said since you touched me." She started kissing me again, giving those little moans that drove me crazy.

"That's not why I brought you here, sweetheart," I warned, pointing to the horizon. "I brought you here so you could relax a bit. The investigation at your company is still ongoing, and since we can't go out like we'd like to, I thought I'd bring you to see the sunset..."

"Which goes perfectly with kissing." She entwined her fingers in my hair and pulled me to her lips. I could feel the heat radiating from them, spreading throughout my body.

"You can't help yourself."

"You provoked me." She bit my mouth. "It's been almost two months, and I feel good enough to cause trouble in a prison. I'm in perfect shape. When are you going to touch me right again? I miss you so much," she pouted and climbed onto my lap, lifting her dress until her panties brushed against my hard member.

"Jasmin," I called, alarmed, looking around.

"No one's watching." She leaned in, kissing me fiercely, and I couldn't think of anything else the moment I felt her tongue in my mouth. "I want you inside me, Christopher." She ground against me, and damn, if she kept doing that, I'd end up coming in my pants.

"Let's just... play a little, okay?"

She nodded, breathless.

I squeezed her ass and dug my fingers into her flesh, pulling her closer to me. I slid my hands down her bare legs, entering her thigh, vowing that I wouldn't go beyond small touches until I found her soaked panties.

"Damn, baby!" I swore against her soft skin as I slid the straps of her dress down.

"I told you I missed you." Her rosy breasts popped into view, and she threw her head back as I captured the hard nipple with my mouth, lavishing attention on each one.

Our breaths oscillated in a mix of desperation, longing, and lust, creating a symphony of moans, growls, and sounds revealing our pleasure. I penetrated her with two fingers, playing with her sex and shuddered at how warm she felt inside. Jasmin began to grind on my fingers, emitting low, constant noises, like a little cat purring on top of me. Seeing her like that was maddening.

"Christopher!" I lost control the moment she trembled in my arms as her orgasm hit her. Her sex closed around my fingers, and when I realized it, I had already unzipped my pants.

She smiled, surprised when the erection pressed against her belly. I held her face and kept her gaze on mine as I slid into her very warm pussy. She closed her eyes as I began to push and bit her lips, tilting her head back.

"What a delight!" I growled against her skin as I felt her tighten around my cock in that tight embrace. I entered her inch by inch, feeling her pleasure drip down my flesh.

"Let's take it slow, I don't want to hurt you."

"You won't," she breathed out, dizzy, closing her eyes. I held her hips and began thrusting slowly. Strange sounds rose from my throat. She tightened around me each time I thrust into her, and I almost closed my eyes from the delicious sensation coursing through my veins, but the desire to watch her with her legs spread, my cock buried inside her, was stronger.

"Oh, baby!" she whimpered when I went in deep.

"Does it hurt?" For a moment, I misunderstood what she said and stopped moving.

"For God's sake, man, don't stop!" she ordered, making me laugh.

A smile that disappeared as soon as she moved up and down the length of my erection, moaning that loud, deep sound only she could make, and at that moment, I couldn't care less if anyone heard. I was too focused on the masterpiece that was Jasmin, with her messy hair, flushed face, and her swollen lips bitten, lost in our pleasure.

"Christopher," she moaned loudly, and I had to lift her off me before it was too late.

Jasmin collapsed in my arms, panting, and I held her close, running my fingers through her hair.

"You are perfection in its purest form." I kissed her lips for long minutes.

"I love you, my Wolfie." She buried her face in the curve of my shoulder. "Thank you for bringing me here." Her eyes roamed over the countless city lights, which slowly stood out as night fell.

"My love, you said you made two decisions today after leaving the appointment," I teased, playing with her hair, twirling it around my finger slowly. "One of them was going to the prison. But what was the other?"

"I'm moving out of the Cahill mansion," she suddenly announced. "The doctor suggested a change of scenery until the nightmares stop completely. According to her, certain triggers, like living in the space where a tragedy occurred, can cause night terrors." An idea had been simmering in my mind for a few days, but I hadn't yet found a way to put it into words. But now, in this situation, it seemed like the perfect moment. I squeezed her hands with mine and let her finish. "The truth is, it was just a suggestion, but I already felt an immense urge to move out of that place long before all this happened. Even though it's not the crime scene, the memories of everything I lived through there with Claire and Carla are still too vivid, like each wall is reminding me of them." She blinked and started rubbing her hands together, anxious. "I don't want to stay there anymore, and my father will have to understand. I'll start looking for an apartment today."

"I have the perfect solution for that." I raised my eyes to her face, fearing she wouldn't like my idea at all.

"What is it?"

"How about... moving in with me?"

"What?" She widened her very green eyes, and I grabbed both her hands, bringing them to my lips, kissing each one tenderly. I was more nervous than ever.

"I've been considering this idea while I couldn't stop thinking about a memory of you that I've kept locked away since the day you left the hospital."

"What memory?"

"The first time I saw you dance. Half-drunk, on top of a crowded club table." I chuckled, the images fresh in my mind.

"Why do you keep that memory?"

"Because that's when I fell in love with you, sweetheart," I admitted. "Everything about you drew me in. Your free spirit, the beauty of your movements, and how you seemed to fly when you danced. The courage you had to steal my bike and everything we went through after that day." I looked down at our hands. "I was afraid when I realized what I was feeling for you, Jasmin. And that fear grew since you left the hospital." Her tear-filled eyes were fixed on every word. "I know our time as bodyguard and VIP is over, but I still want to be there when the nightmares come. I want to hold you and soothe you, I want to see you dance and inhale the scent of your perfume that drives me crazy. I want to pull you off the roof every Tuesday and hear your cursing when you get scared, and for God's sake, I want you to hit Phantom with a frying pan more often." She burst into laughter. "I want you to sleep in my arms every night so I know you're safe. I want to make love to you every second of our free time." I traced a path across her face, outlining the curve of her lips with the tip of my finger. I felt exposed, driven by the urgent desire to have her in my arms forever. "You may not need me as your bodyguard anymore, sweetheart, but I need you as my woman. And knowing that, I've been making plans to include myself in your life, every night. Because I don't think I can go a whole day without you." I smiled awkwardly, staring at our intertwined hands. "It sounds ridiculous, doesn't it?"

"There's nothing ridiculous about it," she said with a choked voice. "And I may not need Wolf as my bodyguard anymore, but I need Christopher Holder as much as I need air to breathe. With your humor as low as my breasts and your tendency to lose keys." The cheeky woman raised my keys between her fingers, and I couldn't help but burst into loud laughter.

"I have an apartment a few miles from Hill and Cahill. High security, lots of comfort and space. You'll be close to your work, and I can take you there every day," I rambled on. "I might be rushing things, but what in our relationship hasn't been rushed?"

"If I say yes, you know you only have two options." She balled up my shirt in her fists, and I couldn't contain the wave of excitement that overtook me, waiting for her answer. "Hire a cook or cook for me."

"We'll have both, of course. I like my kitchen the way it is. I never planned on setting it on fire, so we'll keep you far away from it." I kissed the tip of her nose. "I also suspect Ruth and Judith come as part of a combo package with you." I laughed, and she joined in. I pressed our foreheads together and felt her shaky breath brush against my skin. "It's a big step, my love. Don't feel pressured to say yes."

"It would be perfect to sleep in these arms every day." She squeezed the muscles of my triceps and bit her lip. "It's all I want. To work at my father's company and be recognized for my projects, to travel on vacations, to walk on a beach on my days off, and to be free for the first time, alongside someone I love. The answer is very simple, Wolfie. Of course, I'll move in with you."

A painful yet pleasurable sensation filled my chest, and I kissed Jasmin with all that emotion. That young woman completed me in a way that was different, deep, and unique.

Jasmin, with all the chaos she brought, was exactly what I needed to know true happiness.

I never knew I needed love until I found it.

"Do you think your father will kill me?"

"Most likely." I laughed out loud.

Never had a death threat sounded so perfect.

CHAPTER THIRTY

Jasmin

A Few Days Later...

The sunset bathed the hills in a warm, intense orange. The shades of green blended among the treetops, giving me a sense of freedom I had never felt in my life.

"Are you sure this is the best decision you'll make, daughter?" My father intertwined his arm with mine, lost in the landscape before us.

Christopher had talked to my father the same day I accepted his invitation and asked for permission for us to live together, presenting a list of criteria that would keep me safe. I thought it was quite sweet after the initial outburst my father had, and I was extremely happy when he understood that this decision had to come from me.

"I'll be fine, Dad. It's time for me to stand on my own two feet." I leaned my head on his shoulder. "Are you sure you don't want to do the same? This house has so many... memories."

"Yes, it does. But I don't know if I can let go of it yet. This is where I lived the best years of my life with your mother; I didn't want to part with this place for that reason. There hasn't been a woman I've loved more than your mother. Claire was a good companion, or rather, pretended to be. But love? I only feel that for one person today. And I never imagined living here could cause her so much pain." He turned to me. "I ask you to forgive me for not noticing sooner."

"Dad, you couldn't have known. I think I didn't really know either." I bit my lip. "Either way, you're my only family. You're all I have, and it will always be us against the world, got it?" He stroked my face with a sad, unfathomable look.

"You have no idea how much I regret not noticing what those vultures were doing to you at that company, daughter. I understand why you didn't tell me, but it's unacceptable. Even if you weren't my daughter, those idiots had no right to mistreat you." He squeezed my hand.

"Seeing a woman excel in the field of science still causes an impact today. We face persecution and discrimination just for being who we are. But the daughter you raised doesn't bow her head to any man, especially those prejudiced assholes... sorry, Dad." I regretted it immediately and was surprised when he laughed.

"I'm going to miss you, daughter." He looked at the horizon again. "Wolf seems to be a good man. I like him more every day, but don't be fooled; it doesn't matter how big that man is." He glanced over his shoulder and watched Christopher engaged in an animated conversation with Shaw and Lyon. "If he hurts you, nothing in this world will stop me from going after him. And I've already warned him about that." My eyes welled up with tears from the tight knot in my throat, and I hugged him.

"We'll see each other every day at Hill and Cahill. We'll have lunch together too. I plan to go back to work on Monday, and you're welcome to visit me whenever you want. You should count on seeing me every weekend; I'll never be far away, and..."

"Daughter," he interrupted me, "this is your life now; you need to take care of it. Don't worry too much about your old man here; I'll be fine. And rest a little more before you go back to work; I want you to be well to start training you. One day you'll take over the whole company, and until then, we'll spend a lot of time together."

"I don't think I can wait that long, Dad." I smiled at the hills.

"Why not?"

"They say that when you have an idea, you need to put it into practice as soon as possible before the essence is lost completely. And I had an idea for a new project after the J.A.S."

"Your mind doesn't stop for a second, does it?" he inquired, curious.

"I take after my father. What can I say?" I shrugged, and we laughed together.

"What's the new project about?" he asked, intrigued.

"About trucks with microwave weapons." He narrowed his eyes.

"Why am I not surprised? You've always been obsessed with that project."

"Yes, it's true I'm passionate about them. So I thought about creating a smaller model, maybe implementing a..." I stopped speaking when I noticed his eyes wide open, with that expression of someone listening to an expert about to suggest a good investment. "I think that will wait until Monday."

"Are you really going to make me wait until Monday?" he shot back, pretending disbelief.

"If I don't, you won't even let me into that place on Monday. I'm already super relaxed, Dad, and since we're talking about new projects, I also want to create a social project in our company. I know we already help some institutions across the country, but I want to manage something focused on the homeless people living here in Chicago. I know some shelters that I would love to help, maybe even create our own." I remembered the shelters that Wolf and his brothers managed, and never had an idea seemed so phenomenal. He watched my face carefully and smiled.

"You've never looked more like your mother than now. She always dreamed of doing a project to help people, but she never had the time for it, and I, bitter from losing her, never thought about following through on any of that." My father's gray eyes sparkled, and he hugged me. "I'm happy you'll do it, and I'll support you in everything you need."

"Thank you, Dad. I love you."

"I love you too, my daughter."

We stayed embraced for a while, watching the sun hide on the horizon, and a smile appeared on my lips with the warm feeling that washed over me as I saw the hill rise among the clouds as if it were touching a part of the sky.

"Sometimes I feel like they are watching over us," I said.

"I know they are, and I can only thank them for it."

Wolf

"IS EVERYTHING READY?" I asked over the phone, more anxious than ever.

"Yes, everyone is here," Ghost confirmed on the other end of the line.

"Great, we're almost out of here." I exhaled, restless, and glanced over my shoulder just to confirm that Jasmin was still playing with her hot chocolate, occupying one of the tables in a café at the mall. "Are you sure this is the best option? What if she doesn't like it?"

"The girl has spent her whole life surrounded by these people. Of course, she'll like it. Trust my advice, brother; when have I ever steered you wrong?"

"That time we were going to Cuba and..."

"Don't you dare finish that sentence." We laughed together. "Just trust me, okay? Snake just arrived."

"Okay, we'll be there soon." I hung up and leaned against the counter beside me, watching her.

Her light hair was tied up in a high ponytail, gracefully showcasing her rosy cheeks. My heart raced just looking at her, sipping her hot chocolate calmly and peering into her bag where she had stashed a pair of old, worn ballet flats. Then her eyes lifted, and she became captivated by everything happening around her, an excitement that was delightful to witness.

We spent the day shopping for what she deemed "basic and necessary" for the move, and even though I disagreed with almost everything she picked—seriously, what's the point of a hot pink armchair?—I followed along with a certain joy. It was incredible how Jasmin looked at everything around her with a unique simplicity and curiosity. I only realized how profound and complex that was when she freaked out at the sight of a small amusement park set up next to the mall. That was when I understood how deprived she had been of a normal life.

Jasmin had never traveled anywhere, and I wanted to show her the beautiful world she hadn't had the chance to see. I felt an urgent need to give her everything she had never had because of the dangers she had always faced.

I would take care of her with my own life without hesitation, and I already started asking my father to reassign me to one-day missions so I could be home at night. I feared that Jasmin might have one of her nighttime episodes alone, and just the thought terrified me. I would return to missions as soon as I was sure that, if I needed to spend a night away, she would be okay.

I walked over to her with the certainty that Jasmin's happiness was my priority.

"Are you ready to see our apartment, sweetheart?" I sat beside her, and she quickly turned her bright green eyes in my direction.

"Our..." she tasted the word. "I really like that." She leaned in and placed a chaste kiss on my lips. "I can't wait to get there."

"Me neither."

Jasmin

"WOW!" I OPENED MY LIPS as we stopped beside a tall, elegant gray building. We got out of the car, and Christopher asked a valet to park the vehicle.

"I usually park the car myself, but I don't want to start by introducing you to the parking garage, so, Miss..." He opened the transparent door of the place, which was very refined and luxurious, and bowed for me to pass through.

I entered the spacious lobby, which had decorative drywall, and walked alongside Wolf until we reached a tall counter where a man was distractedly examining a logbook on the counter.

"Oh, good evening, Mr. Holder," he greeted kindly as soon as he saw us.

"Good evening, Lucien." The man's eyes flickered between me and Christopher, looking confused by what he saw. "I want you to meet my... girlfriend." He lowered his gaze to me and possessively wrapped his arm around my waist. We exchanged a knowing look that burned me inside, as much as that word. *Girlfriend*. "Jasmin Cahill. Starting today, she's going to live with me, so please update the team about her arrival."

"Yes, of course, sir, right away. And welcome, Miss." He opened a genuine smile that made some lines appear on his face.

"I'll send the necessary documents," Wolf added, and the man nodded as he guided me toward the elevator.

Christopher pressed me against the metal walls as soon as we stepped into the elevator, and the doors closed. His lips sought mine slowly, deliberately. I gasped against his mouth, feeling euphoric about everything we were experiencing.

"Was I too hasty, sweetheart? I've never dated anyone before, and... is it a proposal, right? But damn it, I forgot the proposal." He started to get lost in his own thoughts. "Do you want to date me? Is that how it works? Should I do this inside an elevator?" I kissed him, holding back the laughter that bubbled in my throat at the sight of his desperation.

This was as new for him as it was for me.

"I accept, love. Of course, I accept." I brushed my lips against his.

"I want to make it clear that I'm adopted, and considering my father is a confirmed bachelor, I don't have a single example of how to make this work and..."

"Chris," I called him when I noticed he was getting anxious again. "We're in this together, remember? I'm not exactly the best reference either." The elevator stopped on the 16th floor, and he took a deep breath before stepping out.

"Alright, but I plan to rephrase that proposal," he warned as we walked down the corridor where four doors were scattered, and an overwhelming silence enveloped the place. Not even the elevator made a sound, which worried me deeply, and for a moment, I froze in place. "What's wrong, sweetheart?"

"This place is too quiet, Christopher. Just listen." I stared at the polished floor. "You can't hear a single noise. How are we going to... you know. I can't stay quiet; we'll get kicked out of the building. I don't want to cause any trouble, and..."

"My angel..." He hugged me from behind and pressed his lips to my ear. A warm, pleasant laugh brushed against my skin right after. "Don't worry about that; the apartments have soundproofing." He placed a chaste kiss on my neck. "You can moan for me as much as you want." I closed my eyes as Chris's low voice penetrated every cell in my body.

"That'll be a huge help," I commented when we stopped in front of the last door in the corridor. Christopher held my hand before opening it, his gaze filled with apprehension.

"It seems we're both freaking out about the endless possibilities of living together, and I know we may encounter difficulties on this new path, but I want to face each one of them by your side. I want to be the best version of myself," he suddenly said. "I hope to be worthy of your love, sweetheart."

"You already are, my Wolf. That's all I want, all I need." He kissed my forehead slowly and pulled me into a hug.

"Then welcome to your new home, Miss Cahill." He entered the code on the electronic panel, and in the next instant, a commotion began.

"Surprise!" The word echoed through the place, which was packed with people. I widened my eyes at the sight of the living room decorated with balloons and streamers in gray, white, and black, matching the black walls of the space.

"Oh my God!" I brought my hand to my mouth when I realized everyone was there.

My father stood next to Mr. Holder, my... *father-in-law*, who, by the way, was a very handsome man, and right behind them were Lyon, Ray, Shaw, and Wood, who was arm in arm with Ruth. I smiled at them and soon felt euphoric when I spotted Judith waving at me. In another corner, Ghost was watching me with a smile next to Snake, who was eyeing me with his usual narrowed and somewhat suspicious look.

"It was a bit last minute, but I hope you like it," Wolf whispered behind me.

"All of this is perfect, Chris." I smiled and looked at him, who wore a beautiful sideways smile.

I hugged each of the guests, stopping when I reached my security team.

I scanned each of the four, and a painful knot formed in my throat. Soon they would travel to Israel, and even though my father wanted to ensure they still worked with us, I would be without seeing them for a long time, and I was already missing them so much. After all, these men had been my only company for years.

"Thank you for being here." I hugged them warmly. "You are part of my story."

"It was a pleasure to keep you alive, Miss," Shaw said, earning an elbow from Lyon, which made us all laugh.

"Miss Cahill." The firm voice made me freeze in place, and I turned to greet the famous Reid Holder.

He visited me twice in the hospital, but we hadn't had the chance to talk about my relationship with his son, and when I faced him, I thought I would feel fear in front of the man with a rigid, well-defined jaw and impeccably gray hair that only enhanced his beauty. But when I looked into his deep, clever eyes, all I felt was gratitude for what he had done to save Christopher when no one else wanted to help him, and before I could control myself, I had already thrown myself into the man's arms, squeezing him in a hug with teary eyes.

"You are such a good man." I sniffed into his shoulder. Wolf was talking to my father but kept his eyes on us, now looking at me with an expression that seemed to say a loud "what the hell is going on there?".

"Dear, I fear you're confusing me with someone else." Holder laughed as I released the hug.

"I'm not confused," I assured, wiping my eyes. "I just hadn't had the chance to tell you how much I admire you for everything you've done for Christopher. He's an incredible man because he followed in your footsteps."

"That's very kind of you." He glanced at Christopher, who had now joined his brothers in an animated conversation that only they seemed to understand. "Those three are the reason for my premature gray hair," he joked, "but I can say that nothing Christopher has been through in his life, none of his achievements, or everything he's gained through hard work and dedication, absolutely nothing has brought him as much joy as meeting you, Miss Cahill."

"Jasmin... You can call me Jasmin." I pressed my lips together, happy to be standing before him.

"Jasmin, we still haven't had the chance to introduce ourselves properly." He smiled kindly and extended his hand to me. "I'm Reid, father of those three crazies, and your father-in-law." I threw my arms around his neck again, squeezing him in a hug.

"Thank you for welcoming me into your family."

"Thank you, dear, for bringing true happiness to my Christopher. I've never seen him smile so much, and I hope you both are very happy." I thanked him again and noticed he hadn't let go of my hand. "I heard rumors of a story I'd love to hear directly from you." I froze for a moment.

"What story?"

"Cahill," he called my father, who came over with Wood and Lyon at his heels, and soon everyone was gathered around me. "Jasmin, I heard that two of my sons, the most reputable bodyguards in my company, got beaten up with a frying pan." My father almost spat his drink from laughing. "Could you tell us that story in detail?"

"It would be a pleasure."

"Dad!" Ghost and Snake complained from the back of the room, but no one listened. Everyone was focused on the story.

"It all started when I was surprised by Ghost and his cotton feet." Reid laughed loudly, and I was filled with pure joy.

Looking at the crowd around me, encouraging me to go on, giving me strength to face whatever came, I realized I had never truly been alone. I had just been suffering too much to see the incredible people who did everything to make my day better and keep me safe.

In the end, family goes far beyond blood ties. It's the bond of love that unites us; it's the hope that never leaves us alone.

I smiled as I realized that all my family was in that room.

"I HOPE YOU LIKED IT, sweetheart. It was my way of making you feel more comfortable." Christopher hugged me as soon as all the guests left.

"I loved it so much that I can't even express it, but I didn't have time to see your house."

"Our," he corrected me with a kiss.

"Right, our."

"Come with me, I'll show you around."

He wrapped his arms around me from behind and showed me every corner of the apartment in shades of black and gray that made the space feel darker. There were two large bathrooms. In one of them, a bathtub was set up, and I could only imagine myself in it for hours.

The entire decor was dark; there weren't as many pictures as in my father's house, and I loved that detail as much as I hated the pictures at Hill House. Christopher showed me the rooftop balcony that overlooked the entire city, and we ended our tour in one of the three bedrooms.

"This is our bedroom." He nodded toward the door, and I peeked in, sensing that, like the rest of the house, it had dark walls and sober furniture.

"Would you mind if I painted one or two walls? I'm not sure if sleeping in a room like this is relaxing or suffocating." He laughed behind me.

"You can do whatever you want, my love." His hands rested on my waist, pulling me back against him.

My face heated the moment I felt his firm erection against my butt.

"I loved having our families here today, but I never wanted a visit to end so quickly," he whispered in my ear. "Let me show you what it's like to sleep in a room like this, Miss." I let out a startled squeal when he lifted me into his arms and kissed me passionately. "I'm crazy with desire, sweetheart."

"Then make love to me," I urged between his lips, and I saw his eyes transform into two bright, intense stones as he closed the door behind us.

The dark room felt warmer as he carried me to the bed in his arms. Our breaths fused in an intense kiss. Christopher laid me on the sheets, ripped off his own shirt, and came over me, wild and hungry. I arched my body as I felt his tongue travel down the valley of my breasts, rising to penetrate my mouth, sucking and biting my lips firmly in a rhythmic way that made me burn. I squeezed my thighs together, desperate for the constant throb that made me feel the moisture forming there.

I tangled my fingers in his smooth hair, messing it up, and I moaned when I felt the weight of his body against mine, as if our souls were merging right there. Christopher slapped his hand on the mattress and reached for a lamp beside the very large bed, turning it on.

"I want to see your eyes when I'm inside you," he whispered against my mouth, and I gasped, diving into a river of warm, deep waters.

Our eyes danced a slow, mysterious, violent music. I parted my lips and moaned deeply when his fingers closed around my delicate nipples and squeezed them, torturing them slowly. His free hand wrapped around my ass and moved up to my waistband, slipping into my pants and pulling the fabric down until he completely freed me from it. His fingers traveled across my skin, compressing it, marking me.

"Love..." I whimpered. His firm fingers invaded my folds, opening them.

He brushed his thumb over my swollen clit and descended between my lips until he slid inside me. The sound that rose from my throat was more like a mewl. His rough lips trailed down my neck, leaving a hot trail like hell until they reached my breasts. I felt Christopher's wet tongue playing with my nipples while his fingers explored me. Every corner, every detail. I could feel him infiltrating my skin, taking me to another reality where our bodies met in a unique dance, just ours.

He lowered his lips further, opening my legs and pulling me closer to him. I dug my fingers into the sheets as his tongue penetrated me slowly, and I began to roll my hips, meeting his mouth. My breath was erratic, and every inch of my body felt like it was on fire. Christopher sucked me hard, with pressure, gripping my ass and pulling me even closer to his lips.

"What a delight!" I found myself shouting and moaning, arching my body as intense pleasure took over.

Christopher came over me again, pressing his body against mine. I bit my lip and looked at him. His bicolored eyes stared at me in wonder, and a strong feeling embraced my heart. I touched Christopher's chest and flipped our position, ending up on top of him. I traced my fingers down his waist to the edge of his pants and opened them. We got rid of the fabric, and Christopher grabbed my wrist, trying to pull me to him, but I refused.

"I want to try something," I whispered, locking my eyes with his.

I slid my nails down his chiseled chest, not breaking our gaze until I wrapped my fingers around his thick, pulsating member. He growled as I moved my hand up and down slowly. I leaned closer, savoring the citrus scent that intoxicated me, and descended my lips down his neck, showering him with kisses, licks, and bites across his skin.

"Jasmin..." he gasped as I descended between his legs. I wrapped my hand around his cock and blew gently on the thick head. "Fuck!" he cursed as I touched him with the tip of my tongue.

I wanted to give him all the pleasure he gave me. I wanted Christopher to feel the piece of heaven he always gifted me. I sucked the head carefully, swirling in a back-and-forth motion. Christopher began to grunt and curse, making my insides clench. I could feel desire dripping down my legs. I ran my tongue the length of him and took him into my mouth, licking him, swallowing him as much as I could. His fingers tangled in my hair, guiding a steady rhythm. His pleasure filled me and made me even hotter. I kept sucking him until I felt his hands on my shoulders.

"Jasmin, my love, come here before I come in your mouth." He pulled me before I could complain and turned me onto all fours, leaving me open for him. He pressed his lips to my ear, and I could feel the tremor in his hand as he aligned himself with my entrance. "Has it been 30 days?" he asked, and I instantly knew what he was talking about.

A few days after I left the hospital, I started taking my birth control again. According to the doctor, after 30 days I would be completely protected from an unplanned pregnancy. I hadn't completed the correct time when we had sex in the car, but now...

"It's over now..." I managed to say while drowning in the delicious sensations he was provoking.

"I want to fuck you like this, angel. Pure." He slid his hand over my ass, whispering indecent words as he penetrated me with a finger from behind. His fingers slid in and out, soaked. "I want to feel you squeezing me inside of you." He brought his fingers to the center of my ass, wetting that sensitive spot. The touch ignited me. He moved his other hand down, reaching my swollen and wet intimacy, teasing my clit.

I grabbed the headboard, spreading my legs wider. I was going to come, I was sure of it, and just as I was about to explode with pleasure, Christopher thrust deep, all at once. His fingers slid up my waist and tangled in my hair, pulling it. He withdrew slightly and thrust again, slower this time, but then quickened the pace. I closed my eyes, biting my lips, panting and moaning.

"Fuck, you're so hot!" I felt a firm slap on my ass, and his hand wrapped around my neck with a delicious, dangerous pressure. His cock stretched me, moving in and out with force, filling me until I lost myself in another orgasm. I trembled and gripped the sheets. Christopher thrust once more, letting out a hoarse, trembling sound, and buried his mouth in my neck, sinking his teeth into my skin, marking me in every possible way.

"THIS IS DEFINITELY my favorite room," I whispered between gasps, lying against his chest. Christopher laughed and pulled me closer, our bare bodies entwined under the sheets in a delirious intimacy. "The apartment is perfect."

"You're perfect. My Jasmin..." He kissed the tip of my nose and traveled down my face to my neck, which by now must have been marked again after the passionate love we shared, causing me to giggle. "I love you, sweetheart."

"I'm completely crazy about you. I love you so damn much." He chuckled.

"Yeah, me too. So damn much," he whispered into my hair and nestled me in his arms. Our breathing began to return to normal, and a question popped into my mind—one I had completely forgotten to ask.

"Chris, can you tell me something?"

"What do you want to know?"

"Where do you keep that motorcycle?" I bit my lips.

"Jasmin!" I laughed in his arms, and he held me even tighter.

"I'm just kidding; I promise I won't steal it again."

"Show me a driver's license, and you can ride it." I propped myself up on my elbow and looked at him. "Under my supervision, of course. It's a collector's item, as I've mentioned once or twice."

"Are you serious? You'd really let me ride it again?" I opened my eyes wider but narrowed them the moment I realized the whopper of a lie he told. "Once or twice? You could rewrite the Bible with how many times you reminded me of that." He laughed, and I fell back into his arms.

"I just don't let you ride it right now because I'm afraid you'll get hurt." He caressed my face. "Motorcycles are dangerous. Just a small mistake can lead to something terrible. With the right instruction, you can ride it safely."

"I think that even though I know how to ride other bikes, I got really lucky when I took yours."

"You're right. It's an aggressive and heavy bike. Thank God you managed to get it to that beach safely." I nodded in agreement. "I'll be the first to hand over the keys to my Spirit when you get your license, if you promise to take good care of it." His fingers slid down my skin and brushed against my breasts, making my core pulse again. "Until then, how about riding it with me?" His deep, firm voice touched me.

"Now?"

"In a bit." His fingers tightened around my nipple, making me gasp a soft moan.

I closed my eyes, surrendering once more to the man I loved, unable to imagine a more incredible happy ending than this. In the arms of Wolf.

***

"ARE YOU READY?" HE asked as he put on his helmet, and I straightened up on the high seat of Wolf's Spirit, admitting I felt euphoric at the prospect of riding it again.

"All set, Captain."

He started the bike, and the engine roared beneath us, making it tremble.

"Wow, I didn't remember it made such a loud noise."

"Want to back out?" he teased.

"I don't know what that word means." I smiled inside the helmet as I felt Christopher's fingers cover mine, which were wrapped around his waist.

"Hold on tight, Crystal. The fun is about to begin."

And he revved the bike, leaving one of my euphoric screams behind.

EPILOGUE

Jasmin

6 months later...

Aoraki Mackenzie Reserve - New Zealand

"*Jasmin Cahill, the heiress of the Hill and Cahill conglomerate, one of the largest high-tech weaponry companies in the United States, made history by launching a protection system based on a wide-spectrum magnetic defense network. This was hailed by government experts as "A revolution for the electronic age, where wars of this level are becoming increasingly common, given that a country's power lies in the secrets its government keeps from enemies." We cannot allow our data to be breached, and the J.A.S. is undoubtedly the most comprehensive system I have ever seen. Congratulations to Hill and Cahill for gifting us yet another success, and to Miss Jasmin Cahill, who has proven to us that the next generation of the conglomerate is in good hands.*"

I reread the newspaper once more as we disembarked from the plane and got into a rental car, filled with a strange excitement.

"Why did you bring this?" I asked Christopher, who was taking the wheel while I settled into the passenger seat beside him.

The handsome specimen was dressed in a tailored navy suit that accentuated his eyes, one of the rare models he had that wasn't completely black, while I had opted for a golden dress with a deep slit in the back.

"I can't stop reading it." He smiled and leaned in my direction, planting a chaste kiss on my lips. "Are you ready?" He glanced at the road ahead.

"Yes, but I wish I had at least brought my phone with me."

We took a few days off after the J.A.S. launch, and Christopher decided to surprise me by keeping all the details of our trip a secret. In the end, we landed in New Zealand.

New Zealand, for God's sake!

I had never left Chicago and had no idea what to expect.

"It's part of the deal. No phones." He pointed out. "And there's one more detail." He smirked slightly as a blindfold appeared in his right hand.

"Are you going to blindfold me?" I said, slightly choked up.

"It'll be worth it, love." He positioned it over my eyes and tied it. "Do you trust me?"

I smiled at the question.

Christopher had become my safe harbor, my partner, and with each passing day, I loved him even more. Our routine was hectic but precious. Wolf still wouldn't take any missions that required him to stay overnight. Before that, he wanted to make sure that the night terrors had really disappeared, and I loved him even more for it. It had been three months since I'd had a crisis, and I could guarantee that I was living one of the most precious phases of my life.

"I trust you," I replied, fully aware that it was the absolute truth of my soul.

It wasn't long before we stopped again, and Wolf helped me out of the car without removing the blindfold from my eyes.

"I've learned so much from you these past months, my love," he whispered in my ear as we continued walking. I could hear other noises and sounds around us, but I couldn't identify what they were. "I learned that you definitely run the risk of killing someone when you enter the kitchen. That shoes have the power to multiply, that I can fall in love with yellow rabbits, blue pandas, and all kinds of pink little creatures, plus discovering that pots and appliances can be used as weapons."

"What happened with the vacuum cleaner was an accident. I swear I didn't hear the Ghost approaching, poor thing."

"I warned you he should stomp his feet." Wolf laughed behind me and suddenly stopped. "I also learned that sleeping embraced with someone is infinitely better than sleeping alone, and that there are people who complete us in such a perfect way that it's almost scary." He began to untie the blindfold. "I also discovered the beauty in the stars, and every time I look at them, I only think of you. Today, the only fear that runs through my heart is the fear of losing you one day, Jasmin, my star." He removed the blindfold, which fell away, revealing an unbelievable scene.

"Christopher..." I gasped, incredulous, when I realized we were in front of a small castle with very high stone walls, atop a hill where the mist created a magical scene.

There was a small square table right at the edge of the hill, overlooking a forest that sparkled under the countless stars of the place, with two plates arranged in a beautiful setup, where a candelabrum held four lit candles on the table.

"A candlelight dinner," I commented more to myself than to him, looking up at the sky in awe. I had never seen stars so close to the naked eye in my life. They created a road of shining stones across the sky and seemed so close that I had to resist the urge to raise my hands to see if I could touch them.

"What place is this?" I stammered, lost in immeasurable beauty.

"This is one of the best places in the world for astronomical observation." He pointed to a gigantic telescope situated at a strategic point on the hill. "One of the ten places I plan to take you to stargaze." He placed his palm at the base of my back; I couldn't even see if there was anyone nearby I should greet. The moment my eyes met Christopher's, everything else faded away. "Will you dance with me?"

"But there's no music playing." He chuckled softly.

"An expert once told me that there's music everywhere. You just have to pay a little attention." I smiled. My eyes burned, and I bit my lips to hold back the urge to cry when he brought my hand to his heart. "Right here, can you hear it? It sings to you every day."

I leaned in and rested my head on his shoulder, dancing with Christopher under the light of countless stars for what felt like an eternity.

"I love you so much," I whispered after a while.

My heart was his, and his was mine. I had never received anything so precious before.

Wolf

One month later...

JASMIN WAS STILL SLEEPING when I got out of bed to answer a call from Ghost. My brother had received a mission to provide security for a VIP at a major event in Italy. Apparently, the VIP was an important and highly influential man, both in the United States and abroad. What worried me was, after all, why would Ghost call me in the middle of a mission in another country? It was concerning, to say the least.

"Zion?" I asked, apprehensive.

"Hello, brother!"

"Is something wrong?"

"Oh yes, definitely." I tried to pick up on any difference in his voice, but Ghost was an expert at hiding behind that confident and cheerful tone in a way that almost irritated me. "Do you still have that hideout in Calabria?"

"I do. I'll send you the location of the keys. But why do you need it? Did something happen to the VIP? Is he okay?"

"It's hard to say, but if he survived, he's going to be a bit annoyed because I took something that shouldn't belong to him." I narrowed my eyes.

"What? What kind of crazy story is this, brother? You... stole from the VIP?"

"Yes."

"For the love of my holy patience, Ghost, what did you steal from that man, damn it?"

"A prisoner. Isn't it exciting?"

"A PRISONER?"

Did you love *Reluctant Protector*? Then you should read *Dark Instinct* by Amara Holt!

Dark Instinct: A Heart-Pounding Romance Thriller

Zion is no ordinary bodyguard. Known as **Ghost**, he's a Class A protector famous for his **lethal precision**, silent movements, and **ruthless efficiency**. His cold, disciplined exterior hides a darker side—a deadly instinct he's fought for years to control. But when he discovers a young woman imprisoned in his VIP's basement, every ounce of his **self-restraint** shatters.

Alena was once full of **dreams** and **hope**—until the day she was kidnapped and betrayed by the very man who should have protected her. Held captive and brutalized, she's lost her past, her identity, and any hope of survival. But just when all seems lost, a mysterious, **fierce protector** storms into her life, determined to save her at any cost.

As Zion unleashes the **dangerous** part of himself he's always feared, he must face powerful enemies, shadowy secrets, and his own **dark instincts**. Alena is broken but not defeated, and together they will fight for survival in a world where trust is fragile and danger is ever-present.

With **gripping action, scorching passion,** and a plot full of twists, **Dark Instinct** is a **high-stakes romance thriller** perfect for fans of **alpha heroes, dark secrets,** and **unstoppable desire.**

About the Author

Amara Holt is a storyteller whose novels immerse readers in a whirlwind of suspense, action, romance and adventure. With a keen eye for detail and a talent for crafting intricate plots, Amara captivates her audience with every twist and turn. Her compelling characters and atmospheric settings transport readers to thrilling worlds where danger lurks around every corner.

Milton Keynes UK
Ingram Content Group UK Ltd.
UKHW042036031224
452078UK00001B/172